Oddjobs

Heide Goody and Iain Grant

Pigeon Park Press

Paperback ISBN: 978-0-9933655-3-9
Ebook ISBN: 978-0-9933655-4-6

Cover artwork and design copyright © Mike Watts 2016
(www.bigbeano.co.uk)

Published by Pigeon Park Press

www.pigeonparkpress.com
info@pigeonparkpress.com

Monday

Rod's mobile and house phone rang at the same time.

He was up and out of bed, reaching for both phone and trousers before the second trill. He looked at his phone. It was not yet midnight.

"Campbell."

"The alarms have gone off at the Library." It was Dr Spence. Ingrid. "The Vault."

"Something's tried to break out?"

"In."

Rod pulled on an already-buttoned shirt while he swiftly digested this.

"Is there any kind of incursion scheduled?"

"Not this week."

Rod stepped into his boots. "Do we know what it is?"

"Human. We have security at the doors," said Ingrid, "but I didn't think it wise to send anyone down until someone with authority was on site."

"Authority. Hilarious."

"You know what I mean."

"Aye, I do. I'll be there in four minutes. Start counting."

He killed the call and whipped his jacket off the bedside chair.

Rod had dressed one-handed and in the dark. He could have turned the light on – there was no one else to be disturbed – but he didn't require it. He had practised dressing one-handed in the dark. He couldn't say what specific situation might call for this (just as he couldn't be certain when he might need to make a phone call with his nose, pick a lock with a spoon or escape out of his third floor apartment via the window) but he was sure he'd be grateful he'd bothered to practise when any of those situations arose.

Rod headed out. En route, he collected with barely a break in his stride: his ID card, a clip-on tie, car keys, a strawberry protein shake, his Leatherman multi-tool and, from the shelf above the front door, his Glock 21 pistol.

Tie on, pistol holstered and protein shake open, Rod headed down the stairs. He clipped his Library ID card to his breast pocket. Library security were real sticklers for that kind of thing.

A person with a keen interest in civic buildings would know that the Library of Birmingham was the largest public lending library in Europe; that it had been designed by a Dutch architect; and built with a façade of gold cladding overlaid with huge interlocking steel circles that made it look like a robot birthday cake. They might also know that it was opened to great fanfare and then, due to local government funding cuts, almost immediately had its hours slashed so that it was open for the briefest of windows. Getting a book out of the library required the determined stoicism of a Soviet housewife queuing for bread during the cold war. Someone with more esoteric interests and a higher security clearance would know that those interlocking circles were a copy of Dee's Ward of Perfect Intersection made from tungsten-magnesium alloy with a selenium core and that the Library's public opening hours had nothing to do with local government cuts.

Dr Ingrid Spence was waiting for Rod in the ground floor lobby, tablet in hand.

"Three minutes, forty-eight seconds," she said.

"And it would have been five seconds less if Security Bob had been quicker with those doors."

They walked together to the bank of lifts.

"You know, getting from bed to office in four minutes isn't an entirely appealing quality," said Ingrid. "Unhygienic some might say."

"Wet wipe face scrub in the car and a sodium-toothpaste mouth-bomb of my own devising. I've begun developing a five-second flosser made from an egg-slicer."

"Sounds dangerous."

"There were some teething problems, aye."

In the lift, Ingrid swiped the hidden card reader and the doors closed. Rod looked at her slip-on crocs, baggy grey jogging bottoms and loose T-shirt.

"They get you out of bed too?" said Rod.

4

"I was working the night shift," said Ingrid. "These aren't pyjamas."

"No. I wasn't... It looks..." The T-shirt had a cute cartoon cat and dog above the slogan 'Life is Meaningless and Everything Dies'. "It looks classy. So, what happened, doc?"

Ingrid gave him an ironic glare of annoyance and tapped her tablet.

"Alarms went off twenty minutes ago. One of the rear doors was forced open. Security were alerted. I only called you when the Vault was accessed."

"How?"

"Manual keypad entry in the back stair. I would have called Greg but he's..."

"Dead, yeah. Have you called Vaughn?"

"And what would he have done?"

Ingrid tilted the tablet towards him. CCTV footage of a section of corridor, a slight figure in trailing clothes running away and off screen. Rod dialled it back.

"Is that a knitted scarf?"

"And a big flappy coat."

"We've had a break-in by Doctor Who."

"Looks like a woman."

"They were going to get around to gender-free casting eventually."

The lift doors opened onto a white, brightly-lit corridor that terminated against the glass airlock doors of the Vault. Three Library security types stood in readiness. One had a pistol drawn. Rod wasn't sure what the guy expected to do with it. The only individuals he would conceivably be allowed to use it against were his fellow guards or himself.

"Anything?" said Rod.

"Nothing since we got here," said one, an ex-soldier called Malcolm. "Nick thought he saw something but..."

Rod swiped his card at the first airlock door and presented his face to the biometric camera.

"You going in alone?" said Ingrid.

"Just for a look-see." Rod stepped inside. He looked back pointedly at Nick and then at Nick's gun. "Put it away, mate. If there's some sort of trans-dimensional face-sucker on the loose, I'll give you a signal." The door began to close. "Probably featuring a lot of muffled screaming and some frantic arm-waving."

"I've not seen you here before," said the man on the next couch over in the buffet car.

The man – Mediterranean or possibly Middle Eastern complexion, modest but stylish grey suit, huge bald-spot, the NHS glasses of a young Michael Caine – had an English accent, an empty tumbler in his hand and a lazy, almost foolish smile on his face.

Morag checked her watch and smiled. Five minutes to midnight. The cosmos, that vast indifferent bastard of a universe, had well and truly put the boot in today and apparently it was not yet finished. Morag smiled because if the universe was laughing at her, there were worse things she could do than laugh along.

"Is that the train equivalent of 'Do you come here often?'"

NHS specs frowned.

"Dear me, no," he smiled. "I'm not coming onto you. Gods, no. I'm one sudden move away from a hernia and I've never got the hang of seduction. No, I meant you see the same faces on this train, week in, week out. It's like a little travelling community. And you..."

"You've not seen me here before," said Morag, nodding apologetically. Okay, so only ninety-nine percent of the universe was out to get her, the other one percent was avuncular and slightly camp bald men.

"Is that whisky?" she said, pointing at his glass.

"Was. Glenfarclas. Not a bad drop." He caught her eye. "Yes, even Sassenachs can appreciate the good stuff. Glass? My treat, dear."

"I don't know. I've a big day tomorrow and I should get some sleep."

"In my experience, there are two kinds of people. Those weird machine people who actually sleep on the Caledonian Sleeper and those who travel anaesthetised."

Morag looked out of the window at a dark world, smeared with occasional lights.

"Where are we?"

"Not yet past Carstairs."

"Well, if we're still north of the border," she said.

NHS specs pushed himself off the leather sofa and went to the small but crowded buffet bar. Morag looked at her fellow train passengers, the business folk and the tourists. She wondered how many of them were also being sent into exile with the threat of face-melting tortures and a slow death if they ever returned. No, probably not many.

"Big day then?" he said, returning.

"Hmmm?" She took one of the tumblers from him. "Slainte. Yes, well, I've been promoted."

It was late, she wasn't good at hiding her emotions, and the subtext in her words was as clear as if she had done accompanying hand gestures.

"Oh, I've had that kind of promotion," he said. "Sudden? Not even enough time to clear your desk? Sent to the corporate equivalent of a Siberian gulag?"

"Birmingham," she said.

"Close. A sideways move then or, God forbid, a backwards one dressed up as promotion?"

"No," she said, unnecessarily defensive. "It's definitely upward. I'm sure I'll be very good at it." The Glenfarclas warmth spread through her. "I can turn my hand to anything."

"Ah, the confidence of youth," he said.

She laughed at that.

"Away with you. I'm closer to forty than twenty."

"Pfff. And we're closer to Norway than London. That doesn't make us flat-pack building Scandawegians."

Morag looked into her glass.

"I've never been to Birmingham," she said.

"I don't think anyone goes *to* Birmingham," he said. "Not deliberately. I'm sure it was a big manufacturing powerhouse in its day, back when we used to make things in this country. It's a big city, the biggest outside the capital, I think. Didn't they used to build cars there or something? British Leyland."

"That's a kind of tree."

"Yes, you are definitely young."

"Don't they all have funny accents?"

7

"Says the redheaded lass with the Highlands burr." NHS specs held out his glass and she dutifully clinked it with hers. "You'll be fine. The Brummies will take you to their ample if unattractive bosom. It's a has-been town, a nowhere place. A cultural wasteland, I'm sure. But that's not a bad thing. There's security in dullness. What can go wrong in a city where nothing ever happens?"

Shelf-lined aisles stretched away in three directions. The Vault, fifty feet below street level, extended beneath much of Centenary Square outside the Library and even under the dual-carriageway on the other side. Rod strongly suspected that, when the commissioning ministers shared their brief with the architects, they had simply said, "You know that warehouse bit at the end of *Raiders of the Lost Ark*? Like that but underground, with wipe-clean surfaces, energy-saving light bulbs and decent air-con."

Rod stood, listened for any sounds above the near-hum of a modern building, and then set off left. Although it was one of the core functions of the Birmingham consular mission to the Venislarn, Rod had little professional interest in the Vault, or the Dumping Ground from which much of its collection was harvested. He worked mostly in clean-up and court liaison. The Vault was the province of eggheads like Ingrid or regulation freaks like Vivian Grey. He was vaguely aware that most of the shelves were filled with documentation: witness statements, field reports from other agencies, plus the diaries of madmen and the theses, research papers and personal accounts of those who had strayed too close to the abyss. Ahead of him was the section holding the Vault's physical artefacts.

He heard a sound. A short squeak, like rubber soles on tile.

Rod slowed, approaching quietly.

He passed cases of reinforced glass containing objects that had been fashioned by either the Venislarn or those who had glimpsed more of their science than any human ought: a selection of one-sided objects, a dog-eared and unedited manuscript of *The Carfax Monographs*, a pile of Tiny Blue Innumerables, an eye-bending four-dimensional Julia Set composed from the remains of the mathematician who had been foolish enough to unlock it.

Another squeak, this from a side corridor hung with paintings, photographs and even a tapestry or two. There was no abiding theme to the collection, apart from the fact that no sane person would have any of them hanging on their living room wall. Beneath a batik print of something that looked a bit like a hedgehog, a bit like a beetle, and a lot like the handiwork of a deranged vivisectionist stood a stout metal tank. It had a circular door like a bank safe, albeit a bank safe with a porthole in the door. And, looking in through the porthole, a length of rolled up canvas in her hand and oblivious to Rod, was a young woman – probably just a teenager – wearing a shapeless knitted scarf, chunky earrings and a Paddington Bear duffel coat. She looked like a size-zero actress on her way to audition for the role of 'kooky undergrad'.

"Excuse me?" said Rod.

The young woman jumped.

"Oh!" She put a hand to her chest and then laughed. She was a pretty girl. No, more than that. She was beautiful, her student shabby chic infused with an enchanting movie-star glow. "I didn't see you there."

Beautiful or not, she was irritating.

"What are you doing?"

The young woman seemed momentarily perplexed. Then, remembering herself, she unfurled her canvas banner. In wonky lettering were the words 'Hands OFF our libraries! No CUTS to jobs and Services!! '.

"You're..."

"Izzy," she said.

"A protestor?"

"That's right." She waggled her banner. "You can't call it a library if it's always closed."

"How did you even get down here?"

"All these books locked away where no one can see them. It's a crime. What is this anyway?"

She pointed at the book in the sealed pressure chamber.

"It's the Bloody Big Book."

"I can see that but what is it?"

"It is *the* Bloody Big Book. The Wittgenstein Volume. The Book of Sand. How did you get in here?"

9

Rod stepped forward. The young woman slipped something from her huge sleeve and, before he could reach her, she had slapped the other end of the handcuffs around a metal upright on the safe.

He growled, exasperated.

"All this amazing stuff locked away," she said. "You can't do this."

"So this is your stand against the man?"

"It should be on display, freely available, anyone —"

"And you don't know who the man is," Rod interrupted.

"There's even a mummy back there. I didn't know we had a mummy in the library."

Neither did Rod.

"Mummy?"

The woman, Izzy, jerked a thumb over her shoulder.

"All kind of weird and leathery."

"Did you touch it, lass?" said Rod.

"I've not damaged anything."

"Right," he said, removed his tie clip and, with a twist, separated it into two needle-nosed blades.

Izzy looked at him worriedly.

"Lock picks," he said.

Sometime previously, the Caledonian Sleeper had crossed into England but it seemed perverse to stop drinking just because of that.

"Right, my turn." NHS specs shifted on the sofa. The effects of alcohol, tiredness and the gentle rocking of the train tried to drag them both from the vertical to the horizontal but they were fighting it. "I'm going to guess yours."

"I told you, I can't tell you what I do," said Morag. "This is how this whole conversation started."

"Are you embarrassed to tell me, dear?"

"No."

"So, you're not allowed to tell me?"

"Yes."

"Are you like a spy?"

"Um. No."

"Not MI6 or MI5?"

"No."

"Private sector?"

"We're not playing this game."

"We've already started."

"No, not private sector. Even if you get it, I can't tell you."

"So, you work for the government? Central government?"

"I suppose."

"And you have offices in Edinburgh and Birmingham?"

"Yes."

"And other major cities."

"The big ones."

"Is this a military thing?"

"Not really."

"Not really. It's a national security thing though."

"Yes."

"Borders and customs?"

She laughed at how close to the truth he was. "God," she said. "Look, my glass is empty."

By chance, one of the buffet staff heard her in passing and paused. Resigned to her drunkenness, she ordered refills.

"Immigration," said NHS specs. "Do you run one of those internment camps for illegal immigrants?"

"If only it were that easy."

"I got it right?"

"No. Not at all."

"But it's some sort of central government preparedness thing?"

"Preparedness thing?"

He shrugged.

"Disaster planning? Flood defences? Preparing for that flu outbreak that's going to kill us all? Maybe... maybe you're building missiles to take out an asteroid that's on course for earth?"

Morag put a hand on his forearm and instantly worried that he – like so many men – might take a gesture of bonhomie as something more, although she was quickly coming to the opinion that he might be gay.

"All good suggestions. And seriously, that's as close as you're gonna get."

He nodded.

"So, are we all going to die soon?"

She gave him a look.

"Hey," he said. "Maurice and I recently bought gym memberships. I'm just curious to know if we're wasting our time."

The waiter appeared with two tumblers on a tray.

"We're all going to die," said Morag and sipped her whisky. "Eventually."

"Of course. But we shouldn't have to die before our time, of something unpleasant and avoidable. That's my sales pitch, my professional philosophy."

"And ours too. Absolutely."

Rod believed the universe had its own natural rhythm: cause and effect, gag and punchline, the long drop and the sudden stop. When someone says "Don't look behind you but –", it is a universal certainty that heads will swivel. When Rod had lost his 6omm anti-tank mortar on that fateful night when he was separated from the rest of his patrol outside Al-Qa'im, it was an iron-clad guarantee that he would need it before the night was through. So when a ditzy young woman mentioned a mummy that she "did not touch," Rod immediately prepared himself for its appearance.

It stepped out into the corridor fifty feet behind the handcuffed protestor and stumbled ever so slowly towards them.

"On cue," said Rod.

"What?" said Izzy, fingering her earrings nervously as she watched him try to pick the handcuff locks.

"Nothing," said Rod.

The mummy had apparently learned how to walk from decades of zombie movies, shuffling in the gait of a man in callipers who had just wet himself. Its bandages were wide and scab brown as if the creature had been wrapped in enormous, dirty sticking plasters. Its head was featureless, a mottled mass of coverings.

Rod had yet to pick the handcuffs. If they had been standard police issue, they'd have been sprung already but these were something else and they weren't about to give just yet.

He took a step back and put a call through to Ingrid. "Do we have a mummy in the Vault?"

"No, Rod. We do not."

"Are you sure?"

There was a pause while Ingrid thought.

"Hey," said the protestor. "Are you going to ignore me?"

"You chained yourself up, lass," said Rod. "Be patient. Look at the pretty paintings."

"No mummy," said Ingrid. "We do have a hibernating scion of the *Uriye Inai'e. Kerrphwign-Azhal*."

"Uh-huh."

"But it's locked away in a secure case."

"Er. You might want to rethink that last statement."

"Who painted this one?" said Izzy, pointing at a surrealist image in which amorphous pink and grey figures embraced, or possibly ate each other, against a blood red landscape. "I think I've seen something like this before."

"Like it but not that one," said Rod.

"If it looks like a mummy then you're safe," said Ingrid, on the phone.

"Why wouldn't it look like a mummy?" said Rod.

"If it looks like a mummy that means it's still chewing."

The mummy stopped in an archway. Its brown bandages bulged fatly. It looked like the Michelin man had lost some weight while dossing in the sewers. Izzy caught Rod's eye and was about to look round.

"It's a Conroy Maddox," said Rod.

"What?" said Izzy.

"This painting. A local lad. It's one of a series of paintings Scotland Yard confiscated during World War Two."

The mummy, *Kerrphwign*-whatever, seemed to be having some trouble. Its bandages (which were clearly not bandages) rippled and started to unfurl.

"Why?" said Izzy.

Rod glanced at the painting.

"The official line is that they suspected Maddox of being a fifth columnist and sending coded messages to the Nazis through his paintings."

13

"So that's not true?"

"No. They were seized because they are an impossibly accurate rendering of the Venislarn Apocalypse."

"The what?"

"The end of the world, lass."

They weren't bandages at all. They were limbs, appendages, like giant tongues or the bodies of flat worms. They opened out, revealing red undersides bristling with yellow teeth.

"How can it be an accurate rendering?" said Izzy. "The world hasn't ended."

"Give it time."

The creature had five limbs, possibly seven, definitely a prime number, joined together around a cluster of eye stalks. The eyes looked human. They looked... borrowed. The teeth too. Definitely human. It slapped an arm onto the wall and swung itself upwards, letting the ancient but still juicy remains of its last human meal fall to the floor.

Rod spoke into the phone.

"It... er, *Kerrwi... Kervph...* Kevin, has stopped eating."

"Are you sure?" said Ingrid.

"I can see its leftovers."

"Who are you talking to?" said Izzy.

Kevin hung in the archway from three limbs. Its eyestalks regarded Rod wetly.

"It's staring at me," he said.

"*It* is a she!" said Izzy huffily.

"Probably still hungry," said Ingrid.

Rod's right hand drifted towards his holstered pistol.

"Please tell me it's fair game."

"One of the *Uriye Inai'e*? Imagine the reprisals. No, Rod. You cannot kill it."

"I'm not seeing other options."

"We can subdue it with a prayer of supplication. Once it's fed again."

"I'm not right happy about that, since the only food in sight is us."

"Are you a virgin?" said Ingrid.

"I... what?"

14

"It only eats virgins. Their hearts specifically."

"It's a fussy eater?"

Izzy frowned. Rod clicked his fingers to keep her attention.

"I need to ask you a question in a moment, lass. Pay attention." Into the phone, "Are you sure? This chap does not look like a fussy eater."

"Sure," said Ingrid. "There was one in Sao Paulo a few years back. I read a paper."

"A paper..." Rod looked at Izzy. "Right. That question."

"Yes?" said the manacled protestor.

"It's gonna sound odd."

"Uh-huh."

"And perhaps a little pervy."

"Oh?"

"Are you a virgin?"

Izzy, quite reasonably, looked at him as though he were mad.

"Are you hitting on me?"

"Who the hell hits on someone by asking them if they're a virgin?"

"I don't know. Maybe it's a Christian thing."

Kevin swung slowly along the ceiling towards them with the confident lazy lope of an orangutan, flat tentacle over flat tentacle, leaving behind a series of slimy prints and a circle of indents where its teeth had bitten into the plaster.

"It's not a Christian thing. It's not an anything thing. I just need you to answer the question. And quickly."

"No. I'm not telling you." She drew her coat around her tightly, protectively. "And, besides, what counts as a virgin?"

"Well, that's obvious. It's someone who hasn't done it."

"You'll need to be more specific."

Rod screwed up his nose in irritation. If the silly woman hadn't cuffed herself to the Bloody Big Book, he could have simply dragged her away to a safe distance for a bit of regrouping and rethinking but, no, she had to chain herself up, make things difficult and ask stupid questions like...

"What's a virgin?" he said into the phone.

"What?" said Ingrid.

"Is it a... a penetration-based criteria?"

"Penetration-based criteria?"

"And can you lose it by yourself? And... and lesbians..." He abandoned that sentence before he strayed too quickly away from the realms of his own experiences. "Ingrid. I'm going to need some clarification here."

"You're not a lesbian, Rod."

"Not me!" he hissed. "Is there nothing from that Brazil incident?"

"I will need to get back to you on that."

Rod huffed. Kevin was barely ten feet away from them and dangling silently from an air vent grille, its tentacle-mouth-arms reminding Rod very much of the inside of a meatball and sauce sub sandwich he had once eaten and quickly regretted.

"Izzy," he said, gripping the woman's arms. "I need an answer."

"Why?"

"It's genuinely a matter of life and death."

"Whose?"

"Well, if you're a virgin, yours. If not, someone else's. Everyone else's."

The woman wasn't budging.

"I don't have to answer a personal question like that and I'm going to call the police unless you step back and tell me what is going on."

"Right," he said with restrained fury. "There's this... entity, Kevin. One of the Venislarn. And, don't look behind you but –"

Izzy looked round. Of course she did. It was the rhythm of the universe.

Izzy screamed. Kevin wrenched opened the air vent and slid upwards through the narrow opening and into the bowels of the Library.

"Bugger," said Rod with feeling.

"I'm not a virgin!" sobbed Izzy.

"Aye, so I gather."

Regret was a stupid emotion, Morag thought miserably.

She stood in the central concourse of Birmingham New Street station, beneath a vast glass atrium that let in too much hateful morning light. She couldn't be sure if she was hungover or still drunk. She was ready to lie down, vomit and then sleep for a century, so probably a mixture of both.

It was stupid to regret spending the entire night drinking with Derek. She'd done it, it was done and she was going to have to live with it. Just as it was stupid to regret her last act working for the Edinburgh consular mission. The deed was done, the bitch was dead and, flee though she might, hell itself was certain to descend on her soon enough.

"No regrets. Fuck 'em."

She plodded around the station with her pathetically small pull-along suitcase. She wandered in and out of shops, playing a sort of retail Russian roulette, in which the loser was going to have to 'clean up in aisle one,' and bought chewing gum, deodorant spray, two cans of Irn-Bru and the saddest looking Cornish pasty she had ever seen. She felt a surprising kinship with that pasty.

Morag then wandered out of the station and into the pedestrianised shopping district. Seven in the morning and the only things open were sandwich bars, a twenty-four-hour supermarket and a Wetherspoons. Morag sat on a bench, ate the pasty, downed an Irn-Bru, chewed gum, surreptitiously sprayed herself and wondered what the hell to do next.

She opened the uCab app on her phone, found the nearest taxi and selected it. She met the cab on a steep side road called Temple Street and all but rolled into the back seat.

"Library of Birmingham."

The bearded taxi driver grunted and pulled away. Morag fumbled with her seatbelt, then gave up and watched her new home city glide by. Repurposed Victorian banks and square office buildings, mostly redbrick here rather than the grimy sandstone of Edinburgh, quickly gave way to brutalist glass offices, dual carriageway and railway arches.

"Is it far?" said Morag. "The library?"

The driver grunted wordlessly again.

"Right," said Morag.

They passed over a canal bridge and hit a queue of traffic. Police cars and orange barriers blocked the road ahead. Morag saw cops in hi-vis running along the brick-paved towpath.

"Something going on?"

Morag heard the buzz of a helicopter somewhere overhead though she couldn't see it or be bothered to look. Over to her left, huge modern buildings squashed up against the canalside, the National Indoor Arena on one side, a building identified as the National Sea Life Centre on the other.

"Aren't we like a hundred miles from the sea?" said Morag.

The driver grunted.

"Maybe the cops are chasing an escaped octopus," she suggested. "What do you reckon?"

The driver grunted.

"You Brummies talk too much," Morag muttered.

"Okay, so what does this Kevin look like?" said Nina.

"He's all arms and teeth," said Rod.

"I've met guys like that."

The Sea Life Centre had been closed off even before it had opened and its night security staff bundled away behind a police cordon that stretched around the canalside and Brindley Place. Rod stood by a crab tank and looked down and over the zig-zagging walkways that rose up between the fish tanks and touch-and-feel rock pools at Nina Seth, who stood in the ticket hall.

"I'm not talking about a gropey Bee Gee," called Rod. "Think psycho-starfish as big as me."

"That's big, big man."

"Aye."

Nina was young, small of frame and not authorised to carry a firearm. She couldn't stop Kevin from eating her for breakfast, if it so wished, so she was lucky she did not match its particular dietary requirements. She had sworn that she was no longer 'pure' an hour before, although this was just a formality. Coffee break conversations on Monday mornings had made it very clear what Rod's junior colleague got up to at weekends. Rod considered himself to have active hobbies and leisure pursuits. Listening to Nina describe hers was itself exhausting.

"You know I'm not a clean-up specialist, Rod," said Nina. "Or an investigator. Resource allocation, that's me. This would be a job for Greg."

"He's dead."

"I know."

"Vaughn says they're sending a new investigator down from Scotland today."

"Wonderful," said Nina.

"And Ingrid is only tech support."

"I know."

"So," said Rod, "until the Argyle and Sutherland Highlander arrives, please allocate your resources into finding Kevin."

"Who we are not allowed to kill." Was that fresh disappointment in Nina's voice?

"No. Tag him with tracer spray, nothing more."

Rod pointed to the entrance to the ray tank section. "I'll sweep this way. Stay in contact."

"I'm going to check out the penguins," said Nina.

"Any particular reason?"

"I like penguins."

Rod nodded.

"Oh, one last question," said Nina.

"Uh-huh."

"What the hell's a Bee Gee?"

Morag pressed the intercom buzzer and waited. A grey-bearded security guard shuffled unhurriedly across the lobby floor.

"Library's closed," he mouthed through the glass.

Morag held her Edinburgh consular mission warrant card up for the man to see. He squinted at it as though she had just presented a doughnut as identification. The man's bushy eyebrows waggled indecisively for a bit before he opened the door.

"Are you expected?" he said.

"I hope so."

"Who are you here to see?"

She shrugged.

"Whoever's in charge. I've been transferred. Promoted," she added hurriedly. "I'm Morag Murray."

"I wasn't told we were expecting anyone."

"Really?" she said wearily. "I mean, if *you* weren't told... Maybe I should just go away again."

He either hadn't been issued with a sarcasm-detector or chose to ignore it.

"No, that's fine," he said in a tone that indicated this situation was anything but. "You'll come this way."

He led her past an empty coffee shop to a bank of lifts. He gestured her into one, swiped his own ID card against a perfectly unexceptional square of lift wall and pressed for the seventh floor.

"Not coming?" she said.

He stepped back from the closing door.

As the lift rose, Morag rubbed her tired eyes with the heels of her palms and then inspected her appearance in the mirrored wall of the lift.

"Looking rough there, Morag," she told herself and yawned.

She ran her fingers through her hair, decided there was nothing to be done about the remains of yesterday's make-up and was halfway through reapplying some deodorant when the lift stopped.

Morag fumbled the deodorant out of sight and stepped out into a white corridor. A hatchet-faced woman with her silver hair drawn back into a tight ponytail and a mobile pressed to her ear paused in her pacing, eyeballed Morag sharply and then resumed pacing. Morag sidestepped her and went up to the glass-fronted reception desk.

The receptionist wore large false eyelashes, Betty-Boop kiss curls and a clip-on library ID that said Lois Wheeler. She smiled at Morag. It was a genuine smile but it lasted only a microsecond, as though she didn't have the energy to sustain it any longer.

"I'm Morag Murray," said Morag and presented her warrant card.

"So you are," said the receptionist, Lois, cheerfully.

"I'm starting today."

"Starting?" She blinked. "As in starting starting?"

"Yes."

"Oh."

Morag grimaced. "The security man downstairs didn't know anything about it either."

"Security Bob doesn't know anything but I'd have thought someone would have told me... Do take a seat for a minute while I sort you out."

Lois picked up a phone and dialled. Morag stepped back from the glass and regarded the seats beside the lift. They looked far too comfy. She feared that if she sat down, she'd be asleep and drooling on her lapel in under a minute.

"Finally!" said the hatchet-faced glarer. "Who are you?"

"Mor—" replied Morag before realising the woman was on the phone. Morag gave an awkward cough and looked away.

"Then listen," said the woman. "I am enquiring about a death. No, no name. Yes, you can, Mr Williams. You can. You record all deaths in the city and collect relevant information and I seek a body that meets my requirements."

The woman tapped her toe impatiently while the man on the other end spoke. Morag pretended to read a poster that reminded staff to shred all printed documentation. Some comedian had cut a ragged fringe on the bottom edge of the paper.

"Grey. Mrs Vivian Grey. You have already made the call back and you know I have authorisation. Do not waste our time by continuing to question it. Now, to the body. I need to know the names of any recently deceased who were virgins. Virgins, Mr Williams. I am sure you *do* know what I mean."

Lois the receptionist rapped on the glass to draw Morag's attention.

"We'll take a wander down to Mr Sitterson's office and get this sorted out," she said. "I'll pop round."

"Do you not record such things?" said the imperious Mrs Grey. "The name 'Register Office' implies that you keep a register of important details. How is such a detail not important? And I could easily imagine it being noted on most autopsies. No?" The woman pursed her lips irritably. "Clearly, a lapse on your part then. I will need to examine the bodies myself. A hospital mortuary will be fine. Which is largest?"

Lois appeared from a side door.

"This way, bab," she said to Morag.

She swiped them through a security door and along the corridor.

They almost instantly bumped into an unkempt woman in a cute 'Life is Meaningless and Everything Dies' T-shirt.

"Lois," said the T-shirt woman, "do you know what room we've got the student protestor locked up in?"

"Miss Izzy Wu. Room Three. Rod wanted to sit in on the questioning."

"I just need to check that she didn't touch anything else in the Vault."

"That's between you and Rod."

The T-shirt woman slipped past.

"It's all go today," Lois said to Morag. "Bit of a to-do in the Vault last night."

"Something serious?" said Morag.

"Complete shitstorm, I should think. That's how it usually is round here. Wait here a moment." Lois knocked on a door and popped her head in. "I've got the new starter here, Mr Sitterson."

There was a pause.

"Ms Murray," said Lois, prompting.

"Ah, the Caledonian Sleeper," said a reedy voice. "Yes, we were expecting her. She will need a full induction."

"Okay. Who's doing that?"

Even though Morag couldn't see either of them, she could read the silence between them.

"Fantastic," said Lois icily. "I'm sure everything else can wait."

There was a faint scrape of metal.

"We have arranged short-term accommodation. Bournville. Be sure to pass her these."

"Do you want to come and meet her?"

Another pause, a lengthy one. "Later, Lois. I have a lot to... contemplate."

"Of course."

Lois backed out into the corridor, closed the door and stared at it for a moment. Then she turned to Morag.

"You know those times when you just want to punch something very very hard?"

"I do."

Lois smiled humourlessly. "But, we shan't do that, shall we? We'll just comfort-eat instead. Coffee? And cake?"

"God, yes," said Morag.

Nina pressed her fingers to the glass and followed the faint drifting trails of blood. She put her phone to her ear.

"Rod, where are you?"

"With the otters."

"Otters aren't sea life, are they?"

"I don't think they snuck in illegally or anything."

"I'm in tropical fish. Kevin's been here. Munched his way through the cast of *Finding Nemo* by the look of it."

"I'm coming down."

"You said this thing only eats virgins."

"Maybe he's just playing. Pulling-the-wings-off-flies sort of thing."

"Nice." Nina proceeded cautiously through the tropical fish section. The walls and ceiling were clad with fake rock and lit in shifting blue and green light. It was hard to take matters seriously when one was tracking a monster through what amounted to a cheap science fiction film set. Nina gripped her tracer spray gun tightly as though it was something more protective than a can of paint.

The path through the tropical aquarium led on to the ocean tunnel. Nina stepped inside and scanned the enormous tank about her. Smaller fish darted about in nervous clouds. A giant turtle skulked in the shadow of a rock. Half a shark bobbed above her head.

"Yep, been here too."

A shadow swept down and encompassed the tunnel directly above her like a nightmare parasol. Toothed tentacles and a posy of lidless eyes pressed themselves against the acrylic glass.

"He's here," she said, as calmly as she could. "The Kevin has landed."

"Tropical fish?" said Rod. She could hear him running.

"The sea tunnel thing," she replied.

"Are you safe?"

The glass ceiling creaked faintly as the Venislarn worked its teeth against the reinforced plastic.

"Momentarily, I'd say," said Nina. "Do we have a plan?"

"Vivian's gone to find a virgin sacrifice."

"Really?"

"Really."

"And until then?"

"We sweet talk it in remedial Venislarn."

"Remedial?" said Nina scornfully. "Unlike a certain ex-squaddie, I actually bothered to learn Venislarn."

"Champion. Then charm his pants off."

"That I can do." Nina put her hand on the glass. Kevin quivered. Red, toothy flesh bunched up over her hand.

"*Slor'han azh perrigh-forl. Skeidl hraim*," she began and then proceeded to explain why she wasn't his type.

The Queen Elizabeth Hospital is a vast nine-storey monument to modern healthcare. It serves the city of Birmingham and is also the nation's one-stop shop for war-wounded members of Her Majesty's armed forces as evidenced by the constantly busy helipads on the roof. However, much to Vivian's annoyance, the gigantic hospital was too good in its mission to heal the sick. Either that or the hospital administrators were canny enough to send its patients home to die. The mortuary, though it had capacity for many more, contained less than a dozen corpses.

"I expected a much larger field to select from," she told the attendant. "I calculated you should have close to a hundred pass through here each week. I am very disappointed."

"Disappointed," said the attendant, nonplussed.

"I need to see their records."

"Whose?"

"All of them. Chop chop."

As the attendant scuttled off, Vivian opened a corpse drawer speculatively. She regarded the wrinkle-faced dead man.

"What percentage of the population are virgins?"

"Pardon?" said the returning attendant.

"Out of nine, ten, eleven corpses... what is the likelihood of one of them being a virgin?"

"I couldn't speculate."

"Of course you can," said Vivian. "You are perfectly capable of it. You just don't want to. What do the notes say?"

24

The attendant looked at the plastic wallets in his hands. "We don't record that kind of thing."

"You have next of kin or somesuch on there. Let us start by discounting the ones who have children."

The attendant spread the wallets on a counter.

Sitting down had been a mistake.

Lois had left Morag in a small meeting room with nothing but the Birmingham consular mission staff handbook for company and gone off in search of refreshments. Three of the room's walls were white and featureless. The fourth was entirely taken up by a window that offered views of the large civic square outside through the interlocking ring façade of the Library.

Morag was almost entirely overcome with the need to sleep. Ten in the morning. She hadn't slept in over thirty hours and, yes, she had definitely progressed from drunk to regrettably sober. The white walls offered no diversion. The view of the square, with its tiny figures of city folk coming and going (all of them blissfully unaware that their world was a thin sheet of ice floating on a broiling hell of alien gods) was like a soothing screensaver to Morag's tired eyes. And the staff handbook... She didn't even dare open it to page one in case the paper-based soporific sent her tumbling over into coma territory.

Instead, she slapped her cheeks, pinched her skin and tried any number of other more obscure techniques to keep herself awake. She had her hands clasped above her head (the theory being that if she nodded off they would fall and smack her) when Lois returned.

"Praying isn't going to save you now chick," said Lois.

"God. Sorry," said Morag. "I was just stretching. It was a long journey down and..."

Lois slid a tray onto the table.

"Let's see if we can't fix that with caffeine and sugar. Ingrid — She's our Venislarn expert. We bumped into her in the corridor. — She's always banging on about budget cuts crippling our service, but cuts don't seem to have reached the executive biscuit budget. Look: Kit Kats *and* Penguins *and* mint Viscounts. I didn't even know you could get them anymore."

Morag poured herself a large cup of coffee and emptied four sugar sachets into it.

"You have no idea how much I need this," she said, before taking a large and unladylike slurp.

"I can guess," said Lois. "Well, this induction isn't going to induct itself. Induct? Induce? You induce babies. Is that the same thing?"

"I don't know."

"Both things often end in screaming and tears and someone needing a good slap. Or maybe that's just me." She opened the staff handbook folder. "We'll need to go through the policies and procedures, I'll need to issue you with a photo ID and then get you to fill out a gazillion forms."

"I have only transferred down from Edinburgh –"

"Beautiful city."

"I'm sure most of this is the same."

"One of the things Vaughn did when he took over was rewrite all the consular policies. It'll be better if we go through this. It's one of the few things he's actually done."

Lois flicked to an employee hierarchy diagram. She tapped the top box.

"Vaughn Sitterson. Our consular chief." She looked at Morag.

Morag read her expression and nodded: it was okay to say it.

"The man's a massive wanker," said Lois with stoic cheerfulness. "He sits in his office. No one knows what he does."

"Apart from rewrite policies."

"Apart from rewrite policies. He's only been in post a month. Maybe he's still in shock. Greg Robinson used to be our consular chief and lead investigator. Refused to let that last one go. Died on the job."

"I'm sorry."

"At least he got out before the Soulgate. We have about eighty employees in this consular mission. About half of them work specifically with the Vault or the Dumping Ground. That's our, er, regional specialism, taking other people's crap. We've also got people working on international co-ordination, religious liaison, a couple of guys in sales for the day when we *will* have to sell this to the public, a whole office on interagency cooperation, us cheerful

26

souls in admin... And then, the sharp end of things: the response team. Your lot."

"My lot."

Lois's finger slid down the chart.

"We've got two response teams in the city. You'll be on team A. There's two of you on investigation. Rod Campbell is a sound bloke. Ex-SAS, six-foot-six of pure muscle but really isn't a knob about it. He's also your clean-up lead and the only firearms officer in the team. You've got Nina Seth who mostly handles housing, property and resources. Spends a lot of time dealing with the half-breed things in Deritend. Fish-chavs the lot of them. And then you've got Vivian Grey – *Mrs* Vivian Grey – who handles registration, regulations and compliance. This handbook is her Bible. She's such a stickler for the rules and scary with it. It's like she's got, you know..."

"Autism? OCD?"

"I was going to say a broom up her arse, but okay."

Lois flicked forward.

"Right. Sickness, Absence and Death in Service Policy."

"I am merely suggesting that, when an autopsy is carried out, it would not add much time to the post-mortem examination to pick up a torch and check to see if the woman is virgo intacta."

"I couldn't say," replied the mortuary attendant.

"There appears to be a lot you cannot do," said Vivian. "One wonders if you are capable of anything at all."

She picked up the patient notes and gazed dismissively at the three bodies that had been pulled out of their corpse drawers. She added a note to the list of ideas she'd scribbled on the front of the notes.

"If only the dead could speak," said the attendant philosophically.

Vivian did not dignify the unhelpful comment with a reply. She pulled out her phone and called Rod.

"Found us a virgin's heart yet?" he asked.

"Not yet," said Vivian. "The hospital notes are woefully lacking in detail. I might have to find a live one."

"That would be a shame. I suppose children are, by and large, technically virgins."

"It had occurred to me," she said. "Unfortunately, this place is plumb out of dead children."

"How thoughtless of them."

"There are other places I could try. There are always dead children somewhere but the question is how fresh they need to be."

"You're not thinking of digging up dead kids, are you, Vivian?"

"If it resolves our problem, I don't see why we shouldn't."

"It could be considered insensitive."

Vivian looked at the notes she'd written on the front of the patient file and added a question mark next to 'Cemetery'.

"Sentimental claptrap," she said. "Dead bodies are better than the last resort."

"Which is?"

"Maternity wing."

"Aye," said Rod slowly. "Babies would be worse."

"Worse than children? But they're easier to transport. Presumably the mothers would be less attached to them than they would one they have had for longer."

"Mmmm. You never had children, did you?"

Vivian considered the smiley face she'd drawn next to 'Random baby'. Maybe it wasn't as good an idea as she thought.

"I'm not the selfish type, Rod," she said.

"Selfish?"

"I tread lightly on this world. I have no intention of leaving behind a massive carbon footprint and some diluted genetic copies of myself."

"Quite right. Let's leave children out of it for now. If we need to placate Kevin –"

"*Kerrphwign-Azhal*," said Vivian.

"Him – with a live sacrifice, let's look for an older one. Perhaps someone closer to death."

"Where would you suggest I look?"

"Roman Catholic priests are traditionally celibate."

"Not according to the tabloid press."

"Nuns?"

"There was a house of Carmelites in Hall Green."

"Good."

"But the last pair got too old to care for themselves and were shipped out to a community in Northumbria. I checked."

'Nuns' was already crossed out on her list.

"We could fly them in."

Vivian considered it. "That depends on how much time we have. When do you estimate it will start actively hunting?"

"Be buggered if I know. It's been happily causing fishy carnage in the Sea Life Centre this morning."

"And what is it doing now?"

"Hmmm."

"You lost it, didn't you?"

"Its precise geographical location is currently unknown. But it's a known unknown. We're on it."

"You are a fool, Rodney Campbell. I am going to find a suitable subject with which to placate it. I suggest you track down the *Uriye Inai'e*. And swiftly."

"As I said, we're on it," said Rod. "Give us a call wh– What? Okay. Nina says that if you're looking for virgins, just go to the Nostalgia and Comics shop with a net. I think that's being unnecessarily prejudiced."

"No," said Vivian thoughtfully. "The sad, lonely nerd angle is worth pursuing. Maybe ask Nina to do a social media trawl for comic geeks, real ale aficionados and what is that thing with dice where they pretend to be elves and wizards?"

"Dungeons and Dragons?"

"Excellent." Vivian added it to her list. "Get to it. I'm going to try one more line of enquiry here."

Vivian ended the call. She turned to the attendant.

"Do you have a ward where you keep all the terminally ill ones?"

"Terminally ill ones?"

"I assume you would consolidate them somehow, if only for the sake of efficiency."

The attendant seemed lost for words for some reason.

With the aid of uncounted cups of coffee, Morag ploughed through the staff handbook. She read and declared her understanding of what she should do if she was infected with a Venislarn parasite, what to do if her colleagues were wounded, possessed or transformed by a Venislarn encounter, what her employer considered a "reasonable level of mental illness" and ineligible for sick leave. She confirm her understanding of the Equal Opportunities Policy, the Safety in the Workplace Policy and the Whistleblowing and Summary Execution Policy. She learned the different sirens that would sound in the event of a fire (a ringing bell), a Venislarn incursion (an intermittent klaxon) and the end of the world (bell and klaxon together).

"We need an alarm for the end of the world?" she said to Lois. "Why? What are we expected to do about it?"

"Very little I should imagine," said Lois. "It's to be sounded when the Soulgate closes. I think I would want to know when there's finally no way out, not even by suicide." Lois stared at nothing for a moment and then smiled brightly. "Not for a few years yet, eh, bab? Another biscuit?"

"I'm good," said Morag.

"I'll have yours then," said Lois and unwrapped a Penguin. "Forms," she said around a mouthful of crumbly chocolate biscuit.

Lois produced a sheaf of forms. Morag stifled a body-trembling yawn and started to fill them in.

"Pecuniary Interest Declaration?" read Morag.

"Vaughn brought it in."

"Does he think we're going to getting backhanders from the Venislarn?"

"I'm sure someone will try to make a profit from them somehow before the end. Smile!"

"What?" Morag blinked at the flash and Lois reviewed the picture on her phone screen.

"Staff ID," said Lois.

"Seriously? You didn't give me any warning."

"I do prefer a naturalistic look."

"Jesus." Morag took Lois's phone and looked at the picture. "I look like a scarecrow. A zombie scarecrow. A zombie scarecrow who's just been turfed out of bed at 2 a.m."

"I'm a dab hand with Photoshop," said Lois.

"I don't care if you're a bloody magician. That's an awful photo."

"You'll see."

Morag was about to protest further but was distracted by Lois passing her a small bunch of keys with a plastic tag.

"What's this?"

She read the tag. *Flat 2, 27 Franklin Road.*

"We know this has been an abrupt change for you so we've rented a furnished flat for you. Just for the short term. Bournville is nice enough. They have a festival in the park each year which is a laugh. And it's just up the road from Cadbury's."

"Cadbury's?"

"Seriously? The chocolate factory."

"Oh, right."

"Last form and then I'll give you the grand tour."

Morag looked at the form. "Spiritual Audit. Cute." She hovered over 'atheist' and then ticked 'agnostic'. She ticked 'baptised/christened'. "Last time I ate blessed food or water?"

Lois nodded.

"Apparently, *Yo-Morgantus* can smell that stink on you, even if it's been years."

"What's that cookie dough stuff you get at Sikh weddings?"

"Kara Parshad. That counts."

Morag wrote 'two years' as a best guess.

"Who's *Yo-Morgantus*?" she asked.

"A Venislarn prince. You'll have to be presented to him at court."

"Sounds formal."

"He has veto on all humans who work with the Venislarn."

"He dictates who you can hire? Like some mafia boss?"

Lois nodded.

"We exist at his sufferance."

"And if we don't comply? Or he takes exception to your hiring choices?"

"*Yo-Morgantus* eats." She laughed. "Don't worry. It really is just a formality." Lois pointed out of the window and across the city. "Can you see that multicoloured building? The one that looks

31

like a game of Tetris? That's the Cube. *Yo-Morgantus* owns the top floors. They've got a restaurant there. Nice steaks but far too expensive for my tastes." She gave Morag a reassuring smile. "Trust me. *Yo-Morgantus* will like you."

"How do you know?"

"Oh, you'll see. Right, last bits. I need you to sign the declaration that you've not sold your soul or other intangibles or are, in any other way, beholden to a Venislarn faction."

"No problem."

"And I need to make an official record of your Abyssal Rating. Vaughn might be a wanker but he won't put his people up against anything they can't handle."

"Um." Morag thought. "It was four but I have, er, met one of the August Handmaidens of *Prein*."

"Really? That's a seven, I think. You met one?"

"Met one," said Morag. "Last night."

"Last night?"

"My last act as officer at the Edinburgh mission."

"Wow. What did you do?"

"Pissed myself with fear," Morag lied.

"Who wouldn't?" Lois gathered the papers. "And now the tour. We'll do the offices, the holding cells, the Vault, the support crew and even perhaps the actual Library. I'll introduce you to all the people who you'll need to make friends with and probably point out a couple of cockwombles with wandering hands who should be tasered if they get within ten feet of you."

"Sounds good."

Lois led her out into the corridor. "You've seen this place from the outside," she said. "Those rings are a magnesium-tungsten alloy with a selenium core."

"They don't build them like they used to, do they?"

"Apparently, it's a good ward against some of the lesser Venislarn. I think most would go through it like tissue paper. There are other wards and sigils built into the structure. Even the escalators are aligned as spirit flow channels. I'll be able to show you some when we get to the basement."

Morag saw a petite, dark-haired woman in a sharp trouser suit and a revealing blouse walking swiftly towards them.

"Lois," she said. "You seen Vivian?"

"Not since she went out in search of a heart."

"Who's this? The new investigator?"

Lois made the introductions.

"Morag, this is Nina Seth. Nina, Morag. Nina's in a hurry because the shit's hit the fan and her legs are so tiny she has to run to keep up with normal people."

"Freakish giants, you mean," said Nina with an impish smirk.

Nina pointedly looked Morag up and down. "Are you a virgin, Morag?"

Morag gave this some thought.

"You know, I don't think that question was on any of the forms," she said. "Everything else. Not that."

Douglas Hamilton, surfacing through layers of sleep, drugs and discomfort, woke to discover a woman at his hospital bedside. She sat beside the quietly beeping life monitor. She was on the far side of middle age and had the look and manner of a severe headmistress. The screen curtains were drawn around the bed.

"Mr Hamilton," said the woman. It sounded like an accusation.

"You're real?" he croaked. His throat was dry, as always.

"Very real, Mr Hamilton."

"Some of these painkillers they have me on. They have very groovy side effects."

"I am no hallucination," she said. "Or dream."

"Who are you?"

"My name is Vivian Grey. Mrs Vivian Grey."

"Not a doctor?"

She shook her head. "I need you to answer a ques—"

"Where's my jelly?"

"Pardon?"

"Jelly. My jelly."

"Yes, it wasn't the actual words I didn't understand, more the overall meaning. Never mind. I need to you to —"

"There's pots of jelly in the fridge. For my throat."

"I understand. I will call for the nurse in a minute."

"What do you want then?"

Douglas tried to shift on the bed, but was too weak to do more than rock from one shoulder blade to the other. He found the bed controls and tilted the headboard up.

The woman, Vivian, leaned forward and looked at the monitoring equipment beside Douglas's bed.

"I am very interested in you, medically. I need your help. Actually, it is not so much your help I need as it is your heart."

"Yeah. The side effects. I could have sworn you said heart. Is this an organ donor thing?"

"In a manner of speaking."

"I filled out a form weeks ago. I particularly wanted to donate my corneas."

The woman smiled like someone who had learned how to do it from a YouTube video but not previously tested it out on another human being.

"You like the idea that your eyes will go on seeing after you have gone."

"No," he said. "I stipulated an open casket funeral in my will and I want to freak the shit out of everyone."

The effort of speaking was too much and brought on a weak but prolonged coughing fit. Vivian waited for him to stop and offered no assistance.

"It's not that kind of organ donation," she said. "I want your heart and I want it rather urgently."

Douglas grunted. "I'm riddled with sodding tumours. Bones, blood, I'm fucked. Come back in a week and it's all yours."

"Yes, I need it more urgently than that."

He blinked at her.

"Simply put," she said, "I need your heart today. Before nightfall, I imagine. Yes, this would entail you being dead, a handful of days earlier than you intended."

"Shit," said Douglas. "I know the hospital is keen to free up beds but that's really cold. Are you going to tell me there's a little girl in the Children's Hospital who's gonna die if she doesn't get my heart tonight?"

"No, Mr Hamilton. I am not with the hospital. But, yes, funnily enough, there's a little girl or maybe a little boy, or maybe a full grown adult who is going to die soon if I don't have your heart."

34

"My heart? Why me? Is it something I've done? If it's because I complained about that guy in the next —"

"It's actually more about something you haven't done. You are a virgin, Mr Hamilton. You are a virgin, aren't you?"

Douglas blushed, or at least felt his cheeks tighten; he wasn't sure if his body was even strong enough to push the blood to his face.

"A —"

"Virgin, Mr Hamilton. Could you confirm it for me?"

Douglas heard footsteps beyond the cubicle curtain; one of the ward nurses by the sound of it. He considered calling out for help.

"I mean, it's not like I don't like... people," he heard himself say to the woman. "It was just finding... the time. And the right person."

"Do not fret, Mr Hamilton. The whole experience is wildly overrated and probably would have offered you less pleasure than..." She gave him a quizzical look. "What gives you pleasure, Mr Hamilton?"

"Netflix," he said.

She nodded, understanding perfectly.

"*Buffy*," he said. "*Angel*. *Firefly*. Lasagne. Jelly. Where's my jelly?"

"Soon," said Vivian. "Sex, I can assure you, does not hold a candle to Netflix or lasagne or, quite possibly, jelly. You really haven't missed much. It is positively awkward, as poorly engineered as a Heath Robinson contraption, unpleasantly messy and far less efficient than relieving one's basic animal urges manually."

"I'm confused," said. "You want my heart because I am... inexperienced?"

"Yes, Mr Hamilton."

"Why?"

"I'm not sure you would want to know."

Apart from the constant buzz of background pain, Douglas's throat was moving from the painfully dry to gargling with razorblades territory. His finger hovered over the nurse call button but he didn't press it.

"Did you know that waiting to die is really boring?"

35

"No."

"I've not got much left. But I've got my curiosity."

"You really want to know?" Vivian pulled a 'don't say I didn't warn you' face.

"There is a creature on the loose in the city. *Kerrphwign-Azhal.*"

"Pardon?"

"*Kerrphwign-Azhal.*"

"Gesundheit."

"Let's call him Kevin."

"And what's...?"

"Kevin. Kevin is one of the *Uriye Inai'e* which, for want of a better word, is a family of Venislarn."

Douglas stared. "English, please," he said.

"It's a giant predatory starfish. All mouth and teeth and appetite."

"Like an actual starfish? From the sea?"

"No. From elsewhere."

"It's alien?"

"Yes, but not in the way you think."

"Some inter-dimensional nonsense?"

"Nothing as clean or simple as that. More like a demon."

"Is it a demon?"

"No."

Along the ward there was an anguished shout and the clatter of a metal bedpan.

Vivian consulted her wristwatch furiously, visibly bit down on an angry comment and adjusted her skirt.

"There are beings, the Venislarn. That's actually an earth word for them. Their names for themselves are many and varied and have far too many glottal stops and strange vowels. They are invading our world – have already invaded our world. They will destroy us all. Not because they are evil or because they hate us. Those are human concepts. They will do it because they will do it. Every living thing on our planet, including seven billion humans, will die in prolonged and screaming agony. Indeed, there is a day – an event – in the indeterminate future, generally referred to as the Soulgate. When that moment comes, even death will not offer an escape and the soul, consciousness, mind-state of everyone still on earth will be trapped in an eternal hell of colourful, inventive and unbearable tortures."

"That's ridiculous."

"But true. I work for a government agency – one of many around the world – tasked with managing the Venislarn threat."

"You're fighting them."

"No, Mr Hamilton. Do pay attention. They will destroy us. This is cold concrete fact."

"But?"

"Our role is to oversee the process and ensure it goes smoothly."

"What?"

"Yes, it is the end of the world. Yes, we are all going to die. But we are British. These things still need doing in an orderly manner and there is certainly no excuse to get all emotional about it."

Morag, grateful at least that the exercise kept sleep at bay, followed Nina Seth down the canal towpath. Derelict factories lined the canal on one side, swanky new apartment blocks on the other. It was some time past noon and the sun was hidden behind office blocks.

A large and almost perfectly circular mass of feathers floated on the surface of the otherwise deserted canal.

"Did a swan explode or something?" said Morag.

"Goose," said Nina. "I think Kevin's getting hungry. Or angry. Or both."

"And it went in there?" said Morag, pointing.

The canal continued into a brick tunnel beneath a high wall.

"Rod says one of the coppers saw it coming this way."

"I can't see any light at the end," said Morag.

Nina nodded and stepped onto the narrow, railed path that hugged the tunnel wall.

"A hundred metres maybe," said Nina. "Then it comes to Snow Hill station." She looked back at Morag. "Tunnels start overlapping. Railway, road and canal." She hand-jived a series of sandwiched layers. "And then there's the railway arches and these cool side tunnels. A real labyrinth. Actually, I think I know of a dungeon a little way off from here."

"Dungeon?"

"Dungeon," said Nina with a grin. "I'll show you sometime."

"Sometime," agreed Morag cautiously.

Morag followed her in. The brickwork curved over her head and she walked with one hand constantly to her side to avoid scalping herself against it. It was soon sufficiently dark that she took out her phone and used it as a light. The black still waters caught the meagre beams and reflected them off the low roof.

"You have stuff like this in... Edinburgh, was it?" said Nina.

"No. Scotland's grim enough as it is. We don't have to take it underground. Shit. What's this?"

"Shit."

"No, look."

Morag cast her phone's light to the ceiling.

"Graffiti tags," said Nina indifferently.

"Look!"

Nina put her hands on her hips and looked. The intersecting lines and weird angles seemed to shift under the phone's light. The overall design was not unlike a Celtic knot, wrapped into a triangular pattern that, quite possibly, didn't have three sides.

"That's a Venislarn symbol," said Morag.

"We're a bit outside of *samakha* territory," said Nina. "The fish-boys do a lot of tagging. They think they're Original Gangstas. I tell them, 'this ain't LA and you have gills'. It's sad really."

A faint knocking echoed up the tunnel. Nina heard it too and hurried onward. The tunnel abruptly widened out into a cathedral-sized space, it was fifty feet high and lit by daylight from the tunnel end ahead. The rumbling of trains could be heard above and around them.

At another time, Morag might have marvelled at the scale of the Victorian civil engineering about her — it was probably Victorian. It usually was — but her attention was more immediately grabbed by a man in red Nike running shorts and vest standing directly ahead of them. He was staring up in fearless curiosity at something hanging from the dank wall high above his head. At first glance, one might have mistaken the thing for tattered plastic sheeting. A second glance would have disabused anyone of such ideas. The teeth, the pulsating flesh, the bouquet of eyes at its centre... They were far from subtle clues.

The man – the idiot – was gesturing to it as though trying to coax a cat from a tree.

"Oi, mate!" shouted Nina. "Get away from there!"

He looked round and took out his headphones.

"What do you think it is?"

"You are in danger, mate. Move away!"

"Really, it's nowhere near Hallowe'en," he said. "Is it art?"

"What?" Nina put her phone to her ear, making a call. Morag stepped forward, can of tracer spray in her hand.

"Sir," she called, calmly, loudly, "that thing is dangerous."

He frowned. Neurons were finally firing in his Cro-Magnon brain.

"What? You don't mean —"

The Venislarn, Kevin, dropped on the runner, the momentum of its fall wrapping tongue-limbs around him in an eye-blink.

"*Azbhul!*" swore Nina softly.

Kevin twisted, tightening its hold. The runner's feet, luminous yellow flashes on his trainers, still poked out from the unholy mass of flat tentacles. They teetered and tottered and spasmed like a crappy en pointe ballerina.

"Was he a virgin?" said Nina.

"I don't know," said Morag. "He didn't have time to show me his official virgin registration card."

Nina muttered something quickly into the phone and then fell to her knees to begin a prayer of supplication, their one hope of returning Kevin to its dormant state.

"*Uriye Inai'e. Uriye Inai'khi rhul'eh. Qa-qa urh lhau-ee,*" she intoned solemnly.

The Kevin/runner mash-up began to make a noise. It sounded like someone blowing through a blade of grass. It sounded like a human voice that had been worked on for a long drug-fuelled weekend by a sound engineer. It sounded like the noise bagpipes would make if bagpipes could scream.

"It does not sound happy," said Morag, stepped briefly forward, and sprayed the creature before retreating again.

39

Kevin tightened its leathery grip on its victim, like a window cleaner's chamois wringing itself out.

"*Uriye Inai'e. Zhay te ayvh-ee shau.*"

The bagpipe shrill rose in pitch and volume. Kevin squeezed tighter, tighter, and then...

Morag's Uncle Ramsay had been a deep sea welder in his day and had spent his career at the bottom of the North Sea or any other sea where pipes needed laying or repairing for the oil industry. His tales of life spent living in pressurised chambers on the seabed seemed to fall into two main categories: Dutchmen's fondness for fellatio and what happened when pressurisation chambers went wrong.

The human body, when all is said and done, is a solid skeletal frame clothed in squishy fibres, jellies and liquid – all held in place by the tensile strength of skin. The human body is a water-filled balloon, and when it is put under sufficient pressure with only a small opening to escape through, only one thing will happen.

It was pretty much as Uncle Ramsay had described. The runner's lower legs came apart in a red mess as several gallons of blood, organs and crushed bones exploded onto the path. Then the gore-covered starfish unfurled into the mire and goo.

"Not a virgin," said Morag hoarsely.

Kevin pinwheeled on tentacle tips and dropped into the canal. It disappeared with a fat 'ploosh,' leaving behind only ripples and a rapidly dispersing cloud of blood.

"This is not good," said Nina.

"I know," said Morag. "I saw it."

"I meant that Kevin is clearly getting desperate in his hunger." She looked at the runner's shoes poking out of the human soup. A spaghetti loop of headphone wire was draped over them and a tinny dance beat could just about be heard. "Either that or he's a complete dick."

"My guess? Both," said Morag. "It'll just keep picking at the human buffet until it finds something it likes."

Nina gazed in the continuing direction of the canal.

"The Gun Quarter and then Aston. It's going to be a long time before it finds a virg–" Nina stopped, mouth open.

"Thought of something?" said Morag.

"Before all that," she said, "this canal passes right by Birmingham Children's Hospital."

She pressed her phone to her ear again.

"Rod. I've just had a really horrible thought."

"Does it even matter then?" said Douglas. "Don't get me wrong. You get used to futility in this place. I heard a woman complaining to the nurses that the jelly's bad for her husband's diabetes. If his heart lasts another day it'll be a miracle, but she's worried about his healthy eating."

"What do you mean, futility?" said Vivian.

"You need a heart to feed to this creature. Kevin."

"That's not its real name, you understand."

"And, eventually, it will find someone. Someone dies. And then, in the end, everyone dies. What's the point? You're not actually saving anyone."

"Oh, I think you know the answer to that already, Mr Hamilton."

Douglas coughed and gasped at the pain. Vivian held the plastic pot of orange jelly for him and supported his hand as he fed himself a teaspoonful.

"I am not enamoured by metaphors or analogies," said Vivian. "I find they tend to be used by those incapable of explaining themselves plainly. But given your situation, it seems apt that you should regard me – us – as being in the business of end-of-life care. Humanity is our patient. It is riddled with a necrotic infection, or cancers if you prefer. The patient will die. While some comfort the patient, help it come to terms with its own mortality, the surgeon works on the patient. A gangrenous finger is cut off to save the hand. An enflamed appendix or diabetic foot is removed to relieve pain. The foot is dead. The appendix or finger does not live on and still the patient will die. But it is a better death."

"A better death..." said Douglas emptily. "Am I just an infected finger you're going to cut off and feed to the monsters?"

"Yes," said Vivian. "And we will do it humanely and painlessly."

"But I'll still be dead."

"Yes."

"So, why the fuck would I let you do that?" Douglas gestured faintly with the spoon.

"You'd be saving the life and sparing the torment of another human being."

"Yeah..." Douglas pulled a face and shook his head a fraction. "Not my... my bag, really."

"And I can pay you a considerable sum of money," said Vivian.

Douglas opened his mouth to point out the ludicrous flaw in that offer but was overtaken by another thought.

"How much?"

"A hundred thousand?" she suggested.

"And I'd have – what?" He looked at the clock. Nearly five in the evening. "A couple of hours in which to spend it?"

"You have family you care about. Loved ones. People you care about."

Douglas thought it over, relishing every second.

"No. No. And no. I'd go so far as to say, I'd rather spend a hundred thousand on making various people's lives utterly miserable."

Vivian took a pen and a notepad from her handbag. "You have some specific people in mind?"

Rod hissed as he overshot the turning.

He'd circled through the maze of one-way roads and sliproads around the Children's Hospital for five minutes or more without actually getting there. Up ahead, the road rejoined the dual-carriageway flyover and, if he continued, he would be sucked into the city's tunnel system again.

"Bollocks to it!" Rod grunted, pulling on the handbrake, and swung the car through a No Entry sign. He pressed the accelerator and sped the wrong way down a one-way street.

He clipped the wing mirror off a beeping Mercedes, startled (nearly terminally) a radiology technician on a zebra crossing and swung once more the wrong way onto Steelhouse Lane. Twenty seconds later, he braked hard whilst turning right and skidded to a stop in an ambulance bay. He stuffed a 'Police Emergency' note in the window, got out and headed towards the main entrance. Nina and a red-headed woman were coming from the other direction.

Nina gave him a lazy wave of greeting.

"Satellite picked up the tracer signal in this general area," he said. "That was good work with the spray, by the way. Morag, isn't it?"

"Hi," said Morag.

"If you don't mind me saying, you look cream crackered. Has Nina made you run all the way here?"

"I'm fine," said Morag unconvincingly. "It's been a long, long day. So, do we know where Kevin is now?"

Rod shook his head. "If it's here, the tracer signal is being swamped by the radiology equipment and such. We're going to have to sweep the place ourselves."

"And listen for screams."

"Are we getting police support?" said Nina.

"No," said Rod.

"What? They cordon off and evacuate the bloody Sea Life Centre but not the Children's Hospital. I mean, I like penguins but I wouldn't have said they're more important than kids... Well, I would, but that's a personal thing."

"Evacuating the hospital would, and I'm quoting Vaughn here, 'be lengthy, expensive, endanger lives and draw too much media attention'. Calling on the police... It's a give and take thing. And he's not going to call in that favour again until we have a confirmed sighting."

"Tit," said Nina.

"No, he's right," said Morag. "We can do this."

"And we've not heard from Vivian yet," said Rod.

"So, we're probably going to have to step back and watch Kevin kill a kid anyway." Rod clearly let something show on his face.

"What?" said Nina.

"He'll eat them, aye," he said. "Wrap them up like a mummy. But, I spoke to Ingrid. She's been doing some more research."

"Shit," said Morag.

"You don't know what I'm going to say yet."

"Um, let's see. You will find a new definition of pain and suffering as you are slowly digested over a thousand years."

Rod's mouth dropped open.

"Unlucky guess," said Morag.

Vivian ran through the extensive list on her notepad. "So, we're arranging for pigeons to... defecate on your neighbour's car every week. That's doable. And a screaming baby to move into your flat when you've gone. Not by itself of course. What else? Chocolate covered Brussels sprouts for trick-or-treaters to be distributed on your behalf at Halloween, and a horse racing event to be publicly sponsored in the name of your anti-gambling local councillor. That's all clear. So, who is this Fox Studios person?"

"She cancelled *Firefly*."

"That is a television series, correct?"

Douglas Hamilton gave her a sharp glare. "Best bloody TV series that never was."

"We will have to see what we can do there. Now, you said you would like to arrange something for your niece."

"A clown on her birthday, every birthday."

"Does she like clowns?"

"No."

"No, of course not. Anything else?"

"More jelly."

"That is not a problem."

"And give me time to think of some more things."

Vivian flipped over to the next page of her notepad and pressed the nurse call button.

Exhaustion piled down on Morag once more.

Last night's alcohol had finished having fun with her body and left behind an empty shell of a woman. Morag's hangover wasn't a stomach-churner or migraine assault. It was the sapping of all nutrients and energy and willpower from her body. She felt dead on the inside.

She thought she had powered through it and was now out the other side, but all it had taken was her new colleague, the man-mountain that was Rod Campbell, to point out how tired she looked and the walls of self-delusion had come tumbling down.

Right now, she would have sold a kidney for a strong Americano or a Kit Kat. Or a soft bed and a lump hammer to knock her out. She would have gladly offered both kidneys in exchange for all four.

Ahead of her, Rod and Nina's conversation skated across her consciousness, words from a near dream.

"I hate hospitals," said Nina, staring up at the 'Use Hand Sanitiser' signs near the entrance. "They're just fucking mazes and smell of old people."

"This is a children's hospital," said Rod.

"Still smells of old people."

"I love hospitals."

"Sicko."

"You want to know why I love hospitals?" said Rod.

"Little hospital shop!" said Morag suddenly as she recognised what was directly in front of her.

"Not exactly," said Rod.

"No. I'll be just a minute," said Morag and dashed inside.

Lucozade, Red Bull, Monster, Coke. Such beautiful capsules of caffeine and sugar.

"Morag?" called Nina.

"One minute!"

There was a distant scream.

"Let's go!" said Rod.

Morag hurried to the counter with three random cans and tried to find her purse.

There was a not-so-distant alarm.

"Shit." She flung a random note at the shopkeeper.

"Keep the change."

It was only when they had reached the end of a corridor, climbed two flights of stairs, run through a surprisingly located rooftop garden café and found a further corridor that Nina realised that the alarm had stopped and that Morag was no longer with them.

45

"We've lost her," she said. Rod skidded to a halt. "I think she's still back at the shop," Nina said, but Rod was not paying any attention.

He was studying an electrical panel by the stairwell. It displayed a multilevel plan of the hospital dotted with LED lights.

"You know why I like hospitals?" he said conversationally as he studied the plan. "It's like toilet paper. You don't realise how much you love them until you need them and they're not there."

"Is this one of them soldier things?"

He tapped the panel with his forefinger. "What do you mean 'soldier thing'?"

"Like 'aye up lass, I 'ad to crawl through t'Gobi Desert with only one leg and used a venomous cobra as t'tourniquet.'"

He gave her his best wounded look. "I don't know what that accent was supposed to be. It was like *Last of the Summer Wine* with added hiccups. And, for the record, it was the Syrian Desert and it was a fascinating story in which human ingenuity triumphed, lives were saved and a working saline drip was fashioned from jeep brake lines, Mountain Dew and Dioralyte."

"Tell it if you want to," said Nina.

"The moment has passed, thank you. The alarm was floor four. Hepatology. Let's go."

Once she accepted that she had lost her new colleagues, Morag stopped trying to chase them, opened a can of Boost and chugged it down.

"Tangy." She wiped the dribbles from her chin. Outside, an air ambulance purred past and overhead.

Morag didn't have the energy to traipse through the hospital willy-nilly in search of the Venislarn. She marshalled what wits she still possessed and thought on the matter. Kevin might just take victims at random until it chanced upon a virgin's heart. Or, if it had any discerning senses, would it head towards the greatest concentration of victims, the largest wards? Or would it seek out the fattest and juiciest hearts?

There was a teenage cancer ward listed on an information board.

"Fat and juicy teenagers?" she said and then had to give an apologetic look to an elderly woman who happened to be passing.

The teenage cancer ward was on the third floor. Morag threw the empty can on the floor, popped open the next and made for the nearest stairs. As she reached the first floor, something in her peripheral vision dragged her attention down the corridor.

It was just a door, a door swinging shut. She paused, trying to fathom why it had drawn her eye. She had just seen a door close and glimpsed someone passing through... *the top edge of the door.*

"Ah."

She ran to the door and stepped from the clinical cleanliness of a modern hospital into the wooden panelling and stained glass of a nineteenth century chapel. A dozen pews lined the room before an altar and the pipes of a church organ. A lone figure in a blue dressing gown sat in the front rows; there was no sign of Kevin.

"Hi," said Morag. The boy looked round. He had a nasal feeding tube taped to his cheek.

"Hi," he said.

"You didn't just see anyone else come in here, did you?" asked Morag.

"No. My mum's just gone to get my inhaler."

"Uh-huh." Morag scanned the ceiling and then crouched to search the gaps between the pews.

"What are you doing?" said the boy.

"Looking for monsters."

"Monsters?"

"Mmmm."

"In church?"

Morag got down on hands and knees and looked across the whole floor. "I usually look under beds, obviously, but thought I'd shake things up today."

"There aren't any monsters under my bed."

Morag knelt up and looked at him. The boy's expression was very serious. "Course not. That's because we do our job properly. What's your name?"

"Biljit."

Morag stood and dusted her knees down. "How old are you?"

"Seven."

47

"Well, Biljit-who-is-seven, I think I can say this place is clear of monsters." She turned to go. "Except..."

She gazed about the room once more. "Except," she looked heavenwards, "I know you bastards. You'd love to do it here. Piss all over the church's carpet."

A shadow unfolded itself from the arch above a stained glass window.

"Biljit," Morag whispered.

"Is that a monster?" he said.

"Nah. Just an octopus that escaped from the Sea Life Centre. Biljit, I'd like you to cover your eyes now. I'm going to use a powerful light to, er, stun him."

"Why?"

"Cover your eyes, Biljit," she said firmly.

The boy raised his hands over his eyes peek-a-boo style.

Kevin opened up, tentacles unfolding like daisy petals. Albeit a carnivorous, blood-stained daisy.

"What kind of octopus is it anyway?" said Biljit.

"A God-damned ugly one."

Kevin rolled arm over arm until it was positioned over the room's one door and regarded them with its many eyes.

"I don't think I like octopuses," said Biljit.

"You have impeccable taste."

Kevin, limbs splayed, quivered. It was *sniffing*, savouring the smell of its meal.

"*Bhul* that, Kevin," said Morag. "You're not having him. *Fa'slorvha pessh khol-kharid!*"

Its weight shifting like dripping slime, Kevin descended onto the tops of the pews and rolled towards the two humans. Its gnarly and scabrous hide creaked as it folded over each chapel seat. Morag, quite awake now (probably more because of her imminent demise rather than the advertised effects of a popular brand energy drink) positioned herself between Kevin and Biljit. Kevin latched two legs onto the frontmost pew and raised itself up like a boneless chimpanzee. Its eye cluster was close enough to touch. Brown eyes, grey eyes, blue, green, each supported on a narrow extrusion of raw and bloody fibres. Human eyes.

Fuck that, thought Morag.

She held out her hands, defenceless.

"I'm not your type, I'm afraid," she said. "I don't know if you can even tell who I've been with and how often. — In fact, there was some dispute over a knee-trembler in a bus stop in Inverness that I'd value your opinion on. — But I'm definitely not to your tastes."

A single flat tentacle, blood red and ragged like a badly cut steak, reached out slowly towards her. Morag swallowed hard.

"But you're not having him," she said. "You will have to go through me first."

A second tentacle reached out parallel to the first, the pair making to encircle her head.

"My card's marked anyway, Kevin. Do you know what I did last night? Um, yesterday? I met one of the handmaidens of *Prein*. In Damnation Alley, Edinburgh. You know what I did?"

Something moist – saliva? blood? – dripped from Kevin's tentacle and onto the front pew.

"Kevin, I put a double barrelled shotgun in her mouth and blew that gallus bitch's head clean off. That's right. Handmaiden of *Prein*. Boom. They sent me down here to get me away but it's only a matter of time..." She stared him hard in the eyes. Not all of them. That would have been tricky.

"I hope you understand what I've said. And I hope I give you *bhul*ing indigestion."

The chapel door banged open. *"Kerrphwign-Azhal!"*

Kevin reared and turned.

"What's happening?" said Biljit, eyes still covered.

It was the silver-haired and hatchet-faced woman Morag had seen in the office reception that morning. Grey. Mrs Vivian Grey. She had a clear plastic bag in her hand that held either the world's worst packed lunch or a human heart. She emptied it out into her hand, bloody and wet.

"Perisa ghorsri Yo-Azhal."

Kevin ran, staggered, flopped across the pew tops.

"Vashan, vashan," Vivian exhorted and then, at the last moment, threw the lump of meat into the Venislarn's maw. The creature's limbs folded up about the offering, overlapping and

encircling as they all crowded in. It rolled to the ground, a giant leathery football.

Vivian went down on her knees.

"*Uriye Inai'e. Uriye Inai'khi rhul'eh. Qa-qa urh lhau-ee Uriye Inai'e. Zhay te ayvh-ee shau.*"

Morag too knelt down and bowed her head and joined in the lengthy recitation of prayer. At some point, she fell asleep.

"An encounter with the Venislarn can really take it out of you," said Rod, passing a pint of something the colour of mud to Morag.

"Exactly," she agreed. "That's exactly it. I wasn't asleep."

"Oh, I know."

"I was just having a moment."

She sipped the drink. It smelled like an old lady's wardrobe and tasted like creosote. She would hazard a guess that it was one those 'real' ales and, given that Rod also had a pint of the same, was part of a rich cultural heritage she ought not to insult.

"What's this?" she asked diplomatically.

"Brew Eleven. A local classic."

"Liquid cobwebs," said Nina unflinchingly.

"Madam's Red Bull and vodka," said Rod and thrust a glass at her. "A load of chemical shite."

Nina and Rod had insisted they come to a place called The Old Contemptibles, a pleasingly old style pub to celebrate Morag surviving her first day on the job.

"Won't Vivian be joining us?" asked Morag.

Rod winced. "Vivian isn't exactly your social type."

"Crusty old sow," said Nina. "We'd be lost without her but she'd rather be back at the office filing the paperwork on this one than…"

"Celebrating our success?" suggested Morag.

"Than anything," said Nina.

"Ingrid says she'll be joining us later when we move on," said Rod.

"Move on?" said Morag. "I'm kind of jiggered. I need to get some food and crawl into bed. I'm starving."

"Ah." Rod dug in his suit pocket. "Almost forgot."

He threw two foil packets on the table. Morag picked one of them up. "Perky Porker's pork scratchings?"

"There's nothing better than a pint of Brew and a packet of Perky Porkers," said Rod.

"He's right," said Nina. "Having literally nothing would be better than a pint of sock juice and a bag of hairy pig scrotums."

Morag resisted only a moment. Her brain had abdicated in favour of base desires. She opened the packet, stuffed a curl of roasted pig fat in her mouth and washed it down with the only alcohol to hand.

Four pints later, Morag was in a cosier frame of mind and, by means she could not recall, their surroundings had transformed from the polished wooden panels of the pub to a curry house with neon-lit prints of Indian mythology and slippery leather seats.

"Two poppadoms apiece, mate," Rod was saying to the waiter.

"Here comes Ingrid," gestured Nina. "Be prepared to talk shop all evening."

Ingrid – technical support or Venislarn expert or something, Morag vaguely recalled – had swapped her cute cat and dog T-shirt for one that read 'I am silently correcting your grammar as you speak'.

"Is this me?" she said, gesturing to the empty seat.

"We're just ordering drinks," said Rod.

"Beer, please."

"They have a nice Long Horn IPA on draft."

"I'll have something I've seen advertised on telly," said Ingrid. "Proper beer."

"Proper! Morag, you'll join me in a pint of the real stuff?"

"I think I might also have a... a telly beer."

"Traitor," he said, but was grinning as he said it.

"How's your first day?" Ingrid asked Morag.

"Over," said Nina firmly.

"Looking forward to being presented at court?" said Ingrid.

"We didn't have a Venislarn court in Edinburgh," said Morag.

"Smaller city. Birmingham's a kind of critical nexus point for the Venislarn. Big incursions back in the day which led to the setting up of the Dumping Ground, which now means we have more activity here. Self-fulfilling prophecy."

"Fascinating," said Nina coldly. "But back to important issues, if you had a hundred grand and only a day to spend it, what would you spend it on?"

"Propping up our meagre mission budget," said Ingrid.

"No," said Nina unhappily.

"No?"

"No. You're spoiling the game."

"What game?"

"The 'what would you spend a hundred grand on' game."

"It's a game?"

"It's a conversation starter."

"I'm sorry, homey," said Ingrid, taking a bottled beer from the waiter. "Am I harshing your buzz?"

"Ladies, please," said Rod.

"But, Rod," Nina moaned. "She's talking shop. And she's trying to be 'street' again."

"Word up, brethren," said Ingrid, which made Morag snort with laughter in her beer.

Ingrid chinked her bottle against Morag's.

"The court thing is a formality. Besides, *Yo-Morgantus* will definitely like you."

"Lois said that earlier," said Morag. "Why will he like me?"

"You'll see."

"She said that too." Morag looked at her menu and couldn't remember if they'd already ordered. "Lois called me babs. Is that a Birmingham thing? I assume her accent is a Brummie one."

"She's more Black Country," said Rod. "Not quite the full yam yam mind. Nina's a Brummie."

"Am not!" said Nina.

Morag could see it was easy to get a rise out of Nina and her colleagues knew it.

"Course you're Brummie," said Rod. "You were born and raised in Handsworth."

"Yeah, but it's not like I have the accent or anything."

"Really? What's the number after eight?"

"Nine," said Nina.

"Noine?" said Rod.

"I say 'nine' not 'noine,'" Nina protested.

"Noine not noine?"

"Why do you have to take the piss, Rod?"

"Whoiy? No idea."

"I don't make fun of your stupid accent."

"Nut'in' wrong with it, that's why."

"And the more you drink, the more ridiculously northern you sound."

"Bollocks," he replied.

"It's true," said Ingrid. "You sound like whatsisface when you're drunk."

"Who?"

"That actor who always gets killed in whatever movie he's in."

"Who?"

"You know. He died in *Game of Thrones*."

"Half of them die in *Game of Thrones*."

"Anyway," said Ingrid, "you're not the most northern member of the team now," and pointed her bottle at Morag.

"Edinburgh," agreed Nina.

"Actually, I'm from Fortrose," said Morag. "It's on the Moray Firth. That's along from Inverness," she explained to their uncomprehending faces.

"Nice place?" said Ingrid.

Morag shrugged.

"We've got a cathedral which got demolished in the sixteenth century, an award-winning public toilet and, oh, a bit out of town is the Clootie Well."

"Clootie Well?" said Nina.

"Mmmm. Mystical site thingy. You're meant to wash an item of clothing in the well, hang it from the trees and it'll cure whatever ails you."

"Does it work?"

Morag thought about her parents for a moment.

"Nope."

"Anyway, Scotland isn't northern," said Rod.

"Rod," said Nina kindly. "There's these things called google maps and if you look toward the top of the screen –"

"It's a different country," he said. "Doesn't count."

"Sean Bean!" exclaimed Ingrid loudly.

"Hmmm?" said Nina.

"Head cut clean off in *Game of Thrones*. And he gets shot up in *Lord of the Rings* after he goes mad and tries to kill Frodo."

"He's from Sheffield," said Rod.

"And?"

"I'm clearly from Rotherham."

Morag picked up her beer and found it was already empty. "Are we getting another or shall we get the bill?" she said. This was met with laughter.

"What?"

"We haven't ordered yet," said Nina.

"I'm sorry. So tired."

"And you've had a tough day," said Ingrid.

"So, let's get some more in and order food and *then* get the bill."

"Aye," said Rod and gestured to the waiter for more drink. "You know," he said, "I'd be all right with going out like Sean Bean."

"In what way?" said Ingrid.

"Dying nobly. Or for a cause. I don't know, even if it's a shitty death, to die for a reason. That's more than most of us can expect."

A sudden sombreness descended on the table. Nina toyed with her glass silently as the waiter brought refills.

"Your colleague..." said Morag. "Greg?"

"In the line of duty," said Nina.

"How?"

Rod stuck out his bottom lip and shook his head. "Couldn't say. There wasn't much of an autopsy."

"Some said that the *Nadirian* has taken up residence in the city," said Nina.

The name meant nothing to Morag.

"That's hearsay," said Ingrid.

"Point is," said Rod, "he died."

He raised his pint.

"I have no mouth," he said.

Morag almost smiled to see that some traditions were universal across the consular missions.

"And I must scream," they chorused in solemn reply, drinks held high.

There was food. There must have been because Morag had smears of it down the front of her jacket.

And there was a taxi. She might have called it with her uCab app but she certainly couldn't remember telling him where she wanted to go. However, she was thoroughly inebriated for the second time in twenty-four hours and was heading towards forty hours without proper sleep, so the mistake was probably hers.

The taxi pulled up in a dark street. "Thissit?" she asked.

The taxi driver looked at her in the rear view mirror and said nothing.

"My new home?" Still nothing. She tried hard to focus on the driver.

"Didn't you have a beard this morning? Or have you all taken a vow of silence?" Morag slid out of the taxi and just about kept her feet under her.

Twenty-seven Franklin Road was directly in front of her.

"Super. Better have a mahoosive feather bed, y'hear."

She got the outer front door key in on the sixth attempt, clawed her way hand-over-hand to the flat door. This one proved trickier. There were only three keys on the ring but she couldn't get any of them to fit properly. She jammed the smallest one in, failed to get it to turn and whacked the door with her fist.

"I just want to sleep, ya bastard."

She thumped the door again and this did the trick. The door popped open and she fell in. The open plan lounge — sofa, battered armchair, whopping great television on the wall — opened onto a kitchen-diner. Not only fully furnished, it had a lived-in look, a cosiness, ready for occupancy. The lights were on, the book shelves were fully stocked, even the fruit bowl on the coffee table was piled high with Terry's Chocolate Oranges which were one of her favourite five-a-days.

"Excuse me."

Startled, Morag whirled and connected the heel of her palm with the nose of the thickset man behind her. He cried and staggered back.

55

"Who let you in, you twatting bawbag?"

"That really hurt!"

She shook her fists out angrily and adopted what she imagined was a threatening martial arts pose. Morag knew no martial arts, although she and her dad had watched a lot of Jackie Chan films when she was a child.

"I've had the second worst fucking day of my life today and the worst fucking day of my life was fucking yesterday and I haven't got any fucking time for creepy fucking housebreakers!"

Before the weird burglar guy could even react, she grabbed him by the shoulder of his dressing gown, shoved him out the front door and slammed it shut.

Morag threw the catch on the Yale lock and slid on the security chain.

"Fucking cheeky fucker," she said passionately to the closed door. "Fuck."

She staggered to the sofa. What she needed to settle her nerves was a glass of something strong or, failing that, a chocolate orange and a little nap. She sat down, contemplated the chocolate oranges and then decided that what she really needed to do was vomit and call it a night.

She threw up in the nearest receptacle and then flopped on the sofa, her head finding a fat cushion by pure chance.

Dressing gown, she thought as she slipped away. Weird.

Tuesday

Billy knew the power of names. He had many names himself.

William was the name his mom – his human mother – had given him. She had wanted to have him baptised but the feds wouldn't let her, but still, William was the name his mom had given him.

He did not know who his father was, which of the *samakha* had sired him upon his mom, but *Kari Trahald* was the name whispered to him in the murky depths by *Daganau-Pysh,* the True Father of all the *samakha*.

When he'd slit the head from Eazy Boy and become the leader of the Waters Crew, he'd taken the name B Shark and made sure people learned to fear it, because he knew the power of names.

But behind his back and very rarely to his face, everyone called him Billy the Fish. He fucking hated that name but, in his heart, he knew it was the name that would follow him to his grave. He was Billy the Fish, as pale and silvery as the moon, except for two big round yellow-black eyes.

He had a coracle and he rowed quietly on the canal in the pre-dawn. To the humans it was the Warwick and Birmingham Canal, but this stretch was, in truth, the *Daganau Vei,* the home of *Daganau-Pysh.* It was known to local residents as The Waters. It was narrow but deeper than the earth and deadly cold. Billy paddled it with large feet dangling over the side, but never a ripple did he make.

Billy moored up silently by the grimy towpath and went to an alley in the brick wall that you would not have seen if you had not known it was there. The alleyway was as narrow as the mortar between two bricks and simultaneously wide enough for anyone to walk through. Billy followed it through twists and turns, ignoring the broken gateways and padlocked doors that led off it and led to places both near and distant.

At the alley's end was a door. Billy stepped through and, when he closed it behind him, it was a clearly a doorway into the part-demolished shell of an old factory. The doorway was papered over with decades of posters for local nightclubs and had clearly not been opened in half a century.

Billy was outside *samakha* territory, outside what they called Fish Town, and in the human city. B Shark or not, here he had to tread carefully. He pulled his cap down low and pulled the collar of his Dodgers jacket up to cover his gills and hurried to the arches of the railway bridge.

In a seamless patch of black brick, he pulled out the one loose brick. There was a folded piece of paper inside.

"There are enough mysteries in this world without us creating new ones."

Rod looked at Vaughn Sitterson across the consular chief's desk. Vaughn didn't look back. He never looked back, never made eye contact. If the eyes were the windows of the soul, then Vaughn's soul had been shuttered and bricked up years ago.

"I don't like unanswered questions," said Vaughn.

"No," agreed Rod.

Vaughn also didn't like unexpected visitors, employee expense claims, any form of genuine human interaction or, it would appear, any colour more daring than charcoal grey. Pale skinned, with mousey hair that looked thin enough to blow away in a strong breeze and a suit that was so ordinary it almost defied description, he seemed to aspire to invisibility. It was as though the man was in training to become a ghost and, until that day came, he would hide his gaze behind a tablet or computer screen or, in this case, behind a summary report on the previous day's events.

"Vivian's report is quite thorough," said Vaughn.

"Naturally," said Rod.

"But I must ask... Do we have any idea how this young woman —"

"Izzy Wu."

"Yes. Ridiculous name. Do we have any idea how this young woman managed to access the Vault and wake a hibernating *Uriye Inai'e*?"

"Questioning her is the first thing on my list this morning."

Vaughn made a show of looking at his watch even though Rod suspected he full well knew the time. "We have detained her for thirty-two hours and you've not yet questioned her?"

"We were sort of busy."

"We're all busy, Rod. We have a major audit of the Dumping Ground this week and I have to contend with the very real prospect that our operating budget will be slashed this year."

"She's not going anywhere."

"She has rights."

"No, she doesn't," said Rod.

"No," agreed Vaughn. "I was speaking figuratively. I just don't want her..."

"Sitting around, cluttering up the place?"

Vaughn inspected the summary closely. He had been doing so for five minutes straight. Any more and he might bore a hole in the paper. "And how has your new colleague settled in?"

"Morag? Aye. Seems to be made of the right stuff. Tagged Kevin so we could —"

"Who?"

"Kevin. The Venislarn. So we could track it to the Children's Hospital and she shielded a young lad from it. Physically inserted herself between them. I like that."

"Needlessly sacrificing herself?"

"Putting her life on the line for others."

Vaughn nodded, apparently approving of this. "And did she go to the new accommodation we arranged for her last night?"

"I saw her get into a taxi," said Rod.

"Did she have any comments on it this morning?"

Rod made a noise.

"Yes?" said Vaughn.

"She's not yet come in."

Vaughn made another show of looking at his watch. It was a physical tic; he probably had no control over it. "I think you'd best give her a call then," he said. "Find out what's happened to her."

Morag did not wake up when her mobile rang. She had been in the process of waking up for maybe an hour or two already, consciousness rising like something dark, terrible and rotten

59

coming up from the seabed, wrapped in seaweed, barnacles and muck, up into the cruel and revealing light.

There were things she was aware of before waking. She was on a sofa and it was a comfy sofa. She had vomited into a bowl of Terry's Chocolate Oranges before sleep and her mouth was now a sticky, horrible, dry mess. If she moved, the hangover loitering at the back of her skull would yawn, stretch and break out its claws. But, by God, she had slept deeply and slept well and that felt good. And she had lived to see one more day than she expected and that felt better.

Her mobile was ringing. She found it in the pocket of her jacket, which she was using as a blanket. "Hello," she said.

"It's Rod."

"Rod?"

"Rod from work."

Morag made a noise and sat up. There was no bowl on the coffee table. Not one filled with Terry's chocolate oranges, not one filled with vomity chocolate oranges. There was however a mug of milky tea on the table. Morag reached out for it. It wasn't exactly hot but it was warm.

"Morning, Rod from work," she said and downed the tea. She swilled her teeth with the last of it.

"I was just phoning to see if you'd settled into your new digs all right," said Rod.

Morag looked about herself, at the dog-eared novels on the bookshelf, at the slightly creepy and entirely out of place set of pinned butterflies and moths on the wall, at the ironing board piled with ironing in the corner, at the front door, the broken security chain and the smashed wood around the lock.

"Um," she said. "I'm here. I think."

"Good. I s'pose, really, you ought to be here."

She rubbed away what she hoped was sleep from the corner of her eye.

"What time is it?"

"Nine."

"Crap. Sorry."

"Well, I'm sure you can be forgiven. Once."

"Sorry. Yes. Give me an hour. I think an hour."

"Not a problem."

"See you soon." She ended the call. She realised there was a man stood warily by the kitchen diner counter. He was broad shouldered and, if he hadn't had been broad shouldered, would have been fat rather than stocky. Also, although he appeared to be quite young, he had one of the bushiest beards she had ever seen. He wore a brash checked shirt. If he was going for the hipster look, he had missed it by inches. If he was going for lumberjack, he had pretty much nailed it. It took Morag a few seconds to recognise that the look on his face was fear.

"I'm going to go out on a limb here," she said. "This isn't my flat, is it?"

He shook his head.

"It's yours."

He nodded.

"This is twenty-seven Franklin Road."

He nodded.

"Flat two?"

He shook his head.

"There we go. I broke in and kicked you out of your own flat last night."

"Yes," he said. He was well-spoken, which kicked his hipster score up a fraction.

"I am sorry," she said.

He gave a magnanimous shrug.

"I threw up all over your chocolate orange collection," she said.

"Yes."

"Very sorry," she said. "Do you like chocolate oranges?"

"Yes."

"A lot, I guess."

"I do."

"It's the kind of thing your auntie buys you for Christmas."

"It is. They were. She does."

"Does she? I have an auntie."

"Small world," he said.

"I'm extraordinarily sorry. I'm Morag. I'm your new neighbour. Flat two."

"That's upstairs," he said.

"Makes a lot of sense. I wasn't thinking straight last night."

"No. I'm Richard."

"I am sorry, Richard."

"You said. It's okay."

"No, it's not," she said with feeling. "You had to break down your own door to get back in."

"You slept through it."

Morag looked at the door. The security chain was just snapped. "You must be very strong."

"I must be."

"I need to make it up to you."

"You must."

"At least let me replace your chocolate oranges."

"Sounds fair," said Richard.

Morag became suddenly and acutely aware of herself. She was wearing the clothes she had put on the day before yesterday. Those very clothes were decorated sparingly but noticeably in biryani, Brew Eleven and vomit. She had not had a shower in a very long time.

"I'm a disgusting mess," she said out loud.

Richard nodded.

"Thanks," she said.

"You're welcome," he replied.

"I need to..." In pointing upstairs to where her flat presumably was, she realised that her little pull-along suitcase that really didn't contain enough was still at the Library. "I need to get creative," she said.

Morag picked up her shoes and walked to the door. There were splinters of wood from the door on the floor.

"I'm not sure I've expressed how very sorry I am," she said.

"I think you have," said Richard.

"You've been very calm and understanding."

"That's the kind of guy I am," he agreed. She paused, stopped, turned.

"You know," she said, "I do think the next time someone tries to break into your flat, you really shouldn't be so calm and understanding."

"No?"

"No. I'd really bust some moves on them."

"Thanks for the advice," he said.

She stepped out into the hall. "Upstairs?" she said.

"Upstairs. Not to the top. The crazy old cat lady lives on the top floor."

"Crazy old cat lady."

"That's what everyone calls her." Morag nodded and, with her little keys in hand, went upstairs.

Billy returned to Fish Town by a different route. Ways in and ways out were not the same. The way in was via a butcher's which had unidentified offal and flies in the window. The butcher looked at him but said nothing as he passed through a bead curtain to the rear of the shop, down steps streaked with sluiced blood and onto the grimy towpath of The Waters.

Billy untied his coracle and rowed silently out. He had pimped the coracle with a purple paint job, silver trim, neon down-lighters and a kick-ass stereo with eight-inch speakers set into the coracle walls for those Friday nights when he'd cruise up and down The Waters, playing phat tunes for all the honeys.

Not now. Now, he paddled soundlessly down the length of The Waters, through geography that did not appear on city maps. He tied up at an old banana wharf, climbed the rotting stairs by the side of the low corrugated iron roof and knocked on the door.

A woman opened the door. Human, like Billy's own mom. Sickly looking, ragged and unhappy. Like Billy's own mom.

"Morning, Mrs Jones – ggh!" he said, ending on an involuntary gill gasp. "Is Jamie in?"

Mrs Jones gave him a shrewd look. "You're up early, William."

"Early bird catches – ggh! – the worm, Mrs Jones."

She made a noise, closed the door a fraction and then shouted. Jamie – Jay-Jay – appeared blinking his big big eyes.

"Whut time is it, B? Ggh!"

"We got work to do, dog," said Billy.

"What kind of work?" said Mrs Jones suspiciously.

"School work," said Billy.

Mrs Jones knew they were up to something – there was no school in Fish Town – but she said nothing. Jay-Jay put on his cap and attempted to dodge his mom's kisses.

"Ggh! Bring your bat," said Billy. Jay-Jay had a wicked aluminium baseball bat that had yet to be christened.

"What's he need that for?" said Mrs Jones.

"Sports," said Billy.

Flat two was, as advertised, furnished. It looked like a page from an IKEA catalogue circa 1995. Closing the door behind her, Morag stripped off her outer layers and made straight for the bathroom. There was a shower, there was a bath, there were towels but there was no soap, shampoo or any personal grooming products at all. It was a flat, not a hotel.

Morag searched the kitchen. There were a number of sprays and bottles under the sink that would probably be effective cleaners but would also probably burn off her skin or cause her hair to fall out. She selected washing-up liquid as a poor substitute for soap.

Morag showered and dried and emerged smelling like a lemon-fresh kitchen.

She put her blouse and underwear in the tumble dryer in the unscientific hope that a dose of dry heat might remove the sweaty smells. She then turned her attention to her jacket and skirt. In desperation, she returned to the kitchen cupboard. Mr Muscle Advanced Power promised to tackle tough kitchen grease and, buffed in with a scouring pad, turned a number of light stains into larger and darker stains on her jacket sleeves and deadened some of the B.O. Power Force Window & Glass washed away some unpleasant trails but its 'vinegar cleaning action' brought those B.O. smells right back.

The Triplewax car wax was a mistake, just a mistake.

She had entered the flat looking like she'd had a fight in a curry house and smelling like an alcoholic bag lady. She left the flat looking like she'd borrowed her clothes from a car mechanic and smelling like a petrochemical factory.

She checked her reflection in the mirror on the first floor landing.

"Look like an old boot," she told herself.

There was a shuffling sound from up the stairs. Morag peered up but saw nothing.

Morag spotted an elastic band in the landing window shelf and used it to tie back her lank hair. Next to it was a short bottle of pump action spray. It featured a picture of a jaunty ginger cat.

"Ideal for treating anxiety and stress in pets."

She gave an experimental spray. It smelled a bit herbal, a bit earthy. It was a lot better than eau de chemical works. She doused herself liberally, put it back in the window and headed down and out.

Morag, following her phone's instructions, walked around the tree-lined perimeter of a grassy park and towards the nearest train station. When she stopped on a bridge to get her bearings, a cat brushed up against her leg and meowed.

Morag sighed. She wasn't a cat person, but it was good to know that she was doing her bit to relieve the anxiety of Birmingham's pets.

The Waters Crew met under the Heath Mill Lane bridge, seven coracles bunched together into a single raft. The last of the morning mist still clung to The Waters. Pupfish yawned and gulped for air.

"What is it then?"

Billy eyed him coldly. "You in a hurry, dog?"

"I'm just saying, B. You got us all up early and I'm – ggh! – eager."

Billy gave him a slow nod. "Eager? Aight. It's good you're eager because today's the day."

"What day?" enquired Jay-Jay.

"Our day. Our moment, dog. I've just had a message from our contact. One of our – ggh! – people has been taken by the feds."

"Man, that's whack," said Kid Fry.

"Nah, it's all part of the plan. They ain't got nothin' on her. But we need to sever some links, cut some bitches loose."

Billy hunkered down low. The Waters Crew leaned in. "Jay-Jay. You and Death Roe are going to take out the jeweller. Quick, fast, now."

"Fasho," said Jay-Jay.

65

"Ain't I going?" said Pupfish.

"You're too – ggh! – dumb. You'll only fuck things up."

"I ain't dumb."

"Dumb as your hood-rat mom," said Jay-Jay.

"Hey."

"Your momma's so dumb, the smartest thing to come out of her mouth was my dick."

"Man!" whined Pupfish but now Fluke joined in.

"Your momma's so dumb – ggh! – she thinks seaweed is marijuana for fish," he said.

"Enough," said Billy.

"Pup, your momma's so dumb, she tried to kill *Daganau-Pysh* by drowning him," laughed Jay-Jay.

A large, flat silent bubble broke the surface of The Waters. Everyone watched the ripples roll out across the dark surface. A joke too far.

"Enough," said Billy with quiet forcefulness. "Today, we step up to the mark. It's not just about the cheddar, homies – ggh! It's about power. It's about becoming names. Legends."

"Like Tupac," said Fluke.

Billy ignored him.

"Jay-Jay and Death Roe, the jeweller," he said. "The rest of you, I need you down at the film studio."

"Me and my swinging dick about to become movie stars." Tony T grinned wide.

"We – ggh! – don't have a zoom lens that powerful," said Fluke.

Billy took out his knife. It had a thin filleting blade, as long as his forearm.

"I saw this movie about the Japanese mafia."

"Yakuza," said Skinny Pete.

"Right. And, when one of them screws up, he has to cut off his finger, like to say sorry – ggh! – and give it to his boss."

All eyes were on the knife.

"No one's gonna screw up, are they?" said Billy.

"No way, dog," said Jay-Jay.

"Good." Billy put the knife away.

"Fish fingers," said Fluke but he wasn't laughing anymore.

66

"True dat," said Pupfish.

Rod picked up the phone while looking through the catalogue of the Vault's contents. Over three thousand items listed, including the freshly returned Kevin, and no knowing yet what else the idiot protestor had disturbed.

"Campbell here."

"Rod. It's Morag."

"Everything all right?"

"I can't get in."

Rod held back a sigh. "We could have really used you today. Hit the ground running, er, again. But if you've genuinely not recovered from yesterday then –"

"No, Rod," she said. "I am here, outside. I just can't get in."

"Can't?"

"This security guy..."

"Bob." Rod growled. "Stick the daft bloody apeth on."

There was an inaudible exchange and then the phone was passed over.

"Let her in," said Rod. "Don't care, Bob. Let her in." He shut the catalogue in exasperation and just waited for the man to just stop talking. "On my authority, Bob. Rod. It's Rod. You know it's me. I will come down there and slap you silly if you do not let her in now."

He stood up, preparing to make good his promise, and then stopped abruptly.

"Cats? What do you mean, 'cats'?"

Out of the lift, Morag went straight to the reception desk. "Lois, I need my suitcase from yesterday."

"Morning, bab."

Lois tried to appear like she wasn't looking at Morag's soiled clothing. She wasn't very good at it.

"Suitcase," said Morag.

Lois nodded. "Now, I put it somewhere very safe, didn't I?" she said cheerily.

"Good," said Morag.

"And in a mo I'll remember where that was."

"Kind of got a major wardrobe malfunction here."

"It doesn't look *that* bad," said Lois.

"The fact you used the word 'that' and said it in a silly voice tells me it does look that bad," said Morag.

"It will come to me," said Lois. "But I do have your ID card. Here. No more trouble getting in."

"Morning," said Rod, sweeping through. "Morag, we're interviewing in room three. Now, if you can."

"Lois is getting something for me."

"She can bring it through, can't she?" He looked directly at her.

How wonderful was the typical man, thought Morag. She looked like she'd been dragged through a janitor's cupboard backwards and he didn't even notice.

"Of course," she said. She followed him down the corridor.

"What's this about you being followed by a horde of cats?" said Rod.

"Oh, nothing," she said. "I think they liked my perfume or something."

"You smell very clean," he said.

"Er, thanks."

Morag looked at her new ID card. "Jesus!"

"What?" said Rod.

She showed him.

"That's a nice picture," he said.

"Well, yes..."

Rod swiped and opened a door.

The interview room was a windowless but warmly lit cube of a room. Venislarn protective glyphs were etched into the doorframe. At a table sat a young and miserable woman, toying unhappily with her chunky earrings. Morag instantly thought that no woman that pretty could ever be that miserable. There was something utterly fascinating about her elfin face, glamorous even.

The two rounds of buttered toast on the table in front of her sat entirely uneaten. To the side, Rod placed a pair of handcuffs and a rolled-up canvas banner.

"Izzy, this is my colleague, Ms Murray. She and I have a few more questions for you."

"I'm not answering any more questions," said Izzy moodily. "Not until I've had my phone call. I'm entitled to a phone call."

Rod and Morag sat. "Who would you call?" said Rod.

"My boyfriend."

"Uh-huh. Bet he's worrying about you. What's his name?"

"Benjamin. When do I get my phone call?"

"The sooner you answer our questions, the sooner this will be over. I need you to explain how you broke into the Library Vault."

"I told you once."

"And when you start telling us the truth, I'll stop asking. I pride myself on being able to turn my hand to anything," he said and picked up the handcuffs. "Give me enough time and I reckon I could near break in anywhere, get past security doors, crack keypad locks, even open handcuffs without the keys. But you..."

"You couldn't pick them the other night," said Izzy, raising an eyebrow as she picked at her nail polish.

"I was under pressure," said Rod. He snapped the handcuffs around his left wrist, took off his tie clip, twisted it into two needle-like halves and paused with one over the cuff lock, looking at Izzy. "I should think you felt the pressure the night before last. So, while I pop this open, why don't you have a rethink and tell us how you really did it?"

"I told you. I levered open the back door and I went down the stairs and there was a keypad and I pressed buttons until it opened," Izzy huffed like a child forced to eat their greens.

"I saw the CCTV, Izzy," said Morag. "The first six buttons you pressed were the right six buttons."

"Lucky guess," said Izzy.

Rod twisted and dug with the lock pick. "No one's that lucky," he said.

"How's that lock coming?" said Izzy.

"Coming," he said without much conviction.

"You knew the access codes," said Morag. "You knew exactly where to go."

"I was protesting," said Izzy. "Standing up for our local library service."

"You don't even have a library card," said Rod. "We checked."

"I don't need a library card to enjoy the library or to know that it's important."

"Someone gave you the codes, Izzy."

Izzy nervously fingered her earrings. They were silver, or possibly white gold, thick pieces embossed with an intricate looping knot design over which Izzy traced her fingers.

"Who told you the codes?" asked Morag.

"Just tell us and then you can go back to your boyfriend," said Rod and grunted as the handcuffs failed to give.

"I can't," said Izzy.

"Can't tell us?" said Morag. "Why can't you tell us?"

Izzy's stressed fidgeting with her jewellery intensified, as though the pattern on her earrings were an endless race track for fingers. Now she accelerated to F1 speeds, round and round the overlapping lanes, bouncing off the three – no, four – corners. No, three.

Morag reached forward and grabbed Izzy's wrist.

Dr Ingrid Spence's T-shirt said, 'There are two kinds of people: those who can infer from incomplete data'.

She considered the earrings for some time.

"I've seen a design like that before," said Morag. "A piece of graffiti in one of the canal tunnels."

"It's definitely Venislarn," agreed Ingrid.

"So, our protestor friend is a lying cow," said Rod. He still had the handcuff on his wrist and worked at it constantly.

"Or this is an amazing coincidence," said Morag. "Rod, do you think we should just get someone to cut that off?"

"If I can't pick it, I want to know how our friend Izzy got out of it later without any keys."

"No, it's embarrassing, Rod," she said.

Ingrid closed the earrings in her fist. "The design is a zahir."

"A what?" said Rod.

"A zahir," said Morag. "Is it dangerous?"

"It's not quite a Langford Basilisk," said Ingrid.

"Are you two just making up words?" said Rod.

"This is a minor zahir," said Ingrid, "but enough exposure could prove fatal."

"How?"

"The pattern is visually fascinating. The eyes follow it. Like the Coventry ring road, once you've been drawn in, it's almost impossible to get out. You ever seen something or heard a tune and not been able to get it out of your head? It's like that."

"I remember a training exercise in Beersheba," said Rod. "Joint exercise with the Israeli Defense Forces. A forty-mile hike with full packs. I was following behind an IDF trooper, Roni her name. Shapely lass and no mistake. All through the heat and the pain I just stared at her jiggling arse, followed it all the way home. Focussed on it 'til there was nothing else in my mind, 'til the rest of the world had gone away. Got me through the hike." He smiled. "I can still picture it now, clear as day."

"Yep," said Ingrid. "Well, the zahir is just like that. Sort of. Not really."

Rod shrugged. "Closest I've come to being obsessed by anything."

"Sure," said Morag, watching his continuing struggles with the handcuff.

"The more powerful basilisks actually exploit mental architecture," said Ingrid, "infecting the brain with a Trojan reboot loop or the human equivalent of the Blue Screen of Death. The obsession becomes everything. The victim sees it in their dreams and thinks of nothing but it when they're awake. They lose the ability to perceive any form of external reality. They stop talking, they stop eating, they stop moving."

Rod leaned back and looked through the narrow window at Izzy. He was saddened and surprised. He vividly recalled how, on first meeting her, he was taken aback by her beauty. Now, he just saw a thin young woman who really ought to take advantage of the food laid before her.

"She's changed," he said.

"The effect of the zahir casts a glamour," said Ingrid and Morag grunted in agreement. "Our eyes are drawn to her, to the zahir she wears."

"So what next?" said Morag.

"Since our girl isn't talking, this is our lead," said Rod.

"I'm not sure how," said Ingrid.

"Let's have a look."

"Careful."

Rod took one of the earrings from her and turned it over. "Maker's mark," he said, circling a series of indentations on the reverse. "I'm willing to bet this is local."

"The Jewellery Quarter?" said Ingrid.

Rod nodded. "Time to pound the streets, newbie," he said to Morag and gestured for them to go.

"You in front," said Morag. "Now that I know you're a perverted arse-ogler."

"Only on punishment marches," he said.

In reception, Rod pressed for the lift. Morag turned to Lois the receptionist.

"I think you've got some explaining to do," she said, as politely as she could. It was only her second day after all.

"I'm looking for your luggage as we speak," said Lois and then, aware that she was sitting at a desk and doing no such thing, added, "In my mind. Mentally retracing my steps."

"Not about that. About this." Morag held out her new ID card.

"Did I spell your name wrong?"

"No. The picture."

Rod was looking over her shoulder. "It's a nice one. You look like thingy out of whatsit."

"Scarlett Johansson in *The Avengers*," said Morag.

"That's the girly."

"That's because this *is* a picture of Scarlett Johansson in *The Avengers*!"

"I would admit there's a passing similarity," said Lois.

"It's her! Not me! You think I don't know my own face?"

"I did say I'd do a little Photoshopping," said Lois.

"Yeah. I thought you meant airbrushing, not cut and paste."

The lift arrived with a 'ding'.

"It looks just like you," said Rod.

"Then your eyesight must be defective," Morag snapped and got into the lift. "Too much staring at arses probably."

Nina entered the Library, mildly diverted by the trio of moggies sitting on the pavement watching the building expectantly.

It was nearly eleven o'clock but Nina worked flexi-time. There was no official policy or procedure that allowed officers to work flexible hours but Nina did it anyway and ignored anyone who said she couldn't. It had served her well in the two years she'd been with the Birmingham consular mission.

Coming the other way across the lobby were Rod and Morag, bickering like an old married couple. Rod was preoccupied with something on his wrist. Morag was wearing the same clothes she'd been in the day before, had her hair pulled back in a Croydon facelift and looked generally like crap.

"No, it is offensive," Morag was saying.

"How can it be?" said Rod. "I'm saying that you looked good. I *like* Scarlett Johansson."

"Point is, I *don't* look like Scarlett Johansson," said Morag. "So what you're really saying is that you don't know what I look like. You haven't even looked at me."

"I thought you didn't want me looking at you."

"At my bum! Heaven help me, Rod. I'd expect you to know what my face looks like. If I went missing and the police asked for a description, would you tell them I looked like Scarlett Johansson, just without the rubber catsuit."

"I think a rubber –"

"Don't even finish that sentence! It's like you're saying all gingers look the same. It's practically racism. And would you stop fiddling with that bloody handcuff."

"Morning, Rod," Nina chirped, sipping her take out coffee. "Morning, generic ginger person."

Rod sighed. "Nina. As a woman, please tell Morag that if people think she looks like Scarlett Johansson, she should take it as a compliment."

"They look nothing alike," said Nina.

"Thank you," said Morag.

"I think people shouldn't quibble when folks are being complimentary about their appearance," said Rod.

"You look great," said Nina.

"Really?" said Morag.

"You've got that whole skanky accountant look going on. Bold perfume too."

"Uh-huh," said Morag.

"What's with the jewellery?" said Nina of Rod's handcuffs.

"Man is trying to prove a point," said Morag.

"Give me a minute," said Rod.

Nina reach for the locked cuff. "You haven't even got lock p–" Rod began and then the cuffs came away in Nina's hand.

"How?"

"I could explain," said Nina.

"But?"

She shrugged and walked towards the lift, drinking coffee.

"Highest concentration of jewellers' businesses in Europe," said Rod as they walked down Vyse Street to the next shop on their list.

"You don't say?" said Morag.

"Birmingham was built on the manufacture of small things – buttons, pins, jewellery. That and guns. Over half the jewellery in Britain used to be made here."

Beyond the modern shops and Warstone Lane Cemetery, Vyse Street was a road of tall Georgian terraces. Every other one was a jeweller's shop. Many of the rest had simple plates by the door, advertising the specific expertise of the workers within.

"A city of metalworkers," said Rod.

"You should work for the tourist board," said Morag.

Rod shrugged.

"My flat's round the corner. It's just stuff you pick up." He stopped by the door of a jeweller's. "Whereas you appear to have picked up an entourage."

The half dozen cats that had followed them down the street wound themselves around her legs. There was a pair of tabbies, a stumpy tortoiseshell, a grey with no tail and three black cats which were somehow each a *different* shade of black.

"You a cat person?" said Rod.

"I suspect I smell like a cat person," said Morag. "This new spray I put on this morning..."

"Maybe I should just take this one," he said. "You stay and appease your followers."

Rod went inside.

74

Morag was not a cat lover really. She admired their self-sufficiency but truly couldn't understand the idea of a housemate who didn't contribute to the chores. She didn't hate them either. She wasn't so low as to resort to violence to drive them away. Instead, she told them all to piss off and, when that seemed to have no impact, resorted to harsh language that would make an Edinburgh schemie blush. Cats, it seemed, were made of stronger stuff.

Rod all but skipped down the steps.

"Knew someone would know," he said. "Hylton Street. A jeweller called Ben Shipston."

"Benjamin the boyfriend?" suggested Morag.

Hylton Street was a loop of a side street almost entirely occupied by the rear doors of shabby workshops. A peeling blue door beneath boarded-up first floor windows held a small brass plate that read 'B. Shipston, Lost Wax Casting'. The edges of this door were cracked and splintered. Rod prodded with one finger and the door swung in.

"Always an interesting development." He undid his jacket and unclipped the leather strap on his holster but did not draw.

"Shall we?" he said and stepped inside.

Morag went in after him, followed by a handful of furry deputies.

"Jesus! Leave me alone, would you?" she hissed.

The door led to a dirty uneven set of stairs. A small ancient window let in a pale dusty light above. The air smelled musty and damp.

"Mr Shipston?" called Rod. "Your front door was open."

There was no sound but their own footsteps and a minor spat between the pair of tabbies. At the top of the stairs was an open workspace. Bare floor boards and ceiling beams. Crumbling brickwork. There was a desk, a strongbox set into the wall and three workbenches set out with jeweller's tools and orders at different stages in manufacture.

"This place probably hasn't changed in a hundred years," said Rod. "'cept maybe the electric lights."

"And the dead body."

"Hmmm?"

There was a body.

Wedged between two workbenches was a man, or at least his legs and torso. The bloody ruin of his head looked like a failed pitch for a headache advert. There were powerful splash marks on the wall behind the corpse. Some of the trails were still wet.

"Fresh," said Rod.

"How fresh?"

"Last few hours, I'd reckon."

Morag looked at the jewellery on the workbenches. "It wasn't a robbery."

She turned over a couple of pieces. Some of the designs hurt her eyes, like magic eye pictures. "Venislarn designs. He was making zahirs."

"Don't look like your usual occultist." Rod's experience told him that much.

"In what way, apart from the lack of a head?" she asked.

"Not rightly sure. I just haven't encountered many occultists in Converse sneakers and skinny jeans."

A tortoiseshell cat leapt up onto a workbench and began licking at a damp patch.

"Your feline friends are contaminating a crime scene."

"Damn." Morag picked the moggy up and dumped it on the floor. Her nose twitched. She bent down and sniffed the patch. "Fishy."

He sniffed too.

"You think it was fish?" she said.

"I don't want to know what it is if it isn't fish."

"*Samakha*?" she suggested.

He raised his eyebrows thoughtfully.

"There's a fish ghetto between Digbeth and Deritend," he said. "This is across town for them, although the canal does cut under Summer Row not far from here."

"Some of these markings do look like a *samakha* graffiti tag Nina and I found yesterday," said Morag.

Rod took out his phone. "I'll call this in and see if Nina's got an opinion on the *samakha* angle."

Morag reached under the bench and pulled out another phone. She woke the screen.

"Locked. Biometric thumbprint. Might have been a problem if it required a retinal scan, but he still has his thumbs, see?" Rod gestured towards what he hoped was a thumb.

Morag turned the dead man's hand so it was upright and pressed the phone against his still warm thumb.

"Thank you."

Nina picked up Rod's call.

"Wassup, kinky cuffs?" she said.

"We've stepped into a murder scene. We're at fourteen Hylton Road."

"Human?"

"One Benjamin Shipston, we think. We'll need police and black ambulance at some point. Morag has this theory that it's a *samakha* hit job."

"That's not their style really."

"No, but there's some circumstantial evidence and there are designs here that look like *samakha* gang tags. Didn't you say the Waters Crew were starting to act too big for their boots of late? This new twerp leading them. Free Willy?"

"Billy the Fish."

"That's the chappie."

"They're just kids, Rod."

"The Library. They might have put that daft lass up to it."

"The protest thing was just a ruse? Wouldn't surprise me. That Izzy girl certainly isn't all knitted scarves, falafels and lefty morals."

"How come?" Rod swapped phone ears.

"Those cuffs. There's a trick catch under the cuff. They're not standard issue. They're purely for... recreational use."

"Marital aid, you mean?"

"If that's a coy way of saying they're a sex toy, then yes. Some of the sex shops in Brum sell them."

"I don't think I want to know how you know this kind of stuff."

"Yes, you do," said Nina, "you're just too prudish to ask."

"Oh, sweet hell," whispered Morag.

"What?" said Rod.

Morag showed him the picture gallery on the phone. "I think this zahir business just got a whole lot worse," she said.

After ending the call, Nina spun round in her chair, drawing her feet up and leaning back thoughtfully.

"Do you know why Thomas Jefferson invented the swivel chair?" said Vivian, without looking up from her work.

The response team office in the Library was open plan with a stunning view of the miserable maisonettes and tower blocks of Ladywood. It had four desks and, theoretically, operated a hot-desking policy. This tended to mean that every person's crap didn't just occupy one desk but any desk they had ever sat at. However, Vivian's desk was Vivian's desk and no one dared hot-desk it.

"Not a clue," said Nina.

"Do you think he did it so he could move easily between two positions while drafting the Declaration of Independence or *do you think* he did it so he could spin on it like a demented toddler?"

Nina spun and thought. "He could do both."

"Well, you are neither Thomas Jefferson nor a demented toddler. Stop it." Vivian treated her to one of her cold hard stares. Most of Vivian's stares were cold and hard but this one was deliberately so.

"Vivian? You know the Waters Crew, do you think they're capable of murder?"

"Billy the Fish killed Eazy Boy. It's common knowledge."

"No, I meant kill a human."

"Eazy Boy was half human. The Waters Crew are all mixed background, not a true *samakha* among them."

"I know that and I'm not being racist – hashtag Fish Lives Matter, and all that – but do you think they'd kill someone, a non-participant, perhaps part of some gangland deal?"

Vivian stopped to give this some thought. "Billy is a slippery customer –"

"To be expected."

"And he thinks life owes him more than it does. The boy loves his mother. He wants to get her out of Fish Town."

"She made a rehousing application last month. Dickens Heath. The new builds."

"That's purely for the unholy offspring of *Yoth Mammon*."

"I know. She won't get in and, if she did, they'd eat her alive."

Vivian held her pen in both hands, testing its strength, as though she was preparing to snap it.

"I have a scheduled visit to Fish Town on Thursday to check registration documentation. I could move it forward, knock on a few doors and ask a few direct questions."

"That would be really helpful," said Nina. "I was going to do that myself but you have a way with them."

"A way?"

"Like a scary headmistress. I've seen it. All those wannabe gangstas, caps off, looking sheepish, calling you 'Mrs Grey'."

"It is my name."

Nina contemplated her colleague. "You don't normally change your schedule in order to be, you know, helpful."

Vivian gave her a rare look of genuine human emotion.

"I need a break," she said and cast her pen down on her paperwork. "Mr Hamilton, our virgin heart donor. Do you know how many funeral directors are willing to perform an open casket funeral for a man with no eyes?"

"Not many?"

"No."

"Vivian. He's dead. He won't know."

"I will," said Vivian firmly, standing up.

Nina picked up the handcuffs on her desk.

"Well, in that case," she said. "I'm going to visit some sex shops while you go tickle the trout."

Vivian glared at her. "What?" she asked.

"What?" said Nina.

"Tickle the...? Is that some sort of sexual reference, Miss Seth? Please don't discuss your filthy acts of self-abuse in the –"

"What?" said Nina, confused. "It's a fishing thing, isn't it?" She started to doubt herself. "When you put your hand under and rub its..." She attempted a hand action which probably didn't help.

"Filthy," said Vivian and left.

Rod and Morag had searched for and bagged up all potentially Venislarn items and left the crime scene to the police detectives. Morag flicked back and forth through the photos on the late Mr Shipston's phone and googled on her own phone while Rod drove. There had been roundabouts and several tunnels and Morag had already lost all sense of what direction they were heading in.

"Okay," said Rod. "So, Izzy Wu breaks into the Vault, possibly with the help of or under the instruction of Benjamin the boyfriend."

"Correct," said Morag.

"Who is – excuse me, was – making jewellery based on Venislarn designs, in particular the hypnotic zahirs."

"Also correct."

"Probably based on those images," he gestured blindly at the phone.

"Probably."

"Tattoos."

"Indeed."

The images on the phone were all close-ups of tattoos in black ink, lines, swirls and sigils that, even on the phone screen, seemed to writhe and strain against the confines of two dimensions. Tattoos on wrists, on thighs, larger designs between pale shoulder blades. The lighting in the pictures suggested they were nearly all taken in the same place.

"Occultists."

"Gang tats?" replied Rod.

"Most of these look like women."

"Branding of property?" said Rod, darkly.

"Or maybe they're just idiots who don't know what they're getting tattooed with."

"Like those people who think their tattoo is the Chinese symbol for 'power' or 'peace' but it actually says 'chicken noodle soup' or 'dumb Western tit'."

Morag grunted, a half-laugh.

"Zahirs are dangerous. They're weapons. And someone's strapping them to human flesh. I can't help but think that will end spectacularly badly."

She flicked back to a photo of a tattoo being applied. A hand in blue latex held the ink gun. Poking out of the cuff was a wristband tattoo: two orbs, one of them the earth, wrapped in a ribbon. There was writing but the image was too blurry to read.

"Seen anything like that before?" said Morag and held out the phone to Rod.

Rod took his eyes off the road for a second and smiled.

"Birmingham City Football Club," he said.

"Oh, okay."

"Our tattooist is an old school Blues fan."

The taxi company office was at the end of Gibb Street, in a curve of street that was apparently inaccessible from both ends. It was unmarked, apart from the word 'TAXI' and a phone number painted above the closed metal grille door: '0121 427 20--'. The last two digits of the phone number had been violently scraped away. Vivian gave the sticky door a firm shove and stepped inside.

"Taxi?" said the figure sat in the gloom behind the counter.

Vivian showed him her ID.

"Taxi?" he said again.

"Let me in, Obie."

Obie had less of the *samakha* look about him. His shiny skin, large and sad eyes, and wide, downturned mouth could almost be mistaken for those of an unfortunate soul with a bad diet, worse genes, and a soul-crushing job (such as, say, managing a low-class taxi cab office).

He stubbed out his cigarette, slid off his stool and opened the bolts on the door behind the counter. Beyond was a narrow back alley between crowded terraces.

"I am going to *Daganau Vei*," she said.

"Taxi, taxi," said Obie subserviently. He closed the door, pulled a handle on the opposite side and opened the door again — this time onto a set of damp steps. Vivian disapproved of such fish magics.

"Better," she said.

"Taxi," said Obie, happy to oblige.

She took the steps carefully. They led directly onto the canal and it would be monstrous bad luck to fall in. *Daganau-Pysh* never turned down free food.

The *samakha* who had been accommodated in the converted warehouses and densely packed houses had set about building on and extending their homes with the zeal of the nouveau riche and the planning concerns of slum landlords. Roofs had become attic apartments. Apartments had sprouted balconies. Balconies had gained roofs of their own and rickety upper floors. Upper floors had merged to form bridges with their neighbours. Bridges had criss-crossed in networks and, even where the weight of the structure threatened to drag the whole down into The Waters, every open space was home to additional buildings or some sort of stall or structure. The whole conjoined mess of buildings would have burned down years ago if it hadn't all been so damp.

As Vivian stepped onto the towpath she was aware that eyes watched her from behind shutters, that distant telescopes were trained on her. Humans were not unknown in Fish Town — there were registered service folk who were allowed access, and some foolish individuals who had sold themselves to the *samakha* — but government officials always drew attention. A human woman in a ragged shift pushed a pram along the towpath, her offspring wriggling in the tub of water it carried. People who were half-human, half-*samakha* solemnly propelled their punts and coracles along The Waters. A true *samakha* observed Vivian from a dark doorway, its webbed paw on the doorframe. Several more were just visible beneath the surface of The Waters, lidless eyes staring up, gill slits palpitating.

Vivian walked along the path, took one of the more reliable wooden bridges to the other side of the canal, and climbed up to a second floor address. The door opened as she approached. Courtney O'Keefe was all nervous smiles, running her bony fingers through her dirty, cotty hair.

"Mrs Grey. I saw you coming and I put the kettle on."

"Good morning, Miss O'Keefe," said Vivian.

She entered the mildewed front room. A pan of water was starting to heat on a primus stove. There were two mismatched cups on the table. Vivian saw the unpleasant stains inside them and imagined even boiling water wouldn't kill those germs.

"You've come about my application," said Courtney.

"No," said Vivian. "I've come to speak to your son, William."

Courtney didn't look up from the cups. "Why?"

"I have questions to ask him."

"What's he done?"

"That would be one of the questions I have for him."

She made for the inner door.

"My housing application...?" Courtney poured the hot water.

"Has not been processed," said Vivian.

"But it's been months."

"Five weeks. And it has not been processed."

"But when?"

Vivian gestured ahead. "Is he in?"

Courtney shook her head and then sniffed back a sob. "Why do you do this to us?"

"Do what?" asked Vivian honestly.

"This – living in this place – it's hell."

"No, Miss O'Keefe. I have seen hell. I have stood on its shores. This is not hell."

"This miserable fucking place. I can't imagine anywhere worse."

"Then you have a surprising lack of imagination. Can you tell me where your son is?"

"Fuck you, you old cow."

Vivian ignored the woman's outburst and started down the short hallway.

"I might as well kill myself then," yelled Courtney. "Living in this shithole. Suicide. What's the difference?"

"Actually, Miss O'Keefe, apart from the obvious, there are some notable similarities. If you wanted to kill yourself, there are indeed places you can go, interviews you can go through, forms you can sign and, having made an informed choice, seek an end to it all." She turned to address the shorter woman. "When the *samakha* laid claim to you, do you remember that we interceded on your behalf? We counselled you to reject their offer. We explained what would happen. And then you signed our forms to say you freely consented to this."

"But I didn't know. A person can change their mind, can't they?"

Vivian nodded. "I should think that some people, in that Swiss clinic or wherever, moments after drinking down the bitter pentobarbital, think very much the same." She opened the door to Billy's bedroom. It was cramped, cluttered and untidy. The bed was unmade, the sheets grubby and crusty in places. There was an unsavoury organic stink to the place. In these matters, it was like any teenager's bedroom.

There were cardboard boxes of various shapes and sizes stacked along the wall. Translucent white DVD cases filled them to the brim.

"Did something fall off the back of a boat?" asked Vivian, but there was no reply from Billy's mum.

Vivian opened a case. The disc inside was blank. A portable DVD player sat on top of the tallest pile of boxes. The case crackled as Vivian took out a DVD. She put it in the player. The player whirred. There was no menu, just the movie.

Vivian watched the detestable scene unfold in stoic silence.

"Give it to me, baby."

"You're gonna have to unwrap your present, honey. Use your tongue."

"Is this a double knot?"

"What you up to, Mrs G? Ggh! Sneaking about a man's crib, huh?" said a voice behind her.

It wasn't Courtney; she had gone. It was her boy, Billy the Fish. Vivian noted the knife held casually in one hand. The giant *samakha* with huge drooping barbels behind him was unarmed. The ugly youth with mismatched eyes beside them, held a metal baseball bat. Vivian saw a smear of blood along its side.

"Sneaking?" said Vivian. "Sneaking? This is my jurisdiction, William. Where did you get these DVDs? From whom did you buy them?"

"Buy them?" said Billy and grinned.

"Oh, we've moved into manufacturing, have we?" She pointed a finger at the bat wielder. "You are Jamie Jones."

The fish boy nearly caved in under her stare but managed to grip his bat tighter and say, "What of it?"

"You and I need to talk."

"'Bout what? Ggh!"

84

"Does your mum know you're a killer now?"

Again, it was nearly enough to break him. "Mrs Grey..." he began to wheedle.

"You're not taking Jay-Jay anywhere," said Billy.

Vivian ignored him and looked at the giant behind them.

"Tyrone. I've got no argument with you. Go on home. These two, however, are in *big* trouble."

Billy eyeballed his tall friend and the big lunk stayed put. "You're nuttin but a toy cop, Mrs G," said Billy. "You think you can push us around, toy cop? I'm a – ggh! – a playa now. Rolling in onion booty and dead presidents."

"Dead presidents," said Vivian.

Billy rubbed shiny fingertips together.

"William, this is the UK," she said. "We don't have dead presidents."

"No, but..."

"We got the queen on ours," said Tyrone deeply, speaking for the first time.

"That's not the point," said Billy.

"We should call 'em dead queens, B," said Jamie.

"She's not dead," said Tyrone.

"Course she's dead, dog," said Jamie. "She's been on them, like – ggh! – forever."

"She's not dead," said Tyrone.

"Call 'em Elizabeths. Ggh! Got me a pocketful of Elizabeths. Sounds kinda —"

Billy shoved him hard.

"Shut it!" He turned his blade towards Vivian. "You shouldn't have come here, Mrs G. Big mistake."

She shook her head minimally. "The mistake is yours, William. You live here under my sufferance."

He sneered. "I am the spawn of *Daganau-Pysh*. Ggh! I'm untouchable."

"No, William. No one wants to touch you. That's different. As far as *Daganau-Pysh* is concerned, you're a filthy half-breed, a mulatto. You're worth nothing to him."

Billy the Fish trembled with rage.

"And you're worth less," he said.

85

Vivian nodded. "Maybe."

She pulled out her phone and began to dial. Billy slapped it out of her hand.

Vivian rarely felt afraid. It wasn't an emotion she had much use for. But Billy had overstepped a line that the *samakha* did not cross.

"Take her," he said.

"Take her where?" said Jamie.

Billy hissed, deep in his throat.

"Give her a pair of concrete Converse. Then a – ggh! – long walk off a short pier."

After a morning of driving round the city, Rod and Morag were parked up, waiting.

Rod was considering the survival paracord bracelet on his wrist and wondering if there was any mileage in weaving a length of monofilament wire into it to make a James Bond-style garrotte. Morag, following the conversation on the way over, was googling tattoo fails and had found a rich stream of misspelt and poorly punctuated tattoos.

"Too cool for shool," she read.

"He didn't need no education," Rod agreed.

Morag flicked on.

"No regerts," she read.

"That tattoo being one them."

"No ledge is power."

"Hard to argue with that." Rod fiddled with the air blower to de-mist the car windscreen from their breath.

"My mum is my angle."

"You're making these up."

Morag showed him her phone.

"And so many misplaced apostrophes. My old English teacher would explode. Do they not spellcheck these?"

"I like to think there's a street gang somewhere with deliberately misspelled tattoos who kill people who point out the mistakes."

"Unlikely."

"I said I'd like to think it. Didn't say it was true."

"Can't they sue the tattooist?"

"It's like sign writers. The customer gets what the customer asks for."

Morag made a disagreeable noise. "I don't understand why people do it. I think you've got to be seriously shallow to think you can have a personality painted onto your skin."

Rod cleared his throat meaningfully.

"Really?" she said. "Where?"

Rod rolled up his sleeve. "Had it done the week after I was airlifted out of the Syrian Desert."

"And here I was thinking it was going to be an 'intimate' tattoo." Morag read the thick gothic script on his upper arm. "Carpe diem."

"The thinking man's YOLO," he said.

"But you were in the SAS."

"I can neither confirm nor deny."

"You're not allowed tattoos."

"Aye. It was also my sort of resignation note. What I'd seen beneath that desert was enough to shake all my assumptions about the world and what I was doing with my life."

"What happened?" asked Morag.

"Lois not tell you?" he said. "Surprised. Queen of gossip, that woman. I got separated from my patrol outside Al-Qa'im. This was back in the Second Gulf War. The big one. We were helping the Americans put a stopper in the flow of military hardware coming across the border from – Ay up, what's this?"

Morag looked up. Down the road, the door to the previously closed tattoo shop opened. A man and a woman, both of them thin as rakes, stepped out.

"You think it's our Bluenose tattooist?" said Rod.

"It is," said Morag.

"You reckon."

"Look at that fresh tattoo on the woman's arm. Venislarn."

Rod tried to get a good look. "You know," he said, "I'd be able to see better and feel a flaming bit less conspicuous if there weren't a pair of ginger toms sat on the bonnet, pawing at the windscreen."

Rod tried putting on the windscreen wipers to startle the cats, but they pounced, wide eyed upon the moving blades, clearly enjoying the game.

"Sorry."

"Didn't say it was your fault."

"Oh, it is," said Morag. "This body spray..."

Rod sniffed and shrugged.

"Are we going to collar these two, then?"

The tattooist had the woman's elbow in a firm grip as they walked away.

"I'd be interested to see where they're going," said Morag.

"Aye," said Rod. "Me too."

Nina wished sex shops didn't smell.

Night Pleasures on Milk Street had clearly made an effort to be welcoming and respectable. It wasn't a dingy and foetid cave of suspicious cinematic delights and dubious sex toys overseen by a miserable troll who had been ground down by the day in day out of peddling smut to furtive men in long coats. Night Pleasures was a bright, cheery and well-organised grotto of erotica and filth. Light samba music played in the background and the shaven-headed woman behind the counter greeted Nina with an upbeat 'Afternoon!' when she entered. But the smell...

Nina browsed a little. The DVD selection had been organised with ruthless precision.

She had a pretty good idea of what she'd find in *BDSM*, but paused to examine what *Double-Stuffed MILF* might contain, so to speak. She skated quickly over *Diaper Fantasies* but the sheer scale of the *Vocational* section took her breath away. Plumbers, nuns, milkmen — all available, complete with their specialist equipment.

There was even a selection of porno reworkings of a popular series of magical movies. Nina was quite tempted to get *Harry Poked-her and the Prisoner of Ass-to-Spank* out of sheer curiosity.

In an age when the porn industry had almost entirely moved online, a place like this had to survive on personal service and giving the customer exactly what they wanted.

Nina was impressed. It was just a shame about the smell.

She supposed there wasn't much to be done about it. All that rubber and latex and leather. All those little jars and tubes of lubricants and spray. People didn't complain that carpet shops had that carpet shop smell, or that IKEA had that furniture shop smell. Maybe she shouldn't complain about sex shops having that sex shop smell. It wasn't like they could prop open the door to get the air circulating.

"You all right there, love?" called the shopkeeper.

"Yep, just browsing," said Nina and held up a copy of *Harry Poked-her and the Orgy of the Penis* as evidence. *The Shawspank Redemption* slid forward to take its place.

The shop did sell handcuffs and other items for recreational bondage but not exactly the same cuffs that Izzy Wu had used. Nina went to the counter.

"I wonder if you could help me?" Nina asked.

"I'll try," said the shopkeeper.

"My friend, Izzy, bought some handcuffs. I'm not sure if they were from this shop."

"Have you seen our selection in the alcove?"

"Yes. I was looking for some exactly the same as hers."

"Exactly?"

"Yes," said Nina. "This is one of those 'dead rabbit' situations where I need to replace them before someone notices."

"Can you describe them?"

Nina pulled a face.

"No, I'm..." She dug in her pocket for a phone. "This is Izzy. Do you, perhaps, recall selling them to her?"

The shopkeeper looked at the phone and then immediately looked up into the corner of the room at a CCTV camera. An interesting development, thought Nina.

"I could ask Tony," said the shopkeeper.

"Tony?"

"He runs the shop sometimes."

"That would be lovely," said Nina, sweetly.

"Bear with me." The shopkeeper came from behind the counter and went to a curtained-off door. There was the rattle of keys and the woman was gone.

Nina paused a moment or two, twiddled with a penis-shaped toothbrush on the counter and then followed the woman. The hardboard door behind the curtain had a Yale lock but the shopkeeper had left in on the latch. Careless. Nina cautiously pushed it open. A set of stairs led down. A purple-green light lit the lowest stone steps.

"Okay."

She made her way down as quietly as possible. Beyond the turn in the stairs, the steps continued on down more than a storey. Nina could just about make out voices ahead.

"— about one of Ben's girls," the shopkeeper was saying.

The next voice was deep and guttural and Nina couldn't make out the words.

"I don't know," said the shopkeeper. "What do you mean she's not in the shop?"

Nina reached the bottom step. The sub-cellar was large. Curved brick arches like whale bones supported the ceiling. Near to, brick dust covered the floor. Further in, plaster walls had been put up and concrete flooring laid. Hooks had been drilled into the ceiling to support light rigs. A fuse board had been set into the wall and leads ran from it to recording equipment, mixing desks and computers.

She had walked onto a film set.

A red velvet sheet had been thrown over a concrete platform in the middle of the room. The naked woman laid upon it stared dreamily at some markings on her forearm. The *samakha* between her thighs made a noise like a vacuum cleaner trying to suck up jelly. Nina couldn't tell if either of them was really putting much effort or emotion into their performances.

Off to the side, four barely dressed women lounged on bean bags. Two of them were passing an e-cigarette back and forth. All had tattoos, Nina noted.

"Well, I'll be..." said Nina.

A third *samakha* – cameraman, director and sound guy all rolled into one – turned from his conversation with the shopkeeper to see Nina. He wore a Yankees baseball cap, black shades and enough sparkling fake gold chains to give someone bling blindness.

"What da *bhul*?" baseball cap said.

90

"No, no," said the shopkeeper startled. "You can't be here."

"It's okay," said Nina. "I know Tony T. Tony T knows me."

Tony T took off his sunglasses and squinted. "Ggh! *Muda!*" he said.

"I don't get it," said Nina. "You wear those things indoors. They don't even cover your eyes. Your eyes are in the wrong place for... To hell with it. Excuse me. You. Yes, you. Could you perhaps quit doing the nasty with Debbie Does Dolphins there. That, that noise is really off-putting." The *samakha* on the platform didn't even pause in his ministrations.

Nina turned to Tony T. "Jesus, does someone need to say 'cut' or something?"

"Oi! Pup!" shouted Tony T. "Quit it! The feds – ggh! – are here!"

The samakha stopped and looked up. "Ggh! What?"

"'What' he says," sighed Nina.

The other naked *samakha* was on his feet. He had a nervous energy about him, probably an inkling of the trouble that he was in, and Nina couldn't be sure if he had decided between fight and flight.

"Easy, big boy," she said. "Is that a crab stick you've got there or are you happy to see me?"

The fish boy visibly wilted at her words. The shopkeeper was making a faint keening sound, as though she was about to burst into tears.

"This has nothing to do with me," she said. "I had no idea."

"You had no idea the Waters Crew were running a fish porn movie studio in your basement? I've got to admit, it's really surprising. Not what I was expecting. I came down those stairs and saw this and, I've gotta say I was shocked, *bhul*-me-sideways shocked." She held up a warning finger to the nervous *samakha*. "That wasn't a request, by the way."

"Listen, please," said Tony T. "We weren't – ggh! – doing no harm."

"I'm all for freedom of creative expression," said Nina. "And I even admire your entrepreneurial spirit, but I've got a couple of issues. I don't think any of these other women are registered as *samakha* associates."

"Oh, come on, dog."

"And then there's the small matter of your gang's involvement in an attempted break-in at the Library."

That was it. Clearly, enough blood had returned to his head to allow the tall, nervous one to make a decision and he broke. But he didn't make to run past Nina; he turned, thrust aside a hanging sheet and fled naked through a door that Nina hadn't noticed.

"Hell!" she spat.

Before she could give chase, though, the *samakha* was back: staggering, screaming and swatting at – Nina had to double-check – yes, at a black cat that had inexplicably become attached to his groin. Its teeth and claws were pinned to his fish-and-two-veg. Intriguingly, he was followed in by Rod and Morag pushing a pasty man and woman before them and trailing a short retinue of stray cats behind them.

The cats immediately hissed at the *samakha* lads. The one on the platform, Pup, leapt to his feet and covered his exposed codpiece.

"Nina," said Rod.

"How did you get in?" Nina asked.

Morag gestured behind them. "A lock up in the railway arches. Followed these two."

Nina pointed upwards. "Sex shop. Where Izzy bought the cuffs, or maybe her boyfriend."

"Help me!" squealed the cat-savaged fish boy as he rolled around on the floor in the grip of an enraged pussy.

"I'm going nowhere near that," said Rod. "Now what the bloody heck is going on here?"

"Our friends have been filming their own dirty movies," said Nina, "and, by the looks of it, not just for their own entertainment."

Pup shifted unhappily as cats circled him hissing.

"These girls drugged up?" Rod looked at the waiting women.

Morag crouched beside the women on the bean bags. None of them had been remotely startled by the interruptions. The two smokers were still passing the e-cigarette back and forth, zombie-like.

"Zahir tattoos." She had to make a conscious effort to close her eyes and pull her gaze away. "God, I don't know but these could be high-power stuff."

"Zahirs?" said Nina.

"What better way to keep your... your cattle in line? Get them hooked on viral images. Drag their tiny minds into cages."

Nina looked at the women. They weren't just skinny movie fodder; they were skin and bones, their wills and minds lost in recursive visual loops. She threw an angry glance at the tattooist but the look on his face revealed that he was a victim of his own creations.

"I'm phoning Ingrid," said Rod. "We're going to need some sort of containment here."

"And we'll need to register all these people as Venislarn associates," said Nina.

"If they live that long," said Morag.

Nina felt fury rise within her. "Tony, you complete low-life. You absolute bottom feeder."

"What?"

Nina gestured angrily at the used women. "Who gave you the zahirs?"

"Ggh! I don't know what you're talking about."

"Don't," she said firmly. "It's time to fess up, Tony. Get a grip! I don't want you to make it any harder than it has to be. It's in your hands, don't blow it."

"I'm not blowing – ggh! – nothing," said Tony fearfully.

"Good. Because I want to get right down to it. I want everything you've got and if you're not going to give it to me then I'm going to have to take you in hand. I hope you grasp my point."

"I grasp. I grasp," said Tony T.

"Good!" Nina, wiped her mouth with distaste, "I want names. Who gave you these designs? Who gave you the access codes to the library vault? And who are you selling these DVDs to?"

"I don't know. Ggh! Really, miss, I don't."

"B Shark handled everything," groaned the cat-mangled feller on the floor.

"B Shark?"

"Billy?" said Rod.

Tony T nodded.

"And where's he?" said Nina.

"Don't tell her," said Pup. "Don't."

"Where?" growled Rod.

"Fish Town," said Tony T. "With the fed woman. Ggh! Mrs G."

Vivian was starting to wish Billy would get on with it and actually kill her.

They had tied her hands with old net twine in a dilapidated boathouse at the far end of Fish Town, near where *samakha* territory re-joined the regular geography of the human city. The floor of the boathouse – by accident or design, she couldn't tell – sloped down to the meet the canal's dark waters. There was no current and no wind, but glutinous waves lapped at the boards.

She had never seen *Daganau-Pysh*, Venislarn lord of the deep, god of unfathomable reaches. Those few humans who had glimpsed him had tended to be robbed of the wits and vocabulary to describe what they had seen. She wondered, with a certain detachment, if he would meet her expectations.

Billy the Fish sat on a rotten crate that looked as if it had spent a century at the bottom of the sea. He was toying with his long knife and watching her. His two henchmen, Tyrone and Jamie – Death Roe and Jay-Jay – skulked behind him in the shadows. She might be tied up but a whole afternoon of watching her had allowed a bit of the fear and respect to creep back into their faces.

"Hypodescent," she said.

"What's that, bitch?"

"Your word of the day, William," she said.

"You being funny – ggh! – bitch?"

"Do you know what it means?"

He glared at her. Fishy eyes tended to glare anyway; he couldn't really help it.

"*We* used to have an empire," she began. "The British. Not quite like the one that the Venislarn are building on Earth. Well, maybe quite a lot like it. And we colonised a quarter of the globe so they say. And our soldiers and businessmen and explorers had children with the people they conquered. I doubt love played much part in that. In Australia, in Africa, in India, children were born. Half-British, genetically. White and black. White and Aborigine. Fifty-fifty. How do you think we, the British, treated them?"

Billy said nothing.

"Did we welcome them as our own?" said Vivian. "No. We categorised them with their mother's ethnic group. We might have called them mulatto or half-breeds but, in truth, they were lumped with the 'lesser' race. They were tainted with the degenerate genes of their mothers. Hypodescent: automatically associating a child with the subordinate race. Do you see where I am going with this?"

"Talk, bitch," said Billy. "You'll be – ggh! – dead soon."

"You are not human, Billy. You could not walk our streets without people screaming in fear and hiding their children from the sight of you. And yet, are you true *samakha*? No. *Daganau-Pysh* might be your great-great-granddad but you are nothing to him. You are an afterthought."

Billy was on his feet. "You tryin' to rile me, Mrs G?"

"No," she said. "It had simply occurred to me that, apart from your poor dear mothers, we are the only people who understand you."

"You?" Billy sneered. "Ggh!"

"The 'feds'." She would have put air quotes around it but her hands were tied behind her back. "We understand each other and that's why you won't kill me."

"I got me a pocketful of Elizabeths – ggh! – and more honeys than I've got arms and —"

"So, three."

"— and the youngins respect me. Ggh! They know I'm a made man."

"Booya," said Jamie supportively.

"You make and sell dirty movies, William," said Vivian.

"For the greater glory of *Daganau-Pysh*."

"He must be so proud."

"*Muda!*" shouted Tyrone abruptly, barrelling into Jamie to get out of the way of a cat that had just wandered into the boathouse.

"What the...?" said Jamie.

Billy was confused. "Ain't no cats allowed in."

He stopped. There were footsteps outside, running feet. Billy closed the gap between them and grabbed Vivian as the side door flew open and Rod stepped in, pistol raised.

Acting rather than thinking, the enormous Tyrone swung at Rod with his fist. Much faster, Rod leaned out of range and slammed his pistol side-on into Tyrone's face. The big lad went down, clutching his flat (and now much flatter) nose and cursing in Venislarn. Jamie had dropped his baseball bat and put his hands up before Tyrone even hit the floor.

Vivian felt something cold and sharp against her throat.

"Back off, man!" Billy shouted. "Back off!"

Nina and Morag were right behind Rod and, bizarrely, so was a small herd of cats.

"Put the knife down, Billy," said Rod, loud, clear and calm. "Let Mrs Grey go."

"Screw that!" he yelled back. "You're not taking me."

With a hand grabbing her shoulder and his knife pressed tight against her throat, Billy dragged Vivian backwards, down the sloping floor to the open end of the boathouse.

"Do *not* move!" shouted Rod. "I *will* shoot!"

Water lapped over Vivian's feet. It was cold, like death.

"Shoot," said Vivian. "Do it."

With a yank, Billy dragged her back further around the edge of the doorway. The boathouse abutted the back of a warehouse and a makeshift wooden jetty had been erected along its edge, a handspan above the water. Billy stepped back onto the walkway but he didn't take Vivian with him. He span her as she rounded the corner and flung her out and away into the canal.

Vivian heard the beginning sounds of a yell and then she was underwater. Cold black wrapped around her.

Daganau Vei. The lair of the deep god.

Vivian kicked with her legs and strained futilely against the bonds that tied her arms. If this had been an ordinary canal, her feet might have already touched bottom or at least ploughed through the silt and muck. There was no bottom. Without sight, she could sense the gulfing depths below her, she could feel the pull of their crushing gravity.

A vast smoothness brushed her leg.

Vivian screamed soundlessly through gritted teeth.

Something looped under her armpit and she struggled for a moment before she realised it was a human arm. It pulled. It lifted.

Vivian broke the surface, yelled and gasped. She and her rescuer went down once more but finally resurfaced.

"Here! Here!" Morag was shouting.

It was Nina who had jumped in after her. Vivian coughed and muttered with feeling.

"What?" gasped Nina.

"Idiot," said Vivian. "You're an idiot."

Nina grunted. Vivian felt herself passed to other arms. Boards scraped painfully against her side as Morag hauled her onto the walkway. Vivian hauled her legs out of the water quickly.

"Get out, get out!" she snapped at Nina.

Having the young fool die in her place would be more unbearable than being *Daganau-Pysh*'s lunch.

Along the walkway, a door slammed. Vivian coughed up canal water. Billy the Fish had slipped through a doorway into the warehouse. Rod rattled the handle, shoulder-barged it and yelped.

As Nina rolled onto the walkway, Vivian saw a wide, shallow bow wave move past and along The Waters. Morag was attending to her bonds. Nina wheezed and spat. Vivian suspected that no one else had seen the wave.

"Rod!" she called. "Rod!"

Rod wasn't looking. He gripped the door handle, dug his fingers between door and frame and, with a roar, ripped it open. Amid exploding splinters, the door opened and bounced back on its hinges. Behind the door was a plain brick wall.

Rod turned, a furious at the *samakha* magic, and shook out his painful fingers.

"Rod!"

The bow wave breached and a limb as long as a tree reached out of the water. Not an octopus or squid tentacle but a muscleless frond of translucent tissue like the arm of a ghostly anemone or the trailing stinger of some giant jellyfish. Rod backed away; it wasn't interested in him. The tentacle rapidly insinuated itself around the wooden door, barely touching it until it tightened. It effortlessly snapped the door off its hinges and hoisted it into the air.

A letterbox in the door flipped open and grey fingers poked through.

"Lord *Daganau*! It's me, father! Don't!" It was Billy, on the other side, in the space that the door led to. The tentacle tightened, loop over loop, like a boa constrictor. Wood creaked and splintered.

"I did it only for you! For your glory! Ggh! Father! Father! *Yo-Daganau-Pysh! Ffer sla'vhen byach karken'ah! Hrifet! Hrifet!*"

The door cracked and, for a moment, bled and then it came apart in shards that rained silently onto the water. The tentacle withdrew and was gone.

Nina propped herself up on her elbows.

"That was some weird shit."

"There!" said Morag and Vivian's arms were free.

Vivian inspected her wrists. "That was a stupid thing to do, Nina," she said. "You could have died."

"YOLO, Vivian. YOLO." Nina wrung out her sodden sleeves. "But, Jesus, I look a mess."

"You look fine," said Morag.

"Oh, really," said Nina.

"You've got that whole skanky detective look going on." Morag slipped off her jacket and passed it to Nina. "Bold perfume too."

The Grand Central shopping centre above New Street Station catered to all desires and tastes, assuming those desires and tastes didn't mind spending a lot of money. Fortunately, Morag was in a philosophical frame of mind and was happy to max out her credit cards. She bought new clothes to last her to the weekend, enough bathroom products to last until Armageddon (or next month, whichever came sooner) and a big pull-along case to take them home in.

She took the train to Bournville and, on her meandering walk back to Franklin Road found a petrol station with an integral supermarket. She stocked up on pizzas, pasties and microwaveable macaroni cheese. She grabbed milk and tea bags, and looked without success for a bottle of something horribly alcoholic to curl up with for the evening. She took her purchases to the till and, as the cashier scanned everything, asked him if the market had a drinks section.

He smiled. "Not in Bournville."

"Sorry?"

"It's a dry village."

"Say again?"

"Dry village. All this area was built by the Cadbury family when they built the factory. Quakers, see? You can't buy booze anywhere within the area. It's the law."

"It's inhumane," Morag whispered.

"Less than a mile to Cotteridge centre. Pubs and offies galore there." The man pointed along the road.

Morag shook her head. Then she saw a display of blue and orange boxes at the side of the till.

"Oh, I'll take them though."

"How many?" said the shopkeeper.

"All of them," said Morag.

The cashier scanned and bagged all twelve. "You do know that they're not real oranges? They don't count towards your five-a-day or nothing."

The game was a welcome distraction as Rod and Nina walked back to the office.

"Seawhores."

"Good one. Blowfish Job."

"Ha. Er, Halibut Plugs."

"Eww. Okay. Moby's Dick."

"Nice," said Nina. "Touched In Her Special Plaice. Plaice as in _"

"I get it. I get it," said Rod. "Let me think."

"Chocolate Starfish," said Nina.

"It was my turn."

"You're too slow, old man."

"Um. Deep Trout."

"Deep Trout?"

"As in _Deep Throat_."

Nina swiped the blank wall of the lift. "Never heard of it."

Rod looked her in the eye. "It was a classic porn movie."

"Does classic mean old?"

"It means classic. Nineteen seventy-something. The whistleblower on the Watergate scandal, Deep Throat, took his name from the film."

"Water-what?"

Rod huffed.

"You're doing this on purpose now. Watergate scandal. Richard Nixon."

"Is he the one who was on *Doctor Who*?"

The lift pinged open.

"Flaming Nora, Nina. You do know there was a world before the year two thousand? It's called history. It's quite important, you know."

"It's all in the past, Rod. Move on." She shrugged happily. She wasn't a tall woman and the oversized gym clothes she had swapped into to replace her wet clothes made her look even smaller.

"Remind me again how old you are?" said Rod. "Twelve, was it?"

Nina swiped them through the door. "So, work-head on. With Billy dead, where's your investigation going next?"

Rod stroked his chin.

"Our friend, Izzy Wu, was asked to break into the Vault by her jeweller boyfriend Ben, who was killed by the Waters Crew and had links to the tattooist who inked their porn starlets to keep them in line. All of them worked for Billy the Fish, who is now dead. And none of the other half-brained mackerel have a clue about the finer details of the operation."

"Exactly."

Rod stopped beside Izzy's detention cell. "I don't know how much of value we're going to get from little miss clueless here." He opened the door.

Izzy Wu was slumped in the corner of the room, head lolling, eyes half open.

Nina knelt beside her, lifted her head up and felt for a pulse under her jaw. "Izzy. Izzy, wake up." There was no response.

Rod took something from the young woman's hand, a crumpled square of paper. He smoothed it out and saw a drawing.

At first he didn't understand. It was just a squiggle, spiky lobes twisting around a segmented stalk, like a spiny conch shell sliced end-on. But there was something about the pattern...

"She's breathing," he heard Nina say. "I don't know what's wrong."

The shape on the paper almost made sense. If he followed this line along, the way it met with these other lines surely meant...

"Rod?" said a voice, far away.

His gaze followed the inward curves and the zahir opened up to him, layers peeling back to reveal the deeper mysteries within...

Somewhere, much further away now, a voice spoke and a hand touched him.

The word *zahir* struck his consciousness. He faintly knew the word meant something, something dangerous and if, if... (Bloody hell! He knew this! It was on the tip of his tongue!) If... Yes. If he followed this line then the other intersections would come together and make a complete circuit –

The image was snatched away. Rod gave a cry and fell back.

Nina tossed the screwed up piece of paper into the far corner. Rod gasped for air and batted away at the remnants of the image that still clouded his vision.

Nina grabbed him. "Rod! Rod!"

He tried to focus on her.

"Come back!" she said and shook him.

"Nnh!"

"Wake up, man!"

"'m awake," he mumbled.

She sighed in relief. Rod lay on his back and put his hands to his head. A part of his brain that he couldn't control tried to remember the hypnotic layout of the zahir, but it had gone.

"A Langford Basilisk," said Nina. "Damn."

Rod lay there for a time and concentrated on breathing. Eventually, he felt he had returned to himself enough to speak.

"Hardcore Prawn," he said.

"Yep," said Nina. "That's a good one."

Morag threw her sweaty, chemical, funky, cat-attracting clothes straight in the washing machine and spent an excessive amount of time under the flat's power shower before dressing in straight-from-the-shop clothes. It felt good in a way that few things did.

Feeling human again, she gathered up the dozen chocolate oranges she had bought and made her way downstairs to flat one. A cat was sitting by the front door studying her. It did not run up to her, rub itself against her or meow. That felt good too.

The door to Richard's flat was closed, but the lock was still broken and the door swung open as she pushed it. There was no one in the living room. She called out a hello but there was no response. She could hear tinny music coming from another room but there was no sign of her neighbour.

The fruit bowl was back on the coffee table, clean and empty. She could just leave her apology present in the bowl and sneak out again. It would be a pleasant surprise.

She tiptoed across. To her side, there was a creak of floorboard and something implacably hard struck her in the face. Terry's Chocolate Oranges flew everywhere.

"Fuck's sake!" she grunted.

"Oh," said Richard and dropped the colander he had whacked her with.

"Christ!"

Her mobile phone started to vibrate. She ignored it and put her hand to her nose. There was no blood. It stung so much she really thought there ought to be. "What did you hit me for?" she snapped.

"You surprised me," said Richard.

"It was meant to be a nice surprise!"

He looked at the chocolate oranges strewn across the carpet. "Those were for me?"

"An apology. Fuck! Am I bleeding? Can you see blood?"

"No," said Richard. "There's some red..." He gestured generally at her face. "Circles."

"You hit me with a fucking colander."

"I was draining green beans. Green beans are good for you."

She went over to the wall and tried to inspect her reflection in the glass of a pinned butterfly case. The eyespot designs on the

102

butterfly wings stared back at her. She couldn't see any marks on her face.

"I think *I'm* the one who owes *you* an apology now," said Richard.

"You think?"

"But you did say I should, and I quote, 'really bust some moves' on people who break into my house."

"Not on me!"

He made an awkward face.

"I don't know what to say now."

She exhaled the remnants of her surprise and anger.

She went over to him. "Hi," she said and held out her hand. "I'm Morag Murray. I'm the idiot who lives in flat two."

"Hi," he replied and shook her hand. "I'm Richard Smith. I'm the idiot who lives in flat one."

"Well, Richard, I think I'm going to go back to my flat and inspect the damage to my face."

"Okay. I can assure you it's minimal."

"Maybe sometime we can do the whole new neighbours thing properly. Get pizza in or something."

"Okay," said Richard. "When?"

Morag wasn't expecting a question at that point. "Um. Er. Tomorrow?"

"What time?"

"Well, I do work late sometimes. I'll definitely be home by ten."

"Then it's a date," said Richard.

"It's not a date," said Morag.

"No, it's not a date," he agreed emphatically.

"Goodnight," she said.

"Goodnight," he replied.

Morag returned upstairs, probing her tender skin with her fingertips. As she entered the flat she remembered her mobile. She had voice mail.

"Morag, it's Bannerman." Bannerman was the Edinburgh consular chief. "I hope you've had a positive couple of days in Birmingham." Morag laughed at that. "I have some... news for you. The incident on Sunday night. Damnation Alley. The Venislarn know and they've made their intentions known." Morag felt a tight ball of nausea twist inside her. "They're coming for you tomorrow," said Bannerman solemnly. "If you need to call me, I am available anytime, anytime at all."

Morag let the phone drop. She stared numbly at a flat that wasn't her home in a city that she didn't know.

The Venislarn were going to kill her tomorrow.

Wednesday

Morag woke up and did not die.

She dressed and left for work and still did not die.

She caught the train, bought something unhealthy to eat for breakfast as she walked to the office and still she did not die.

She swiped herself into the Library, said good morning to Security Bob and continued to not die.

In the office, Nina Seth put a piece of paper in her hand. Morag looked at the word-filled grid.

"For this morning's session with Chad and Leandra. And you'll need to put five pounds in the pot."

"What pot?"

"First one to get a line wins a fiver. First one to get them all wins the pot."

"I don't understand."

"It's straightforward stuff, Scarlett Johansson. It's just to break the monotony."

"Um. I think I'm going to die today, Nina."

Nina grinned. "It's not that bad. It's just Chad and Leandra."

Morag went to the kitchenette to make herself a cup of tea.

"You are to be presented to the Venislarn court later this morning," said Vivian without any kind of preamble, social niceties or any indication of human warmth.

"This morning?" said Morag.

"As the official registrar of all Venislarn beings, I am to take you there and make introductions."

"To the Venislarn court."

"Yes."

Morag thought about it. "That's the one at the top of that building."

"The Cube. An unnecessarily garish and hollow edifice if you ask me."

"*Yo-Morgantus*," said Morag.

"Are you telling me these things or asking?" said Vivian irritably.

"Vivian."

"Yes?"

"I think I'm going to die today."

Vivian regarded her carefully. "A quarter of a million people die every day," she said. "Our line of work holds considerable risk. I don't know if you enjoy the stereotypically unhealthy diet of your fellow Scotsmen and you are – let me see – forty?"

Morag's mouth wouldn't work for a good second.

"I am... safely in my thirties," she said. "That birthday is some distance off still."

"There is a percentage chance that any of us might die on any given day. Wednesdays are statistically one of the safer days. This morbid belief is not due to a horoscope reading or similar?"

"No," said Morag.

"Oh. If it had been then that would have raised the chances of you dying. A subconscious desire to fulfil the prophecy. Besides, I would question the continued readership of any newspaper or magazine telling said readership that they are going to die."

Rod came by the kitchenette and clicked his fingers.

"Giving you fair warning, the door is open and I'm making a beeline for the best pastries." He steered Morag away and down the corridor. "We're doing a thorough check of the Vault contents later this morning, on the off chance that anything else Izzy Wu might have touched would give us a clue."

"I'm to be presented for *Yo-Morgantus*'s approval this morning."

"Fair enough."

Rod held the meeting room door for Morag.

"And I think I'm going to die," she said.

"Then you'd best tuck in. Seize the day."

A tray of Danish pastries sat beside the drinks on the meeting table. At the head of the table stood a flipchart on which someone had written 'Selling the Apocalypse – think outside the box!'

"Excellent," said Rod and crossed out the words 'outside the box' on his grid sheet. "Got one before we even start."

Morag looked at the peculiar buzzwords and phrases on the sheet Nina had given her. "No one would really say these words," she said. "Would they?"

"Now," said Rod, "some might say that Chad and Leandra are a right pair of Home Counties wazzocks and that any amount of shite pours out of their mouths..."

"But..." Morag prompted.

Rod looked at her. "But nothing. Chuck us one of them cinnamon swirls."

Apart from Chad and Leandra who led the session, there were five of them there. Nina, Rod, Vivian, Morag and a twinkly-eyed man who smiled easily and was introduced to Morag as the Venerable Silas Adjei.

"I'm an archdeacon in the Birmingham diocese and the regional inter-faith Venislarn link officer," he said, shaking her hand.

"That is a mouthful," Morag said.

"Most people make do with Silas," he said.

"Okay, team." Chad clapped his hands together. "We're all here, we're all refreshed. Welcome to the dreamnasium. Get ready for a workout."

"Fuck me," whispered Morag in disbelief and then immediately turned to the archdeacon to apologise. Silas smirked silently and shook his head.

"If you recall last month's session," said Leandra, "we talked about how we could view our marketing goals through a grief analogy matrix."

Morag scrabbled for a pen and crossed 'analogy matrix' off her chart.

Leandra wrote the letters DABDA down the flipchart. "Denial, anger, bargaining, depression, acceptance," she said.

"And the point is that when we go public with the Venislarn," said Chad, "we move the population through these stages as quickly as possible."

"Find speedy resolution at each stage and then move on, yes," said Leandra. "But we must have resolution. Can't have people bouncing back and forth, unresolved."

"This morning's session therefore is to get your insider's perspective on how we use the grief analogy matrix to raise Venislarn brand awareness."

"Is this the best way to work out how to go public?" asked Nina.

"It's as good approach as any, Nina," said Chad. "Our current train of thought."

"Either get on or get out of the way," said Leandra.

"Oh, I'm definitely on the platform, Leandra," said Nina, deadpan. "But I'm just checking the route before I get on."

Leandra nodded approvingly.

Rod leaned over to Nina and whispered. "You are *not* allowed to cross them off if *you* were the one who said it."

"Spoilsport," she whispered back.

"So," said Chad, "that day comes. The Venislarn are wheeled out onto the public stage, the 'absolute horror at the heart of the universe' —"

"Oh, the horror, the horror," said Leandra in a pantomime voice.

"— is made known to all," said Chad. "What's the initial reaction going to be from the populace?"

There was a long silence.

"Terror," ventured Silas. "Abject fear."

"Good, good." Leandra made a note on the flipchart.

"And excitement," said Nina.

"Okay." Leandra refrained from noting that particular suggestion. "Care to handhold us through that one?"

"We've just been told that the world is going to end at some point," said Nina. "There will literally be no tomorrow."

"You mean figuratively," said Vivian.

"I was using the word 'literally' figuratively," said Nina. "So, there are no consequences. We have just been granted complete freedom to do what we like. The world is suddenly ours to trash, like when your mate's parents are away and she's decided to throw a house party. Freedom. Excitement."

"Terror," said Silas.

"Are you putting Nina's idea down?" asked Chad with a sad face. "Or are you building on it?" he asked with a happy face.

"I would like to *colour* Nina's statement by pointing out that the overwhelming majority of people will be afraid, not only of the

108

Venislarn but of the idiots who think the end of the world is an excuse for a party."

"But a likely first response would be....?" Leandra gestured to the first D on the flipchart.

"Denial!" said Chad.

"Can we mindscape what that would be like?" said Leandra.

"People will think it's a conspiracy," said Vivian.

"Revealing the Venislarn will be a conspiracy?" said Silas. "Surely, a conspiracy's what we have now. Going public would be uncovering the conspiracy."

"And people will see it as somehow covering up a greater conspiracy," Vivian countered.

"Misdirection," agreed Rod, reaching for another pastry. "Stage magic. An MP's sexual indiscretions hit the headlines and cause scandal for the government and, incidentally, at the same time, the government sneaks through some crafty legislation that, I don't know, legalises child murder or summat."

"And I think that would be a good thing," said Vivian.

"Child murder?" Morag turned to face Vivian.

"Allowing the populace to think they are being lied to. I have an ambivalent attitude towards child murder. No, we should allow the people to think it is a lie. We should encourage that very thought. It was how Greg – Vaughn's predecessor – dealt with major incursions in the city."

Morag gave her a questioning look.

"If there was an incursion within the city that could not be wholly covered up," Vivian explained, "Greg would have us throw confetti on it. *Figuratively*," she said to Nina. "Draw people's attention to it and, at the same time, embellish the story and the evidence until it becomes utterly ridiculous. Do you recall those people who reported a giant spider in the basement of their flats only for it to turn out to be an abandoned float from the Lord Mayor's Show?"

"That was funny," said Nina.

"A gestating *Dinh'r*. You may be aware that back in the nineteen-seventies there was a twenty-foot statue of King Kong in the Bull Ring markets."

"I've seen pictures," said Rod.

"Commissioned, constructed and put in place overnight to explain away sightings of a wandering *Kobashi*. And as for the Birmingham tornado of 2005..."

"That was a real tornado," said Nina.

"Was it?" said Vivian, leaning back. "Was it really?"

"Okay, let's not get into analysis paralysis here," said Chad. "This train of thought is going places and fast, like the TGV. A Team with Great Vision."

"So far we've got people who are fearful, disbelieving and possibly excited," said Leandra. "We need to get the populace all on the same page."

Morag crossed out 'on the same page'.

"We present them with incontrovertible proof," said Silas.

"We put up posters saying 'You are all going to die. Get over it,'" said Vivian.

"We get *Yo-Morgantus* to headline at Glastonbury," said Nina.

"Brave ideas but I think we need more value-add," said Leandra.

Rod did the world's most surreptitious fist pump and crossed something off his bingo card.

"Surely it's better to have them in denial than the next stage," said Morag.

"But anger is a stage we must get through," said Leandra.

Rod sniffed. "Maybe, in the end, we need to fight them."

"But we have run all the simulations, checked all the calculations," said Vivian, "and have proven that resistance is truly futile."

"There is always hope," said Silas and moved to take the last Danish on the table.

Vivian beat him to it. "No, there is not."

"Ah, to hell with them," said Nina. "When that day comes, let's nuke them 'til they glow then shoot them in the dark."

"And compound the misery of those humans still alive?" said Rod. "Maybe not."

"The Strategic Arms Limitation Talks were a direct response to the Venislarn threat," said Vivian. "The Berlin Wall wouldn't have come down if it wasn't for them."

"Berlin Wall. They were, like, an electronic band or something, right?" said Nina.

"Beg pardon?" said Rod.

"Like, um, Kraftwerk or the Pet Shop Boys. David Hasselhoff played with them, didn't he?"

"There are so many nuggets of purest wrong in what you've just said, I don't know where to start."

"I bought you a book on twentieth century history for Christmas," said Vivian.

"It's a book," said Nina.

"You could try Wikipedia," suggested Silas.

"Pfff. Can't trust Wikipedia. It's just stuff written by people."

"Point is, people will still want to fight them," said Rod.

"Generations of humans have been raised on a diet of cinema in which good triumphs over evil," said Morag. "Plucky heroes and human ingenuity will win through."

"Then Hollywood needs to change," said Vivian. "Replace idealism with pragmatism."

Silas gave her a gently condemning look. "You want to sell defeat and death as virtues?"

"Absolutely. Write that down, Leandra."

"Perhaps you want the media to kick-start a wave of suicides?" said the archdeacon.

"Ideally," said Vivian. "Suicide is preferable to being alive when the Soulgate comes."

"Killing ourselves is never the solution."

"Codswallop. It is the solution to a wide range of problems. What we perhaps do not want is for it to be messy, painful and an inconvenience to others."

"Inconvenience?"

"Last month, a young man threatened to jump off the Paradise Circus walkway. The traffic had to be stopped, which caused tailbacks across half the city. That is an unacceptable inconvenience."

"I might be mistaken, Mrs Grey, but you seem to be saying that some people being stuck in traffic is more important than the deep-rooted mental suffering and anguish of the suicidal young man."

"Seem nothing. I'm saying it outright. His suffering might be a thousand times that of any driver affected but he was one man. The net suffering of thousands of local commuters was far worse. We need to provide the means for the suicidal to exit this world quickly, quietly and without fuss. I imagine it's what most of them want."

"Euthanasia clinics," said Morag.

"Oh, do we need to go to that expense?" said Vivian. "There are plenty of high places that are away from urban areas and which offer a cast iron certainty of death. I think people just need to know about them."

"People could review them on TripAdvisor," said Nina.

Rod thought on this. "At what point? I mean, you'd have to do it before you actually... You know."

"People could do it as a memorial thing. 'My sister flung herself off Beachy Head and died instantly. No splatter. Five stars.'"

"This is repugnant," said Silas.

"Sorry, Rev," said Rod.

Silas held up a hand in acceptance, no offence taken. "I do think we shouldn't be talking about such *final* acts when a peaceful solution could yet be reached."

"Bargaining," said Chad, pointing back to the flipchart.

"The Venislarn are not open to negotiations," said Vivian.

"I have spoken to their representatives," said Silas. "They are rational. They have desires. They can be reasoned with."

"Not the true Venislarn," said Morag. "The elder gods, the deep ones who will consume our world, they are either mindless or beyond our comprehension. The ones we speak to are either their offspring or parasites or... or God knows what. Who did you speak to?"

"One of the *presz'lings*."

"The equivalent of talking to a flea and thinking you're talking to the dog."

"People have made bargains with the Venislarn," said Nina.

"Really?"

"I know someone – no, I'm not saying who – who has provided services to the Venislarn in exchange for a one hour warning when the Soulgate comes."

"What good is an hour?" said Leandra.

"Long enough to find a gun."

"Or a high place that offers a cast iron certainty of death," agreed Rod.

"But let's cast our net wider," said Chad. "Bargaining with the Venislarn is low-hanging fruit. There are other psychological forms of bargaining."

Morag was distracted for a moment, not only by the idea of casting a net to catch low-hanging fruit, but by notions of death. Bannerman had said the Venislarn were coming for her today. Would she be better off finding a quick death for herself before she let them get their claws into her?

"I'm not going to talk about bargains with God," said Silas. "I'm not here as a salesman."

"But religiousness is going to shoot right up the charts when the Venislarn make themselves known," said Rod.

Silas nodded. "One concern is the uncontrollable nature of the religious zealotry we might see."

"Apocalyptic cults. Bizarre rituals. Human sacrifice. Naked orgies in the ruins." There seemed to be a certain enthusiasm in Nina's voice.

"Are you sharing my concerns or compiling a wish list?" said Silas.

Nina treated it as a serious question. "I really don't see why, if the end of the world is coming, we can't have a bit of fun. I don't *want* the world to end but, since it is, I'm pretty sure I want to enjoy it."

"That's a very irresponsible attitude."

"Now, Silas," said Leandra, "this is a safe idea space. There are good ideas, there are better ideas and there are solid gold spray-on butter ideas. But there are no wrong ideas."

"Yes, there are," he said, not unpleasantly. "There are wrong ideas, immoral ideas and there are stupid ideas."

"Of course." Leandra was less certain. "I just meant in this space..."

"No," said Silas, politely but firmly.

Morag leaned over to Rod and pointed at 'spray-on butter' on her bingo sheet with a bewildered look on her face.

"Leandra loves spray-on butter," he whispered. "Wishes she'd invented it. Always mentions it."

"Okay!" Chad clapped his hands once more. "Let's get a thought shower down on the page to collate our key suggestions based upon our discussion so far." He ripped the page off the flipchart.

"Let's sell the Venislarn apocalypse to the masses," said Leandra.

"Make tentacles sexy," said Nina.

"How?" said Morag.

"*Hows* can be bridges or barriers," said Leandra. "How do you think we can make tentacles sexy, Morag?"

"Do I have to answer that question?"

"Get Brad or Angelina to get one surgically attached," said Nina. "Make it a fashion statement." She picked up her tablet and started browsing.

"Mass sterilisation," said Vivian.

Chad could only stare, surely even Vivian wouldn't seriously suggest...

"Whip out the ovaries of every woman of breeding age. We need to get the human population to an absolute minimum before the Soulgate. I should imagine a Tory government could pass laws that make sterilisation a criterion for income support applicants."

"Sterilise the poor," said Chad.

"Or pay women to have abortions," said Vivian. "Either would work."

"I hope you're joking, Mrs Grey," said Silas.

"I only know one joke," said Vivian. "This isn't it."

"The idea of encouraging or enforcing the termination of human lives –"

"Before they've begun."

"It's morally abhorrent."

"If we have any love for our fellow man, it's morally imperative, archdeacon. You're being squeamish, not moral."

"Your proposals represent the most superficial form of utilitarianism."

"There's no call for personal insults. Perhaps you would like to explain your moral justification for consigning hundreds of millions of future children to an eternity in hell?"

Silas raised a finger. "Point of clarification. The Venislarn are not devils. They are not gods. The Soulgate is not hell. Eternity is the province of God."

"I think we should just make everyone's final years, months, whatever as cheery as possible," said Rod. "Encourage people to live for the now."

"YOLO," said Nina.

"The Canadian office are so pleased with themselves for coming up with that one," said Leandra snidely.

"How about libido-suppressing drugs in the water supply?" suggested Vivian directly to Silas.

"Better," he said charitably, "but this covert meddling in people's lives is still quite unpalatable."

"Surely, the whole point is to meddle because people can't be trusted to do the right thing themselves," said Morag.

"Drugs are not the only way to limit population growth," said Rod.

"Absolutely not," agreed Chad. "Easy access to contraception, online pornography, morbid obesity, and women choosing to have children later in life are all factors behind the falling birth rate in the western world."

"We've worked very hard on some of those," said Leandra.

"And in the States, the federal government diverted millions into that purity ring, virginity pledge organisation."

"Got it!" said Nina and flipped her tablet for all to see. "I give you... Tentacular!"

Morag looked at the hastily photoshopped line-up of pretty young men, standing before a smoky pentacle-and-squid-thing background.

"Wow. Someone's been duck-paddling in the meeting," said Chad. "Tentacular, eh?"

"Mmm-hmmm," nodded Nina. "Tentacular are a new five-piece boyband. Five generous portions of bare-chested hotness. They sing about love, longing and the unspeakable horror underpinning our universe. They make tentacles sexy."

"A boy band?" said Morag.

"Don't say you're not excited by these."

Morag looked closely. "Well, I kind of prefer my men to be... well, actual men, to be honest."

"They'll be a worldwide phenomenon and there'll be copycat bands."

"Managed carefully, we could engineer a cultural paradigm shift," said Leandra, genuinely taken by the idea.

'Paradigm shift' was on Morag's bingo card. She was two buzzwords away from a line. The fates had decreed she was going to die that day but Morag was still surprisingly excited by the idea of winning five pounds.

"That is indeed visionary," said Chad. "It's great what can come out of an open source ideas forum like this."

"Maybe," Leandra said to Chad, "it's time to bring out the plushies."

Chad nodded.

"Okay," he said to all. "There's been some good ideas in the room and some good energy. Leandra and I would like to share with you some prototypes that came out of a focus group meeting in Belfast last month. We want eyeball reactions, from the eye to the gut to the mouth. No sugar coating."

Together, they brought out a half-dozen paper shopping bags from under the table and handed them out. Morag opened her bag and took out something pink and fluffy and misshapen beyond the realm of all known shapes. She turned it upside down, back and forth and was still none the wiser. Adages about an infinite number of monkeys with typewriters sprang to her mind. This cuddly... thing would be the first aborted product of an infinite number of monkeys with sewing machines. There were googly eyes sewn onto it and a row of card-stiffened tartan spines.

"Is this meant to be *Yoth Mammon*?" she said in sudden recognition.

"Well done," said Leandra.

"*Yoth Mammon* the corruptor, the defiler of souls, the dredger in the lake of desires?"

"Yes."

116

"With cute little eyes and... and this is a smile. *Yoth Mammon* doesn't smile."

"The Belfast group thought it would play better with a smile."

Archdeacon Silas held a winged Wind of *Kaxeos* at arm's length. "You've made cute little effigies of major Venislarn," he stated simply.

"Toys," said Chad. "You know, for kids."

Rod's offering looked like the result of an unholy one-night stand between a cushion and a cow's stomach, all tubes and tassels.

"*Yo-Morgantus*?" he said.

"Correct," said Leandra.

"Do the gods know you have turned them into Cabbage Patch Dolls?"

"This is just the developmental stage," she said. "Not ready to roll out."

"Aye, well don't be surprised if he doesn't take to it."

"What is this meant to be?" asked Vivian, holding hers up between finger and thumb.

"That's the – let me check – yes, that's the *Nadirian*," said Chad.

"The *Nadirian* is said to take on whatever form the observer expects to see," Vivian pointed out.

"Then it's an entirely accurate likeness," said Leandra smugly.

"This smacks of idolatry and worshipping false gods," said Silas. Nina walked her *Zildrohar-Cqulu* across the table as though it were an EU-fire-regulation-compliant Godzilla on its way to Tokyo. "But my sister's children would love them," said Silas. "I assume this is to accustom us all to their appearance?"

"*My Little Venislarn*," suggested Morag.

"So," said Chad, "do you think these toys are going to have a positive brand impact?"

"We're looking for a steep uptake with a pebble-free runway," said Leandra. "The Buzz Lightyear effect."

Morag crossed out 'steep uptake'. One to go!

"Hideous," said Vivian simply.

"Thank you," said Leandra. "Honesty is good."

"Misguided."

"Good. Thank you."

"Based on false premises and executed with no consideration of the bigger picture."

"Lots of opinions there," said Leandra with a forced smile.

"Wrong-headed, naïve, stupid and –"

"Okay, Vivian," Leandra cut in. "Let's not front up our idea shelves with just your thoughts. We're sharing opinions here but we're also sharing the floorspace."

"I do see a contradiction here," said Silas. "You've already discussed ways of encouraging the public to seek oblivion – to seek death – and yet, simultaneously, you are encouraging acceptance of the Venislarn, a lessening of their fears."

Rod nodded. "On the one hand you're saying 'don't worry, be happy' and, on the other, you're saying 'kill yoursen'."

"Be happy. Kill yourself," mused Nina. "That could work on a T-shirt."

Rod looked at her. "I can't tell when you're being sarcastic and when you're being serious."

"Neither can I," she agreed. "Curse of our times. But death and happiness don't have to be opposite ends of the spectrum. We should get a member of Tentacular to commit suicide."

"Your fictitious boy band?" said Vivian.

"Everything's fictitious until someone makes it happen," said Nina.

Rod whispered to Morag. "She does this every time. By the end, she's talking more dribbling arse gravy than Chad and Leandra. I can't tell if she's joining in or taking the mick."

"Tentacular should get their first couple of albums under their belt, maybe their first world tour too, and then Zeke, the cute quiet one, should announce his intention to kill himself. He's not crying out for help. He's not got mental health issues. He's moving on to oblivion because the time is right and it's what he wants to do. It will be beautiful. Every stage of it will be documented. He'll do a poignant farewell track with his bandmates and, afterwards, after the beautifully choreographed funeral, Tentacular will record another album in his honour and do the 'Oblivion Be Mine' tour."

Chad frantically copied a shortened version on the flipchart.

"This is sick," said Silas.

"It might just work," said Vivian.

118

"I think I'm dreaming," said Rod.

"I know," agreed Leandra, completely failing to understand.

"So, you've convinced a million screaming pre-teens to top themselves, Nina. How are you going to reach out to everyone else?" asked Rod.

"Money is always a good incentive," said Vivian. "If life insurance payouts were government subsidised, for example."

"You could make the Darwin Award an actual award," said Morag, deciding to join in with the silliness.

"Give out cash prizes to people who top themselves in ridiculous and amusing ways," said Rod.

"You've Been Fatally Framed."

"And we could get media pundits to advance nihilistic viewpoints."

"Let's commission Will Self to write a series of sneering articles in the broadsheets about the futility of existence."

"Doesn't he do that already?" said Silas.

"Ingenious," said Leandra.

"This is positively an idea blizzard," said Chad.

Rod suddenly slammed his hand down on the table. Everyone looked.

"Bingo," he said softly, holding up his card. "Read 'em and weep."

The Cube was a fifteen-minute walk from the Library, but Vivian found that Morag was dragging her heels, in a slight daze, her eyes following the white-grey clouds that scudded across the sky.

"I am sure that, without too much additional effort, you could manage a faster pace," said Vivian.

"Sorry," said Morag. "I was just... taking it all in. Savouring it."

Vivian contemplated the dull skies, the brown canal waters beside them, the indolent urban ducks on the towpath, the grass growing through cracks in the brickwork. Vivian wasn't sure that there was much to take in or whether indeed, taking in any of it was advisable. The towpath from Holiday Road ran up to the rear of the

Mailbox, once the Royal Mail sorting office and now given over to hotels, shops and bars that catered to people with more money than sense. Restaurant-lined pathways connected the Mailbox proper with the not-strictly-cubic Cube. The architect had apparently stated that the glass body of the Cube reflected the city's jewellery-making past and the multi-shaped and multi-hued box of shapes around it spoke of the city's more industrial heritage. To Vivian's eyes, it still looked like a twenty-storey conservatory covered in titanic Lego bricks.

"We've just sat through the most bizarre meeting with two people who are handsomely paid to come up with insane ways to sell the Venislarn to the public," said Morag.

"We have," Vivian agreed.

"Life is strange, isn't it?"

"Compared to what?"

"Do you ever wonder what it all means?" Morag sighed.

"No," said Vivian without hesitation. Morag stopped in her tracks.

"Meaning is created in the minds of intelligent beings. The 'it' you are referring to is the universe including those self-same minds. It is logically impossible, like trying to fit a gallon into a pint glass. Is this to do with you dying?"

Vivian was aware that her tone was far from sympathetic but she didn't have the energy or the ability to do anything about it.

"Yes," said Morag.

"And why do you think you are going to die today?"

"I've been told. I have enemies."

Vivian laughed drily. "We all do." She looked at Morag straight in the eye. "Do you want the truth? A lot of things in this world hurt us and cause us pain. A small number of things do not. The only meaning to life involves avoiding the former and finding the latter. Death is the end of all of them, the good things and the bad ones. There is no more meaning than that."

They walked on in silence for a bit.

"Do you know we have the Wittgenstein Volume in the Vault?" asked Vivian.

"The Bloody Big Book? Yes."

"You should read it sometime," said Vivian. "Then you will understand."

"I'm going to die today," Morag pointed out.

"True. Then don't read it. You have probably got better things to do with your final hours."

In the white tiled aisles far below the Library, at the very spot where Rod had first found Izzy Wu, Dr Ingrid Spence showed the Vault catalogue to Rod and Nina. Ingrid's T-shirt had a picture of Bruce Willis in *Die Hard* mode with a speech bubble that read 'I got enough friends'.

"Close to four thousand items," said Rod. "Are all accounted for?"

"They certainly were at the last audit," said Ingrid. "But when that young woman broke in..."

"How long did she have?" said Nina. "Ten, fifteen minutes."

"She was here for a reason," said Rod. "She was sent here. Someone gave her the codes. They'd have also given her instructions."

"You came down here and apprehended her, Rod. From here to the detention room to the secure hospital she's now drooling in. She stole nothing."

"That we saw," said Rod. "Some of the items here are very small."

"She could have swallowed rings, trinkets, scales, scrapings or eyeballs," said Ingrid.

"Scrapings? Seriously?"

"Or taken a page from a book. Just one page."

Rod looked at the reinforced chamber holding the Bloody Big Book and then crossed to look through the porthole. The heavy book inside was laid open to a centre page. Of course, it was always open to one of the central pages. When a book had an infinite number of pages, any page was as equally and infinitely far from the beginning as it was from the end.

"There's no way she could have accessed it," said Ingrid.

"Ah, let's not rule anything out just yet," said Rod. "But this is where she came. This is where we start looking."

Nina went to the case containing the Tiny Blue Innumerables. The sparkling stones sat on a black velvet square.

"Maybe she stole some of these."

"I doubt it," said Ingrid.

"Really? When was the last time you counted them all?"

"Nina," Ingrid began, "they are Tiny Blue Innumerables. By their very nature, they cannot —" Ingrid stopped herself and pouted at Nina's idiot grin. "A joke. I see."

"Maybe she didn't steal anything," said Rod.

"That's what I said," said Nina.

"Maybe she just moved some things."

"Why?"

"Ooh," said Ingrid darkly. "That's a worrying thought."

"What?"

"Well, there are certain things that need to be stored separately. Powerful items that could be dangerous when combined."

"Bullets and guns," said Rod. "Nina and vodka shots."

Rod looked at the painting on the wall above the Bloody Big Book, Conroy Maddox's surrealist painting of the Venislarn Apocalypse. He looked at the obscene carnival of monsters, cavorting and devouring the remnants of the world.

"This is potentially very bad," he said.

"It is," said Ingrid.

"World-endingly bad?" he asked.

"Hm." Ingrid made a seesaw motion with her hand.

The top two floors of the Cube were filled with monsters, crammed together like an art collaboration between Hieronymus Bosch and HR Giger.

The concierge in the lobby, a fat man with uneven patches of hair sprouting out of his scalp, had recognised Vivian and directed them straight to the nearest lift. The ride up seemed to take an age and Morag felt a strange rolling sickness, not quite butterflies in her stomach – more like a bouncy castle full of sugar-fuelled five-year-olds.

The lift opened onto a lobby with a view of the city to the north. Through the Tetris block shell of the building, Morag could see the canal network, the Library off to the right, a few lesser tower blocks off to the left and then a rapidly blurring mass of red, browns and black stretching out to low and distant hills. The air about them was stiflingly hot. Somewhere a heat vent droned.

"*Yo-Morgantus* is expecting us," said Vivian.

"Right," said Morag fatalistically. "Let's get this over with."

"He won't kill you," said Vivian.

"That's optimistic."

"No. *Yo-Morgantus* will like you."

"You're the third person to say that. How do you know?"

"Hold that thought," said Vivian. She led her to a set of double doors and pushed through into a carnival of monsters.

The hall took up two floors. Weird tassel-like party streamers hung from the ceiling. There were no windows. Black drapes, irregular mirrors, steel tubing filigree and dim orb lights lined the walls, making it look like an eighties nightclub trying and failing to recreate a twenties nightclub. In the centre of the room, tables sat incongruously beside mysterious mounds and uninviting pools of sludge. This space was even hotter than the corridor they had come from. Large heating vents breathed warmly over the entire room.

Presz'lings, *Uriye Inai'e*, *Mammonites*, *draybbea*, *Croyi-Takk* and *samakha* respectively stalked, wheeled, strutted, oozed, glided and lolloped about. In the heights and darker recesses, larger, more singular forms held back and watched their children and emissaries play.

None of this surprised Morag. This was partly because Morag's thoughts were less bothered with unearthly wonders and more with her imminent death. It was also partly because she encountered Venislarn horrors on a daily basis and had a very healthy Abyssal Rating of seven. But, mostly, it was because Morag was already surprised by the humans in the room.

Human servants in the room carried platters and trays. They waited dutifully at their masters' sides and they caressed, pummelled and scourged their betters' hides. This wasn't surprising or particularly unusual. That there were nearly a hundred of them in one space was uncommon but not unheard of. That they were all butt naked was an intriguing aesthetic but, no, the thing that

123

almost floored Morag with surprise was that every single one of them was a redhead.

From strawberry blondes to coppery reds, from deep auburns to fiery orange, every human in the room (apart from the grey-haired Vivian) was a ginger.

"Hell," said Morag softly.

"Or something very much like it," said Vivian. "Come."

They walked forward. Minor Venislarn stopped and glared at them. A stick-limbed *presz'ling* crossed their path and paused as though to bar their way but moved on when they showed no intention of stopping.

"*Yo-Morgantus* likes red hair," said Vivian.

"I can see."

"It is not a visual thing. These are all natural redheads. We suspect *Yo-Morgantus*'s attraction is more to do with the high levels of pheomelanin."

"It's a good theory but entirely wrong," said a red-haired young man, coming up beside them.

He was tall and built like an Olympic sprinter. His nose was wonky and his ears stuck out but he had a beautiful if lopsided smile that more than made up for his other facial shortcomings.

"I'm sure you have a better theory," said Vivian, "but I do not pay attention to the opinions of naked people. It is a little rule I have."

A completely irrational but powerful corner of Morag's brain wanted to shout out, "But he's got a really big penis," but Morag forced it down.

"*Yo-Morgantus* is fascinated by the cultural and religious connotations of red hair," said the man.

"I had considered that," said Vivian, "but I doubt your lord is that well-read. Now, we have an audience with *Yo-Morgantus*."

"And I am to take you to his presence," the man said.

"You are not his emissary. What happened to the woman, Brigit?"

"No, I am not his emissary. My own mistress is elsewhere but *Yo-Morgantus* has sent me nonetheless. My name's Drew."

"Hello, Drew," said Morag.

Vivian sniffed. "Lead on then."

124

Human slaves, skittering beings, and amorphous rolls of fat moved out of their way as they proceeded to the far end of the hall.

"In some cultures, red-haired people were considered the kin of the devil and violently driven away from towns and villages," said Drew. "This distrust has crept into major religions. You are aware that Judas Iscariot had red hair?"

"I didn't know that," said Morag.

"And medieval painters gave Mary Magdalene red hair too. Gingers are betrayers and temptresses, fiery-tempered and highly sexed."

"This is tenuous stuff," said Vivian.

"The *Malleus Maleficarum* — I believe you have one of Heinrich Kramer's original manuscripts in your library vault — says that red hair is a sign of a witch."

"Are you suggesting a fifteenth century treatise on witchcraft correctly identified a link between redheads and this one Venislarn god?" said Vivian.

"Nothing so unlikely," smiled Drew. "*Yo-Morgantus* merely has a special fondness for the degraded and persecuted."

"Persecuted? Are gingers an ethnic group now? I didn't realise that the trials of redheads were to be equated with the historic suffering of the Jewish people or the black community."

"Try spending your life being called carrot top or fanta pants," said Drew.

"Orangutan heid," said Morag. "Jaffa flaps."

"Red man walking."

Drew stopped and turned at the far door. He gave Vivian a look, not an unpleasant one, but the warmth had gone from his expression.

"Miss Murray has an appointment with *Yo-Morgantus*. You don't."

Vivian was about to reply and then reconsidered. "Very well," she said and then to Morag, "I will be here... when you return."

"Nice knowing you," said Morag and followed Drew through.

Alone with him now, it felt even more ridiculous to be in the company of an entirely naked man. As they walked the length of a corridor, Morag could not think of anything to say to break the awkwardness. Instead, she gazed at the downy hollow in the small of Drew's back and said nothing.

Through a final door, they entered another hall-like space. It was curtained and dimly lit like the hall of monsters. Wire-thin streamers hung from the ceiling here too. And the noisy heating system was also at work in here.

The room was otherwise empty.

Drew stood in the centre of the room and turned to face Morag. "So I'm to wait here?" she asked.

"No," he said.

"Oh," she said. "You're *Yo-Morgantus*?"

He shrugged and winked mischievously. He raised a hand to touch one of the dangling streamers. A tiny flash of light, like a spark of static electricity, leapt between streamer and fingertip.

"You can talk to me," said Drew. "His thoughts are mine."

Morag looked up. The streamers, like ribbons of damp saggy paper, like thin lengths of shaved skin, ran up to the ceiling and through a fine mesh grille. She looked about herself. The heating vents... were not heating vents. That hot air was not just hot air; it was breath.

Morag signed a rainbow to indicate everything around them, within the room and beyond its walls, floors and ceiling.

"Am I inside *Yo-Morgantus*?"

"So, you are Morag Murray," said Drew. "There's been a lot of talk about you."

"Who am I speaking to now?" she said. "*Yo-Morgantus* or Drew?"

"I'm not sure what the distinction is," said the man. "I am Drew – or at least I am today – but the almighty *Morgantus* has filled me with his thoughts. I speak my own mind freely but my mind is his." He waved his hands through the dangling fronds. "He takes, shapes, edits and inserts memories and thoughts into my head."

Before she knew what was happening, a streamer descended and touched her lightly on the head —

Morag saw the otter on the pebble shore from some distance but only when she neared did she see that it was alive. Its head lay on its side in the rock pool, half in half out of the water. Bubbles formed

126

on its nose as it breathed. Its rear end... Something had shredded its rear legs and tail, torn away chunks of flesh and fur in a peculiar spiral pattern. There were no sharks in the firth. Had a seal done this? A motorboat? Whatever, the otter was dying, unable to move and breathing its last in a cold rock pool.

Morag looked back up the long beach to where her family sat. Her mother was dandling Morag's baby sister on her knee. Her father was fiddling furiously with his binoculars.

The otter was still breathing. The blood around its wounds was thick and congealing.

Morag, with wind-stung eyes, looked around for a large stone.

— Morag staggered back across the hall floor, gasping.

"Funny," said Drew. "I would have thought the death of your parents, either of them, would have taken precedence over that memory."

"Don't do that again," she said, still breathing heavily.

"Are you telling Lord *Morgantus* what he can and can't do?" asked Drew lightly.

"No. No, of course not."

"Good. Now, what are we to do with you?"

"Do?"

"We sent for you for a reason."

"Aren't all new consular staff presented to the court?"

"Yes," said Drew, "but not all new consular staff are murderers, are they?"

After inspecting it, Nina returned the Unapproachable Stone of *Msgoto* to its alcove, realised it was the wrong way up, turned it round, realised that, no, it was still probably upside down and turned it round once more.

"Anything?" said Rod.

"Nothing out of place," said Nina. "Well, nothing I can see."

Rod turned to Ingrid. "Do we have CCTV in this area?"

"Nope. We can't risk it in most of these areas. Cameras effect a wave function collapse in perception-sensitive artefacts."

"Eh?"

Ingrid sighed. "Some of the magic things don't like being looked at."

Nina glared at the *Shus'vinah* mask on the wall. It averted its gaze and pretended it hadn't been looking at her.

"Fair enough," said Rod, ambling through to the next section. "Change of tack. We know Izzy and the Waters Crew had some powerful zahirs. Maybe she came down here to find others. Have we got some here?"

"Lots," said Ingrid. "There's some physical items, some carved, some natural, including the Buenos Aires coin. But most are in books, illustrations, many of them just border doodles by mad occultists. One of the 'Necronomicons' is full of them. There's even some in the confiscated pages of the Birmingham Qur'an."

"That's the one they found at Birmingham Uni?" said Rod. "And our Izzy was a student, wasn't she?"

"Yes, but I don't know where she studied," said Nina.

"We could find out. Hey." Rod put a hand against a long, empty case. "Shouldn't wotsisname be in here?"

"Kevin?" said Nina.

"*Kerrphwign-Azhal*," said Ingrid.

"How do you manage to roll your 'r's like that?" asked Nina.

"The alveolar trill is just a matter of letting your mouth relax and holding your tongue in a position where it can vibrate."

"I love it when you talk dirty."

Ingrid blushed.

"*Kerrphwign-Azhal* was here but it was requisitioned this morning," she said.

"By who?" demanded Rod.

A strand touched Drew once more. "You know there are members of the court who want you dead?" he said.

"I heard," said Morag.

"They would like to kill you today, now, if *Yo-Morgantus* let them."

"And is *Yo-Morgantus* going to let them?"

Drew grinned. "I told you earlier that *Yo-Morgantus* has a fondness for the degraded and persecuted."

"Yes?"

"It's not because he likes them. It's more that they're... pre-cooked. Surrounding himself with rusty gussets and ginga ninjas who know they're derided and mocked is very pleasing to him."

"I see."

"Do you know the best thing about gingers?" said Drew, smiling broadly.

"Our superior ability to convert sunlight into vitamin D? Our immunity from rickets?"

"They suffer abuse and taunts every single day of their lives and – you know what? – no one gives a *muda*. I don't see a ginger Martin Luther King marching on Washington any time soon, do you?"

"We're indoorsy kind of people."

Drew laughed. "With that sense of humour, we might let you live beyond today. It all depends on how much entertainment value you can provide."

"You want to watch me suffer?"

"You. Them. Anyone. Everything – and I do mean everything – in this city exists for our pleasure. Maybe today, I'll make you fall in love." A strand touched Drew. He grunted in surprise and put a hand to his groin.

Morag fixed her gaze on a point above his left shoulder and refused to look down.

"Put that away before you have somebody's eye out," she tutted, annoyed.

"Maybe tomorrow, I'll kill you." Drew suddenly gripped his own throat and dug his fingertips into his own windpipe. His face reddened quickly.

"Stop that," she said.

Drew – or was it *Yo-Morgantus*? – had to stop in order to speak.

"Again, you appear to be telling me what to do."

"Maybe I don't give a *muda* anymore."

He grinned. "Keep it up, Morag Murray. Keep it up and maybe you'll even live to see the weekend." Drew shuddered, the smile suddenly gone. He looked at Morag with different eyes. "I think that's our lot," he said quietly.

She looked up at the streamer tendrils. Without moving, many of them had recoiled out of reach.

"The audience is over?" she said.

Drew nodded and gestured toward the door. Partway down the corridor, Drew put a gentle hand on her arm and gestured to a side door.

"If you don't mind, I'd like to introduce you to my mistress."

The side room was another huge hall. Morag was beginning to suspect that the Venislarn weren't playing fair with the local dimensions. The room was built from pale stone and lit by bowls of open flame on metal tripods. The whole was like a theatrical set designer's idea of an ancient Greek temple. Drew's mistress squatted hugely in the centre of the room.

Her form was, if anything, that of a gigantic faceless thin-legged spider, but one that was coated in horny plates of armour taken from some deep sea crustacean. The bony exoskeleton was generously dotted with protuberances in the shape of faces – the faces of human babies, eyes screwed shut, mouths wide in silent cries.

It was one of the August Handmaidens of *Prein*.

Morag's legs wobbled for a moment in absolute fear.

The handmaiden took a step towards Morag. Her armoured plates rotated and shifted until one of the porcelain baby faces was directly facing Morag. Morag had read that the August Handmaidens had added the faces to their hides when they first met humans. They hadn't done it to make themselves look fucking terrifying (even though that was the net effect); they had done it to make themselves appear like the locals. The August Handmaidens of *Prein* were Venislarn trying to look like humans.

Drew coughed politely.

"May I present her ladyship, *Shardak'aan Syu*, of the August Handmaidens of *Prein*."

"Pleased to meet you," said Morag hoarsely.

At that point Morag saw that the handmaiden held something in her front claws. It looked like a large leathery ball. The handmaiden rolled it absently from claw to claw.

It was the virgin-devouring Kevin.

A voice spoke. It came from the handmaiden but not from any mouth. It was Morag's own voice.

"My card's marked anyway, Kevin," her voice said. "Do you know what I did last night? Um, yesterday? I met one of the handmaidens of *Prein*. In Damnation Alley, Edinburgh. You know what I did?" Morag realised these were words she had spoken, taken from Kevin's memory. "Kevin," she said, "I put a double barrelled shotgun in her mouth and blew that gallus bitch's head clean off. That's right. Handmaiden of *Prein*. Boom."

Morag trembled. "Well, any quote taken out of context can sound..."

The handmaiden leaned closer and spoke mouthlessly again. The handmaiden's own voice was clear and precise, the deep warm tones of a female newsreader.

"Boom," she said.

Morag dug deep and found a small reserve of anger and defiance. She put her hand meaningfully inside her jacket, reaching for a weapon or amulet that wasn't there.

"You want to come at me, you *adn-bhul* bitch?" she snarled. "Try it."

The handmaiden shifted. Faces rotated.

Vivian was almost barged aside as Morag pushed through the double doors and back into the hall of monsters. "Let's go."

"Is everything all right?" asked Vivian. "Apart from the obvious," she added, indicating the horrors and hallmarks of mankind's extinction around them.

"Yes. Why wouldn't it be?" Morag said.

Vivian looked at Morag's hands. They were visibly shaking.

"Very well," she said.

Rod crossed the office with a piece of paper in his hand. Nina put the phone down.

"You first," she said.

"There *are* items missing," he said.

"Oh?"

131

"Minor stuff. Junk. An earring. A piece of egg shell. A key, a knife, a brooch. None of it powerful or dangerous or meaningful. All of it from one room of the Vault."

"But Izzy had none of it on her."

"So she moved it. Dumped it. I don't know. You said, 'you first'."

Morag and Vivian entered the office.

"Tea?" Morag offered to Vivian.

"I will but I doubt you can make it how I like it."

"I am vaguely familiar with the process," said Morag.

Vivian made a sceptical noise.

"I think some education is in order," she said and beckoned for Morag to follow her to the kitchenette.

"Go on," said Rod to Nina.

"Oh, yeah. You'll like this one. Izzy Wu was at Birmingham University. She was doing a degree in Practical Theology. Guess who her tutor was?"

"Omar?"

"Professor Sheikh Omar."

"Who's Professor Sheikh Omar?" asked Morag.

"A bloody thorn in our sides," said Rod.

"A tit," said Nina.

"I think it's time to go knock on some doors and bust some heads," said Rod. "Who's coming?"

"Me and Vivian and Ingrid were going to oversee the audit at the Dumping Ground today," said Nina. "Kinda keen to check we've not lost anything there either."

"Why would you have?"

"No reason. Just after discovering we've lost stuff from the Vault..."

"Bolting the stable door after the horse has gone," said Rod.

Nina frowned. "We don't have any horses at the dumping ground."

"No, that's..." He didn't bother finishing the sentence. "You coming, Morag?" he called out.

Morag poked her head over an office divide.

"Vivian was going to show me the five steps to making the perfect cup of tea," she said.

"So, no?"

"I didn't say that. I really didn't say that."

Vivian knocked on Vaughn Sitterson's door and entered. The consular chief was sitting at a low table with Archdeacon Silas Adjei, his face buried in a sheaf of notes.

"Lois said you wished to see me?" said Vivian.

"Yes, Vivian." Vaughn didn't look up. "Silas and I were discussing the round table negotiations and ecumenical outreach that we had originally lined up for next month."

Vivian sat, cup and saucer in hand. "Yes?"

Vaughn made an open palm gesture towards her in lieu of actually looking at her. "Silas, quite reasonably, was asking me why they're no longer going ahead."

"We talked about this briefly this morning. Two reasons mainly," said Vivian. "Firstly, they would be pointless."

"You would dismiss peace negotiations before they'd even begun?" said Silas.

"I am trying to picture it," said Vivian. "We are to imagine something like the United Nations, are we? You, yourself sitting down at table to talk with the Venislarn gods, assuming we can find a table that *Yoth Mammon* wouldn't dissolve with her bile and a meeting room large enough for *Zildrohar-Cqulu* to squat in. Presumably some sort of aircraft hangar, one with an Olympic swimming pool in it for *Daganau-Pysh*."

"It would not be easy, true," said Silas.

"And ranged around the other end of the table, would be you, Kevin O'Driscoll from the Roman Catholic diocese, the chairman of the central mosque, Councillor Singh perhaps, one of the priests from Shree Geeta Bhawan or Shri Venkateswara. Are you going to invite the humanists? The Buddhists?"

"You're creating barriers and making jokes, Mrs Grey," said the archdeacon.

She put her tea down on the table and took the opportunity to also stop and silence the annoying Newton's cradle in the window sill.

"I've already told you," she said. "I only know one joke. But let us imagine we have you all sat together, what do you think the first thing is to happen?"

"Enlighten me."

"They would kill you," said Vivian. "To many of them, your faith is a personal affront. Listen carefully, for I am offering a compliment here. You represent power and faith and solace in this physical world. You represent much of what the Venislarn intend to take from us. The Venislarn have not come here for our gold or oil, our water or air. They do not want our land. They do not want a flat screen TV, Nike trainers and a cheeky Nando's at the weekend. They want our minds and other mental intangibles. Insomuch as we can ascribe motives and goals to the Venislarn, they want the bread and butter of the religious business: our hearts and souls."

"So, you agree we are the people best placed to understand and negotiate with them."

"In the same way that geologists are the people best placed to negotiate with volcanoes."

Silas put his hands in his lap. "I'm sorry you have a closed mind on this topic. Can I also remind you that I do take exception to you referring to them as 'gods'. There is one God, with a capital gee. These Venislarn gods, small gee or not, should not be given the same label."

"You have raised that point before, Silas," nodded Vaughn. "I am sure we can draft a policy statement to that effect. Wording can be crucial."

"The second reason there will be no ecumenical outreach or round table negotiations," said Vivian.

"Yes?" said Vaughn.

"We have no money for it. As far back as January, we knew there would be cuts and the funding for this particular vanity project was struck from the yearly plan."

"Ah," said Vaughn with a gnomic nod. "Tis true. Our budget is under considerable strain. And things are looking less than rosy for next year."

"But I read that spending on Venislarn matters is rising globally," said Silas.

"Yes," agreed Vaughn, "but regional budgets are calculated individually according to the ToHo formula which essentially distributes blocks of funding based on the number of major incursions that occur within a set region. We've not had any such events since the Winds of *Kaxeos* tornado of 2005. Locally, we derive additional funding from the management of the Dumping Ground in Nechells and the storage and research facility beneath the Library but that is about all."

"So," said Vivian, "if something truly terrible happens in the city, we'll have enough money for your coffee morning with the unspeakable horrors."

"Here's an idea," said Vaughn in the tones of someone who wanted to make out that they'd just thought of it but had quite clearly been sitting on it for some time. "You know the local Venislarn community well, Vivian."

"I do," she said warily.

"The proposed ecumenical outreach could still be carried out on a 'street' level. In fact, don't we have some of the *samakha* in detention?"

"The Waters Crew. You know we do."

"Excellent," said Vaughn. "Maybe you could set something up on small scale with them. Some kind of workshop or programme of interventions?"

"Or a coffee morning," said Silas, smiling.

Birmingham University sat in green and leafy suburbia, fifteen minutes' drive from the Library. Just from the general direction and the feel of the area, Morag suspected it was quite near to her new home, but she hadn't sufficiently grasped the geography of the city to be sure.

Rod parked in a staff car park beside an Art Deco gallery and put a 'police emergency' note in the window.

"So, do the university know that they have a major occultist and Venislarn artefact dealer on their payroll?" said Morag.

"They don't even know the Venislarn exist, do they?"

They walked through a square archway into the campus proper. Over to one side, a massive red brick clock tower stood before a semi-circle of grand domed buildings.

"You go to university?" asked Rod.

"St Andrews," said Morag. "You?"

"You know when people say they went to the University of Life or the School of Hard Knocks and they just sound like a complete arse?"

"Yes."

"I went to a university so bad that I prefer to tell people I went to the University of Life."

Rod led her to a large shoebox building, the Faculty of Arts. "Professor Sheikh Omar is a lecturer in the department of Practical Theology," he explained as they walked up to the first floor, "but, additionally, he runs something called the Department of Intertextual Exegesis."

"What the hell?"

"It basically means he likes to poke his nose in very bad books and then write new ones." Rod stopped at a nameless door, hammered it three times with his fist and entered.

It was a spacious office, of the kind university academics rarely got to occupy. Abstract pencil and charcoal prints filled the wall around the windows. A tall, balding man in black-rimmed glasses sat at the large, battered desk. A shorter, silver-haired man with a pink cravat about his neck, perched on the edge of the desk. They looked like Morecambe and Wise, if Eric Morecambe had been of Arab descent and Ernie Wise had been on a starvation diet.

"As if by magic the shopkeeper appeared," said Professor Sheikh Omar.

It was only when he spoke that Morag realised she had met the man before. They'd sunk several whiskys together on the way down from Scotland at the beginning of the week.

"Maurice, be a dear and put the kettle on," said Omar.

The little man slid off the desk and slid away into a side room.

"Expecting us, were you?" said Rod.

"Just thinking about you, Rodney," said Omar. "And this is your new colleague from across the border. The Caledonian Sleeper."

"We've met," said Morag, shaking Omar's hand.

"Have you?" said Rod.

"Was that a coincidental meeting then?" said Morag.

"Oh, what is a chance meeting," said Omar, "but the gods recycling the strutters and mummers out of laziness?"

"We're here because we think you've been a naughty boy of late," said Rod.

"You might need to be a tad more specific, Rodney," said Omar. "I mean these..." He gestured at a set of aged papers on the desk before him. "These are mildly scandalous. This..." He touched lightly upon a leather journal. "This is beyond cheeky and these..." He picked up a box of soft toffee squares printed with a tartan pattern and a picture of an Aberdeen Angus. "Positively sinful. Do have one."

Rod threw a photograph of Izzy Wu on the desk. Omar ignored it and held out the box of Highland toffee to Morag. "I got these on my recent holibobs. Go on. Be a devil."

Morag ignored him. Rod pushed the picture across the desk.

"This is Izzy Wu."

Omar made a pretence of looking at the picture. "A student of mine, as you know. Where is she now?"

"The restricted ward at the QE hospital. Not coming out any time soon."

Omar pushed his glasses up his nose. "Not planning to pin this nasty business on me, are you?"

"Pin nothing," said Rod. "She was your student and she was up to her neck in dodgy artefacts and *samakha* gangland dealings."

"Gangland? It's hardly Codfather proportions. Just some wide boys who like to play at being gangsters. Not my scene."

"No? Maybe this is your scene." Rod tossed a DVD case onto the desk. The cover was an amateurish screengrab of a skinny dead-eyed woman being taken from behind by a glass-eyed *samakha*. The title was in Venislarn with an English translation underneath. To Morag's mind, the English didn't quite capture the desperate sordidness of the Venislarn; English lacked the juicy verb forms of the Venislarn language. Omar looked but did not touch.

"Maurice and I prefer *The Great British Bake Off*, don't we, Maurice?" said Omar.

"Soggy bottoms," called Maurice from the other room.

"He's so saucy," said Omar.

"We don't think this is funny," said Morag.

"Then you're not trying hard enough," said Omar. He looked at them levelly. "I have nothing to do with this. If people were going to blame teachers for what their students get up to then there should have been more schoolmarms at the Nuremberg Trials. What exactly are you accusing me of?"

"Bankrolling *samakha* porn films. Handing out deadly zahirs to local idiots. Conspiring to steal Venislarn artefacts from the government. Take your pick," said Rod.

"Ah."

"The Waters Crew have ID'd you," said Rod.

"So, they know me," said Omar. "I do get about."

Rod tapped the DVD case. "I wonder how your bosses would respond if they knew you were involved in this kind of filth."

"Stooping to blackmail and threats?" said Omar. "Rodney. You're better than that. We're friends. Look."

Maurice glided in with a silver tray bearing cups of black coffee in glass cups. Maurice slid it onto the desk. Omar picked up a cup, inhaled deeply but did not drink.

"Rodney. Morag. I am going to do you three favours."

"Three," said Rod.

"I will respond to each of the accusations you had laid before me, I will give both of you a sound piece of advice and I will tell you what you really ought to be doing."

"And do we have to cross your palm with silver?" said Morag.

"Just remember," said Omar. "Remember who your friends are."

"Go on then," said Rod. "Give us your penneth worth."

Omar smiled and put his cup down. "These specialist cinematic efforts really aren't my style. You know this. A fool of a fish called Jay-Jay tried to flog me one the last time I was on *Daganau Vei* but I said no. Billy the Fish had his own distributor. Jay-Jay was just trying to make a bit on the side. The zahirs weren't from me. I have my own charms and enchantments but why would I want to pass them onto my own students? It's hard enough to get them to achieve their grades without turning their brains into caviar. As for stealing from you." He sighed happily. "There's no point going to all that trouble when eBay is only a finger-click away."

Rod made an unhappy noise. "Fair enough. I'm not saying I believe you though."

"Such a cynical Yorkshireman, aren't you? I do wonder if it's something in the water. Advice now," said Omar. "Rod, you want to find Billy the Fish's distributor. His name is Gary Bark."

"Gary Bark. Never heard of him."

"He's registered. You'll find him. Morag, advice for you, sweetheart."

"Yes?"

"Take the afternoon off. Life's too short."

Morag felt his words touch her coldly and, for a moment, all colour drained from the room. She abruptly realised that the abstract charcoal drawings on the wall weren't abstracts at all. They were all careful renderings of pieces of human anatomy, very close up and medically precise. She wavered momentarily on her feet. Rod didn't seem to notice.

"Now, what you really ought to know," said Omar. "Maurice here is not only a master of the coffee pot and an immaculate pastry cook, he also has a gift for augury, specifically haruspicy. The reading of entrails, Rodney."

"At least it's not tea leaves."

"Don't poke fun, you naughty boy. When Humphrey – such a fat ginger tom – brings in a dead pigeon, there's almost nothing Maurice can't read in its remains. Such a skill. Last week, he pulled out the lottery numbers from the remains of my Balti lamb special."

"I get it," said Rod. "What does the future hold, Mystic Meg?" Rod was looking at Maurice but it was still Omar who spoke.

"There will be a major Venislarn incursion in the next two days."

"Uh-huh. Where?"

"Here," said Omar. "Birmingham."

"What kind of incursion?

"Maurice is less certain on that point. But it will either be *Zildrohar-Cqulu* or the *Nadirian*."

Rod nodded doubtfully. "So, gods walking the earth, huh?"

"Indeed."

"Twaddle."

"The entrails never lie," said Omar.

Maurice gave a tiny cough.

"Apart from that time in Marrakesh," Omar agreed, "but you were suffering with Delhi belly, dear. And perhaps had had one too many banana daiquiris, if you don't mind me saying. You'd never catch me making such a fool of myself," he said to Morag. "Clean-living vegetarian that I am. Boring? Perhaps. But at least I've got all my own teeth."

Rod picked up the DVD and the picture of Izzy Wu. "Any further questions?" he asked Morag. Morag shook her head. She had not quite yet recovered from the peculiar turn Omar's words had invoked in her.

"For the record, I think you're full of shite, professor," said Rod.

"Such a colourful turn of phrase," said Omar.

"Don't be surprised if we're back again real soon. And you'd best hope that your cock and bull prediction comes true."

"I don't hope. I fear. Gods can be bad for business."

On the stairs on the way down, Rod asked if Morag was okay.

"You went an interesting shade of grey back there," he said.

Morag shrugged it off. "I've been hearing a lot of dark talk today."

"Earlier, you said you were going to die today."

"Mmmm."

"Care to tell me about it?"

"Well..."

Ahead, Morag saw a figure leant casually against the concrete pillar of an archway, watching her. He had ginger hair and, if not for that, she might not have recognised him with his clothes on.

"Listen," she said to Rod. "I'm not feeling too good. Truly. Would you mind if I caught up with you later?"

"We can go get a drink somewhere. Sit down until your colour comes back."

"No," she said. "I think I do need a bit of time to myself. Maybe I'm coming down with something."

"You sure?"

"Sure."

Rod didn't argue.

"I'm going to follow up this Gary Bark character," he said. "It's probably a wild goose chase but we'll see. Give me a call when you're ready to get back in the game."

Morag waved him off and then walked towards the redheaded man in the archway.

The Dumping Ground's official name was the Venislarn Material Reclamation Centre. Specifically, its truly official name was Birmingham Freight Forwarding and Storage and operated under the guise of a cargo container storage centre but, to those in the know, it was the Venislarn Material Reclamation Centre. But everyone called it the Dumping Ground because it was shorter, snappier and properly reflected the chaos, filth and uncertainty that ruled the place.

The Dumping Ground was hidden away in the Nechells area of Birmingham. It was bounded on one side by the River Rea and on the other by the brick viaducts that brought westbound trains into New Street station. It was further encircled by twenty-foot-high metal fencing topped with coils of razor wire. Finally, the inner area was lined by a veritable castle wall of cargo containers, stacked four high and creating a thirty-foot barrier against prying eyes. Within the metal fort, the Dumping Ground was superficially what it pretended to be: a container yard. Forty acres of compacted dirt, space for over a thousand containers and tankers, all managed from a prefab office by the rail terminal that ran onto the site. The deeper reality was quite different.

Dr Ingrid Spence wore a yellow biohazard suit with the hood down. Unlike most biohazard suits, this one was painted with a variety of catch-all protective wards (including, Nina noted, the words 'please don't eat me!' in Venislarn).

Vivian consulted the clipboard. "Six-five-five. The weird tree of Chippenham."

Ingrid threw the stiff bolts on container 655 and the stockyard worker helped her haul the doors open. Nina shone a torch on the gnarly twisted object inside.

"It's a tree," said Ingrid.

"It's weird," said Nina.

They began to shut it up again. "Wait," said Vivian.

"What?"

"Is it all there?"

Nina frowned at her. "It's a tree. It's there."

"But is it all there?"

"Meaning?"

"What if, for example, a branch had been taken from it?"

"It's still a tree. It's still the weird tree of Chippenham. Are you concerned that someone somewhere has now got a weird *branch* of Chippenham?"

"Whatever properties this tree has —"

"It weeps blood and drives people mad," said Ingrid.

"— then these will also be possessed by the branch."

"But it's still a tree," said Nina. "I mean, how many branches would you have to snap off it before it stops being a tree?"

"That's zen, that is," said the stockyard worker. Ingrid closed the door.

"To answer your question, no, it's not all there," said Ingrid. "There's a weird branch in Hull and another in Bristol."

"Explain." Vivian waited.

"Standard practice," said Ingrid. "Look, over here." She walked over to a trailer tanker, spray painted with the number 430. "What's this supposed to contain?"

Vivian flicked through the papers. "Diluted *shrol'iek* plasma. Thirty thousand litres."

"We were originally sent this by the Highlands team, Loch Morar. We billed them for reclamation, transport and storage and they were able to pay for most of that from central budget. Now, let's say we get too much stock in and have to move thirty thousand litres of diluted *shrol'iek* plasma to Port Talbot. We have to pay for it but can reclaim most of that from central. Not that we use such vulgar terms as profit but we've now made a profit equal to the amount that we've been able to reclaim from central."

Vivian wasn't impressed. "You are simply shuttling the same tanker back and forth and claiming central government funding for it."

"Oh dear, no," smiled Ingrid. "They'd spot that. I said we'd taken thirty thousand litres from Loch Morar and send thirty thousand litres to Port Talbot. I didn't say that we'd got rid of the

Loch Morar shipment. There's thirty thousand litres here and thirty thousand litres in Port Talbot."

"Diluted, isn't it?" said the stockyard worker.

"The devil's in the details," said Ingrid. "I should imagine that one day, we will get another thirty thousand litres back from Port Talbot."

"And you are continually watering it down to boost revenues." Vivian did not approve.

"The Dumping Ground is the Birmingham mission's primary source of revenue, Vivian. It pays for everything else. If we didn't do this, we wouldn't have the Library, the Vault, anything. This is standard practice."

"It is dishonest."

Ingrid put her hands on her hips in a determined pose which was moderately undermined by the fact she was dressed in bright yellow plastics.

"I'll tell you what's dishonest: Birmingham selling itself as a centre for reclamation and research. On paper, this place and the Vault are meant to be international beacons for Venislarn research. With the miniscule budget we get, this place is containment, nothing more."

"It is still dishonest," said Vivian.

"It's quite clever," said Nina. "Have you ever considered putting in an expenses form for the services of a tree surgeon when you inspect them —"

Ingrid raised her clipboard. "Got the invoice right here."

"Dishonest," said Vivian. "You have no moral compass, Nina, so your opinion does not count."

"Whatever you think," said Ingrid, as Nina's phone began to ring, "this is the way of the world. We make ends meet by bending the rules. And we'll be sending weird branches to here, there and everywhere until container six-five-five contains only the homeopathic memory of a tree."

It was Rod calling.

"Yo," said Nina.

"Nina, are you at the Dumping Ground with Vivian?"

"Uh-huh. Having an argument over how many branches you have to take off a tree before it stops being a tree."

"That's a bit zen."

"That's what the guy here said."

"Um, I wonder if you or Vivian could answer a question for me. I'm trying to locate a distributor of occult artefacts called Gary Bark. Sheikh Omar says he's registered but I can't find any record of him."

Nina stuck out her bottom lip and shook her head. She looked at Vivian.

"Gary Bark? Independent occultist. Ever heard of him?"

As Vivian shook her head, the stockyard worker said, "Gary? Who's after him?"

"You know him?" said Nina.

"One of our haulage drivers. He lives in Dudley, but he's been off sick the last four days. Not heard from him."

Nina put the phone back to her ear. "I think we've got your guy. What's he supposed to have done?"

Morag and Drew were drinking in the Birmingham University Students' Guild bar. It actually had a nice pub-style vibe and Morag would have liked it more if they weren't surrounded by pretty twenty-somethings who made her feel positively middle-aged. Drew had offered to buy her a drink. Morag had asked for a juice and then remembered she was due to die later and ordered a pint of lager.

"I don't particularly like being out with other redheads," she said once they were sat down in a booth.

"Prejudiced against your own kind?"

"I don't like being a redhead out with other redheads. It just makes us stand out more, like we're in some special club. Seeing all those people in the court today... One day there'll be one too many and you'll reach some kind of ginger critical mass."

"Nuclear ginger-geddon," said Drew.

"Exactly."

"Actually, I like it. The court, I mean. When everyone is ginger, no one is ginger."

"Ginger power," said Morag, fist raised.

"You're making fun of me."

"Fun of it. Ginger isn't a racial group. It's not a 'thing'. We don't have a proud and rich history. We don't have a shared language or culture. I'm not aware of Ginger History Month or Ginger Pride marches."

"Really?" Drew lounged back in his seat, nursing his bottled beer. "You have to be told something is a 'thing' before you'll accept it's a 'thing'? We're all identified by our labels. If you have a label, you make it your own. If you're black, be black. If you're straight, be straight. If you're transgender, transethnic, otherkin then that's what you are."

"Excuse me? Otherkin? No, wait. Transethnic?"

"Sure," said Drew. "Transethnic."

"Um...?"

Drew put his drink down so he could use his hands to gesticulate. "So, transgender is where you're assigned one sex at birth but you identify as another."

"And transethnic," said Morag, "is... When you're born white but you feel black on the inside?"

"Yes. It can be across broad racial groups or between different nationalities and cultures."

"Like when everyone declares themselves to be Irish on St Patrick's Day."

"You're making fun again."

"Sorry. And otherkin? I will do my very best to keep a straight face and, if I don't, I'll let you buy me another beer."

Drew gave her a playful warning look. "Otherkin, I think, grew out of the elf community." He stopped. "You're smiling."

"Nicely," she argued. "I'm showing interest. You were talking about elves."

"The online elf community."

"That's a real thing?" she said deadpan. "Not made up?"

"They're people who self-identify as elves."

"Pointy ears. Hats with bells on."

"Elves. There are people who feel they are elves."

"But elves aren't real."

"They know that. But that's how they self-identify. And other people identify with other non-human beings. Demons, dragons, vampires. And the umbrella term is 'otherkin. I've even met some Venislarnkin."

Morag's laugh forced its way out noisily through pressed lips.

"You laughed!" said Drew.

"I call bullshit," she replied.

"No, it's true."

"Humans who think they're Venislarn on the inside? I'd like to see how that one plays out when the Soulgate comes."

"It's definitely true." He looked confused. "I'm fairly sure it's true. My memories..."

"*Yo-Morgantus*?"

"And my mistress," said Drew. He turned his head and pulled aside the hair at the back of his neck to reveal a circle of puckered flesh the size of a ten pence piece.

"What's that?" said Morag.

"Sensory feedback. She just plugs into me when we're at it and –"

"Oh, you're her... lover."

Morag knew it happened but she couldn't picture sex between a human man and a ten-foot armoured spider woman.

"Lover. Plaything. Yeah, that," said Drew.

"The Handmaidens of *Prein*. That's a once-a-month thing. Lunar cycle, isn't it?"

"It's more astrological really."

"Huh. I don't know many guys who'd be happy with sex just once a month."

"It's quality not quantity, Morag," he smiled. "When we're together, it's unbelievable."

"But the August Handmaidens of *Prein*," said Morag, curious, "aren't they the ones that, when they're about to come, they kill their lovers?" She made a tentative head slicing motion with her hand.

"Clean off," Drew agreed. "But it's a cumulative thing. When they bond with a lover, each time is more powerful than the last. It can be dozens of times before she finally..."

He drank his beer.

"Yeah, but your time must be coming soon," said Morag.

He shrugged. "Do you know what? I'm looking forward to it. I feel what she feels. It's so *adn-bhul* amazing, I would rather she killed me tomorrow than I never get to be inside her again."

"O-kaaay. A little too much detail now. Your round," she said. He didn't argue.

It was not yet dark outside but day was edging into evening.

"She ate up most of my childhood memories in our first six months together," said Drew when he returned with drinks. "She and *Yo-Morgantus*."

"That's terrible," said Morag.

"You can't miss what you can't remember. And she implants new memories all the time, like it's some kind of practical joke. Currently, my earliest childhood memory is of me doing something utterly degrading with the neighbour's dog."

"And she planted that memory?"

"How would I know?" he said. "Cheers." He tapped his bottle against the rim of her glass. "Whom the gods would destroy, they first make mad," he said. "Henry Wadsworth Longfellow. Now, *that's* an implanted memory. Doubt I ever had that kind of education."

"How do you know?"

"Exactly. Drew's probably not my real name. I spent a month thinking my name was Ron Weasley. I remember at different times thinking I was a girl, a delusional psychotic on a psychiatric ward, and any number of animals. At least I have memories of those things."

"You're messed up," said Morag and spoiled the sentiment by smiling.

"Human condition," said Drew.

"I'm not sure I'd let that happen to me."

"Maybe it already has. *Yo-Morgantus* touched you."

"So?"

"That memory of the otter on the beach. Are you sure that memory's even yours?"

"You... saw that?"

"I know what my lord wants me to know."

"That memory was real," she said.

"As long as you're certain."

147

"I've had that memory since childhood."

"You remember having it since childhood."

"But it *happened*."

"I didn't know you had otters in Scotland."

Morag stared fixedly at the table and tried to put the memory of the dying otter in the context of her childhood. Could she remember why they had come to the beach that day? Could she recall other events from the same time? Her mum with her sister on her knee, her dad with the binoculars... Did those events match the chronology of her life?

The gulf of years and the two beers inside her made it impossible for her to remember clearly. She gave up. "Were you sent to kill me?" she asked Drew. "Or are you just here to screw with my mind?"

"Kill you?" Drew seemed genuinely surprised.

"Kill me. Your mistress sent you."

"No," he said plainly. "When I saw you today, I was... attracted to you. I wanted to see you again. So, on an impulse, I decided to follow you."

"Attracted, huh?"

"People can be attracted to each other. You are an attractive woman."

Morag cleared her throat, which had become suddenly uncomfortably tight. "Okay, you're being embarrassing."

"Embarrassing?"

"If you'd rather I called you creepy, I can do that."

"So you're not attracted to me, Morag Murray?" he asked.

She had a flash image of his naked body and felt betrayed by her own body's response to that image.

"Again," she said, "with the embarrassing slash creepy."

"Sorry," he said cheerfully. "I'm still not sure why you think I'd want to kill you."

"I'm due to die today."

"That's a bummer."

"Yep," she said, drinking. "So, when a man apparently has an irrational urge to come find me, I'm going to be sceptical. Maybe she planted that urge in you."

148

"Very good," he said. "I wouldn't know. We all have irrational urges. We can't say why we feel compelled to do certain things. We can't comprehend the biological drives that govern our lives."

"Sex is weird," said Morag.

"The weirdest," agreed Drew.

"You know, there have been times when I've been, you know, doing it, and... You know that thing when you suddenly see yourself – objectively – and you think, 'what are we doing?' Legs all everywhere. Frantically sticking." She made hand gestures.

"Tab A in slot B?" said Drew.

"Exactly. It's crazy. And I just burst out laughing."

"In the middle of sex?"

"Well, yes."

"And how many long-term boyfriends have you had?"

"And now I'm thinking, maybe *Yo-Morgantus* totally messed with my mind with that one touch. Maybe that's just what I think sex is. Objectively, it seems entirely ridiculous. Makes as much sense as wanting to stick your finger in someone's ear or lick their eyeball."

"Okay, enough with the cheap philosophy," said Drew. "I think this place is rubbing off on you."

"The pub or the university?"

"Either. Both. Pub philosophy or undergraduate philosophy, I can only take so much. The way I see it, if this is your last night on earth and you've got an urge to do something, heck, go and do it."

Morag blinked. "Are you saying we should have sex?"

"Actually, if it was me I'd go play knock-a-door-run, set off fireworks in the street and do a mountain of cocaine."

"Interesting selection." Morag sipped at her pint.

"But, sure," said Drew, "why not have sex with me?"

"Worst chat-up line ever." Even as she said it, Morag realised it wasn't true.

"It's not a chat-up line. It's a question. It's your last night. Why shouldn't you have sex with me?"

"You want reasons?"

"Yes."

Morag drank while she thought about it.

Rod rang and then knocked and then rang again. Then they waited a full minute.

"He's not there," said Nina.

"Or he's not answering."

Gary Bark's dilapidated house stood on the corner of Bath Street and Bilston Street in Dudley. The lights were on in the Beacon Chippy & Pizza across the road and the smell of chip fat wafted across the road.

"I'm hungry," said Nina.

"If I was as skinny as you I'd be hungry too." Rod considered the door.

"You going to do some kung fu or Krav Maga on the door?" asked Nina.

"You can't Krav Maga a door," said Rod. "And no."

He opened the side gate and went round to the rear of the house. He peered in through the kitchen window.

"Can we get chips?" said Nina.

Rod lay down on his back by the kitchen door, put his arm through the cat flap and felt his way up the inside of the door.

"You're not going to fit," said Nina.

Rod ignored her, found the key in the back door and unlocked it.

"Kung fu would have been more impressive."

Rod brushed himself off and opened the door. There was crusty and uneaten cat food in a bowl by the sink and a fusty stink in the air.

"Single men," said Nina, her nose wrinkling. There was a faint noise from further in the house.

"Television?" said Rod.

Nina shrugged.

"Mr Bark?" she called. "Gary?"

There was no reply. "Look," said Nina.

Rod turned away from the fridge door, on which someone had left a note that simply read '474'. A pile of brown cardboard boxes stood in the corner of the kitchen. Nina had flipped the top one open and now held a familiar DVD.

"Mr Bark!" she called again. "We'd like to talk about your fish porn collection."

Rod went out into the hallway and, following the sounds, went into the living room. "Flaming heck!" he exclaimed.

"What?" said Nina.

"Come have a look," he said. "Just watch you don't tread in anything."

Morag had not had much time in which to plan her last night on earth, but she launched into it with glee and abandon.

They took a taxi into town. The uCab driver did not speak once, even when asked to wait outside a Digbeth warehouse while they bought themselves tasteful neon hula skirts to wear. The taxi dropped them off at a city-centre hotel bar where they bought the entire cocktail menu, drank half, and gave out the rest to anyone who would have them. They walked down New Street and persuaded a street vendor to apply henna tattoos to their stomachs and buttocks. They went into the Bull Ring where Morag bought herself a calabash tobacco pipe and, at Drew's suggestion, a pair of smart balance hoverboards upon which they chased each other around the shopping centre until security chased them out. They then sat outside the doors of a nearby church and tried, and failed, to get the pipe to light. On hoverboards, they raced through the evening debris of an outdoor market and, in some Chinatown area, ate Korean barbecue, drank Japanese beer and lost the last two hundred pounds of Morag's bank balance in a Malaysian casino by nine o'clock.

"Now," Morag said, clutching the front of Drew's shirt for support more than anything else. "Now, we can have sex."

"You sure?" said Drew. "You're kind of drunk."

"Only kind of?" said Morag. "Then we must pick up more booze on the way back to mine. *Before* we get to mine. It's a dry village, you know."

The living room lights were off, but Rod could see well enough by the glow of a dozen TV screens set up in a curved bank in the bay window. Cables ran from the screens to a desktop computer, a stack of DVD players and a pair of tripod-mounted camcorders. One camera pointed directly at the single armchair in the room. The other, positioned behind the armchair, pointed at the bank of screens. Rod stepped towards the screens and into thickly-congealed gunk that squelched underfoot. Looking down, he saw that the chair's cushion and arms, and the surrounding floor were covered in translucent white slime.

"Ectoplasm?" said Nina. "Milt?"

His nose twitched. "Oh, how I wish it was ectoplasm."

In the centre of the chair cushion, drowned in goo, something pink and fleshy, no larger than a sausage, flopped and pulsated in fitful bursts. Rod, who had seen things to drive men mad, had seen nothing like it.

Nina's foot nudged one of the wet, screwed up tissues on the sodden carpet.

"I've got a theory about this," she said.

"I don't want to know your theory about this," said Rod firmly.

"Yes, you do. You're just too prudish to ask."

"This," he said, pointing at the sad, pathetic remains of something on the chair. "This is why you shouldn't play with yourself."

"Porn overload," said Nina. "I thought he was just the distributor."

"Testing out the wares, I guess."

Rod reached out to the central screen. Recursive layer after layer after layer of sordid sexual activity and – just off to the side – a fragment of screen in which Rod saw himself. A hand, a face, an eye, leaning into the infinite depths of writhing flesh...

The screens went black.

"What the...?" The lights came on. Nina's hand was on the light switch. The hand other held a plug.

"Enough of that I think."

Rod nodded tiredly. "Aye." He looked at the pink thing on the chair. He wanted to kill it, put it out of its misery. He wondered if there were any flammable liquids under the kitchen sink.

"I didn't have to leave the SAS, you know," he said.

"No."

"You want to go get them chips now?" he asked.

"Not hungry," said Nina.

"Me neither," he replied.

152

"Was that the door?"

"Huh?" said Drew, under the covers.

There it was again, a knock at her flat door. "What time is?" she said, in drunken disbelief.

"Are you seriously going to get it?" said Drew and made his feelings known.

She ran her hands over his shoulders. "Didn't say that."

She tilted her head. According to the bedside radio alarm clock, it was ten o'clock precisely.

The knocking came again, louder.

"Give me two minutes, three at most," said Drew, "and you can yell 'I'm coming' to comic effect."

"Two minutes? Pfff. You overestimate your abilities, sir, and seriously underestimate how pissed I am."

"Is that a challenge?"

In the end, Drew won the bet, not that Morag was complaining at all.

They slept but, at some point, Morag surfaced, untwined her legs from his and went to find the toilet and a glass of water. Drew rolled over as she left the room but did not wake. It was only just past eleven p.m. The day was not yet done.

She paused by the front door. For a second, she thought the Venislarn had sent bloody wedge-shaped slugs to kill her. Then she realised that someone had attempted to feed slices of pizza under her door and through the letterbox.

Pizza. Ten o'clock. Ah, yes.

"Sorry, Richard," she whispered.

In the kitchen, Morag poured herself a glass of water, downed it, poured another and took it and the largest sharpest knife in the house into the living room. She sat in a chair that gave her a view of both the door and the window and waited.

"Ready for you, bitch," she muttered to herself.

Sometime later, the sound of a closing door woke her. The knife fell from her hand and landed on its point in a gap in the laminate flooring.

"*Muda!*" she said and stood up, naked and confused.

She went to the bedroom. Drew was gone, leaving only violently ruffled sheets and a damp patch. She went back to the living room and looked out onto the street. There was no sign of Drew. It was windy out. Black shapes that might have been the tops of trees or maybe weren't moved along the rooftops opposite. It was five past midnight and Morag had not died.

"Bloody liars," she said. "Talking a load of pish."

She cleaned her teeth. As she mulled over the events of the day – seen in the light of the fact that she was not dead, considering the fact that she had blown all her spending cash on cocktails, gambling, hoverboards and a tobacco pipe, and had had reckless unprotected sex with a fellow ginger – a thought occurred to her. Something Professor Sheikh Omar had said. She found her phone and sent a text to Rod.

Seconds later, her phone rang. "Are you still up?" said Rod.

Morag regarded herself in the mirror, undressed, with a mouth of toothpaste foam.

"I guess."

"Good. Grab your coat and get over to Sparkbrook. We're going for a curry."

Thursday

Morag looked at herself in the mirror on the first floor landing.

A quick wash and fresh clothes and she was ready to go out for curry. She was indeed hungry. Sex and alcohol tended to make one hungry. She patted her cheeks and peered closer. Did she look like she'd just had sex? Would Rod notice?

There was a noise overhead. A scraping of something heavy over the floorboards. She looked up the stairs. There was a faint musical sound too, a stringed instrument – a banjo? A ukulele? It wasn't a nice sound. Three days and she hadn't met her upstairs neighbour, the supposedly crazy old cat lady.

Morag walked to the foot of the stairs. The lower half of the door to flat three was covered in thin scratches. A fat black cat sat halfway up the stairs. It looked at Morag lazily and then, almost as if it could barely be bothered, bared its teeth and hissed.

Morag's phone dinged. Her uCab awaited.

"If you were nicer, the other cats would play with you," she told the cat and went downstairs.

The taxi was parked in the middle of the road, engine idling. Morag slipped into the back seat. "Karakoram Balti House in Sparkbrook," she said. "It's a restaurant. You know it?"

The taxi driver met her gaze in the rear view mirror and then pulled away.

It was a silent fifteen-minute journey across the south of the city, through high streets that might have once been Victorian villages and the leafy suburban streets that had welded those villages into the growing city.

The taxi stopped on a high street lined with gaily lit shop frontages. The only businesses that were open were the restaurants. Morag counted half a dozen without even looking. She paid the driver and hopped out.

He swung away and into a car park beside a discount supermarket where a line of cabs waited, lights on.

"Yeah, I bet you talk to them," she muttered. "It's cos I'm ginger, isn't it?"

The name Karakoram was spelled out in loops of pink neon lighting. Inside, a waiter in a waistcoat and bow tie approached.

"I'm here to meet my friend," she said. "Ah."

Rod and Nina sat at a circular table beneath a wall-length photographic print of the Himalayas at sunset. There was a scattering of other diners in the restaurant, clusters of men dining in trios or pairs.

"Hungry?" said Rod.

"Surprisingly," said Morag, sitting down. "He drag you out of bed too?" she said to Nina.

"It's nowhere near my bedtime," said Nina. "And I skipped dinner, so when I heard there was food in the offing..."

The restaurant menu was a single piece of paper pinned underneath the glass table top.

"So, why are we here, exactly?" said Morag.

"You said you were hungry," said Rod.

"Yes, but..."

"It's as you said." Rod turned to Nina. "Our new colleague's a smart un. We went to visit Professor Sheikh Omar today."

"How is he?" said Nina.

"As camp as Christmas and as dodgy as a late night kebab."

"The usual then."

"Aye. And he was blathering on about how his mate Maurice had read the future in Omar's Balti lamb special. And what do we know about Omar's dietary habits?"

"He's a vegetarian," said Nina.

"So, he lied," said Morag. "What has that got to do with this? Did the mention of Balti just make you hungry?"

"No. You see the only reason he would order a Balti lamb –" He stopped. The waiter had materialised at his elbow. "Right. Drinks?" said Rod. "A pint of what?"

"Cheap and nasty lager," said Nina.

Rod looked at Morag.

"I think a half," she said. "It's late."

"You'll want a pint. Trust me. Three pints of your best lager," he told the waiter. "And we would like to order the Balti special for all three of us."

"The special?" said the waiter. "Which special?"

"*The* special," said Rod. The waiter looked at him. He looked at the waiter. "You do serve the Balti special, don't you?" said Rod.

"It is very hot," said the waiter.

"We like hot food." Rod simply maintained eye contact.

"Yes. But it is very, very hot."

"Good," said Rod with finality. "And make sure you don't forget the chef's special sauce."

The waiter backed away reluctantly.

"Um," said Morag, "does 'chef's special sauce' mean the same thing here as it does in... well, everywhere else?"

"That's your first question?" said Nina. "Not, why is the man ordering for everyone like he's some super alpha dude who's come back to the cave with a dead T-rex?"

"I was going to come to that. If a guy on a date did that, I'd walk straight out."

"Nah," said Nina. "I'd eat it and then walk out."

"Hey, I'm not that kind of bloke," said Rod.

"I know you're not," said Nina. "You're one of the good guys."

"Ta."

"One of those good, polite, kind, boring guys who... how did you ever get in the SAS?"

"You can be an alpha male and a gentleman," said Rod nobly. "By the way, a caveman wouldn't have brought a dead T-rex back to the cave."

"Not by himself, maybe," said Nina. "Him and his mates."

"No, I meant it wouldn't have been possible."

"With that kind of attitude it's no wonder that the caveman went extinct."

"No. Wait. What?" said Rod. "Cavemen didn't go extinct."

"Really?" said Nina. "Well, where are they all now?"

Rod, befuddled, made a general round table gesture. "They're us."

"I don't live in a cave and I've seen your metrosexual manpad."

157

"Manpad? Listen, humankind and dinosaurs were sixty-five million years apart."

"No, I saw this thing on YouTube."

"Must be true then," said Morag, smiling.

Rod's jaw ground to a halt under the onslaught of stupid and only started working again once the waiter had brought the beers and poppadoms.

"The special..." said the waiter, his voice full of servile regret.

"Had better be coming soon," said Rod firmly.

The waiter shuffled off unhappily.

"Back to the chef's special sauce," said Morag.

"Aye," said Rod. "You ever eaten a Balti, Morag?"

"I think so," she said honestly. "I tend to wander all over the Indian menu. Not sure what I'm ordering half the time."

"Balti's the one fried in the little pot," said Nina."

"Right. Yes."

"'Pot' or 'bucket'. That's what the word 'Balti' means," said Rod. "And where do you think the Balti comes from?"

Morag looked at the photographed mountains on the wall and thought of Northern India, maybe Pakistan, Tibet even... "You're going to tell it was invented here, aren't you?" she said.

"It was," said Rod. "Literally around the corner. Back in the seventies. The first Baltis were cooked here and the best Baltis still are."

"In the Balti Triangle," said Nina in a deep and spooky voice.

"Seriously?" said Morag.

"It's the wedge between the Stratford Road and the Alcester Road," said Rod, drawing a triangle in the air.

"Like I know where that is," said Morag.

"Main arterial roads out of the city."

"Is it like the Bermuda triangle?"

"No. It's something stranger."

"Uh-huh." Morag broke off a shard of poppadom and paused in the act of dipping it in the chutney tray. "Is there chef's special sauce in this?"

Rod shook his head.

"The Balti triangle predates the Balti and the first Pakistani immigrants, even possibly the first human settlers of any sort. It's the story of *Kaxeos*."

"I like it when Rod tells a story," said Nina. "Although, I always think it should feature trouble down t'pit or whippets."

"What bit of Yorkshire do you think I come from?" said Rod.

"Eck 'e thump."

"That's not a place. Now, shut up and listen. There was a Venislarn called *Kaxeos*, a god of fire."

"The Winds of *Kaxeos*," said Morag, remembering the surreal session with Chad and Leandra the day before.

"They're his servants. Possibly his children. They're still alive and free and roaming... somewhere. *Kaxeos* was worshipped by the locals."

"I thought you said this was before people came to Britain."

"Exactly. His worshippers, whatever they were, weren't stupid. They worshipped *Kaxeos* but they were afraid of him. So they bound him in chains and buried him, '*and the fires of his body baked the earth into stone*'. But that was not enough. To ensure he would never be freed, they dug out the major organs and reburied them in three separate chambers (or 'pots') arranged around his body. '*They bound him in a triangle powered by his own magic.*'"

"So there's a god buried beneath us, providing underfloor heating for the local borough?"

"And more besides. *Kaxeos* is a powerful being, psychic or something of that ilk and practically omniscient."

"So, if anyone knows anything about possible incursions in the next forty-odd hours, he will."

"And that's why we must eat the Balti special," said Rod.

"I'm just here for the free food," said Nina. She smashed the pile of poppadoms and grabbed a handful of fragments. "Chef's special sauce or not, free food is free food." She fed them into her mouth like crisps. "I've swallowed worse stuff in my time."

Rod looked at his hand as he reached for what remained of the poppadoms.

"I'm sure I have, but I can't remember washing my hands since that last job in Dudley." He stood. "Back in a minute."

"Dudley?" said Morag to Nina.

"Long story," said Nina. "Long... sticky... messy... dirty story."

Going to the toilets in a curry house is rarely fraught with danger.

Rod had long accepted the mysterious shittiness of men's toilets. Restaurant, bar, café, pub... It didn't matter what establishment or how plush and well-maintained the general premises, the men's toilets were always filthy, poorly repaired and generally awash with a good half inch of piss on the floor. It was part of the natural rhythm of the universe. Women's toilets (he was given to understand) might well be as fragrant and as inviting as a country health spa but there was no such thing as a clean gents. It was as though trained apes came in every half hour to piss over every surface and, if they were feeling particularly dutiful, smear crap on cubicle walls.

Therefore, the only danger Rod anticipated facing was getting his shoe laces soaked in another man's piss or, worse, after washing and drying his hands, finding the door handle slick with something wet and unknowable.

He did not expect to be about to enter the gents and be distracted by the sound of voices conversing in Venislarn along the corridor. He did not expect that, upon opening a door to take a look, he would see two men, deep in conversation over a parchment covered in Venislarn astrological charts. He certainly didn't expect one of the men to shout and then something hard and heavy to connect with the back of his head and clout him into unconsciousness.

Rod woke and, before opening his eyes, took an automatic audit of his senses.

Touch: he was lying on a hard surface. Not metal or wood. Smooth under his fingertips. Tiles or stone. There was a tightness across his chest and across his thighs. He was tied or strapped down, and firmly too.

Sound: He heard three people talking. Men. Rod was a poor linguist but he was fairly certain they were speaking a creole of Venislarn and some other language. Urdu? Bengali? Rod really didn't have a clue. It could have been Swahili or Serbo-Croat for all

160

he knew. But the echo of the voices told him that the room he was in was small and sparsely furnished. A kitchen store room? A cellar? The echo had an additional dimension to it, a distinct hollowness, as though there were a chimney or a corridor close by.

Smell: Rod did not like the smell. Musty. Organic. It was not directly offensive, and yet it spoke of things that had not been cleaned in a very, *very* long time.

Someone pulled open his jacket and reached for his pistol. Rod opened his eyes. The man had a round face and an ugly, oiled handlebar moustache like a cartoon villain. And now he had Rod's pistol.

"That's mine," Rod said.

Ugly 'tache grinned. A younger man — wielding a meat cleaver, Rod could not help but notice — double-checked and tightened the leather straps binding Rod's legs to the counter. The third man in the room was the waiter who had taken their order. He looked at Rod with a terribly sad expression on his face.

That's nice, thought Rod. That's nice that he at least feels sad that he's tied up one of his customers in a dank room with a bloke with an ugly 'tache and a bloke with a shiny cleaver.

The room *was* dank. The floor, walls and the boxy shelf Rod was tied to were covered in tiles that might have once been white but, like meth addicts' teeth, had darkened to an uneven tortoiseshell colour. In the floor beside Rod's head there was a square sunken shaft and the tiles around its rim were a diseased fungal brown.

"I hope this isn't a food preparation area," Rod said. "A poor food hygiene rating can shut a restaurant overnight."

Ugly 'tache turned to the waiter. "*Scha'pheri bha fur ghurri spayn'ogn?*"

"*Rho-lergisko'l. Rho-lergisko'l,*" said the waiter. "*Des Kaxeos ma Yo. Fnah-Yo.*"

Rod's grasp of conversational Venislarn was on a par with his Pashto and his Arabic: limited to inventive swearing and pleading for his life. He didn't know what the two men were saying but he was prepared to wager that they were deciding what to do with him.

"If it helps, I am a remarkably generous tipper for a Yorkshireman," he said.

"*Hoh'ch me rhu ap Yo-Zildrohar. Aklo byach, so-khor,*" said Ugly 'tache indifferently.

"You do know who I am?" said Rod.

Cleaver tucked his weapon into his belt, went to the edge of the square pit and lowered a length of wire like a plumb-line into the hole.

"You do know why I am here?" said Rod.

The waiter approached him. "We know," he said. "You have come to steal the wisdom of Lord *Kaxeos.*"

"Steal? We know the Venislarn. They know us. We come as ambassadors and, mate, to be honest, this..." He attempted to gesture about him with bound hands. "This is seriously not on."

"We are servants of Lord *Kaxeos,* Mr Policeman, and Lord *Kaxeos* does as he pleases."

"He does. But you. I don't know you," he said, holding down the anger inside him. "I haven't seen any of your faces on registration papers and that means you answer to me."

Cleaver pulled up his line. On the end was a cylindrical container now dripping with pale brown slime that might have been mucous or ichor or...

"I always wondered what was in the chef's special sauce," said Rod.

Ugly 'tache laughed. "*Perrhe'ri tamade dras'n-orgh, muda khi umlaq.*"

"Oh, yeah?" said Rod. "You think you'll be laughing when *Kaxeos* finds out what you've been doing to his guest?"

The waiter twitched his head as though he had an itch behind his ear that he didn't want to scratch.

"Lord *Kaxeos* knows all," he said.

"Well, I'm certainly not happy about all this," Rod said and then addressed Ugly 'tache. "And don't think I don't know what some of those words meant, you *adn-bhul muda khi umlaq.*"

Cleaver whispered something to the waiter. The waiter peered at the cylinder full of slime and nodded. Cleaver put the cylinder and line aside, picked up his cleaver and took hold of Rod's hand.

"Don't you bloody dare!" Rod said through gritted teeth.

It took him a moment to realise that Cleaver was trying to unfold his fingers. Rod fought against him.

"*Whe'dhna oyi*," said Cleaver.

Ugly 'tache smacked Rod across the bridge of his nose with the butt of his own gun. In that instant of white pain, Cleaver stretched out Rod's fingers and pressed them flat against the counter.

"You evil bastards," Rod grunted. His vision swam and he struggled to focus on the waiter. "I'm going to scream this bloody house down."

The waiter nodded, understanding, patient and sad. "Soundproofing," he said simply.

Cleaver adjusted his grip and brought the blade down at speed. Rod didn't know if he started screaming before or after the cleaver struck. He didn't truly feel anything until he saw Cleaver hold something up, pink and bloody and the size of a cocktail sausage.

Rod grunted, yelled and thrashed. His hand hurt – of course, it bloody hurt – but more than that, he felt the wrongness in his hand. He fought down the urge to vomit, channelling his anger and fear and nausea into some lengthy and loud swearing which featured the invention of the previously unheard-of 'ankle-grabbing cockbadgers!'

Cleaver inspected the ruined tip of Rod's finger and then dropped it down the square shaft. Almost instantly, there was a deep rumbling from far below. Like the roar of a trapped beast or the rumbling of a stomach bigger than worlds.

"Did you hear that?" said Nina.

Morag cocked an ear. "A train?"

"Trains don't run past here. Maybe it was an earthquake."

"In Birmingham?"

"We have them. There was one when I was kid. Registered five point oh on the wotsit scale. I don't remember it really. I do remember the tornado."

"The one Vivian mentioned? That was in, what, 2005?" said Morag.

"Mmm. It was at the beginning of the summer holidays," said Nina. "I was at my auntie's house off the Ladypool Road when the tornado came by, tearing up trees and flinging cars across the road. It ripped tiles off the roof of the house and blew out of the upstairs windows."

"That must have been terrifying," said Morag.

Nina shrugged and stuffed the last of the poppadoms in her mouth. "Of course, if what Vivian says is true then it was a god. Or godling. Or godlings, plural. The Winds of *Kaxeos*."

"Vivian seems quite knowledgeable on such things," said Morag.

"Well, if you had been alive since, like, World War One, then you'd know a lot too."

The waiter came to their table pushing a two-tiered wooden trolley. He unloaded three deep metal bowls of reddish-brown curry and two oval platters of pilau rice.

"It is very hot," he said.

"Thanks," said Morag.

The waiter backed away, blinking nervously, as though he had just deposited live bombs on the table. Nina swiped a portion of rice onto her plate and scraped half her Balti on top.

"So, you settling in all right?" she asked.

"To the job? To Birmingham?"

"Either. Both."

"It's been a manic few days," said Morag. "I left Edinburgh on Sunday. I've only had one full night's sleep in my own bed since then. It's Thursday now, isn't it?"

"Time be time, man," said Nina.

"The flat they've put me up in is nice. I'm sandwiched between a crazy old cat lady and a man who posted pizza through my letterbox last night."

"It's nice they've put you up somewhere at all. When I started with the mission..." Nina paused. "That first week, I was completely balls out petrified."

"They throw you in at the deep end?" said Morag, serving herself some food.

"No. Not that. Um, Vivian. She's fucking terrifying."

"I can see that."

"Vaughn just didn't speak to me for the first month."

"Not met him yet. Not even sure he really exists."

Nina laughed. "And even Rod," she said.

"Rod's nice," said Morag.

"Sure. Once you get to know him. But, on first impressions he's like some scary Navy SEAL drill instructor. Greg was nice. He was the boss back then. You never got to meet him. He was the nicest of them all. But, still, I was the newbie and they were all so... old. I mean that's not such a problem for you."

"Gee, thanks. I'm not quite at retirement age yet."

"I know," said Nina. "But I mean, you and Vivian. At least, you two can talk about your menopauses or whatever."

"How bloody old do you think I am? Shut up before I slap you down, squirt," said Morag, but she was smiling. She toyed with her food. It smelled good; rich, fatty and fresh. "I admit it," she said, "I think Vivian's scary."

"God, she is."

"She's *Mrs* Vivian Grey, isn't she?"

"I think Mr Grey was one of our lot."

"Was, huh?" said Morag.

"Maybe that's why she turned into such an ice queen."

"No," said Morag after some thought. "I think she was always like that."

"Uh-huh," said Nina and shovelled a forkful of food into her mouth.

"I see it like this," said Morag. "Most of us, when the world doesn't conform to our expectations, we get angry or depressed. I think Vivian just gives life a hard stare and waits for it to get its act together. Bet she was like that when she was a toddler. 'No, mother, this birthday cake just won't do. Go back and do it properly.'" She stopped. Nina's face had turned an interesting colour. "Are you okay?"

"Hot," Nina coughed.

"He did say."

"Really hot," she whispered.

Morag took a little of the Balti on her fork and ate it. The chilli zing took a good few seconds to kick in but, when it did, it sent a violent warmth down her throat and up to her brain.

165

"Mmm, spicy," said Morag and took another mouthful. This was perhaps a mistake as the first mouthful had not yet done its work. Chilli-infused energies wrapped around the inside of her mouth and all but paralysed it. "Yes. Hot," she said hoarsely and reached for her pint. The act of drinking felt good but the beer did nothing to dampen the heat. "Where's Rod?" she said. "There's no reason why we should suffer alone."

Nina looked in the general direction of the toilets. "I dunno. He's probably just fallen in."

Rod concentrated on breathing and tried to think straight. They'd left him, still strapped to the counter. The waiter had tied a napkin around Rod's injured hand. Rod couldn't angle his head to see if he'd done a good job of it or not. The counter was wet beneath Rod's wrist. His hand was a ball of pain, a football-sized sphere of scalding misery.

The pain was interfering with his thought processes but Rod had been forged by nearly two decades of pain and death, mostly other people's, and he wasn't about to lie down and feel sorry for himself.

"Right. Right. What have we got? What have we got?"

The room was mostly featureless. There was another counter across from him. There was nothing on it but the rusted remains of some butchery machine, maybe a bacon slicer. The door at his feet had a metal pull handle, like a walk-in freezer. The door looked stout. There were rivets in its metal surface. Rod tried to angle his foot across to reach the door. They had bound him well. His foot could barely move and the door handle was a good two feet away.

"Not that," he said. "What else? What else?"

Two parallel pipes ran across the wall above the door. Gas pipes? Water pipes? He wasn't sure and there was no reaching them.

"What else have you got?"

The straps about him were leather and had buckles with double rows of eyelets. If he was to escape, he was going to need to undo them or cut through them or wait for Cleaver to chop him up and escape piece by piece.

Rod took a personal inventory. Ugly 'tache had taken his gun. That left him with, on his left hand, a survival escape ring (containing a coiled hacksaw blade); in his left trouser pocket, a Leatherman multi-tool, assorted coins and two powerful magnets disguised as coins; in the secret compartment in his left boot heel, a pair of powerful lenses which could be assembled into a rudimentary telescope; in his right trouser pocket, his key ring including two skeleton keys, an hourglass key fob engraved with 'Greetings from Skegness' that, mixed in with the sand, contained two grams of explosive francium held in a vacuum; on his right wrist his watch with in-built compass, depth gauge, altimeter, laser pointer, GPS beacon, high tide indicator and sunrise/sunset sweep arm plus his survival bracelet woven from paracord with the additional interweave of monofilament wire he had recently added; in his right jacket pocket, a tobacco tin containing fishing wire, wax-headed matches, needle and thread, superglue, water-purifying tablets, a square of Kendal mint cake and a condom (for carrying water supplies or, in extremis, contraception) plus his wallet which held cordite-infused dollars (the company didn't do any other currency) and a credit card survival tool containing a magnesium alloy fire starter and an LED torch; in his left jacket pocket, his mobile phone, a pen with a one-shot taser built into the nib, a propelling pencil with a sharpened steel lead, a fold-out sheet of idiot-proof Venislarn ideograms, wards and sigils and a nub of chalk to draw them with; finally, on his person, his tie (threaded with steel wire for zip line escapes), his tie clip lock picks and a waistcoat that could be pulled apart to make a hammock or an impromptu fishing net.

The ideal tool was the escape ring with hacksaw on his left hand but his fingers, caught in the radius of pain, were not responding to his command. With his right hand, he unclipped his watch — he had spent many an evening practising this wrist-snapping feat — and, because he could, activated the GPS beacon. He then reached further back and tugged at his survival bracelet with his longest fingers.

"Come on, mate. Come on."

His fingers brushed against the end of the monofilament and he pulled on it.

"So, how long have you been with Birmingham mission?" Morag asked.

She ate another forkful of the curry. It was quite extraordinarily hot but it was – and she had no idea what she meant or felt when she thought this – it was a *good* hot. The heat filled her cheeks and her belly and her head and, though she was probably imagining this, brought a rosy sharpness to her vision.

"Two years," said Nina. "It's been good. I really enjoy it. Apart from the end of the world stuff, obviously."

"Obviously."

"But even then I just like the fact that I know the Big Secret. I know. My mum doesn't know. My sister doesn't know. My old teachers and all those spoddy girls at school who made fun of me because I thought that Mick Jagger was prime minister during World War Two."

"Mick Jagger? That well known politician?"

"Shush, you. Point is, I know the Big Secret."

"Even though it's a deeply horrible secret."

"Ah, but that too has benefits."

"I'm all ears," said Morag. "The benefits of knowing that our world is being consumed by omnipotent alien gods and that, at some undisclosed future point, we will be plunged into a literal and eternal hell. Go for it."

"Simple," said Nina. "My sister worries about being able to buy a house and get on the property ladder. I don't, 'cos alien gods are going to eat the world. My friends worry that they're getting old and fat. I don't 'cos alien gods are going to eat the world. Credit card bills? Alien gods. International terrorism? Alien gods. Turning up to work on time? Alien gods."

"You're right," said Morag. "I don't worry about any of those things."

"See? Benefits."

"So, two years in and you're already in the response team. That's... surprising."

"Oh?" said Nina heavily. "Don't I strike you as the right sort?"

"I didn't say that."

"No?" Nina emptied the rest of her Balti onto her plate. "I can't feel my lips anymore. Should I worry?"

"It's good stuff this."

"Chef's special sauce."

"Yeah. You can say that as much as you like, still doesn't sound right."

Nina drank beer and mushed her lips together experimentally. "I know what you mean though," she said. "Response teams, it's mostly eggheads and soldier boys and... whatever you are."

"Thanks," said Morag. "So, how did you wind up in this role?"

"I bring something unique to the mission, apart from the stone-cold-bitch-and-sex-kitten vibe."

"What's that?"

"An Abyssal Rating of ten."

"Shut up."

"It's true. This girl isn't scared of nothing."

"Except Vivian."

"Except Vivian," Nina agreed. "I came to their attention after I'd signed up to take part in a series of dangerous experiments for a deeply dodgy Birmingham academic."

"Professor Sheikh Omar?"

"That tit, yes," said Nina. "He was paying. I like money. I didn't stop to think. Picture a chair, restraints, loads of things – electrodes – all over my head and then a slideshow of the ugliest psychosis-inducing Venislarn buttfaces you ever did see."

"I'm surprised you came out the other end, sane or alive."

"There were six of us who signed up for that experiment," said Nina and said it in such a way that there was no need for further questions. Nina raised her pint. "I have no mouth."

"And I must scream," said Morag.

Nina lowered her glass and then raised her hand again. Up and down.

"I'm getting trail blur," she said.

"You're getting what?"

Nina waggled her fingers as she waved her hand. "You know, like when you've taken too many shrooms."

"Not really," said Morag.

169

She scraped out the last of her bowl onto her rice. Morag studied her own hand. She wasn't getting any kind of blurring to her vision. Far from it. She looked at her plate and saw the one hundred and thirty-seven grains of rice remaining on it. She looked around and saw the room in a rich, fiery red and pinpoint clarity. "I think I can see in infrared," she said.

"That's not normal," said Nina.

"No," said Morag slowly. "It's not. Have you eaten here before?"

"Nope." Nina chased the remains of her food around her plate. "But it's good, isn't it?"

"Very good. Rod brought us here to find something out."

"Where is Rod?" said Nina.

Morag felt a fuzziness in her head and shook her head as though she could physically dislodge it.

"He's been gone a while," said Nina.

"Nineteen minutes and six seconds," said Morag automatically and then, "I shouldn't know something like that. I thought we came here to question someone but..."

"The knowledge is in the curry," said Nina.

"This really hot curry."

"But it's a good hot, isn't it?"

"Chef's special sauce. I remember reading..." She closed her eyes and reached for the memory. "I remember reading a book, when I was six, about how Indian monks would burn or freeze themselves to attain enlightenment."

"Knowledge through pain."

Morag took a deep cleansing breath. "I didn't even know I still had that memory." On one level, Morag felt drunk. The world was passing her by and her mind couldn't alight on one thing for more than a moment. But, on another level, she was experiencing a clarity and certainty unlike any she had known. Facts and knowledge rolled over her and she felt that she could simply reach out with her mind and pluck any truth she wished from the air.

"*Kaxeos* is psychic," said Morag.

"Practically omniscient," said Nina and then, "I didn't know what that word meant until now."

"And we're inside the triangle. We're directly above him."

Nina ate the last of her curry. "Seriously, I can't feel my face anymore."

Morag reached over and took her hand. "I've realised something else," she said.

"Uh-huh."

"You see that table of four guys by the door?"

Nina leaned slightly to see behind Morag. "Uh-huh."

"One of them was the taxi driver who brought me here."

"So?"

"The man next to him?"

"Yes?"

"The taxi driver who brought me to the Library on my first day."

"They're taxi drivers, they know each other."

"The guy in the booth over there. Half-moon glasses."

"Yes?"

"That's the taxi driver who took me to my new flat after we went out for food and drinks on Monday night."

"So, taxi drivers come here."

"*I never told him my address.*"

"You were drunk," said Nina.

Morag put her phone on the table. "I've got the uCab app on my phone."

"I've got that," said Nina. "Really handy."

She opened the map page and tapped the icon to find taxis for hire in the local area. Dozens of car icons appeared in overlapping clusters in the area immediately surrounding the Karakoram Balti House.

"Hundreds of them," said Morag.

"Okay, that is weird," agreed Nina.

"It's beyond weird."

"Want to hear something weirder?"

Morag automatically gathered up the last of her curry and ate it. "What?"

"There are twenty-two diners in this restaurant apart from ourselves."

"Yes."

"And three staff at the counter."

"Yes."

Nina fixed her with a serious gaze. "Apart from our waiter, in all the time that we've been here, have you heard a single one of them speak?"

Morag looked round. Men ate slowly or drank coffee. Nina was right; none of them were talking. They didn't even raise their eyes to look at each other. They just sat and ate and drank. A chill ran through Morag.

"Rod *has* been gone for a long time."

The orb of shocking pain around Rod's hand had receded somewhat but the sickening, sticky stump of bog-standard pain it left behind was just as much of a distraction.

He managed to unravel a length of wire from his survival bracelet and, gathering a bundle of it in his hand, threw it up towards his head with a forceful hand flick. On the second attempt, he got it to fall across his face. Then, suffering only minor nicks to his tongue, he wrapped it around his front teeth and, with a combination of head jiggles and wrist pulls, began sawing at the leather strap over his hands and midriff.

As he sawed, he tried to get an objective view of the situation: here he was, within the triangle, in a building located over one of the three chambers housing *Kaxeos's* confiscated innards. He was prepared to bet that the pit beside him was the entrance to one such chamber.

He had been to the restaurant before, in the company of Greg, a month or two before his death. They had eaten the special and the pair of them had been rewarded with, if not quite visions, certain insights into local Venislarn activities. It would have been the same special Balti that Sheikh Omar and his little friend, Maurice, sampled recently.

Rod had not lied to his captors. He had come with openness and honesty to gain wisdom from the hot and spicy oracle of Sparkbrook. The consular mission knew *Kaxeos*. *Kaxeos* knew them. There should have been no need for violence or mistrust. Something else was going on. The situation, locally or globally, had changed...

There was a feeling of give by Rod's wrist. He flexed his arm and pushed outward, snapping the remains of the leather strap and almost ripping out his two front teeth. The movement brought renewed pain to his left hand.

Rod reached up with his freed right hand, found the buckle across his chest and undid it. He sat up, dragged the tangle of wire from his mouth, reached down to free his legs and, only then, looked at what had become of his left hand. The napkin the waiter had tied round it was now a sodden red mess. Rod pulled it away and regarded his hand: four and a half fingers (or three and a half fingers plus a thumb). The top joint of his little finger was gone and the wound was bleeding profusely.

He reached into his jacket for his tobacco tin and simultaneously stuck the ravaged digit in his mouth. While he sucked the wound, he one-handedly took out the superglue and unsealed it.

"So, you got a little taste, did you?" he said to the hole in the floor as he squirted glue liberally over his tiny stump. The glue stung but began to seal the wound instantly. He blew on it to help it dry. His breath was blades of ice. The glue dried and the bleeding slowed to an oozy trickle.

"Rod is off the menu," he told the hole. He felt like using stronger language but this was possibly a god or a part of a god he was addressing and he wasn't one for offending all-powerful Venislarn.

"And now for the dramatic escape," he said.

His phone had no signal. The door, locked, had no lock on this side. Nor did it have hinges or any accessible screws or other moving parts. There were no air vents, grilles, windows or other openings into the room. Rod looked down the hole. It descended into impenetrable darkness within six feet and Rod had no intention of going for a little explore.

He inspected and then dismantled the defunct bacon slicer and came away with a heavy square blade. "So, no way out," he said. "And I can't get a message out."

He looked at the dark slime-edged shaft. "But you could, lord, couldn't you?"

Rod regarded the pipes that ran above the door, from one wall to the other. "Gas or water?" he asked philosophically. "What do you reckon, lord?" Rod raised the square piece of blade and brought it over in a double-handed slam which ripped the pipe in two.

"The curry, then, allows communication with *Kaxeos*," said Nina.

"Communication. Communion," said Morag.

"Communion curry."

"*Kaxeos* is a god of fire."

"And knowledge."

"Fiery knowledge."

"The spark of intelligence."

"He can reach out to others telepathically."

"And control them?"

"So, he knows our intentions," said Morag.

"He knows we mean no harm."

Morag nodded. "You know how some of the smartest people you know make the most stupid mistakes?"

"Oh, yeah."

"I've just eaten a whole bowlful of smarts. Watch this for stupid," she said and stood up, wobbling slightly, drunk with knowledge. "Evening all," she said to the restaurant at large. "May I assume that I am addressing *Kaxeos*, most venerable of the Venislarn?"

Wordlessly and as one, the twenty-odd diners stood and faced her. The synchronicity and silence was eerily unpleasant.

"Um," said Morag.

"Freaky," said Nina.

"*Yo-Kaxeos*," said Morag, "we have come to seek your wisdom and advice but..." She looked at the implacable and emotionless faces. "Have you done something with our friend?"

"*Yo-Kaxeos skruv'en ist mezzhor*," said two dozen voices as one.

"Ooh, goose bumps," said Nina.

"*Ouril skruv'en ist mezzhor*," said the men.

"Freed?" said Morag. "Why? How?"

174

"Ouril skruv'en pes beschro'ne."

"Eat," said Morag. "That doesn't sound good."

Nina was on her feet. "You mindless arseholes had better not have fed our Rod to your god."

The nearest men stepped out from their tables and moved towards the two of them.

"I think their god might still be hungry," said Morag.

It was a water pipe. Rod had had a half-formulated plan of what to do if natural gas had started jetting out but that plan involved singed eyebrows as a bare minimum. This was better. Water gushed from the ruptured pipe, cascaded over him, pooled on the floor and poured down the tiled shaft. Rod hoped that, whatever aspect of *Kaxeos* lived at the bottom of that hole, it would object to a spot of god-sized waterboarding and reach out telepathically.

It did.

Within a minute, the door was flung open. Ugly 'tache stared at the water on the floor and then at Rod and then Rod drove his fist into the man's stomach. As Ugly 'tache doubled up, Rod brought the same fist up and slammed the man's bottom jaw shut with a noise like a tree branch snapping. As Ugly 'tache staggered back, Cleaver ran at Rod, swinging his blade wildly. Rod ducked him easily and brought his whole arm around in a haymaker sweep. The blow knocked Cleaver from his feet. Momentum and wet tiles carried Cleaver onward, slipping and sliding the short distance to the hole, down which he vanished feet first.

Ugly 'tache stumbled into an upright position against the corridor wall. There was blood on his split lip. He pulled Rod's pistol from his waistband. Rod moved forward, slapped the gun hand aside and, taking the man's face in hand like a basketball, bounced his head off the wall. Rod caught the pistol as Ugly 'tache dropped it and put a bullet in the man's foot for good measure.

He flipped the pistol up to point at the waiter along the corridor. The sad-faced little man put up his hands. "No violence, please," he said.

"You're saying that now, hmmm?" said Rod, holding up his mutilated hand as a counterpoint.

From the pit in the waterlogged room, Cleaver began to scream. It wasn't a nice scream and it didn't sound like it was going to end anytime soon.

"I think it's time we settled the bill," said Rod and, with a waggle of the pistol, shepherded him back to the dining area.

The entire restaurant was on its feet. Morag and Nina were backed up against the counter, facing a small crowd of blank-faced men.

"Nobody is to do anything reckless," said Rod, advancing with pistol aimed, "or I'm literally going to take off and nuke the entire site from orbit."

"Figuratively," said Nina and then looked at Rod, in his sodden suit. "*Muda*, did you actually fall in?"

"I'm not right happy at this very moment," he replied.

"These taxi drivers are all under *Kaxeos*'s control," said Morag. "What happened to your hand?"

Rod ignored her and wheeled on the waiter. "Explanations. Quickly. I've had some deeply unsanitary surgery and want answers before A and E."

The waiter wrung his hands pitifully. "*Kaxeos* must be freed. Before..."

"Before what?" demanded Rod.

"Before the city is destroyed."

"Destroyed," said Morag. "The incursion Professor Omar mentioned?"

The waiter nodded. "Tomorrow," he said.

A trickle of water ran down from Rod's wet hair. He wiped it away with the back of his injured hand. Suddenly, he was very tired. It was one a.m. and he'd lost the tip of his finger and probably a bit too much blood and he'd had enough.

"Right," he said. He waved the gun at the taxi drivers. "You lot sit down and shut up."

"They're shut up," said Nina.

"Good. Stay that way." He looked at his colleagues. "Think one of you two will need to drive me to the hospital. And you" – he turned to the waiter and waved the gun at his uneaten Balti – "box this up for me. I've still not had my flaming dinner."

Shortly after nine o'clock that morning, Vivian found Nina in Room Two with a sad and sorry looking man.

"Miss Seth," said Vivian.

"Mrs Grey," said Nina, unscrewing the cap on a Boost energy drink. From the mess on the table Vivian could see it wasn't her first of the day.

"I went into Room Eight and found it to be full of taxi drivers," said Vivian.

"Yes."

"And Room Seven."

"Yes."

"And Room Six."

"Guess what's in Room Five?"

Vivian really didn't enjoy the young woman's impertinence. "I assume there's a reason why you've rounded up and detained half the city's private hire drivers."

"Certainly is."

Vivian waited. Nina smiled at her inanely.

"It's too early in the day to play silly games, Miss Seth," said Vivian.

Indeed, in the morning it was too early for silly games, in the later portions of the day she was too busy for silly games and, at all other times, she was simply not in the mood for silly games. The correct time for silly games, she had decided, was any time before seven years of age.

"This is Mr Arif," said Nina. "Until this morning, he was proprietor of the Karakoram Balti House."

"The House of *Kaxeos*."

"Bang on. And Mr Arif has been a very busy man. In a beautiful combination of modern tech and Venislarn powers, he's been calling uCab drivers to his master's home whereupon *Kaxeos* has seized control of their minds and bodies."

"Building an army."

"An army of spies throughout the city. But not only that. Mr Arif has been defiling the chambers that outline *Kaxeos*'s prison and weakening their power."

"Defiling how?" said Vivian.

"The usual. Human sacrifice."

Vivian gave the horrible little man a hard stare. He shrivelled under her gaze. "That is not acceptable, Mr Arif," she told him firmly.

The man whimpered something.

"What was that?" snapped Vivian.

"But we must flee. The end is coming."

"Yadda yadda yadda," said Nina. "Apparently, *Kaxeos* is convinced that the city will be destroyed by some cataclysmic incursion event tomorrow."

Vivian sighed irritably. "I've got to do this ridiculous community outreach workshop this morning with Silas Adjei and the Waters Crew. I had a chance to put it off until next Tuesday but I thought I'd better get it over and done with. If I had known that we'd all be dust and rubble by tomorrow..." She looked at Nina. "I was going to use Room Seven, as it's the largest. Any chance you could have these mindless cabbies processed by ten?"

"Doubtful," said Nina. "I've got to ID them all and work out where to send them. Morag's taken Rod to the hospital and I'm operating on caffeine and sugar."

"Hospital?"

"Lost his little finger."

"Careless," said Vivian.

Morag left Rod in the restricted ward of the QE hospital – on an IV drip of Venislarn antibiotics and antiparasitics while he waited for some consultant or other to take a look at his beshortened pinky. He had insisted he'd be able to drive himself back to the office once the 'fusspot doctors' let him leave, so Morag left his car keys with him and called for a uCab.

Outside hospital reception, she bent to peer in the driver's window.

"Morning."

The taxi driver looked at her and said nothing.

"Jeez, how many of you are there?" she said and got in the back seat. "Take me home."

The *Kaxeos*-possessed taxi driver waited.

"Home," she said. "Don't pretend you don't know where that is."

178

The taxi driver silently put the car in gear and drove off.

"And don't think I'm paying either," she said. "Ever. From now, I get in one of your taxis, it's a free ride."

The taxi driver said nothing. She didn't expect him to.

It was a mere ten-minute drive across a dual carriageway and down alongside the chocolate factory to 27 Franklin Road.

"Stay here," she told the cabbie. "I'm going to need a ride back to the Library in half an hour."

Out since midnight and having got smeared with more than a drop of Rod's blood, Morag needed to change. She went upstairs, threw her clothes into the washing machine (on top of the other, still unwashed clothes she had dumped there on Tuesday) and showered. As she dried her hair in the bedroom, she heard the faint and weird music from the flat upstairs once more. What had sounded like ukulele or guitar in the wee hours now sounded more like a harpsichord or a harp, something static, plucked and resonating. It had a peculiar quality to it, as though it was being played backwards or at the wrong speed. And, accompanying it, an out-of-time thumping, like stamping feet.

"I'm surprised your cats put up with it," Morag said to the ceiling.

As she gathered her things and headed back downstairs, she thought about Drew. She'd had one night stands before but not one where there had been no pretence of staying in touch afterwards. No exchanged phone numbers (real or fake). No promises to friend each other on Facebook or Snapchat. Nothing. Admittedly, spending most of his days naked, Drew possibly didn't have anywhere to keep a phone anyway.

Extenuating circumstances of the I'm-going-to-die-tonight variety aside, Morag wondered if she'd reached a new low in personal sluttiness.

"Not that sluttiness is bad," she said to herself.

"Well, no," said Richard.

Morag gave a start.

"I'm certainly not going to judge," he said, standing in his doorway.

"Jesus," she said. "I did not see you there. You're like some kind of ninja."

179

"Yes, I am," said her neighbour.

"Um. Listen," she said. "About last night..."

"We were going to have pizza at ten," said Richard.

"Right, because we agreed that, didn't we?"

"The whole new-neighbours thing. I did knock."

"I realise. I went to bed early."

"I heard noises."

"I did have a bit of a cough."

"I thought I heard moans."

"Yes. But I think I'm all better now." She shuffled uneasily. "You posted pizza through my letterbox."

"I..." He looked sheepish. "It seemed the right thing at the time."

"Did it really?"

"We said pizza at ten."

Morag wondered if he had OCD or Asperger's or severed heads in his freezer. No, he wouldn't have frozen heads in his freezer; he was too soft and gentle. He had a personality as yielding and as passive as a sponge. He was a teddy bear in human form. She suspected he was just lonely.

"Shall we try again?" she said.

"Pizza?" said Richard.

"Or something."

"Or something."

"We could go out Friday night. I mean, go out for something, not go out together."

"We wouldn't go together?"

"No, we'd be together," said Morag, struggling. "I meant, we could go out together, not *go out together*."

"Right," he said, not giving her any glimmer of comprehension.

"What do you do for fun, Richard?"

"Me?"

"Yes."

He thought about it. "I like chocolate oranges."

"It's not an activity though."

"No."

"Are you a big drinker? A real ale aficionado? Do you go to art galleries? Do you play squash? Go to concerts? Open mic nights?"

"Yes," nodded Richard.

"What, the open...?"

"Mic nights," he said. "I do."

"Music? Comedy?"

"Both."

"You play an instrument?"

"Absolutely." He held his hands out uncertainly, miming something vague.

"Bagpipes?"

He clicked his fingers. "Got it in one," he said.

Morag was momentarily lost for words. "Er, ok. An open mic night somewhere on Friday, possibly featuring bagpipes."

"It's not a date," said Richard, smiling.

"No," agreed Morag, contemplating the evening ahead. "It's really not, is it? Okay."

She sidled past and out the door. The taxi was still there, waiting. She climbed in.

"Take me to work," she said and then checked herself. "Wait."

The taxi driver did nothing, didn't move.

"You're *Kaxeos*, right?" she said. "Or, you're an extension of him. You understand what I'm saying and you know everything that *Kaxeos* knows."

Nothing.

"There's going to be a major incursion on Friday, tomorrow, isn't there? Rampaging gods, pestilence and horror rolling out across the city? Death and destruction?"

The taxi driver made no movement.

"The *Nadirian* or *Zildrohar-Cqulu*. Which is it?"

There was no response.

"You won't tell," she said. She thought. "But you'll take me where I want to go. Okay, sunshine, assuming they're in the city, physically or potentially, take me to them."

The taxi driver looked at her in the mirror.

"The nearest one," she said. "Take me to the nearest one."

Still, the taxi driver was motionless.

She tried it in Venislarn. *"Yo-Kaxeos, pes hroventizh kash-ka* Venislarn-*achlat't."*

The taxi driver pulled away.

"Thank you," she said.

The driver turned left at the end of the road, along the main road to the next turning, left again and left a third time. They stopped. Morag looked out at 27 Franklin Road.

"Yeah, that's really not what I asked," she sighed. She looked up at the old, subdivided house. Three floors. On the top floor the pale curtains were speckled with aggressive mildew.

"Okay," she said slowly. "Back to the office, my good man. To the Library."

Vivian led the five Waters Crew boys into Room Three. The *samakha* gangsters hung timidly behind her as though the room might contain unspeakable tortures or a horror from beyond the stars when, in actuality, it held nothing more ominous than Archdeacon Silas Adjei, Leandra from marketing and a circle of chairs. Although, she thought, clergymen, vacuous PR people and an invitation to sit down and share one's feelings probably featured frequently in many people's ideas of torture.

"I don'ts have to do this. Ggh!" said Tony T. "'Gainst my human rights."

"You have no rights," said Vivian. "In."

Death Roe, Pupfish, Fluke and Tony T — Tyrone, Michael, Harvey and Anthony – trooped inside sullenly, gills fluttering, fish lips pouting.

"Hey, homies," grinned Leandra, giving each a stick-on name badge as they entered. Fluke regarded his suspiciously and sniffed it.

"S'too bright in here," said Tony T. "Gonna hurt my – ggh! – eyes, dog."

"He got rights," said Death Roe.

"Here, let me," said Silas and stood to change the lighting.

Pupfish scrawled on his name badge and passed the felt tip to Tony T.

"Your names in English," instructed Vivian.

"You dissing my heritage, Mrs Grey?"

"No, Tony. I have seen your attempts at writing in Venislarn. It is just embarrassing. Now sit."

Leandra passed a large bowl of chocolate bars along the circle. "Take as many as you like, boys."

"What's this?" said Tony T.

"*Adn-bhul* stranger danger," said Fluke.

"Cougar wants to – ggh! – buy a feel of my codpiece, dog." Tony T grabbed at himself through his tracksuit trousers.

"These real Kit Kats," said Pupfish. "Not the – ggh! – knockoff ones from Lidl my mom gets."

"Everyone calls your momma Kit Kat, Pup," Fluke laughed.

"No, they don't."

"Cos she takes four fingers. Ggh!"

Tony T offered an explanatory mime. The rest of the Waters Crew laughed dutifully. With their leader dead and his lieutenant locked up indefinitely, it hadn't taken them long to find a new hierarchy.

"You will watch your language in front of the archdeacon, Anthony," said Vivian.

"Church man," said Tony T. "I seen your od. He's the one who up and died like a punk bitch."

"And you parade him round with a stick up his – ggh! – ass," said Pupfish.

"Michael!"

"No, it's all right, Vivian," said Silas softly, sitting forward. "Seems you lads do know something about God. He came to earth as a man but the authorities treated him like a criminal and he was killed by those who were jealous of him and hated him for speaking the truth."

"Like Tupac," said Fluke.

"*Muda!*" said Pupfish. "Is everything like – ggh! – Tupac to you?"

"But God, in the form of Jesus. He overturned death. He defeated death. And he rose, having paid for all the evil in the world. Now, that's God, my God. But I know nothing about your backgrounds or your beliefs. And that's what this morning's all about."

"You want to know what – ggh! – we believe?" said Tony T.

183

"Mmm-hmm. It's about dialogue. Conversation."

"And we thought we'd kick things off with some ice-breakers," Leandra broke in chirpily. "Break that ice. Break it down."

No one in the room appeared to share her enthusiasm. Not a soul.

"Everyone's had a chance to take a chocolate bar or two. Or three or four. What we're going to do is go around the circle and everyone – that's *everyone*, Vivian – is going to tell us some facts about themselves, one for every chocolate bar they took."

Pupfish looked at the half dozen Kit Kats in his hands. "Shit," he said, with feeling.

Morag knocked on Vaughn Sitterson's office door, waited for a response of some sort and then, when there wasn't one, piled in.

The man behind the desk jumped to his feet in flustered surprise. His eyes darted everywhere – the desk, the computer, the wall, the door – as though he had just been interrupted doing something unpardonable and was looking for evidence to sweep out of sight.

"I'm sorry, sir." Morag wavered in the doorway. "I knocked."

"I heard," said Vaughn. "I'm just..."

Morag attempted to catch his eye and, when she failed, smiled at him anyway. "I'm Morag. I'm the new investigator."

"Of course you are," said Vaughn.

She shook his offered hand. It was like shaking hands with fog: insubstantial and gone in an instant.

"I thought I might drop in," she said, "seeing as we've not met yet."

"No, we haven't, have we? Very much remiss," he said. "Well, it's good to meet you. Are you sitting? I mean, do sit."

Morag was already sitting. Vaughn sat down and looked at his computer screen. Morag realised that her first impression, that he was bald, was incorrect. He had hair but it was so fine and colourless as to be almost transparent.

"Well," he said.

"I just wanted to say, first of all, that I'm really grateful for the position here. I don't know how much you talk to Jim Bannerman in Edinburgh?"

"We know each other of old." Vaughn shifted his gaze from the screen to papers on the desk.

"I don't know if strings had to be pulled to make this possible. It was a quick transfer."

"It was, but it's all part of the service."

"Is it? And I really, *really* must say I'm particularly grateful," she said with slow and deliberate emphasis, "for the flat you've provided for me."

"Happy to help."

"It's in Bourneville."

"Lovely area, yes."

Morag waited and wondered. If she waited long enough, would the consular chief have to look up to check that she was still there?

"Do you do that for all new members of staff?" she said. "Find them accommodation?"

He moved a sheet aside, looked at the one beneath it and put the original back.

"Not always, Miss Murray. But, given the short notice and the distance you'd come, I thought... we thought..."

"Again, that's very kind, sir," she said. "Have you seen the flat?"

"Seen the flat?"

"You know of it? Maybe it's one that you – we – own."

He frowned to himself and then spotted a piece of imaginary fluff on his lapel and brushed it off. "Is there a problem with the accommodation?" he asked.

"No," she said. "The neighbours..."

"Yes?" he said, perhaps a bit too quickly.

Morag thought of the weird music and the mildewed curtains and the noises that emanated from the flat above hers. "Are they persons of interest?" she asked.

"Not sure what you mean," he said.

Morag swore inside her head. The fucker was going to try and brazen this out. "You referred to me as the Caledonian Sleeper. To Lois. When I first arrived."

"The train you came on?" he suggested.

"Ah," she said. "You see, I was thinking of a different meaning to the word 'sleeper'."

"Are we just making chit-chat now, Miss Murray? I'm sure there's work to be done and I hear Rod is in the hospital."

"A sleeper agent," she said. "One who is planted but is left to settle into their cover and not given any instructions for a significant period of time."

"Work to be done," Vaughn repeated.

"And the best sleeper agents are possibly those who don't even know they are sleeper agents. Even better are those who you wish to plant in an extremely hostile environment but who are conveniently, in a manner of speaking, already dead."

"I do believe you've completely lost me now," said Vaughn.

"I don't think so," she said and stood. She stopped by the open door. "Sir?"

"Yes?"

"Sir."

She waited and he almost managed to look at her. But she did have his attention at least.

"What happened to your predecessor, sir?" she asked.

"Hmmm?"

"How did Greg Robinson die?"

"Have we got that?" said Leandra. "Tony is the farmer. Fluke is the fox."

"Damn straight," said the *samakha* youth.

"Silas, you're the sheep. Pupfish, you're the crate of melons."

"What am I?" said Death Roe.

"You're the helpful bystander. You're going to tell Tony T what to do."

"No one's gonna tell this – ggh! – melon farmer what to do," said Tony T.

Chairs had been placed in rows on either side of the room to symbolise river banks. Fluke and Silas had been given cuddly toys, a fox and a sheep respectively. Tony T held a piece of paper saying 'I am the farmer'. Pupfish's piece of paper simply said 'Melons'.

"Ghh! – just like his mom," said Tony T.

"What?" said Pupfish.

"Nah, he's got – ggh! – better melons than his mom," said Fluke.

"Harvey, be nice," warned Vivian from the sidelines.

"Sorry, Mrs Grey."

"Okay, lads," said Silas. "We can crack this puzzle."

"Do you know what you need to do?" said Leandra.

"Sure," said Tony T. "I got to get my cracker ass – ggh! – goods back from market. Only one at a time. Fox, get in my boat."

"Ggh! That's not a good idea," said Fluke.

"You do what I say."

"Just sayin', dog"

"Fluke, I am the farmer."

"Easy, Darth Vader." Fluke ambled over to Tony T's side and they shuffled across the 'river' between the two chairs.

"That ain't gonna work," said Death Roe.

"Sheep's gonna eat the melons," said Fluke.

Pupfish looked at Silas. "Eat my melons."

Silas shrugged and held out his sheep to Pupfish's bit of paper. "Nom nom nom," he said, smiling.

Fluke cracked up and slapped his knee.

"Maybe we can try again," said Silas. "And this time, I don't want to eat the melons."

"Funny, man," said Death Roe.

"Okay, let's press reset," said Leandra. They wandered back into place.

"I don't – ggh! – get it," said Pupfish. "What's a fox?"

"A fox!" said Fluke. "A bindog, dog."

Pupfish shook his head. "What kind of stupid ass – ggh! – melon farmer buys a bindog from market?"

"Maybe he said he'd get your mom a – ggh! – waste disposal," said Tony T.

"Leave my mom alone!"

"Many done tried and failed. She's so damn needy – ggh! – her *glun'u* got a tractor beam."

"Anthony," said Vivian.

"You can still hear the screams of the dudes it's eaten."

"Enough!"

Tony T shot Vivian a look. She held it and matched it. "Do you want me to take you outside and have a word with you, Anthony?" she said.

He broke within seconds.

"No," he said quietly.

"What?"

"No, Mrs Grey."

"Right."

"So, are we going to solve this?" said Silas.

"It's impossible." Death Roe gave a good impression of a sulk.

"Not if we work together," said Silas.

Tony coughed through his gills. "Fasho," he said. "Pup – ggh! – get your melons in my boat."

"Classic Tony T pick up line," said Fluke.

"You dissin' me, Fluke?"

"I didn't say nathan, dog. Ggh! I'm just a fox."

Nina guided the next taxi driver into Room Two and physically sat him down. "Right. Name?"

He said nothing, just as the sixteen previous taxi drivers had said nothing.

"No name? Okay, I'm going to check you for ID." She opened his thin coat and took a wallet from his inside pocket.

"Let's have a look-see..." She pulled out a wad of notes. "A good day's take. Mind if I look after that for you?"

In a smooth one-handed movement, she folded the notes over her index finger and stuffed them in her own pocket. She then took out his driving licence.

"Hussain Ali. Hello, Hussain." There wasn't a flicker on his lined, unshaven face. "How long have you been working for Mr *Kaxeos*, huh?"

Nothing.

"Is there someone at home who's wondering where you are? Is there a Mrs Ali? Lots of little Alis? No?" She popped her lips, bored, and raised her phone to take a photo.

"Look this way, Hussain. This way. Working with the camera, yeah? Hey." She clicked her fingers repeatedly. "Look! Look! A fare!" As she took the picture, there was a knock at the door.

"Yo."

Lois popped her head in.

"Chief Inspector Lee is here, bab."

"Top banana. Could you get someone down here to watch over Hussain here? He's like a crazy party animal." She looked back to Hussain Ali, as still as a waxwork and considerably less lifelike. "Look at him. Crazy."

Nina sashayed out into the corridor. She felt reckless and restless and suspected she might have overdone it on the bottles of Boost. Chief Inspector Ricky Lee, the local police-Venislarn liaison, was in reception chatting to Morag.

"Ricky," she said. "Still shooting unarmed black kids?"

"Still? We're only just moving on from shooting unarmed Irishmen. You still poking the Dungeon Dimensions with a pointy stick?"

"Every day."

Ricky Lee grinned. Ricky had a goofy grin but he was cute looking guy and had an entertainingly lax attitude to marriage vows.

"You here for the two dozen taxi drivers I hauled in last night?"

"And you wonder why they say you're insatiable. No. Not taxi drivers."

"Something's happened at the cathedral," said Morag.

"Which one?" said Nina.

"St Philips. Pigeon Park," said Ricky. "I gather you've got the interfaith link officer here too."

Nina took them to Room Two. "I'll warn you, they're doing some kinda *samakha* sweat lodge love-in thing. Could be ugly."

She pushed the door open. Tony T was standing on a row of chairs, pointing an imaginary pistol at Fluke.

"Don't you dare, fox. You touch the sheep and – ggh! – I'll pop one in your mother-*adn-bhul* ass!"

Fluke took a step towards Archdeacon Silas Adjei.

"You hearing me?" Tony T shouted.

189

Fluke shrugged. "But I'm a fox."

"Tha's deep," said Death Roe.

"Gonna get me – ggh! – that on a tattoo," agreed Pupfish.

Fluke held out his fox to Silas's sheep. "Nom."

"Boom!" said Tony T. "Now your punk ass is dead, bindog."

"Well, it's nice to see you're getting into role," said Leandra.

Tony T jumped down from the chairs. "I'm just – ggh! – gonna get me a bigger boat."

"Sorry to interrupt," said Nina, "we need to borrow Silas."

Silas's eyebrows went up questioningly.

"Something's happened in Pigeon Park," she said.

Silas passed his sheep to Fluke. "Sorry, lads. I'll be back."

"I'm sure you need me too," said Vivian.

Nina made a noise. "I don't know," she said and then caught the desperate glint in Vivian's eye. "Sure, maybe. I can step in here."

"Church man," nodded Death Roe and gave Silas a fist bump as he left.

"This has got to beat zombie taxi drivers," said Nina to the room once the others were gone. "So, what's this game?"

"It's a lateral thinking puzzle," said Leandra.

"Got to get the sheep, the fox and Pup's melons across the river," said Tony T.

"And Tony – ggh! – keeps getting us killed," said Pupfish.

Nina looked at the papers and toys. "Tony, you're the sheep now."

"Hey – ggh! – I'm the farmer."

"Hey, you bought the farm. Doesn't make you a farmer." This drew a laugh from the others. "Death Roe, you're the farmer now."

Vivian insisted on sitting in the front as Chief Inspector Lee drove her, Morag and Silas round to St Philip's Cathedral. She did this for no other reason than that she always sat in the front of cars. She wasn't a child.

St Philip's, less than half a mile from the Library, had been built in the eighteenth century as a parish church and elevated to cathedral status when Birmingham was made into a city. In Vivian's eyes, it was an entirely unremarkable building but for some fine

190

stained glass by the Pre-Raphaelite Edward Burne-Jones and the fact that it was the third smallest cathedral in the country.

Ricky parked by the iron railings that ran around Pigeon Park, the wide green space that surrounded the cathedral. There were police officers at each of its narrow gates, keeping passersby out.

"Who found the body?" asked Morag, once they were through the cordon.

"Katie Lightfoot, the canon something," said Ricky.

"Canon liturgist," said Silas. "How is she?"

"They've taken her to the station to take a statement," said Ricky. "She's quite shaken, I believe. It's not a pleasant sight."

"And that's what makes you think it's Venislarn," said Vivian.

There was a police van beside the statue of Bishop Gore and a pair of constables in high-vis waterproofs at the cathedral door. They waved them in.

"Do I need to remind you not to touch anything?" said Ricky.

Beneath an iron staircase, a detective talked to a man in a dog collar. Silas went to the man, put a hand on his shoulder and spoke words of comfort that were too quiet for Vivian to hear. In the cathedral proper, Scenes of Crime were sweeping along the pews. Much of the activity was focussed around the altar and the naked body draped across it. There was blood on the stone floor around the altar. A lot of blood.

The altar sat before three large windows of stained glass at the east end of the church. The nativity, the crucifixion and the resurrection. Vivian hadn't realised until that moment that Edward Burne-Jones had been very fond of red. Angelic robes and Roman standards turned the morning sunlight a rich and bloody crimson.

"No head," noted Vivian as they approached the altar.

"Severed." Ricky pointed. "Behind the altar."

Morag was slowing, falling back.

"Problem, Miss Murray?" asked Vivian.

Morag looked pale – well, she was a pale and pasty sort but she looked even paler now. "I... I think I might know who it is."

Vivian was impressed. "You recognise him? Without clothes and, I must emphasise, without a head?"

Morag cut left through the pews to skirt the pool of blood and get behind the altar.

"Maybe he has a distinctive scar," said Vivian reflectively.

"Well, he's a ginger, I can tell you that much," said Ricky.

"Motherfucker!" shouted Morag furiously.

"Miss Murray," Vivian called to her.

"That bastard motherfucking *glun'u* hole!"

"Miss Murray!"

Silas Adjei came scurrying up the aisle. "May I remind you that this is a church!" he hissed loudly.

Morag backed away from the altar, fist in her mouth. The muscular young man lay on his back on the altar. His bloodless arm was draped over one side of the altar, and the cleanly severed stump of his neck rested over the end. His head wasn't the only thing missing. His groin was a concave hemisphere of ravaged tissue; his genitals had been torn out.

"I'm assuming this was Venislarn," said Ricky, "or a really jealous wife."

"I know who did this," said Morag, her voice ragged with emotion.

"You do?"

"*Shardak'aan Syu*, August Handmaiden of *Prein*. You want to put out a photofit? She's about twelve feet tall, has ten legs and is armoured with the faces of screaming babies."

"That makes sense," said Vivian.

"Makes sense?" said Silas indignantly. "Our altar defiled with bloody murder?"

Vivian twirled a finger over the scene. "This is not a murder scene, not specifically. The Handmaidens of *Prein* decapitate their lovers at the moment of climax."

The archdeacon's eyes bulged. "He and a Venislarn were..." He couldn't find an appropriate word and just made a wordless murmur, "...on our altar?"

"Who do you think he is?" Ricky wanted to know.

"His name's Drew. Name *was* Drew," Morag corrected herself quietly. "I don't know his surname or if that was even his real name. We'll have registration documents for him. There won't be any family who are looking for him."

"So, it's entirely in your court." Ricky looked at Vivian, trying not to sound relieved.

"Do they not know what this place is?" said Silas. "Have they no inkling of the offence they've caused?"

"This is, in all probability, a very calculated piece of offence," said Vivian. "It is a message. I do not know if the Venislarn are specifically aware of the purpose of the altar in the act of communion. The body and blood of Christ, made real in this way." She made a noise to herself. "It is probably just a serendipitous coincidence."

"I'm going to kill her," said Morag coldly.

"You'll do no such thing," said Vivian sharply, "and you should know better than to even suggest it. This is a very deliberate act by a member of *Yo-Morgantus*'s court. I would normally expect us to be notified of such atrocities in advance."

"They'd tell you they were going to do something terrible?" said Ricky.

"I believe your lot used to have an equally pragmatic relationship with the IRA," replied Vivian.

"Then I need to go to the Venislarn court." Morag turned on her heel.

"To make enquiries," said Vivian. "Nothing else."

"Naturally," agreed Morag. "Besides, I left my shotgun in Scotland."

"And we shall arrange the speedy removal of this body," said Vivian, "before public interest is roused."

Silas was looking at his phone. "I think it's already too late for that."

Nina skipped down to reception and rapped on the glass. Lois, on the phone, irritably waved her away. Nina pushed the glass aside and scoured Lois's desk area below the reception window.

"Pardon?" said Lois into the phone. "No, madam, I don't know anything about that. I'm not sure what I'd be apologising for."

Nina flicked through the staplers, Post-Its and pens on the desk.

"I'm sorry, madam, but I've no idea why you'd think we'd do that." She scribbled on a Post-It and give it to Nina. It read 'Get Ingrid!'

Nina nodded and scribbled 'Glitter?' on the Post-It and passed it back to Lois.

"Excuse me for a moment, madam." Lois put her hand over the phone. "Glitter?" she said.

"Yes," said Nina. "Do you have any?"

"Glitter?"

"Yes."

Lois blinked. "Glitter?"

"Yes. You know, little bits of glittery stuff. For making cards, Christmas decorations and vajazzles. Gold or silver or whatever you've got."

"I don't have any glitter," said Lois as though Nina was an idiot. "Can you find Ingrid for me? They need a Venislarn medical team over at the Cube."

"What's happened?"

"They're saying *Yo-Morgantus* has been poisoned. By us."

"Why would... How would we do that?"

Lois shrugged. She went to speak into the phone again and then stopped. "Why do you want glitter?"

"Me and the fish-boys are doing arts and crafts, of course," said Nina. "I'll find Ingrid."

They sat at pews to the rear of the cathedral to discuss what was to be done. Vivian, Archdeacon Silas and Chief Inspector Lee had been joined by the bishop's deliverance advisor, Rita Giffen, and Canon Kevin O'Driscoll of the Roman Catholic diocese who, as far as Vivian could ascertain, had come to offer sympathy and have a bit of a nose about.

"We can have the body bagged up and out of the door in minutes," said Ricky.

Silas held out a gently interrupting hand. "There are three priorities that I can see. There is the physical matter of removing the body of this poor dead man and the evidence of what happened here. There is then the matter of the media who are already camped outside and who would love to know that a ritual sex-murder has taken place in the heart of the city's Christian community."

Canon Kevin's face twitched but he said nothing.

"Thirdly," continued Silas, "there is the spiritual attack upon our church. We must respond appropriately to this unholy stain on our church and to the *meaning* of this event. I do not want to do anything that will spread any contamination. What does this attack mean, Vivian?"

"Many of the Venislarn's motives are entirely unknowable," answered Vivian. "We ascribe them personalities and motives much as we identify shapes in clouds. The true Venislarn are entirely alien to us. But their intermediaries and agents: their actions are sometimes open to interpretation. This. This is a territorial display."

"They're claiming this space as their own?" said Silas.

"They have sought out your most important building and then..."

"Pissed all over it," said Rita, the deliverance advisor. "Like a tom cat."

"Rita," said Silas.

"But that's what's happened," said the round and ruddy-faced woman.

"Yes," agreed Vivian.

"So, this is indeed a spiritual attack." Silas shook his head in despair.

"I would not know about such unscientific mumbo-jumbo," said Vivian. "Consider this the planting of a flag, a declaration of conquest."

"Dear Lord," said Canon Kevin.

"In one sense, you should be flattered," said Vivian.

Silas was momentarily speechless. "Flattered?"

"The Venislarn could have done this in the council house, in the centre of the Bull Ring, in the Town Hall. But they chose a church. This church. It indicates the apparent importance of this place and the perceived power of the Church."

"And yet they chose to do it here rather than over at St Chad's," said Canon Kevin. He tried to keep his tone neutral but Vivian could detect an edge.

"You think this should have happened in the Catholic cathedral?" Silas allowed a grim gallows-humour smile onto his face.

"No, Silas. This should not have happened anywhere."

"No."

"But... if one was talking about religious importance and power..." the Catholic said softly.

"Really?" said Silas.

"His Holiness, the Pope, has long accepted the unique role the Church has in combating this invasion. As the largest and oldest branch of the Christian faith..."

"Kevin, this is not the place for such arguments," said Silas.

"I was not arguing, only offering my sympathies that this incident has accidentally befallen your place of worship."

"Thank you." Silas nodded in reflection. "Of course, if you were to actually count the number of Roman Catholics versus Anglican worshippers in the city..."

"Oh, come now!" said Kevin.

"If you're talking about a popularity contest, Kevin, then I'm sure you'd come out –"

"Really?" Vivian did not disguise her annoyance. "You want to bicker about who's got the biggest God?"

The archdeacon and canon held up hands in apology and disagreement.

"Shall I get Mr Ahmed from the Birmingham central mosque?" she said. "I bet he could knock both your attendance figures into a cocked hat. Shall I? I have his number. Yes? No?"

"We are merely discussing the intended meaning, the symbolism behind this attack, weren't we, Kevin?" said Silas.

"Exactly, Silas," said Kevin.

"Good," said Vivian, "because from where I am sitting it sounded like you were arguing over whether the mafia had put the horse's head in the wrong bed."

"We need to perform a service of cleansing and rededication as soon as possible," said Rita.

"These creatures are not devils or demons or any other form of supernatural entity," Vivian corrected.

"And yet you call them gods," said Silas. "Rita is right. If this is a deliberate attack on a place of worship, then it is a spiritual attack."

Vivian looked pointedly over to the bloody floor around the altar. "It is going to take more than a splash of holy water and a few Hail Marys to shift that."

Kevin smiled at Silas's frown.

"Fine," said Vivian, "whatever you C of E lot have instead. A few kumbayas."

"Or a quick harvest festival," suggested Ricky.

"Are you trying to mock the Church?" said Silas.

"Try? No," said Vivian. "Let us elevate our minds above mere religious details and decide what we are going to do with the body. I can get a clean-up crew and a black ambulance over here within the hour but there is a BBC news crew already camped outside."

"We must be rid of them before we can cleanse the church," said Rita, already planning the spiritual spring clean.

"But the damage to the Church as a whole if it is discovered someone has died here would be incalculable," said Silas.

"You would deceive the public?" said Rita.

"I would want to protect their faith."

"Could we not just get the TV people to go somewhere else?" suggested Canon Kevin.

"How would we do that?"

Kevin looked at Ricky.

"Uh-huh," said Ricky. "We may live in a police state but we don't have to keep reminding people."

"I was just thinking a bit of 'Move along, move along. There's nothing to see here.'"

"Not confiscate their cameras and arrest them under some dubious anti-terrorism powers?"

"Or that," said Kevin. "I do believe the cameraman looks a bit Muslim-y."

"Really, Kevin?" said Silas.

"It's usually justification enough for the boys in blue."

"We're not arresting the camera crew, not even if one of them starts shouting 'God is great' in Arabic."

"In the old days," said Kevin to Vivian, "your lot would just arrange a diversion. Start a fire somewhere or blow something up to draw them away."

"That was Greg's speciality," said Vivian. "Master of misdirection. We do not have the time or budget for that now. I do have a solution, however."

"Yes?" said Silas.

"You keep the body here."

"Come now," said Silas unhappily. "Where would we put a dead body?"

"It is a church, archdeacon."

"You do have tombs," said Ricky.

Rita made a disagreeable noise, like she was trying to swallow a hedgehog. "The spiritual significance..." she managed to say.

"This man was ritually murdered," said Silas. "Decapitated. His genitals scooped out like, like..."

"The worst Ben and Jerry's flavour ever," said Ricky.

"That hardly seems grounds for refusing him a Christian burial," said Vivian, "even a temporary one."

"Deuteronomy twenty-three one," said Rita automatically.

"It's unseemly," said Silas.

"Really?" said Ricky. "Beheaded and his jewels ripped off? Sounds like the kind of thing the Romans used to do to Christians."

"I'm not going to entertain comparisons between this man and –"

"St Gustav of Bad Königshofen," said Kevin. "Martyred by some mad Germanic king."

"See?" said Ricky.

"I seem to recall he chopped his own testicles off in a fit of piety but the broad details are the same," said Kevin.

"It's preposterous," said Silas. "You speak as though there are empty tombs where we can conveniently store this man's body."

"Have you actually checked?" asked Vivian.

The lift doors opened and Morag stepped out into the top-but-one floor of the Cube. The air was hot and unpleasantly sweet-smelling.

Dr Ingrid Spence and Rod stood by the window overlooking the city's canal network. Ingrid's T-shirt said '98% Chimpanzee' but it was quickly being covered up by the yellow biohazard suit she was climbing into. Apart from a line of dried blood across his shirt and tie, and the pristine dressing around his left hand, Rod looked back to his usual Herculean self.

Morag looked up. "What are you two doing here?"

"Ah, that famous Scottish warmth," said Ingrid. "Nice to see you too. I was summoned."

"*Yo-Morgantus* is ill," said Rod.

"Poisoned," said Ingrid.

"Who by?"

"Us, allegedly."

"And you're here to find out if there's any possible reason why the Venislarn might throw a hissy fit and desecrate our cathedral," said Rod. "Case closed, I reckon."

Morag stumbled mentally. "They killed him because..."

"Because *Yo-Morgantus* has a dicky tummy and has lashed out," said Rod. "You have an alternate theory?"

Morag thought furiously. The moment she had seen and recognised Drew's body, she had leapt to a single and escapable conclusion: *Shardak'aan Syu*, the August Handmaiden of *Prein*, seeking to torture Morag before killing her, had – what? – given Drew to her for one night only and then ripped him apart. *Here. Want this? Want this? Well, you can't have it.*

The idea was so well-rooted in her mind, she struggled to accept Rod's more reasonable explanation.

"What are you doing here, anyway?" she said irritably. "You should be in hospital or at home."

"Aye, possibly," he said, "but Vivian called and suggested I meet you. Head you off at the pass, as it were."

"Is that so?"

"Said you had a face like thunder and were thinking of declaring war on the court."

"Preposterous."

"That's what I thought," he said with an amused and knowing look in his eye. "Come on then, let's play doctors and nurses."

On cue, double doors opened and a *presz'ling* strode out. Its pole-like limbs walked along ceiling and floor equally as though gravity was merely a lifestyle choice. The prehensile wound-lined protuberance in the centre of its body that was, at once, mouth, anus and ovipositor angled towards them.

The *presz'ling* spoke in Venislarn whilst simultaneously producing a thin, reedy screech that carried a rudimentary English translation.

"*Sogho fer juriska* – Come – *v'zhul cho* – make – *adn-hrifet long'hor* – restitution? – *tye!*"

Ingrid picked up a fat medical kit. "No, *tye presz'ling-fu*. We have come to inspect and treat your lord."

The *presz'ling* sucked air noisily through its orifice, very much like a builder about to tell someone they'd 'clearly had some cowboys in' before giving them an astronomical quote for repairs.

"*Shomph pi-khar* – To follow! – *tye!*"

Rather than lead them into the hall of monsters Morag had entered before, the *presz'ling* took them along to a stairwell and up three flights. The *presz'ling* climbed with disregard for the actual stairs, planting needle-tipped feet on walls, floors and stairs with such ease it appeared like a weightless bundle of sticks falling slowly up the shaft.

As they climbed, Morag once again suspected that the Venislarn in the Cube had tampered with the local space-time dimensions. By her judgement, they were some distance above the building's roof.

The *presz'ling* pushed a door open. "*Ghu'qani* – In – *tye!*"

The space beyond was dark, barely lit at all. Morag could only perceive the vaguest outlines of a huge space. The ceiling was too dark to see, the furthest wall merely an end to what she could see. She knew somehow that this chamber covered the entire roof of the Cube, that this was what lay above the hall of monsters, the audience hall and all the corridors and private rooms. This was the place from where *Yo-Morgantus's* streamer-like tendrils came and therefore that thing on the floor...

The floor was covered in a mammoth cushion of rolling yellow flesh. It bulged and shifted like an oleaginous sea. No, it was like a bouncy castle, albeit a bouncy castle as big as a football field, stitched together from offal, skin and knobbly organic protrusions from which jutted shards of bone, flaps of tissue and the partially absorbed bodies of humans and Venislarn. No, on reflection, it was nothing like a bouncy castle at all, unless it was a bouncy castle dredged from the worst nightmares of someone with a chronic fear of castles.

Ingrid checked the seals on her biohazard suit and pulled the hood into place. She turned to Morag and Rod.

"Whatever happens," she said. "Do not touch him. No skin-to-skin contact."

"Pretty much goes without saying," said Morag.

Rod unclipped his holster and drew his pistol with his good right hand.

"You going to need that?" said Ingrid.

"Just in case. Won't be the first time I've wanted to give a colleague a merciful death and not been able to."

Ricky dusted his hands together as he emerged from the crypt.

"I don't remember why, but when I was at primary school, we used to play a game called 'funerals'. We'd take it in turns to bury each other and then say the words, 'In the name of the father and the son and into the hole he goes.'"

"Your point?" said Vivian.

"None," said Ricky. "Just bodies in holes."

Over by the altar, Scenes of Crimes were scrubbing the surrounding stone for the fifth time.

"That's pretty much the exact opposite of what they're meant to do," he said. "It's weird like..."

"Like a criminal police officer?" said Vivian.

"Ha! We've got *those*. Or like one of your lot working *for* the Venislarn."

"We do work for the Venislarn," said Vivian. "The exact opposite of our role?" She paused to think. "Attempting to bring about the Venislarn Apocalypse before its time and ensuring the maximum amount of human suffering." She looked back to the crypt door. "We will return for the body in the next day or two, once we are certain the media's attention is elsewhere."

"As soon as possible, please." Archdeacon Silas placed a hand on Vivian's arm. "Rita is adamant that we will not be able to use this building for its intended purpose until such time as it's been thoroughly cleansed."

"I am sure it won't be more than two days." Vivian removed his hand. "By the end of the weekend at the latest."

"Weekend? As in Sunday?" he said, alarmed. "But the cathedral? The scheduled services?"

"Yes," said Vivian. "You may have a day of rest. We do not. I am returning to the Library now. I dread to think what Miss Seth has been up to with our *samakha* guests. Will you be joining me?"

Silas threw his arms wide. "This takes precedence," he said.

"Quite," said Vivian. "Then you may wish to reschedule your community outreach efforts for some future time. Next year perhaps. Let us go," she said to Ricky.

"I've still got some details to resolve here," the chief inspector replied.

"Not going to resolve themselves, no?"

"No. Sorry."

"Good, then they will still be here when you get back from taking me."

Ingrid walked carefully out across the surface of *Yo-Morgantus*, Venislarn god and the most puissant (or at least most comprehensibly puissant) entity for more than a hundred miles. She walked with a rolling gait, part lunar astronaut, part mud-wader. Near the centre of the Venislarn's wobbling and burping mass, a ginger-haired woman protruded from the flesh, her left arm and abdomen fused with her god. The woman's eyes tracked Ingrid silently.

Ingrid genuflected to the woman. "*San-shu chuman'n*, my lord, I see you have grown in... stature since we last met." Within the folds of suppurating flesh, something flapped and farted.

Ingrid opened her medic's case, removed the Geiger counter and played it over the Venislarn's body.

"Readings are elevated," she called back to Morag and Rod. "It's a potassium iodide smoothie for all of us later."

She unpacked heat paddles, syringe and pressure cuffs from the case and then knelt. She slid her hands into the nearest folds of fatty flesh and levered them apart.

"I'm just going to take your *ju-falas*, my lord."

As she inserted the heat paddles, Yo-Morgantus reacted violently, shifting and rolling like an earthquake-struck island. Pseudo-limbs erupted bloodily from the surface. Ingrid rolled away as one threatened to loop over her and pull her under where, protective suit or not, she would be lost.

Rod shouted out to her.

"Stay back!" she replied, hand held up in warning. "It's okay. Got my secret weapon."

With toddler-level agility, Ingrid crawled back to her medic's case, plugged her phone into the in-built speaker and thumbed play. Frenetic electric guitar and classical string filled the air. The godquake subsided almost immediately.

Ingrid grinned at the confused look on Morag's face. "Yo-Morgantus and I have a shared love of ELO," she explained. "But only the early stuff with Mike Edwards on cello,"

"I have to ask, why?" said Morag.

"Not sure. He died a sudden and violent death. I think Yo-Morgantus enjoys things on a different level to us."

"Rock and roll drugs overdose?" said Rod.

"Nope. A six-hundred kilo hay bale rolled down a hill and crushed the van he was driving."

"Rock and roll," said Morag. "At least the roll part anyway."

Ingrid proceeded cautiously. She ran lines from the heat paddles to a handheld *yathathana*-scope and drew fluid samples that caused her to shake her head gravely.

Rod gave her a questioning look.

"Well," said Ingrid, thinking on her feet, "Yo-Morgantus's *chet-sakrina* are misaligned to such an extent that they're *svading* with the wrong portions of the *dho-latz* weave. He's rotating – well, *g'rnt*-folding — through a sense-plus *khladish* loop of mal-skeined *hnngis* and *shodar-lan* tissues and this is leading to a *frenz mac-frenz* accumulation of dry *cosht* in the *ghesimal* wallets. Basically, *lo-sjin fofoi pakh lat*."

"In English?" said Rod.

Ingrid shot him a look. "We don't have the nouns or the verbs." She thought for a moment. "Or the grammar."

"Try," said Rod.

"Lord *Morgantus* is not well."

"We already knew that."

"He's probably been poisoned."

"Again, knew that."

Ingrid sat back in a crouch and thought. The half-eaten and comatose woman twitched and brushed her hair out of her eyes.

"You did this," said the woman, her tone dead.

"No, lord," said Ingrid. "I don't know what this is, some sort of plant toxin. Like, erm..."

"You did this."

"No. No." Ingrid racked her brain. She knew this. She knew she knew this. "Wild mandrake! Etoposide phosphate! You've eaten something, you've eaten some*one*. Lord, have you eaten anyone with cancer?"

"Lord *Morgantus* delights in cancers and tumours," said the redhead.

"Yes, but this one was pumped full of chemotherapy drugs. That's what's done this."

"No," said the ginger. "Not these humans. You are playing for time."

Ingrid could feel the Venislarn skin tension beneath her legs begin to weaken. Ingrid started to slowly sink.

"I assure you, lord..."

Morag shouted something.

Ingrid battled against her own suit and the enveloping hollow beneath her to turn to look to her colleagues by the door.

"Kevin!" shouted Morag.

The word initially made no sense to Ingrid. And then she realised what Morag was saying and then she truly understood.

"Lord," she said, putting her gloved hand down to steady herself and finding it sinking in, as though she was pressing against thick custard. "Lord, have you recently consumed one of the *Uriye Inai'e*?"

"Their house is beholden to ours," said the redhead tonelessly.

"You have eaten *Kerrphwign-Azhal*, a noble of the *Uriye Inai'e*," said Ingrid, trying to keep the panic out of her voice as she sank lower. Although she wasn't sure if her legs had been drawn into the Venislarn body, she could not see them for the loose folds of skin about her. "It was hibernating. Lord! *Hrifet!*" Ingrid paddled against the encompassing folds. Rod shouted her name.

"Rod!" she yelled back. "Don't you dare fucking shoot me yet!"

It took Ingrid a full further ten seconds to realise that she wasn't sinking any further.

The redhead looked down at her, the young woman's possessed body angled oddly, like a bad animatronic. "*Kerrphwign-Azhal* was presented as a gift by one of the court."

"And it had only this week consumed the heart of a man dying from cancer," panted Ingrid.

"This was deliberate?" asked *Yo-Morgantus*.

Ingrid held her tongue. There were several answers she could give. She could placate him, she could, with a word, instigate some Stalinist-style court purges or... she could tell the truth.

"I do not know, lord," she said. She crawled without any co-ordination or dignity to where her medic's case now lay on its side and fumbled around for a fat vial. "I do know that this could alleviate your suffering until the poison has gone from your system."

There was no response for a moment or two and then, as though the nightmare bouncy castle was re-inflating, Ingrid found herself being lifted up from beneath until she was lying on a blessedly solid surface.

"Thank you, lord," she sighed.

At the Library, Vivian found Room Two to be empty, apart from a chair on its side and a fine scattering of what appeared to be gold glitter on the floor. In the otherwise empty office, she found Nina poring over a set of papers.

"What did you do with them?" said Vivian.

Nina looked at her blankly.

"Anthony, Michael, Harvey and Tyrone," said Vivian.

"Oh. My fishy friends, my marine amigos. Yeah, I sent them home. It's gone four and we've had a packed day."

"I dread to think."

"No," she countered. "We did really well. First, we solved that stupid fox, chicken and melons riddle by trading a couple of melons for a bigger boat. Then we had a rap battle."

"A... rap battle?"

"Yup," said Nina. "The group decided that Tony T's was best but, really, no one could top my efforts."

"I am so glad I was out of the building at the time."

"It would have blown your mind wide open," said Nina. "Like, kapow."

"Yes, I am sure. Indeed, it sounds like you have had a marvellous time –"

"And then we made cards for our moms."

Vivian closed her eyes. "Sorry? You did what?"

"Made cards for our moms. Hearts and flowers and 'I love my mom'."

Vivian thought on this. "Two things immediately spring to mind, Miss Seth. One, the word is 'mum'. Or 'mother' or 'mummy'. 'Mom' is just annoying. It sounds like an Americanism but, along with the inability to pronounce the words 'bald', 'tooth' or any 'I' vowel sounds, is just an unnecessary quirk of the Brummy accent."

"Whatever you say, mom."

"And..." Vivian gave Nina her most perplexed look. "Cards?"

"It was nice. We used felt-tips and we sent Lois out to get glitter and glue."

"How dreadful."

"I think the words you're looking for are 'thank you, Nina. Truly you are a special snowflake and I couldn't possibly cope without you.'"

Vivian nodded very slowly. "Would you like a cup of tea, Nina?"

"Does it come with a free lecture of how proper tea should be made?"

"Not necessarily."

"Then, yes, please."

In the lift on the way down, the ooze and alien sweat on Ingrid's suit created an acrid and meaty stink as it dried. Rod and Morag pressed themselves into the furthest corners from it. Ingrid appeared not to notice.

"That was some impressive work," said Morag. "Seriously kept your cool."

Ingrid shrugged, a gesture which wafted the stench around.

"I've seen worse," she said, "and I don't mean that in a macho posturing way. This universe is full of terrors."

"Aye, you're not wrong," said Rod. "What's the worst thing you've encountered?"

"Ah, now this does sound like competitive macho posturing," said Morag.

"Worst thing?" said Ingrid. "Books. I've read the Bloody Big Book. Well, a bit. Not all obviously. The terrors described in those pages, the vile secrets that wait for us at the end of a telescope and at the bottom of a microscope. My mind boggles with the unholy shapes and frightening truths."

"No specifics?" said Rod.

"Hmph." Ingrid smiled. "We don't have the language. But, I tell you this, if I could get the bigwigs in power to just glimpse the monsters that haunt my dreams, they wouldn't merely stop the budget cuts; they'd write us a blank cheque."

"I believe that," said Rod. "You, Morag? Worst thing?"

"Worst? I don't know. Most frightening? An August Handmaiden of *Prein*."

Ingrid shrugged casually, politely unimpressed.

"She was about to eat my face," said Morag. "Those pink flesh mandibles opening up in her underside..."

"What happened?" said Ingrid.

"Something changed her mind," said Morag, which wasn't exactly a lie. The shotgun had certainly changed her mind: turned it into molten goo and distributed it evenly around the area. "Rod?"

"First experience was the worst," he said. "Al-Qa'im. As if the night time firefight with gunrunners wasn't enough, I got separated from my patrol among these ruins and –"

The lift binged and the doors opened. Rod and Morag squeezed out as quickly as possible into the fresher air of the lobby.

"I don't smell that bad, do I?" said Ingrid.

"We could lie and spare your feelings," said Morag.

"Oh."

Vivian hovered with cups.

"You don't have a coaster," she said.

Nina excavated a small space patch of desktop on her desk. "There."

"But it could spill and stain," said Vivian.

Nina plonked a copy of the office phone directory down. "There."

"That is the phone directory."

"And I never use it. Put the tea down, Vivian."

Vivian reluctantly placed Nina's tea on the directory. "Thin end of the wedge," said Vivian. "Entropy in action."

Nina stopped what she was doing and looked up at Vivian. "Thank you for the tea."

Vivian didn't move. "What are you looking at?" she asked.

Nina spread out her papers once more. "The paper records for the nine objects we discovered were missing after Izzy Wu broke into the Vault on Sunday-Monday night. We have a knife, an old iron nail, a key, two pieces of jewellery, a fragment of shell, a piece of sheet music, a small pot of *draybbea* bile, and a pottery thing that might be a cat or possibly a badly modelled and really racist tiny Chinaman."

"And you are wondering why Miss Wu would attempt to steal or conceal them."

Nina made a confirming hum. "I see no link between them, apart from the fact that, as far as artefacts go, they are so minor as to be entirely worthless."

"And you are certain of that?"

Nina drew her finger down to the box on one of the forms where the expert assessment had been written. "They're junk. All of them."

Vivian went and sat at her own desk. "Maybe the information is incorrect. Maybe they are more significant than they app– What is this?"

"Hmmm?" Nina looked up.

"What is this?" asked Vivian and held up a folded rectangle of card, covered in pencil doodles and glitter.

"Well, it's a card, isn't it?"

"I do have eyes. I am asking why it is on my desk."

"Fluke made it for you."

"Harvey?"

"Uh-huh. Think he's got a soft spot for you. Like a mother-figure thing."

Nina flicked through the sheets again. Earring, brooch, eggshell, sheet music.

"And what's this supposed to be?" said Vivian, pointing to the artless sketch on the front of the card.

"It's you," said Nina.

"And these?"

"Um. Your melons."

"Do you mean my breasts, Miss Seth?"

"Melons was the word he used. From the game, maybe..."

"No. This will not do," said Vivian decisively. "I will have him in tomorrow and explain how grossly inappropriate this is."

"Woah, there," said Nina, standing up. "That is not cool."

"Those words do not constitute any form of cogent argument. This card is not acceptable and the young man needs to be told."

"No, he doesn't. He really doesn't. You should have seen the effort he took with that. He had his tongue stuck out of the side of his mouth and everything."

"It is offensive."

"Okay, so maybe it's more of a MILF thing he's got for you – or maybe not – but you can't tell someone that their handmade present is crap. It's like... My nanna knits and she knitted this jumper for me for my birthday. It had a puppy on it. I think it was meant to be a puppy. It was green and pink and it was" – she closed her eyes at the memory – "it was so wrong that I didn't want to bin it, I wanted to have it put down to end its suffering. What I did *not* do – that's *not* do — was tell my nanna. I didn't want to hurt her feelings."

Vivian's look was disapproving.

"You are the second person today to advocate deception to spare the feelings of others," she said.

"Hey, we're in the deception business."

Vivian scooped particles of glitter from her desk into the palm of her hand. "I hardly think comparisons between a knitted jumper and the Venislarn hordes are apt."

"True. There's not much chance of me taking *Yo-Morgantus* into the back garden and burning him in a dustbin."

"But the problem with deception is that you might be found out."

"There is that," said Nina. "My nanna did ask me about it, wondered why I wasn't wearing it, suggested I wear it the next time I visited her."

"My point exactly."

Vivian positioned the card on the edge of her desk and looked at it critically.

"In the end, I had to set fire to my car," said Nina.

"Sorry?"

"I set fire to my car," said Nina.

"You committed arson?" said Vivian. "And, one assumes, told your grandma that the jumper was in the car at the time. She didn't ask why the jumper happened to be in the car at the time?"

"It was just one item in a long list that was in the fire. There was my mp3 player, my best coat, my handbag..."

"That's appalling," said Vivian.

"It's okay," said Nina, keen to reassure. "The insurance company paid up for everything and, more importantly, my nanna never found out that I really hated that jumper."

"Excessive."

"Effective." Nina put her hand to her stomach. She was tired. She'd need to crash soon. Yet another full day after an all-nighter and her food intake amounted to a dodgy curry, a dozen bottles of Boost and whatever junk food she had been able to scavenge throughout the day. Her mind was just a buzz of tiredness, false energy and...

"Jesus *adn-bhul* Christ! That's it! That's exactly it!"

"What?"

Nina grabbed the nine record files off her desk. "If I'd pretended I was robbed or faked an accident in which that jumper – just that one crappy jumper – was destroyed, Nanna might have suspected something. Her focus would have been on the jumper. But I burned the car and everything in it. The jumper was lost in the chaos."

Nina crossed to Vivian's desk and put the papers down. "Nine objects stolen. All of them apparently insignificant."

Vivian touched the top papers with her fingertips and slid them aside.

"It is possible that eight of them were simply taken to conceal the importance of the ninth," she conceded, "but that does not explain what Izzy Wu did with them."

"She didn't," said Nina. "She didn't steal them."

"Or where she put them."

"She didn't steal them. She didn't move them. She did nothing."

"You appear to have lost me," said Vivian.

"Those items. We would have known they were missing in the next audit anyway. We would have known what we know now, just not had some Venislarn-groupie to pin it on. Because if we couldn't pin this on Izzy then what conclusion could we have come to?"

Vivian tapped her fingers on the papers. "An inside job. One of us."

Nina nodded. "Because no one else has access to the Vault. Even though the jumper was already destroyed, I had to fake a later crime to account for its disappearance."

"This is a rather alarming theory, Nina."

Nina laughed.

"What's odd is that I happened to recall an event from my life that precisely mirrored what's going on now."

"Hmmm?"

Nina rubbed her stomach.

"I think the power of the chef's special sauce just took a while to work its way through."

Rod drove Morag home. She watched his hands on the wheel.

"I'm not sure you should be driving," she said as they passed by a small urban zoo.

"I'm fine."

"You're missing a finger," she pointed out. "You're down to only ninety percent manual dexterity."

"Half a finger," said Rod. "That's ninety-five percent at least."

"It hurts though."

"Course it bloody hurts," he said with a wry smile. "And I'd be resting it at home if Vivian hadn't thought you were going to start busting heads at the Cube."

"Not a clue where she got that idea from."

"Uh-huh." Rod turned off the main road. "So, the body in the cathedral..."

"Yes?" she said.

"Was it the same guy I saw lurking in the archway at the university?" Morag's mouth dropped open. "You know, they don't just let any old idiots into the SAS."

Morag sighed in defeat. "Yes. His name was Drew."

"Nice guy?"

"Yes. I don't know. I only knew him for a few hours."

"Aye, but that can be long enough if you know what I mean."

She looked at him shrewdly. "I'm not sure that I do."

The next turning was Franklin Road. Rod slowed to a stop. Morag looked out at number twenty-seven. "Apparently, there's a crazy old cat lady living on the top floor," she said.

Rod leaned over to look up at the top windows. "Apparently?"

"She certainly has cats. And a really weird taste in music," said Morag.

"You've not met her yet?"

"Not yet."

"She's probably lovely."

Morag found herself suspecting otherwise. "You go home now," she said. "To your metrosexual manpad."

"Ha!"

"Sleep. Rest."

"I intend to," he said as Morag opened the door. "You, go make friends with the crazy old cat lady."

Morag got out, waved him off and went inside.

The old house was quiet. There was no noise from Richard's ground floor flat. Morag climbed the stairs to the first floor and her own front door but did not stop. She carried on up to the bottom of the short flight that led to flat three.

There was no lazy black cat on the stairs, no peculiar unmusical music or arrhythmic thumping from beyond the door.

Morag crept up the stairs. If asked, she wouldn't have been able to rightly say why she was creeping. But then again... Her new boss had placed her in this house deliberately. As a sleeper agent? That was tenuous. But there had also been the business with the taxi driver who had simply driven round the block when she told him to take her to the nearest Venislarn... And, if there was danger in these flats, then already being marked for death made her conveniently expendable, possibly the main and only reason she had been sent down here. If she was living on borrowed time, she might at least be of some use...

She stood before the door. As well as the cat claw marks around the lower portion of the door, there was a wealth of scratches around the keyhole, as though created by someone or something that only had a rudimentary idea of what locks and doors were.

Morag reached out to knock, changed her mind and put her ear to the door. Nothing, silence. She closed her eyes and listened deeper.

In truth, there was no such thing as silence. Even in an empty house, there were the sounds of the house itself: air movement, the geologically slow settling of the building, the accumulated sound of a million dust particles colliding through Brownian motion. If she listened hard enough, she could hear the house breathing, in and out.

It took Morag some time to comprehend that it wasn't just the house she could hear. There was a breathing sound, a faint and bronchial wheeze. Morag realised it was shifting in an unusual manner, as though it was rising from more than one throat and, a second later, further realised that the breathing sound wasn't coming from the other side of the door but from behind her...

Morag whirled.

"What ya doing?" said Richard.

He had a set of deflating bagpipes under his arm. He was holding them as though he had just beaten an octopus in a wrestling match. The last of the air rasped from the bladder.

"I was thinking of dropping in on my new neighbour."

"Mrs Atraxas?"

"Mrs...?"

"Atraxas," said Richard.

"What kind of name is that?"

Richard shrugged. "From the old country?"

"Those are bagpipes," said Morag.

"That's right," said Richard. "I checked. There's an open mic talent night at the British Oak tomorrow night. I've got my bagpipes, brushed up a few of my one-liners and..."

"Huh!" Morag laughed to herself. "You're going to think it's bizarre but, this morning when you said you played the bagpipes, for a moment I just thought you said it because I suggested it, that you've got some kind of uncontrollable need to agree with people."

"That is bizarre," he agreed.

The silence hung between them.

"Can you play the bagpipes?" asked Morag.

"No," said Richard.

"Where did they come from then?"

"I bought them today."

"Right. So, you were just going to learn how to play them overnight and then perform at a pub open mic night, just because you can't bear to disagree with people?"

Richard's bowed his head, ashamed.

"So, um, I guess you don't want to go to the open mic night with me then?"

"Are you kidding?" said Morag. "I can't wait. It's going to be amazing."

Friday

"The world is going to end. We know that in this job. The Venislarn Apocalypse will come and, on that day, everyone on earth will drown in blood and flame but won't die. It will be hell on earth for all eternity. That day is coming, waiting for us in the future. Today, we're going to get a small glimpse of that hell. We believe there will be an incursion by a powerful Venislarn god. We've few details. We've heard rumours from local Venislarn and gossip from untrustworthy magicians. There's been no official notification from the court, not a word. But let's assume it's going to happen, right? We're not going to stop it. If the Venislarn want it to happen then we have to let it happen. If lives are to be lost, then they're to be lost. But, if we can even find out when and where this is going to happen, then, like with a tidal wave or a volcano, we can warn people, get them to move to higher ground."

"You move to higher ground when there's a volcano?" Nina leaned against the office door, keeping it closed.

Rod cleared his throat. "Higher ground on a different mountain. Point is, our job today is to find out what's happening and get as many of the public away from the point of impact. That's our only goal."

"Thank you. A truly stirring speech," said Vivian without any note of warmth or any sign that she had been stirred in any way whatsoever. "And I am pleased you are so excited to be part of this meeting *I* have called together."

"We," said Nina. "We called the meeting."

"Please, Miss Seth. This is about saving lives and preventing human suffering, not pandering to your ego. We are keeping this matter between us four alone. Nina's theory that the Vault thefts were an inside job seems more than plausible and hints at an even darker possibility: the reason we have not been officially notified of today's incursion is that it is being brought forward or even instigated by a human agent. We already know that one of our hauliers, Gary Bark, was providing services for the *samakha*

215

pornographers. Whoever is behind this plot might have turned other consular employees. I can trust you three and no others at this time." Vivian looked at Morag. "Miss Murray, you are entirely new to the consular mission. I shall assume this means you are innocent of whatever corruption and treachery has infected the mission."

"Thank you, Vivian," said Morag.

"Miss Seth is the author of our pet theory. It would be an act of overwhelming stupidity, beyond even Miss Seth's capabilities, to draw attention to a conspiracy to which she is party."

"And me?" said Rod. "You trust me."

Vivian sniffed. "I am a good judge of character and you are the most trustworthy man I know."

Rod pulled an approving face and nodded in quiet agreement.

"She means men are too simple-minded to be good liars." Nina smiled sweetly at Rod.

"That is unfair. Although, in my experience, northerners tend to be unsophisticated creatures, unequipped for guile and duplicity."

"Gee Vivian," said Rod. "You say the nicest things."

"See? Even your subtlest sarcasm is heavy-handed and transparent. Rod, I would like you to look at the paperwork for the objects stolen from the Vault."

"Oh, you're giving the orders today as well?"

"Are you going to get precious about the chain of command?"

"I'll let you know," he took the papers from Vivian.

"Professor Omar told us that the Venislarn at the centre of the incursion would be either the *Nadirian* or *Zildrohar-Cqulu*. We need research. We need clues."

"So, who's tackling the *Nadirian* and who's researching Zippy-McCoolio?"

"Miss Seth, you are to look into the *Nadirian* –"

"Actually," Morag cut in, "I'd like to tackle the *Nadirian* if that's all right."

"Oh? Any particular reason?"

"Personal interest, that's all."

Vivian gave her a long look. "Very well," she said. "Miss Seth, *Zildrohar-Cqulu*."

"Cool."

"And you?" asked Rod.

"What about me?" said Vivian. "I will be providing managerial oversight, support and supervision." Again there was no hint of irony in Vivian's voice.

"Excellent," he grinned. "My support comes builder's strength with milk and no sugar, thanks."

She held his gaze for a second. "Very well."

"And chocolate digestives."

"Do not push it."

Morag and Nina took the lift down to the Vault together.

"You'll notice Rod wasn't given the research job," said Nina. "Trying to read Venislarn texts brings him out in cold sweats. He can't even say *Zildrohar-Cqulu*, let alone research it."

"I'm guessing the Birmingham mission didn't hire him for his esoteric knowledge." Morag followed Nina through the lift doors.

"Nope. This way."

Morag had only been down to the Vault once and she was still in 'awe and bafflement' mode when it came to the vast underground library-cum-museum.

Nina led her to a large book-lined room with a reading table at its centre. Morag looked at the shelves of mostly brown and mouldering tomes.

"The god section," said Nina.

"You have a lot of books," said Morag.

"This is only one of the reading rooms," said Nina. "We have to keep some of the books separate. They're kind of territorial. And occasionally hungry." Nina passed a tablet screen to Morag. "I'll find us some books. Meantime, maybe you could check if any other sections have intel on our two prime suspects."

"Your tea," said Vivian.

Rod moved his computer keyboard aside and placed a coaster on the desk with his bandaged hand.

"Glad to see someone uses a coaster." Vivian placed down a cup of tea that was the perfect chestnut brown.

217

"Well, if you don't, it's just the thin end of the wedge," said Rod. "Got to have some order in this world."

"Quite so."

"Also," said Rod, "this coaster, the outside dissolves in water to reveal a concealed Japanese throwing star."

"I am not sure if I can imagine a situation in which one might need to a turn a coaster into a weapon."

"Preparing for the unimaginable," said Rod sagely. "That's what we're all about."

Vivian neither agreed nor disagreed but left him to his work. It was a task that had him stumped even before he had begun. Nine missing items and nine pieces of accompanying paperwork that provided only the most cursory of information. There were photographs of the items, names provided for a handful of them and — apart from a list of dates and locations to indicate where they had been found, bought or stored — nothing more. It was a mystery with no breadcrumb trail to follow.

Rod needed a Venislarn expert. He called Dr Ingrid Spence. The phone went to voicemail the first time he rang. On his second attempt, someone or something answered.

"Nnnng."

"Ingrid?"

"Oh, hi Rod," she croaked. Ingrid sounded like she was gargling marmalade with razor blades in it.

"You all right?" he asked.

"Nuh-uh," she sniffed. "Come down with something virulent and mucous-y. I just don't know where it's all coming from. It's like I've got the snot glands of an elephant."

"Aye, you've painted a vivid picture there. You should be at home, resting up."

"I am," said Ingrid. "Me, a bottle of Night Nurse, a dozen Curly Wurlies and a box-set of Xena: Warrior Princess."

"Sorry. I didn't mean to catch you on. Hey, you don't think you caught anything from treating that Venislarn windbag?"

"Not likely," she said and gave a hacking cough. "If I start sprouting tentacles or some newborn Venislarn bursts out of my chest cavity, I'll let you know. Anyway..."

"Yes?"

218

"You called," she said.

"Oh. Aye. I've got these items I need identifying. Explaining. I wanted some background information on them."

There was a protracted wheezing on the line as though Ingrid was trying to hawk something up from the back of her throat.

"Or maybe you're not well enough," said Rod.

"Maybe. Can't it wait until next week?"

Rod weighed it up in his mind: end-of-the-world style incursion versus professional courtesy to his sick colleague. Did the needs of the many outweigh the needs of the one? But then again, if they cancelled sick leave every time there was a Venislarn emergency, they'd be forbidding flu-ridden germ carriers from abandoning their desks all the time.

"No, it's okay," he said. "I'll muddle through. Could have used the brains of the smartest Venislarn expert in the city."

"Smartest Venislarn expert on the payroll at least," she said and hung up.

"Right," said Rod. "Square one. Drawing board. Back to." He stared at the sheets of paper. Nine objects, eight of them probably decoys. One object that potentially held the key to predicting a catastrophic incursion before the end of the day. "We have to solve this without the help of the smartest Venislarn nerd on the payroll."

And immediately his next obvious course of action struck him. He didn't like it. He really didn't want to do it. It took him a full ten minutes and possibly the finest cup of tea he had ever drunk to sufficiently build up the courage and swallow his pride.

He phoned Birmingham University.

When Vivian reached the reading room, Nina had a fat tome open on the table and a phone to her ear. Opposite her, Morag was working through a tall stack of bookmarked volumes.

Vivian tilted her head to look at the woodcut engraving in the book before Nina. The image had the appearance of a photographic double exposure, as though the artist was incapable of settling on one artistic representation of *Zildrohar-Cqulu*. The body of the being was both that of a short-limbed locust-like insect and that of a sinuous lizard with dragon wings sprouting from its back. Its head was that of a hairless and fanged ape, whilst simultaneously being the multi-fronded chitin-covered helmet of the angriest prawn Vivian had ever seen. Locust-ape or lizard-prawn, or locust-prawn or lizard-ape, *Zildrohar-Cqulu* had been rendered with suitable menace.

Nina was nodding to the person on the other end of the phone line.

Vivian followed the Venislarn text on the page and translated out loud to herself.

"*Zildrohar-Cqulu*, high priest of the Temple of Ages, the wielder of wakefulness, the fastness of sleep. Brother of *Ligh'er* the Unnameable –"

"Surely, his name's *Ligh'er*," said Morag.

"Yes," said Vivian.

"Well, that's hardly unnameable, is it?"

Vivian grunted and continued reading. "The tyrant of dreams, the speaker of men's souls, the drinker of song-weave, he of the flame-vision. His house of sleep is — glued? mortared? — mortared with the blood and spirit of his slaves, each accorded a place in his principality in hell."

"Hull," said Nina.

"He's got a principality in Hull?" said Morag. "Suddenly, this guy sounds far less cool."

"He's in Hull," said Nina.

"Pardon?" said Vivian.

Nina jiggled her head at the phone in her hand.

"I'm just talking to Glynn at our mission there now. They have him in storage, sleeping, or whatever it is that Venislarn gods do instead of sleeping. He was brought to the country recently after some natural gas prospector company unearthed him in the South Atlantic."

"Hull?"

"Yes, Hull," said Nina patiently. "Grey, miserable, smells of fish."

"Yes, I know Hull," said Vivian. "I had a brief and unsatisfactory relationship with a junior accountant from Hull. If *Zildrohar-Cqulu* is sleeping under our guard in Hull, then I think we can safely strike him off our list." She looked to Morag. "So, the *Nadirian*."

Nina stepped away to conclude her conversation with the Hull consular mission.

Morag placed her hand on the pile of books. "Dozens of references to beings that might or might not be the *Nadirian*. Funnily enough, descriptions of an entity that appears to be what you expect it to be aren't exactly going to agree with each other. The Venislarn name, *Nadirian*, is a loan word from us. Nadir, from the Arabic *nazir*, the opposite, the other, the reflection."

"All very nice, Miss Murray," said Vivian, "but we need facts, not a lesson in etymology."

"Facts." Morag tapped her tablet. "I've got a handful of facts and a theory with virtually no evidence to support it. Fact one, in the *Emerald Tablet*, Jabir ibn Hayyan asserts that the mirror-god is the father of the *Uriye Inai'e*."

"Yes?"

"Well, we know that prayers of supplication can be effective in calming or subduing them. It worked on Kevin."

"Tenuous."

"Yep. Well, this is even more tenuous. In this commentary on *The Testament of Solomon*, Cassiodorus says that after the shape-stealing demon has eaten, it can be bound and captured in a box woven from ivy."

"Do we have a box woven from ivy?" asked Vivian.

"Shouldn't think so."

"So it is a moot point."

"I suppose."

Morag closed the book in front of her. "Thing is..."

"Yes?" said Vivian.

"In all these books, there are no pictures of the *Nadirian*."

"Because it can take on any shape," said Vivian.

"And yet Chad and Leandra produced a cuddly toy version of the *Nadirian* at Wednesday's meeting."

"I don't think those toys were meant to be true to life."

"But all the others were clearly based on the images we have of them."

Vivian considered this. "You think the toy designer has seen a picture or a document that we haven't?"

Morag shrugged.

"It's either that or we put our trust in prayers and boxes made of ivy."

"Then let us go ask Chad and Leandra and, on the way up, you can tell me your theory."

When she came off the phone from Glynn, Nina saw she had a missed call from Rod. She called him back.

"Are you busy, Nina?" he asked.

"That's a trick question," she said. "I've been caught out by that one before."

"I wondered if you fancied coming for a ride with me."

"I choose to interpret that in the filthiest way imaginable."

"To see Professor Sheikh Omar."

"Oh, yeah," said Nina with a vicious sarcasm that sent her voice up in pitch. "I just love visiting the Josef Mengele of Venislarn studies."

"Woah, did you just make a reference to a twentieth century historical figure?"

"I'm talking about the evil doctor in that *Nazis at the Centre of the Earth* movie. I'm saying the man is an evil fuck."

"I just thought you might be able to persuade Omar to help us. He always had a soft spot for you."

"Yeah. I think I'd like to gouge out his soft spot with a pencil."

"Fine." Rod paused. "I was also going to offer to buy us McDonald's drive-thru on the way back."

"Hotdog!" said Nina in far happier tones. "You should have opened with that. See you in the car."

Morag and Vivian found Chad in the marketing office. He was sat cross-legged on the floor contemplating a large cardboard cutout of a young woman in the arms of a *samakha* youth.

Chad looked up. "Ladies!" he said, delighted. "Welcome to the idea nursery. We never see you down here. Help yourselves to some strawberries or cherry tomatoes." He waved a hand to a selection of red fruits and salad items on the desk. "Leandra and I are on the colour diet. Friday is red."

"You'll get no argument from me," said Morag.

222

"It's good for the blood," said Chad. "My favourite is Sunday. Green. Lots of grapes and kiwis to help the positive flow of *chi*. What do you think to this?" he asked, gesturing to the cardboard cut-out. "It's concept material for a possible book-dash-film-dash-multi-platform-dash-story event."

Morag thought about adding 'dash pointless' but refrained.

"Last decade it was all dark romance with vampires. We've had zom-rom. We've had alien teen romances. Maybe it's time for teen-Venislarn romance. I look at this and I'm thinking *A Love as Deep as the Ocean*. What do you say?"

Vivian eyed the cutout. "*Samakha* have their eyes on the sides of their heads, like fish. "Not the front."

"Focus groups said that the public couldn't accept a romantic male lead who didn't have his eyes on the front of his head."

"But it is factually inaccurate."

"I think we're aiming for a deeper truth, you know?" said Chad. "Leandra was very positive. She said some of those troubled *samakha* youths you had in yesterday had a real energy to them. Do you know if any of them have considered a career in the film industry?"

"Um, quite possibly," said Morag.

"We have some questions for you, Mr de Marco," said Vivian.

"Shoot," said Chad. "It's only through questions that we learn more about ourselves."

"You showed us that hideous range of cuddly Venislarn toys."

"I wouldn't know about 'hideous', Vivian. Customer beta-tests were very positive. We could even have them in the shops for Christmas."

"You produced one of the *Nadirian*."

"Yes, we did." He rooted around behind a desk and came up with a shopping bag. "Not everyone's into the asymmetrical thing but I think this guy has a real charm-factor. Well, I would. Based on a design concept I submitted myself."

He pulled out the toy. It looked like a root vegetable, a misshapen root vegetable with an uneven number of legs and a mouth that was on the opposite end of the body to its eyes.

"We want to know where this... concept came from," said Vivian.

"Ah," said Chad. "The mysteries of the muse. Where do ideas come from? I read this interesting lifestyle piece about Plato. I don't know if you're familiar with his work. He believes that ideas –"

"Did you make it up or did you copy it from somewhere?" said Vivian.

Chad's perma-grin faltered. "Am I in trouble or anything?"

"That depends," said Morag.

"He said it was okay for me to have it."

"Who?"

"Greg. He gave it to me a couple of days before, you know..."

"He died," said Morag.

"Yes."

"What did he give you?" said Vivian.

Chad opened a desk drawer and pulled out a large hardback notebook.

"This."

Nina put her collar up against the wind as they crossed the square to the stairs of the Faculty of Arts building.

"This place bring back bad memories?" said Rod.

"Yep," said Nina. "Puts me in the mood for punching things."

"Hold onto that. We might yet need it."

They went up to the first floor and to Professor Sheikh Omar's office. Rod knocked.

"There's somebody at the door," sang a voice from within.

"You knock?" Nina said to Rod.

"Always. He might not be decent," Rod replied.

"The man is incapable of being decent." She threw the door open.

Professor Sheikh Omar was at his desk. A magnifying glass on a gooseneck stand was positioned over a broad manuscript. The manuscript was leather hide not paper and it was covered in faded pictures, not actual script.

"I've never regarded the Polynesian people as particularly flexible," said Omar conversationally as he peered. "Either physically or morally. But I'm always prepared to be proven wrong." He looked up and smiled. "Care to take a gander? Fair warning, it's a little racier than the old seaside *What the Butler Saw*."

A tinkling of crockery heralded the arrival of Omar's assistant, Maurice.

"Timing," said Omar. "It's almost as if we were expecting you. Oh, Maurice, you read my mind!" Omar picked up the box of chocolates on the tray. "Cadbury's Milk Tray. I would say that I much prefer the chocolate confections of the Swiss or the Belgians but there is something utterly delicious about Cadbury's, isn't there? A beautiful kitsch quality. Some days, we don't want caviar; we just want fish fingers. Don't you agree?"

"We've come to ask you some questions," said Rod.

"No," said Omar simply. "Try again. Sit down, have tea, eat a chocolate or two, and try again."

"We require your assistance with our enquiries," said Rod.

"Close, but not quite," said Omar, his tone hardening a fraction. "One last time. Sit. Take tea with me."

He rolled up the ancient hide as Maurice poured. Rod reluctantly sat and Nina followed a second later. "You know what annoys me most?" said Nina. "That this kind of shit is funded by my student loan."

"A pleasure as always to see you, Nina," said Omar. "Your mere presence, like the rising sun, casts elucidating rays. Rodney, let me tell you what you meant to say when you entered my office."

"Using your psychic powers again?"

"No, my intellect, dear boy. To paraphrase, any sufficiently advanced intelligence is indistinguishable from magic. You need my help."

"Need is a strong word."

"The clock is ticking. You are floundering. And you have even brought the delectable Nina Seth with you as an enticement. You need my help and you should have come in with the humility of a petitioning supplicant."

"You use big words," said Rod.

"Don't feign ignorance. It diminishes you, Rodney. You need my help because I know things you do not and I'm feeling broadly disinclined to help you."

"You won't help stop a Venislarn incursion?" said Nina.

"If they will it, nothing will stop it," said Omar.

"But we can prevent thousands of needless deaths."

225

"No such thing. Death is always needed. It's the grist in life's mill. Maurice and I are taking the old charabanc down to Barry Island for the weekend to get out of the way. Maurice does love the donkeys. I think he feels a certain kinship."

"Ignore him." Maurice finished pouring and bustled the empty tray away.

Omar plucked a chocolate from the box and popped it in his mouth. "Last time we spoke, Rodney, you said I was full of shite."

"I did."

"It would only be natural for a fellow to feel offended by such remarks. Fortunately, I am a forgiving fellow."

"Glad to hear it."

"The thing is, of course, forgiveness cannot simply be given; it has to be asked for."

"Ah," said Rod, understanding. "You want me to grovel. You want me on my knees."

Omar smiled at Nina lewdly. "He's so eager. It's always the quiet ones, isn't it?"

"He's wasting our time." Nina stood up.

"I will help you," said Omar, "in exchange for three things: a genuine and heartfelt apology, a verbal acknowledgement that you have come to me because I have skills and knowledge above and beyond yours and, finally, an understanding that, after today, *you owe me.*"

Rod had been in the job long enough to know what 'you owe me' meant. In the world in the shadow of the Venislarn, debts and favours were true currency and could be called in at any time. Omar wasn't after mere words; he was seeking fealty.

"Not bloody likely," said Rod, also standing. "You know some things – *some* things – because you live in the sewers and are willing to get your hands dirty. Don't pretend you hold some high and mighty position or that we need you."

Nina took a hold of Rod's arm. "We do need him."

"Not that much."

Omar had a roguish glint in his eye. "Too proud. Too proud. I understand. Then I offer another avenue."

"What?" said Nina.

"A challenge."

226

"Like a duel?"

"A game," said Omar. "A game of skill and knowledge. Let's see who the expert is."

"We don't have time for games." Rod headed for the door.

"Time *is* for games," said Omar. "Everything else is filler. We play, Rodney. If you win, I will answer all of your questions. And, yes, I do have the answers you seek."

"And if you win?" said Nina.

"Rodney apologises, acknowledges me as his superior, accepts that he owes me a favour *and* I will still answer your questions."

"I have a bad feeling about this," said Rod.

"He accepts," said Nina.

"I do?" Rod shook his head and then shook Omar's proffered hand.

"So glad," said Omar, opened a desk drawer and removed a long flat cardboard box that was so old and battered its corners were held together with several layers of sticking tape.

"Scrabble?" Rod looked in disbelief.

"Oh, dear boy," said Omar, "not any old game of Scrabble."

Vivian owned a car. It was exactly the sort of car Morag would have expected her to own. It was not small but was modestly sized, built for economy and efficiency over style and comfort. It was pristine, inside and out, and as well-organised as a fascist rally. When Vivian asked Morag if she had clean shoes before she got in, Morag was already checking.

Vivian obeyed the speed limit all the way to Bournville. Morag flicked through Greg's notebook. There were doodles aplenty, and personal and often incomprehensible notes.

"In any other job, if you showed this kind of thing to your doctor you'd be signed off sick for a year," said Morag.

"I do not know of a single person in our line of work who does not suffer from stress, anxiety or depression in one form or another," said Vivian.

"You seem to be holding it together well."

"I was talking about other people," said the older woman.

Morag found herself once again looking at Greg's drawing of the *Nadirian*. It had been executed in biro, in more than one colour as though he had come back to it time and again to refine it. It looked like the man had poured all his doubts, guilt and self-loathing onto the page and given it flesh.

"What kind of a man was Greg?" said Morag.

"Mr Robinson laughed a lot."

"That's nice."

"Misdirection," said Vivian. "He was like Vaughn Sitterson in that one sense."

"Hmmm?"

"Vaughn Sitterson does not like the world to pay close attention to him and foolishly attempts to achieve that by ignoring the world. Greg Robinson achieved the same by making the rest of the world seem more interesting."

"Do you know why he died?"

"Most people seem to think it was suicide."

"He was depressed?"

Vivian gave her a dismissive look. "Happy people tend not to kill themselves."

"No. Suppose not." Morag flicked onward to the page they had discovered together earlier, the one that had nothing on it, apart from Morag's address.

Vivian parked on Franklin Road, a short distance from Morag's home. The afternoon skies were grey and unfriendly.

"You believe that your neighbour is the *Nadirian*?" said Vivian.

"I believe Vaughn believes my neighbour is the *Nadirian*," said Morag. "If I might speculate, Greg knew that Mrs Atraxas was the *Nadirian* and, for whatever reason, chose suicide-by-Venislarn as his preferred way out. Vaughn either knows this or suspects this."

"So you suspect."

"I do suspect."

Vivian locked the car. "Have you ever seen this woman?" she asked.

"No," said Morag. "I've seen her cats. I've heard strange noises coming from her flat. Thumps, bumps and something that's trying to sound like music but really isn't."

"So, you've no idea what this thing looks like?"

Morag came round the car and joined Vivian on the pavement to walk up to the house. "It will look like whatever we think it will look like. It's the whole Stay-Puft-Marshmallow-Man thing."

"Stay Puft?"

"From *Ghostbusters*. The movie. You know, when they're on top of the building and..."

Vivian shook her head. "I stopped going to the cinema after they stopped having intermissions."

"Because?"

"In the intermission, Mr Grey and I used to have a little debate about how the film would end."

"You always won, I bet," said Morag.

"Naturally," said Vivian. "If we are to tackle the *Nadirian*, one of us must go in with a clear mind, refuse to view your Mrs Atraxas as anything other than an old woman."

"That's impossible. That's like telling someone to *not* think of pink elephants. If I try to avoid thinking of a monstrous horror with suckers and claws and orifices in the wrong places, I'm going to think of nothing but that."

"It is a matter of will power."

Morag sighed. "I'm not happy asking a colleague to face danger but if you're confident about this..."

"I am. I will enter her flat, engage her in conversation and, at the appropriate time, employ the *Uriye Inai'e* prayer," said Vivian. "Meanwhile, you will ensure the building is empty and secure. And, if I give the signal to indicate that I have failed, *then* you will call for reinforcements."

"Would the signal involve a lot of screaming?"

"It will be a loud shout at most," said Vivian. "I shall be professional to the end."

They stopped at the gate to 27 Franklin Road.

"She may just be an old woman," said Vivian.

"Here's hoping."

Professor Sheikh Omar unpacked the Scrabble box with slow reverence.

"It was a rainy night in dreary Halifax. Nova Scotia, not Yorkshire. We were hoping to unearth some of Maurice's distant relatives but it had proved to be a dismal endeavour. Our hotel had an unimaginatively stocked bar and this solitary board game. One of the E's was missing. And so, over a bottle of inferior Pinot Grigio, Venislarn Scrabble was born. Later on, we combined it with a Polish and a Danish edition to get a better frequency of letters to represent those pharyngeal fricatives and glottal consonants that make Venislarn such a workout for the mouth."

"Pharyngeal fricatives, sure," said Rod.

Nina patted Rod's knee supportively. "Don't worry, mate. We'll trounce him."

Omar adjusted his glasses. "This is a game between Rodney and myself, Nina. You're not playing. It's his apology I seek to extract."

"But I'm rubbish at Venislarn," said Rod.

"Oh, I am sure your rudimentary abilities will stand up to those of a man who is so patently 'full of shite'."

Rod gave Nina a panicked look.

"Team talk!" Nina declared, and pulled Rod by his lapels out into the corridor.

"How did we get ourselves into this position?" he said. "And why did we agree to this stupid game?"

"Do we need his help or not?"

"Probably."

"Then shut up and listen:

      Scyad fyada crikh'hu,
      Drat cribbe'u nhup mudu,
      Posna-bhapa shuta,
      Pabbe scama shis'kha,
      Faiska-shaska taset glun'u."

Rod blinked. "A Venislarn limerick."

"Yup."

"There were lots of rude words in that."

"Yes, there were. Now, repeat it back to me."

Rod blinked some more. "Our strategy is that I memorise a dirty limerick and hope that I can play some of those words?"

"It is."

Rod gave her a long look.

"Okay. Give it to me one more time."

Morag knocked on the door to flat one. Richard answered almost immediately.

"Oh, you are in," said Morag, surprised.

"I am," said Richard and then, "By knocking, you are usually indicating that you hope to see the person inside."

"I suppose."

"I don't think I would ever knock on a door and hope the person was out. Hello," he said to Vivian, who was standing behind Morag in the hallway.

"This is my Aunt Vivian," said Morag.

"I am her aunt," Vivian confirmed flatly.

"She's agreed to come round and do some tidying at my place while we're out tonight," said Morag, "which is very nice of her."

"It is," Richard agreed. He looked at his watch. "The open mic event isn't on for a couple of hours yet."

"I thought we could go early. Get a bite to eat. Sound good?"

"That does sound good," said Richard. "I'll got get my bagpipes."

"It wouldn't be a proper night out without them."

Richard disappeared.

"Does he deliberately dress as a lumberjack?" asked Vivian.

"I think it might be a hipster thing."

"I have no idea what that means."

Richard appeared with the tartan windbag under his arm. "I'm ready."

Morag looked at Vivian. "Be careful up there."

"I will," said Vivian.

"Is your flat dangerously untidy?" asked Richard.

"This niece of mine has the most atrocious habits," said Vivian and made her way upstairs.

Morag tried to give her a 'call me' gesture but she didn't look back.

"Lead on," Morag prompted Richard. She followed him out and locked the door securely behind her.

As she climbed to the top floor, Vivian opened her purse and removed a pendant on a silver chain. She did not generally approve of jewellery on either men or women but she kept this particular item close. It had been a Christmas present from someone who understood her fondness for practical gifts. She stopped at the bottom of the final flight of stairs. A fat black cat sat before the door to flat three. Vivian dangled the pendant and watched the arrow-head twitch. It moved only millimetres but it definitely twitched, as though it was feebly trying to escape earth's gravity.

There was a Venislarn presence in the local area. The hope that it was just a little old lady in flat three was diminishing quickly.

She went up the stairs. The black cat stretched and hissed at her. Vivian ignored it and the cat had to move fast to avoid being trodden on. It part rolled, part scurried its way down the stairs and out of her way.

Vivian composed herself at the door and fixed the idea of a sweet old lady in her mind before knocking.

There was a scraping shuffle from within – the sound of furniture being dragged across the floor? – and a series of scratchy muttering sounds. Something stroked the door and eventually found the door handle. It turned slowly, creaking.

Rod looked at his seven tiles. He had six consonants and one vowel. Four of the consonants were H's. He made quiet strangling noises as he tried to wrap his mouth around possible Venislarn words.

The day was darkening quickly and Maurice had put the lights on and made a fresh pot of tea. Omar had insisted the Nina sit at the long edge of the desk where she couldn't see Rod's tiles or whisper any suggestions. Omar had presented her with a clothbound book.

"The world's most extensive and accurate English-Venislarn dictionary," he told her.

She looked at its blank cover and spine. "Written by you, I guess," said Nina.

"But typed up by Maurice. I'm all thumbs whereas Maurice has such nimble fingers. Tiny hands, like a capuchin, don't you, Maurice? Come show the lady."

Maurice waved his suggestion away and blushed.

Rod rearranged his tiles and almost dislocated his epiglottis trying to pronounce the resulting word.

"One birthday, Maurice gave me a set of Scrabble tiles engraved with Venislarn ideograms," said Omar. "We managed one game, didn't we?"

"What happened?" asked Nina.

"Do you recall the Birmingham tornado of 2005?"

"That was the Winds of *Kaxeos*," said Nina.

"And I'm glad that's what everyone thinks," said Omar. "We never saw the tiles again, did we? The power of words."

It was an old woman who opened the door, but she did not particularly resemble the image that Vivian had conjured in her mind. Vivian had gone for a Miss Marple-style dignified old dear, perhaps with a blue rinse and lavender perfume, but the woman who opened the door bore more resemblance to one of Macbeth's witches.

Mrs Atraxas – the *Nadirian* — was short and bent. Her hair was a thick thatch of light grey, like a teetering mass of day-old mashed potato. Her face, so round as to appear wider than it was tall, was deeply lined and the colour of toffee. Patches of bristly hair sprouted from her chin. Her dark green cardigan had been buttoned up wrong and her brown skirts were marked with old stains. A pea clung to her cuff, in a thick clot of what appeared to be gravy.

The woman repositioned her wooden walking stick and tilted her head to look up at Vivian.

"Yes?" she said.

Vivian felt a sudden and rare thrill of nervousness as she prepared to speak, as though the act of speaking would force strange images into her own mind and thus unleash the *Nadirian's* protean abilities.

"Mrs Atraxas," said Vivian. "My niece, Morag, has just moved in downstairs. I thought I would just come up to say hello."

"Who?" said the *Nadirian*.

"Morag, my niece. She's moved in downstairs. My name is Vivian."

The *Nadirian* squinted at Vivian like she was a snake oil salesman. "You'll be wanting to come in for a drink then?" she said eventually.

"That's very kind of you."

"I haven't forgotten my manners, not like some," said the *Nadirian*. She turned away and toddled lopsidedly into the flat proper. Vivian followed.

The flat stank of cats. It felt like the air itself was fifty percent cat hair. Cats littered the place, as though there had been an explosion in a cat factory. They lounged on the back of the time-soiled sofa. They curled under the occasional tables, sometimes only a paw or a tail poking out from under the brown lace tablecloths. A series of small bric-a-brac shelves were fastened to the wall in a staggered arrangement that reminded Morag of steps. When she saw a cat run up them and trot around the picture rail to peer down at her, she realised that they were, in fact, steps — positioned for the cats' convenience. Two tawny long-haired cats sat like a lion and lioness atop a Welsh dresser. Another was stretched out flat in front of a closed door, as though it had drawn the short straw and had been given the job of draught excluder.

There was also the cat that sat on the arm of a chair wearing a knitted baby bonnet and a bib.

"I do coffee," shouted the *Nadirian* from the kitchen. "I do not do tea. I do not understand it."

The Venislarn-in-an-old-woman-suit had a curious accent. It had a definite Mediterranean air to it. At one moment it sounded Italian. At another it had a Greek quality. It could have been Albanian or Croatian or maybe the Venislarn hadn't settled on a single accent yet. If Vivian understood the *Nadirian's* powers correctly, she should simply be able to imagine hearing the woman in a specific accent and it would be so.

With the old woman in the kitchen, Vivian slipped her phone from her pocket and sent a quick text.

"This is a... very interesting hat your cat is wearing," she said conversationally.

"I knitted it for him," the *Nadirian* shouted back. "From a pattern I have."

"Does he like wearing it?" Vivian asked.

"He is a cat," said the *Nadirian*. "He wears it because I make him wear it."

The British Oak was an impressively large pub with a stone façade that made it look like a beer baron's castle. Unfortunately, it was pressed up against a busy stretch of high street — which kind of took the grand and majestic wind out of the building's sails. Still, it was pleasant inside and the menu looked better than the kind of pub fare Morag was used to.

The barmaid eyed the bagpipes under Richard's arm suspiciously.

"Are you here for the talent night?"

"That's right," said Richard.

"And can you play them?"

"I've been practising."

She looked at Morag.

"I've never heard a bum note out of them," Morag said truthfully.

"It's not on until seven," said the barmaid. "I'm putting you on first, before it gets busy."

"Thank you," said Richard.

They took their drinks to a corner seat by leaded windows that overlooked the car park. Morag glanced over the menu. She wasn't really hungry and her thoughts were more on the colleague she had left in the lair of the *Nadirian*.

"Well, here's to the neighbour thing," said Richard and held up his pint.

"To the neighbour thing."

Richard took a sip of beer that left a thick white froth on his moustache.

"Classy," said Morag.

"I aim to be," said Richard.

Morag looked at the funny, gentle teddy bear of a man. "I only know Richard Smith the pizza delivery guy and devil-may-care bagpiper slash stand-up comedian," she said. "Tell me a bit about yourself."

"Oh, you know more than that," he said.

235

She wiggled her nose in thought. "I know you like Terry's Chocolate Oranges. I know that if a strange drunk woman breaks into your house, you're too nice to kick her out."

"True."

"I know you eat green beans and aren't averse to whacking women with colanders."

"I did say sorry."

"I'm over it," she smiled. "But beyond that, you are an enigma, Richard."

"I'm a man of mystery," he agreed, "but, to be fair, I know even less about you. Let's see. You like a drink." She raised her bottled beer to confirm this. "You sometimes can't read door numbers. You sometimes forget when you've arranged to have dinner with a neighbour."

"Sorry."

"But you were ill. Um, and you have an aunt called Vivian who, I notice, doesn't have a Scottish accent like yourself."

"I was raised on the Moray Firth. Vivian's always lived in England." There was a buzz from her phone. "Speak of the devil," she said and read Vivian's text.

"How's the cleaning going?" asked Richard.

"Okay," said Morag without much confidence.

Vivian was quite troubled by the coffee the *Nadirian* presented her with. It was as dark as black treacle and seemed to simmer in her cup as though it was reluctant to give up any of its heat. She wasn't certain how the *Nadirian* had made it or how long ago it had originally been brewed. By the smell, she wasn't certain what kind of milk had been added or how far it was past its sell-by date. She couldn't even be absolutely certain that it was actually coffee at all. A tiny cat hair floated on its thick surface.

"That looks lovely," she lied. "Thank you."

The *Nadirian* gestured at a chair with an erratic hand movement and Vivian sat. Immediately, from beneath the chair, a cat wrapped its legs around Vivian's ankle and tried to bite her shoes. The *Nadirian*, who was doing a complicated three-point turn to back into her own chair, didn't notice.

236

Vivian made a show of looking round the flat, at the old furniture and gloomy and dusty corners. There was a glass-topped record player by the window with a stack of long players in brown wax paper sleeves beside it. On top of the Welsh dresser, the lion and lioness watched Vivian malevolently.

"This is a nice flat you have," she said.

The *Nadirian* gave a wobbly but genial nod like a monarch accepting tribute from a foreign dignitary. She dug down one side of her armchair and pulled out a bundle of knitting. She began to knit without even looking at her needles. For a creature in a doddery old body, her hands showed sudden and sinister dexterity.

"You do have a lot of cats," said Vivian.

"They breed," said the *Nadirian* as though it explained everything.

"They must take a lot of feeding."

"Cats feed themselves," said the *Nadirian*. "Rats and mice and such. They bring me food too. Morsels."

"Yes," said Vivian.

"Would you like to see family photographs?"

"Your family."

"My family."

"I would like that very much."

With pink yarn hooked over her fingers, the *Nadirian* pointed with both hands at a fat photo album on the table next to Vivian's chair. The cover was embossed with a photograph of a woman in a gauzy wrap skipping along a tropical beach at sunset. Behind her, the words 'Treasured Memories' rose from the surf in shimmering gold foil.

"Ah." Vivian picked up the volume reverently and placed it in her own lap. She did not open it.

She was extraordinarily mindful that she was sitting five feet away from a god and was preparing to open the god's family photo album. Venislarn images were to be feared, as were the Venislarn themselves. A high Abyssal Rating or not, there were Venislarn images that would fracture the human psyche in an instant and tip the viewer into permanent psychosis. A Venislarn photo album was potentially a very bad thing.

"I am very proud," said the *Nadirian*.

Was that a warning? A threat? Vivian took a silent but deep breath and opened the album. She looked at the first page. She was absolutely certain this was no human family.

"Ah," she said.

A sudden flash of light blinded her and sent a spectrum of entoptic images spinning across her retina.

"Vivian is apparently taking coffee with the *Nadirian*," said Nina, reading from her phone.

"That's brave," said Professor Sheikh Omar.

Rod looked at his tiles and heartily wished he and Vivian could swap places. Supping with a shape-shifting mind-reading god from beyond the stars seemed infinitely preferable to spending another minute trying to pluck meaningful Venislarn words from the gibberish in front of him.

"Mrs Grey is a brave woman," said Professor Sheikh Omar. "A fiery woman. I think if I were ever of the inclination to marry..."

From a chair in the corner, Maurice gave an amused snort.

Rod looked at the board. Omar had already criss-crossed the board with such gems as *karken'at*, *gharri*, *byach-id* and *drasn'eech*. By comparison, Rod had only managed to play *eh*, *fer*, *eh* (again) and, his best play and six-point scorer, *drat*.

Omar leaned forward over the desk. "I wonder what is brewing in that capacious cranium of yours, Rodney."

Rod gave a sudden bark of realisation and laid down three tiles.

"*Muda!*"

"Indeed," said Omar and immediately laid *jaer'khu* on a Triple Word Score.

"Flaming hell," Rod muttered under his breath.

"Come on, Rod. You can do it," said Nina, ignoring all evidence to the contrary.

"Oh, aye," he said sourly. "I'm just lulling him into a false sense of security."

He grabbed four tiles at random and laid them out to stretch to a Double Word Score. Omar studied the resultant word.

"*Hraa?*"

"Aye. That's right. *Hraa*," said Rod.

238

"And, Rodney, what's the meaning of this word?"

"This word? The original meaning?"

"Mmmm."

"It's the name we give to those, um, flange things... on the ends of..."

"It's the measured degree of *muh'yakhe* licence given to a *rhen-dho* courtier in exchange for filial sacrifices," said Nina, reading from the dictionary.

"Like I said," said Rod. "Flanges."

"Very well," said Omar and considered his next play.

"And this one?" said Vivian.

The *Nadirian* peered at the photograph. "That is the white cat."

"I can see that. Does it have a name?"

"It is the only white cat I have ever had so she didn't need a name."

"And what is this she is wearing?"

"It's the field uniform of a captain of the Wehrmacht."

"Of course, it is. I can see that now." Vivian turned the page. More cats. It was an entire album devoted to her cats. A very small number of them were undressed, but the majority had been kitted out in various outfits. They continued the military theme. From the tall bearskin of the Grenadier Guards to the feathered helmet of an Italian *Bersaglieri*, each was rendered in lovingly knitted detail. Vivian flipped to the last page of the military section to find an Imperial Stormtrooper cat. She frowned at the mistake, but of course the *Nadirian* would be unconcerned with the difference between fiction and reality.

The *Nadirian* picked up the Polaroid photo she had taken of Vivian, gave it a final shake and held it out for Vivian to see. It was not a flattering image, Vivian judged; and, like a savage tribesperson, she felt that the creature had somehow stolen part of her soul by taking it.

"It is a good likeness," said Vivian politely.

"It will go in the collection," said the *Nadirian*. She put the picture on the table and the Polaroid camera back down the side of her chair.

The evening light that had seeped around the drawn curtains was completely gone. The only light in the room came from a table lamp with a cloth shade printed with a painting of a coach house, complete with a horse and carriage. The old woman peered at her knitting in its yellow light.

"Would you like to hear something?" said Vivian.

"Like music?" said the *Nadirian*.

"A poem."

The *Nadirian's* round face scrunched up in a peculiar expression.

"People don't tend to read poems anymore," she said and then shook her head at her knitting as though it had suddenly become too much for her and put it down.

"It is an unusual poem but I do like it," said Vivian.

Vivian took a piece of paper from her purse. It was actually a receipt from a cash machine. She knew the *Uriye Inai'e* prayer of supplication by heart but the paper served her ruse. The *Nadirian* gestured for her to read and settled back.

"Uriye Inai'e. Uriye Inai'khi rhul'eh," Vivian recited. *"Qa-qa urh lhau-ee. Uriye Inai'e. Zhay te ayvh-ee shau."*

The *Nadirian* gave a grunt and laced its gnarled fingers together over its round belly, its eyes closed. Vivian repeated the prayer.

The open mic took place in a small function room at the rear of the pub. A short stage had been set up and tables and chairs were scattered around in a Parisian café style. Two middle-aged bikers sat drinking beer at one table. A pair of youngsters played on their phones at another. A woman in a long flowing outfit and a Joni Mitchell haircut sat tuning her acoustic guitar by the fire exit. An audience of five, six including Morag, who was already preparing to tell anyone who asked that, no, she wasn't with the man with the bagpipes.

A beanpole of a man came onto the stage with Richard in tow.

"Good evening everyone," said the beanpole into the utterly superfluous microphone. "Welcome to talent night at the British Oak. First up, we have…"

"Richard," said Richard.

"Richard," said the beanpole. "And he's got bagpipes and five minutes tops."

The beanpole backed away and left the stage to Richard. Richard nervously approached the microphone. He licked his lips and blew into the bagpipes to inflate the bladder. And then stopped.

"What do you call a dog with no legs?" said Richard. "Anything you like. He's not coming."

One of the youngsters scoffed. Morag smiled supportively. Richard pressed on.

"Man goes in a pub. The barman says, 'What are all these mangoes doing in here?'"

One of the youngsters muttered. "Get off," said one of the bikers.

"Is that what your wife says to you?" said Richard.

The biker's mate laughed and elbowed the other in the ribs. Richard gripped the microphone. "My parents used to laugh when I said I wanted to be a stand-up comedian. Well, no one's laughing now, are they?"

A youngster swore softly at the terrible joke but she was grinning nonetheless.

"My parents never liked me. For my seventh birthday, they bought me an abandoned fridge."

There was a smattering of chuckles.

"I can't even get a job. I went for an interview with a blacksmith. He asked me if I'd ever shoed a horse before. I said, 'No, but I once told a donkey to piss off.'"

There was laughter in the room. Genuine laughter. Morag blinked.

"After the accident, I woke up in hospital," he said. "I said to the doctor, 'Doctor, I can't feel my legs.' The doctor said, 'I know. We cut off your hands.'"

Even the heckler raised a chuckle at that one.

"Keep laughing," said Richard, "or I *will* be forced to play the bagpipes."

The *Nadirian* snored loudly once, then settled down, chin on chest, and was still. Vivian paused in her recitation. She sat still for a full five minutes and simply observed.

The creature seemed to draw in on itself as it sank into its torpor. The wrinkles on its face deepened and it looked even less human than before, more muppet than woman.

Eventually satisfied that it was indeed asleep and dead to the world, Vivian closed the photo album of cats in hats and carefully put it aside. She took out her phone, sent a quick text off to her colleagues and then stood to leave.

It was at that moment she recalled that there was a cat wrapped around her ankle and attempting to eat her shoe. Vivian gave her foot an experimental shake but the furry little vice wasn't going anywhere.

Some choice words rose to Vivian's mind. She kept them to herself and made for the door, dragging the cat behind her like a ball and chain.

Nina's phone buzzed. Rod shot her a filthy look and then, apologetically, turned it into an exasperated gesture. Nina silenced the phone.

Rod had six tiles: four X's an E and a Z. There were no more letters in the bag, he was sixty-seven points behind and he suspected Omar would be out on his next go. Rod knew he wasn't going to win but he had to go down fighting.

"That was Vivian," said Nina. "She has placated the *Nadirian* with a prayer."

"She's done what?"

"She's hypnotised it, put it in cryo, whatever," said Nina.

"That's great," said Rod. "Just let me concentrate."

"But it's all dealt with," said Nina. "*Zildrohar-Cqulu* is in Hull and the *Nadirian*'s been put into hyper-sleep. Crisis averted. No incursion in Birmingham tonight."

"You wish to abandon the game?" asked Omar, disappointed.

"Hell, no," said Rod.

"Oh, he thinks he can still win," the professor grinned.

Rod studied the board. There were few places left to go. Frankly, he might as well go out in a blaze of glorious stupidity. He began laying tiles across the latticework of letters.

"What's this?" said Omar. "E-I-X-X-E. *Eixxe*?"

"Not finished," said Rod.

"E-I-X-X-E-Z-E." Omar frowned. "What? You're not thinking of...?"

Rod placed another X on the board. As his finger came up, the tile flipped, as though it had a magnet in its base. Rod picked it up and placed it again. It scooted away from the board square, repelled by some force.

"Are you playing silly buggers, Omar?"

"Quite reasonably, the universe is taking exception to your word choice."

"Eh?"

"Forces beyond those that govern our physical world fear you are planning to spell the final word of unmaking."

Rod put the tile down and held it there with his forefinger. "The forces can fear what they like," he said. "They're not stopping me winning."

"You don't know the final word of unmaking, do you?" said Omar.

"I know all the words, mate. Nina, get ready to check this one in the dictionary."

"Er, Rod," said Nina, "it's not going to be in the dictionary. It can't be."

"It's not a real word."

"The – and I should point out it's an entirely theoretical word – the final word of unmaking can never be written or said. If it is, it... *unmakes*."

"Unmakes what?"

Her eyebrows waggled at him irritably. "Everything, Rod."

"Oh." He shrugged. "Well, maybe I haven't got it here. Maybe I can't spell it. How many letters has it got?"

"Eleven," said Nina.

Rod had two tiles. With them and the spare E on the board, that would make an eleven-letter word. He put down his final X and found that he had to hold that one in place with his finger also.

"Enough," said Omar. "Venislarn Scrabble is only for those who treat the game with the respect it deserves."

"You want to quit?" said Rod.

"I didn't say that," said Omar. "I'm merely telling you to stop."

"I'm only going to stop when the game is over."

"You're being childish now, Rodney."

Rod smiled. He was starting to lose feeling in his fingertips. If he didn't know better, he would think that the two letter tiles were vibrating rapidly in their bid to escape. The other letters on the board started to slide away. Rod had to use all the fingers of his good right hand to hold the line in place.

Rod picked up his last tile.

"This could be the final letter of the word of final undoing."

"The final word of unmaking," said Nina.

"That too," he said. He looked Omar straight in the eye.

"I'm going to play it. I don't know if it's the word of thingy-thingy. It's Russian roulette for me because I just don't know."

"You are playing Russian roulette with the world," said Omar. "Nina, tell him he's being stupid."

"YOLO," she said.

"There's nothing to gain," said Omar, panic seeping into his voice. "Your crisis is over. There's nothing to be won or lost."

"Pride." He held the tile with his thumb over the letter and brought it over the board. His fingertips were hot now. The board around his unfinished word seemed to be fading... Then he realised that the vibrations were sanding away the cardboard. And was that a whiff of smoke coming off it?

"Stop now," Omar insisted. "You'll not only destroy the world but ruin a perfectly lovely weekend in Barry Island for Maurice and me."

"Bugger Barry," said Maurice from the corner.

"Just admit defeat, professor," said Rod and started to bring the letter down. The vibration in his fingers travelled violently up his hand to his wrist but Rod was now in comfortable territory. Whereas linguistic mind games utterly threw him, physical endurance and pain management were right up his street. "This letter *really* doesn't want to be put down," he said.

"Listen to the universe," said Omar.

"The universe has never listened to me." Rod pushed against the ethereal forces that were trying to keep the letter away.

The desk creaked under the pressures. The tile in his bandaged left hand tried to break loose, pressing up against him like a football held underwater.

"Your pride will destroy everything!" shrieked Omar.

"My pride?" grunted Rod. "Or yours?" He brought his elbow up to apply pressure for the final push.

"Enough!" yelled Omar, as he gripped the edge of the board and yanked it from the table. Letters flew in all directions. Several ricocheted loudly off walls and windows. A picture frame shattered. When the force opposing Rod vanished, his hand drove straight into the desk, splintering the table top and sending an agonising jolt through his recently amputated digit. He recoiled with a roar.

"Enough," said Omar.

Rod shook away the pain in his hand. "You've thrown the game," he said with a vicious grin.

"You've wrecked my office," offered Omar by reply.

Richard bounced off stage to as rapturous a round of applause as could be given by six people. Morag was distracted by the text she had just received from Vivian:

NAMIBIAN SUBDUED. PRAYER WORKED.

Morag assumed the word 'Nadirian' had been mangled by Vivian's autocorrect into 'Namibian'.

"So?" he said.

"Um," she said, thoughts still on the text.

"That bad?"

"No. It was good." She did a little mental reboot. "Richard, it was really good. You were actually funny."

He smiled — a toothy flash of childlike happiness in a forest of beard.

"You didn't play your bagpipes though."

"You *want* me to play the bagpipes?" he said.

"I didn't say that."

"I'm sure I wouldn't be up to the exacting standards of a Scot."

"You know we Scottish don't all play bagpipes, wear kilts and know Nessie on first name terms. I think drinks are deserved all round. You were amazing up there and I've just had some good news from my Aunt Vivian."

Before she could react, Richard had angled his head and looked at her upturned phone.

"The Namibian?"

"Sorry, er, yes. It's the name I give a... particularly nasty stain on the living room carpet. I call it the Namibian."

"Why?" said Richard.

Morag thought quickly. "It's in the shape of Namibia," she said. "You know, all..." She drew an intentionally vague outline in the air, given that she had no idea what Namibia looked like.

"And your aunt has eradicated it with prayer," said Richard, his tone even and non-judgemental.

"And elbow grease," said Morag. "Prayer and elbow grease. She's a very religious woman. Now, did I mention that you deserve a beer?"

Maurice went round the office on hands and knees, picking up scattered Scrabble tiles.

Professor Sheikh Omar had the notes for the nine stolen items before him. He looked from each to the next and only occasionally glanced at the splinter-edged hole Rod had punched in his desk. Rod stood over him, flexing and inspecting the grazes on his left hand knuckles and the shiny pink burn marks on his right hand fingertips. Nina sat on a chair in the corner and quietly demolished the box of Milk Tray chocolates.

"This one," said Omar, tapping the paper. "Is it meant to be a pottery cat or a Chinaman?"

"Good question," said Nina.

"It's a bit non-PC if it's the latter," said Omar.

"Just identify them," said Rod. "We need to know why someone might want to steal them."

"I'd steal this one in order to destroy it," said Omar. "For offences against political correctness."

Nina's phone rang. Rod looked at her.

"Yo," she said. "Evening, Glynn. What's that?"

She shot Rod a look. It was not a reassuring look.

"Gone where? Last weekend? But you didn't check."

She pursed her lips unhappily as Glynn spoke.

"Swapped container numbers. Who? Ah. Gary Bark. Yes, we know him. But Birmingham have no record of receiving it. Shit."

"A problem?" asked Omar politely.

"Get on with your job," said Rod tersely.

"No. Thanks for telling me," said Nina. "This could be very bad. Phone me if you find out anything else."

She ended the call.

"*Zildrohar-Cqulu* is not in Hull," she said. "The container was removed without authorisation last weekend by our haulier friend, Gary Bark. They've only just noticed."

"So, *Zildrohar*-thingy *is* in Birmingham," said Rod.

"We can only assume."

"Is the crisis back on?" said Omar. "Maurice. Time to fire up the jalopy, dear."

"You have work to do," said Nina. "Do it."

"Someone stole the sleeping body of a god and has had it brought here," said Rod.

"Gary stole it and brought it to his partners or masters or buyers," said Nina.

"And his death. Either an accident..."

"Or the tying up of loose ends."

"We have to find that cargo container."

"He could have taken it to the Dumping Ground," suggested Rod.

"Hiding a needle in a haystack," Nina agreed.

Omar whistled softly to himself, a strange little melody. "Ah," he said.

"What?" Rod and Nina chorussed.

"This," he said and turned one of the papers around to face them.

"The sheet music," said Nina.

Omar indicated the fragment of music in the photocopied image on the cover.

"*Simple Tunes for Little Hands*," read Rod.

"It's nothing of the sort," said Omar. "It's incomplete but this is one of the five pieces that make up Eliphas Levi's Invertible Hymn of *Sanq'hu*."

"Which is?" said Nina.

"A spell. To awaken gods."

"Bugger," said Rod.

"Crisis definitely back on," said Nina.

Rod drove at speed through the evening traffic. Much of it was going the other way, heading out of the city, but he still had to weave between the lanes and beep and flash the odd vehicle out of the way.

"And I'll say it again," said Nina. "This is why we need blue flashing lights."

"It's not a problem," said Rod, steering sharply to cut between two lorries.

"Flashing lights say we're 'important people dealing with an emergency'. These people just think you're a wanker in a hurry to get home for his tea."

Rod circled a roundabout in the wrong lane, earning several angry honks for doing so, and then slid, tyres squealing, into the Dumping Ground yard. Nina had phoned ahead and the stockyard manager was waiting.

"We've looked," he said. "The cargo container Gary Bark brought in on Saturday was, as the manifest said, filled with *Whurrikin* casings."

There was a tone in his voice, a tone of disbelief and annoyance, a tone that suggested it was out of line for anyone to even suggest that a slumbering god had been snuck into his yard without his knowledge.

"So, they switched it," said Nina. "He bribed a crane operator or something. Containers were switched."

"No," said the stockyard manager. "You can't accuse our men willy-nilly. And, besides, all the containers are marked. They're numbered."

Rod stood stock still, one hand on the roof of the car, the other on the open door. "Four-seven-four," he said.

"What's that?" said the stockyard manager.

"Container four-seven-four," said Rod. "Where is it?"

"I'd have to check."

Rod waved for him to do so and hurry. Rod and Nina followed the man to the pre-fab office in the centre of the yard.

"Four-seven-four," said Rod.

"The number Gary Bark had written on his fridge door to remind himself," said Nina.

"Exactly."

In the office, the stockyard manager ran through a wad of dockets and notes on a clipboard. "Four-seven-four," he said to himself as he riffled through. "Here. Oh. *Whurrikin* casings. Again. Arrived Saturday."

"Where is it?" demanded Rod.

"It should be..." The man stopped himself on the way to the door. "No. It's already been loaded. On a train bound for Cardiff tomorrow."

"So where is it now? Is it on a flatbed?"

The stockyard manager bent and whispered to the only other man in the room. Rod tolerated the hushed back-and-forth for approximately five seconds.

"Where is it?" he said loudly.

The stockyard manager straightened up. "It's on the train. It's on a layover in a siding."

"Where?"

"Beneath New Street station."

Rod nodded. Rhythms of the universe, he thought. You lost something, it was always in the last place you looked. You lost something hideously evil and dangerous, it was always in the worst place it could possibly be.

"*Zildrohar-Cqulu* is under New Street station," he said. "Right in the middle of the city."

"On a busy Friday night," said Nina.

"This has become a lot worse than I feared," said Rod as they hurried back to the car.

"Shit just got real."

He looked at her. "Seriously, Nina. I don't even know what that phrase means."

"It's from that movie."

"I'm aware it's from *Bad Boys*, Nina. You made me watch it."

"*Bad Boys 2*, actually."

"*Bad Boys 2*? They made two of them? I can't believe they made one of them and then thought making another one would be a good idea."

"I can't believe you're discussing the merits of movies when there's a world-devouring god from beyond about to throw his shit down on New Street!"

"A world where there's two *Bad Boy* movies? Frankly, I think he's welcome to it."

Moving quietly so as to avoid accidentally reawakening the now-dormant *Nadirian*, Vivian had managed to drag her feline ankle-warmer to the door where another challenge lay before her, literally.

The draught excluder cat had moved to the entrance door and lay stretched out in front of it.

Vivian bent over to pick it up. The draught excluder opened one eye and swiped at her. Vivian snatched her hand back. There were now two long red scratches in the back of her hand. Vivian considered what to do. She gave some serious thought to kicking the beast.

There was a vase of flowers on the sideboard beside the door. The flowers were dead but there was water in the vase. Vivian slipped her slender hand into the vase until her fingers were wet and then flicked the water at the cat on the floor. The draught excluder writhed unhappily but didn't move.

Stubborn, thought Vivian. Vivian had little time for stubbornness in others.

She slid her foot (the one not already carrying a cat) under the draught excluder's body. It swiped at her angrily but refused to move. Vivian wiggled her foot under further and then, standing on the other foot, lifted the draught excluder away.

It was at that instant that her phone rang. Vivian growled inwardly and shot a glance back at the *Nadirian*. The alien god was still asleep. With a cat on each foot — and one of those in the air — Vivian clumsily pulled the phone from her pocket. She fumbled at the End Call button but the phone rang on.

250

Thinking quickly but not necessarily wisely, Vivian dropped the phone into the flower vase, where it burbled for a second and then went silent. She looked at the *Nadirian* again. It remained still.

Vivian put her foot down. The angry draught excluder had wrapped itself around her ankle and she now wore two cat-shaped slippers. Vivian reached for the door catch, opened it slowly and waddled silently out of the flat, pulling the door to behind her. The cats were still attached.

They were certainly persistently single-minded. It was almost admirable. Of course, that didn't mean Vivian wasn't going to beat them off with a stick the moment they were out of earshot of the sleeping god.

Rod accelerated along a bus lane at seventy miles an hour, clipped a pedestrian barrier at the top of Moor Street and won a game of chicken against a bus coming through the tunnel under the Selfridges building.

"Vivian's not picking up," said Nina as Rod handbrake-turned the car onto the pavement beside New Street station.

"You get hold of Vaughn yet?" said Rod.

"Are we trusting other people now?"

He shoulder-barged his dented door to get it open. Nina joined him on the pavement.

To Nina's mind, New Street station had been originally built sometime in the Dark Ages and deliberately modelled on a Nazi bunker. It had been all concrete blocks and creaking escalators and sinister subterranean platforms. Then, some years back, the forces of newness and shininess had swooped in, ripped out the old evil concrete heart of the monster and replaced it with glass and light and sushi bars and a John Lewis. However, the forces of newness and shininess had not penetrated below ground level and the station still sat on a maze of subterranean platforms.

Next to where Rod had abandoned the car, a four-foot-high wall ran around one of the wide light shafts that allowed daylight and trainspotters to peer onto the tracks thirty feet below the street.

"There," said Rod and pointed.

Nina squinted through the night-time gloom. Beside a static passenger train, the corrugated roof of a freight train was just about visible. "What's the plan?"

"We get down there," said Rod. "We stop it. Or we get that train out of the city."

With barely any effort, he swung his legs up so that he was perched on the edge of the wall.

"I'm not jumping down there," she said. "My ankles will snap."

"Then run," he said and dropped off the wall and down into the pit.

Nina saw him land on a carriage roof, roll, jump again and come down on a platform. Apart from a minor stumble at the end it was Olympic standard stuff.

"*Muda.*" Nina jealously sprinted for the pedestrian entrance to the station, phone in hand.

Morag and Richard left the pub in good spirits, while the Joni Mitchell-alike was murdering *Big Yellow Taxi*. The open mic comedy had been a success. Richard had accepted Morag's praise with humility. They had sunk a handful of drinks between them and had what Morag thought was the nicest and most normal conversation she'd had with anyone for a long time. Richard was easy-going and amiable, showed a genuine interest in her and was a truly great listener. And, possibly best of all, better even than the knowledge they were walking home to a flat in which the *Nadirian* threat had been neutralised – best of all, it had been one of those rare occasions when evening drinks with a single man didn't feature him trying to get inside her knickers.

She breathed deeply and watched the early moon trying to make an appearance between the clouds and the rooftops.

"That was a big sigh," said Richard.

"Contentment," said Morag.

"Not boredom?"

Shadows shifted on high up on the building opposite in the corner of Morag's eye. She looked properly. The shadow shape was gone, melted into the roof but, for an instant, it had looked like something huge with many spider-like legs. Armoured spider-like legs.

"No, not bored," she said.

"You paused," said Richard.

"Distracted," said Morag.

She scoured the skyline for signs of the August Handmaiden of *Prein* and felt a nugget of anger well inside her because this was turning out to be a perfectly lovely night and she didn't want it spoiled by a vengeful Venislarn.

"Morag," said Richard.

"Mmmm?"

"I think we're being followed."

She stopped. "You saw it too?"

He nodded. "Yeah, it's right there," he said and pointed at the taxi that was crawling along the curb ten feet behind them. There was a uCab sticker on the taxi door. Morag's phone rang. It was Nina.

"Hello?" It sounded like Nina was talking from a cocktail party being held in a wind tunnel. Nina also sounded out of breath.

"*Zildrohar-Cqulu!*" Nina said. "He's here! New Street station!"

"But..."

"I know!"

"I'm on my way." Morag hung up.

She turned to Richard. "Really sorry. A work thing. An emergency." She hurried to the uCab taxi. "It was a really lovely evening. Really," she said and got in.

Morag looked at the taxi driver. "I guess you know where I need to go," she said. The taxi driver pulled away without a word.

Nina skidded to a stop in the station concourse and looked around. Outside, she had seen where the train was. Right now, she could point to its approximate location below the marble flooring. How to get there and which stairs to take was another matter entirely.

The station was busy and crowded. Late-working city-types were heading home. Drinkers, clubbers, theatre-goers and the like were pouring in. The cafes, cocktail bars, pizzerias and restaurants on this level and the shopping centre above were doing a brisk trade. And beneath their feet, a giant locust-ape-lizard-prawn was about to go all King Kong if something wasn't done about it.

She had almost settled on which stairs to go for when something in the crowd caught her eye. It was a T-shirt. On the back it read 'Keep Calm and Kill Zombies'. The T-shirt was attached to a blond ponytail Nina thought she recognised. She ran over.

"Ingrid!"

Dr Ingrid Spence turned and blinked at Nina in surprise.

"You're just the person we need," said Nina. "Talk about right place, right time."

Ingrid shook her head, confused.

"Someone's about to perform some summoning-music, ritual thing," said Nina. "Right here."

"Here?" said Ingrid.

"Yeah. You all better now?" she said. "Rod said you were ill."

Nina saw Ingrid had a gnarled and twisted wooden stick in her hand.

"What's that?" said Nina.

An invisible force slammed Nina in the chest, punching the air out of her lungs and sending red spikes up into her vision. She clutched at Ingrid as she fell but her hands didn't want to work.

"Yeah. All better now," said Ingrid.

Rod had landed on the service platform at what he guessed was a midpoint on the freight train. The nearest cargo containers were marked with Dumping Ground serial numbers. This was the right train.

He ran up the platform, reading numbers as he went. Even though he was expecting it, seeing container 474 still sent a chilling jolt through him.

"Bugger," he whispered.

He leapt onto the flatbed and took hold of the heavy padlock on the chains around the locking rods. He removed his tie-clip and slipped the two lock picks apart. Then he saw something shiny and glutinous in the lock. He prodded it. Superglue.

He let it drop and considered the chains. They were too thick to break. He would need a welding torch to break through them.

He pressed an ear to the door. There was no noise from within, none that could be heard above the echoing background noise of a busy train station.

"Plan B." He jumped down and ran on towards the locomotive cab.

A station worker in hi-vis orange waved at him up ahead. "Oi! What you doing?"

"We need to move this train," said Rod.

"You can't be down here!"

Rod ran past him to the locomotive.

"We need to find the driver."

He grabbed the cab door handle and yanked it open. He looked at the body crumpled up beneath the train controls.

"Okay. I've found the driver." He turned to the station worker and flashed his ID. "Can you drive a train?"

"I'm a platform manager."

"Then you need to go find your superior. Tell them there is a terrorist device on this train. The Transport Police need to clear the station. Wait," he said as the man made to run off. "And tell them I'm taking the train out of the station. That way." He pointed.

"Can you drive a train?" said the platform manager.

"I'm a quick learner." As the man bolted off, Rod pulled out his phone and googled 'How to drive a train'.

When Nina felt she had recovered enough to both breathe and move, she attempted to sit up.

"Easy now," said Ingrid and pushed her back in her seat.

Nina gripped the sides of the swivel chair and tried to clear her fuzzy head.

"Ladies," said the barman and placed two champagne flutes before them.

Nina looked around.

"Wh're 'm I?" she said groggily.

"A wine bar," said Ingrid with a smile. "Don't worry," she said to the barman. "She's not drunk. She's just a bit backward."

The barman left them and went to clean the taps further along the bar.

Nina felt her strength coming back to her and reached for the glass of champagne.

"No stupid moves," said Ingrid and rolled the stick in her lap between thumb and fingers.

"Oh please," said Nina. "You get that from *Shit that Villains Say in Bad Films dot com*? What's that thing?" She nodded at the stick.

"A wand of *guirz'ir* binding. Fashioned it myself from a piece of the weird tree of Chippenham."

Nina drank half the glass in one mouthful. "It's got one hell of a kick," she grunted.

They sat on the upper level of the station, the wine bar overlooking the main concourse. "So, you're the bad guy," said Nina.

Ingrid gave her a pretend look of shock and offence. "Me? God, no. I'm the hero."

"Uh-huh. I think I might need that one explained to me."

"Is this the bit where I do my evil villain monologue? No, I didn't keep you alive because I needed the company. I need to know what you know."

"Hmmm?"

"Does anyone suspect me?"

Nina downed the rest of the sparkling wine and waggled her glass at the barman for another. "Suspect you of what? None of this makes sense. You know we're meant to stop this sort of thing, not make it happen."

"I *do* know that," said Ingrid with a quiet anger. "We stand at the brink, against a hell of monsters, and we're meant to stave it off for as long as possible. And with what? A pocketful of spare change and hope?"

Nina watched the barman pour her refill and gave him a cheeky smile in thanks.

"So," she said to Ingrid, "this is a fundraiser."

"I prefer to think of it as a wake-up call."

Rod remembered a time before the internet. Despite what Nina might believe, it really wasn't all that long ago. It was a time when an argument over trivial facts could fuel an entire evening's conversation in the pub, rather than be settled in less than a minute. It was a time when libraries were respected as houses of knowledge and depositories of wisdom. It was a time when any idiot with a computer couldn't just pour their idiot thoughts into

256

the public arena. It was a time when publishing houses, news agencies and academic institutions were the gatekeepers of truth and respectability and one could actually believe the things one read.

It was a time when a man couldn't learn to drive a train in under five minutes.

Google said he was in the cab of a British Rail class 66 diesel-electric freight locomotive. The wikiHow website gave him an overview of the general principles of driving trains, and he found a handy, labelled diagram of the control desk at railsimulator.com. With his phone propped up in the window, he was now watching and copying a YouTube clip of a driver in Norway at the controls of an identical vehicle. He already had the engines started.

"Directional lever moved to forward. Train brake lever off. Locomotive brake lever off. Throttle to notch one." And the train moved.

The internet was a marvellous thing.

"You know, it wasn't my idea," said Ingrid. "Not in the first place."

"Was it the voices in your head?" suggested Nina.

Ingrid gave her a withering look. "Greg," she said. "Greg Robinson."

"That's ridiculous."

"He did it for all the right reasons. We have people to protect, suffering to ease. Doomsday is coming and we will not go gentle into that good night. But we need the resources. You do know how we get our funding."

"The ToHo formula."

"Right," said Ingrid. "Funding is given to regions based on the number and magnitude of incursions. Greg always made sure we had a bigger slice of the pie. You know the Birmingham tornado of 2005?"

"It was the Winds of *Kaxeos*," said Nina.

"No."

"It was a game of Venislarn Scrabble gone wrong."

"Now you're being silly." Ingrid sipped her wine, barely letting it touch her lips.

"It was just a tornado, Nina. Just a tornado, but Greg convinced the accountants and auditors that it was an incursion and we got an extra thousand square feet of room for the Vault."

"But that's other consular missions' money," said Nina. "You're not contributing to the global Venislarn effort by pinching funds from Manchester or Leeds or Glasgow."

"So," said Ingrid, "we need to frighten the government into increasing the overall budget." She took out her phone and thumbed open her messaging app. "There's a cargo container in a train directly under our feet. There's another phone in the container and, when I send it this music file, the other phone will play it and the great dread lord *Zildrohar-Cqulu* will awaken and kill every man, woman and child within a mile radius."

"You..." Nina's lips curled up in disgust. "You're..."

"Mad?" said Ingrid. "Hardly."

"I was going to say 'a complete cunt,'" said Nina.

"Oh, save your abuse for the pillocks in power. Haven't you ever noticed? The politicians always complain there's not enough money for health or education or the environment. But there's always enough for a war." She tapped her phone; message sent. "Let's give them a war."

Rod saw the night sky above the cutting as the train came above ground, half a mile from New Street station. It took him a second or two to recognise where he was: south of the Cube and the Mailbox, with a canal to the left of the train tracks. That put Five Ways and Birmingham University ahead. Two, maybe three, miles to Longbridge on the edge of the city. Five more and he'd be in the Worcestershire countryside, as far from human habitation as he was likely to get.

There was no knowing if the hymn of awakening had already been sung or if he had robbed the singers of their opportunity. His only criterion for success was getting the train out of Birmingham before his passenger started kicking up a fuss.

He pushed the throttle forward to full power.

Morag's uCab taxi stopped on a bridge.

They were less than a mile from where it had picked her up. Morag looked out at the surrounding area and recognised the purple archway at the end of the bridge.

"This is Bournville train station," she said. "I'm going to New Street."

The taxi driver said nothing and sat perfectly still.

"This is my local train station," she said. "I could have walked here. Take me to New Street."

The taxi driver remained rudely oblivious.

"*Yo-Kaxeos, massa-khi nei* New Street station *shu'phro*," she tried.

Nothing.

"*Muda ben ai*," she swore and got out. The taxi pulled away immediately.

Her phone rang. "Hey, Rod. Where are you?"

"Driving a train," he said. There was an edge of boyish excitement in his voice, mixed in with the general mood of grim concern.

"I didn't know you could drive a train," she said.

"The jury's still out on that one. I've got *Zildrohar*-Coo Ca Choo on board. I can't get hold of Nina. Where are you?"

"Stupidly, I'm stuck at Bournville train station."

"Two minutes and I will be too."

Morag went to the side of the bridge and looked along the tracks towards the city. "A *Kaxeos* cab brought me here," she said. "Do you think *Kaxeos* knows something we don't?"

"Bollocks," said Rod with feeling. "I guess it was too much to expect to be able to get out of the city..."

"What's going to happen?"

"Are there people on the platform?" said Rod.

Morag ran for the stairs, waving her arms and yelling at the trio of figures waiting on the platform below.

At first, Rod could only imagine *Zildrohar-Cqulu* waking up and bursting forth from his cargo container womb. The sound of the locomotive engine and of several thousand tonnes of rolling stock rattling along smothered any external noises.

But soon Rod thought he felt a change in the train. There was a new sluggishness to the acceleration, a grinding sensation along one side. He couldn't see there was much to be done about it, just press on the throttle and hang on tight.

And then Rod did really hear it. He heard, above the engine and the train and the tracks, the sound of rending steel and snapping links. And the roar of a titanic beast, its hour come at last, sliding into Bournville to be born.

The locomotive began to tip to one side and Rod had a few scant seconds in which to curse the manufacturers for not fitting the thing with seatbelts.

"Because I bloody said so!" Morag yelled at the one man remaining on the platform.

"I know my rights," he argued. "It's a free country. You can't make me move."

"I will in a minute, when I skelp you one."

Let's see that ID again," said the man. "It's a fake, isn't it?"

"I don't have time to stand here and..." She trailed off and looked along the track. "Oh, I really don't," she said softly.

She grabbed the man's sleeve and ran as the freight train, tilted up at a forty-five degree angle and riding on only one rail, came into the station. Wagons tipped, some having already shed their loads. A half dozen carriages back, a shipping container trailed its ruined top like a comb-over caught in a gale. The great shadow clambering out of it threatened to pull the whole train off the tracks.

The recalcitrant commuter resisted up to the exact moment that the locomotive struck the concrete platform edge and, with its nose as the fulcrum, cartwheeled up and over, dragging flatbed cars behind it. The disintegrating train reared up like an industrial tsunami — and suddenly the man was ahead of Morag, dragging her towards an exit.

Vivian closed the door to 27 Franklin Road behind her.
"All done, eh?"

Vivian looked at the young man who had appeared at the gate. Morag's neighbour, Richard, had a vacant smile and equally vacant gaze.

"A fear of beards is called pogonophobia," she said.

Richard's hand immediately went to his hairy chin.

"If the Greeks went to the effort to come up with a name for it, they were probably trying to tell us something."

Richard nodded, uncomprehending.

"Sorted out the old Africa stain, yeah?" he said.

"Pardon?"

"They can be stubborn things but with a little scrubbing... And a bit of faith, of course."

"I have no idea what you are talking about," said Vivian. "Where is Morag? My niece."

"She had to go," said Richard. "Work called. A taxi picked her up. Just came out of nowhere."

"I see." Vivian stepped into the road to meet the uCab taxi that had just pulled up. "Then I had better see what she is doing."

"I'm sure she's fine," said Richard as she climbed in.

Vivian made a disapproving sound.

"The road to hell is paved with bland platitudes," she told him and shut the door.

Ingrid looked at her watch.

"Problem?" said Nina.

"No," said Ingrid defensively.

"Should something have happened by now?"

"The timing is immaterial," said Ingrid. "Wheels are in motion. The deed is done. At any moment, a —"

She was interrupted by a whooping alarm sound.

"This is an alarm," said a rather self-explanatory recorded voice. "Could all customers please make their way to the nearest exit."

All around, people stood still and looked about themselves in faint surprise.

"So, this is how the world ends," said Nina. "Not with a bang but with —"

"This is an alarm. Could all customers please make their way to the nearest exit."

Down in the concourse below, some people headed off unhurriedly towards the exits, some with overactive imaginations or a keen sense of self-preservation ran for the exits and some, who perhaps didn't think alarms applied to them or suspected it was all part of a reality TV show, stayed exactly where they were.

"Our time is up," said Ingrid and tightened her grip on her wibbly wand.

"I'm afraid we have to evacuate, ladies," the barman was already removing his pinny.

As Ingrid turned her attention to the barman, Nina lunged forward and threw her from her chair. Ingrid rolled, scrabbled for the wand and her phone, and found her feet again in time for Nina to rush her once more. Nina barged her, rugby-style, wrapping her arms around Ingrid's upper body and pinning her arms in place. Ingrid screamed, kicked and stumbled. Nina slammed her against the handrail that ran along the walkway.

Ingrid yelled and kneed Nina in the groin. Nina bent in pain, but it was only momentary. Then she came back at her (definitely) former colleague, striking hard, striking upwards, and pitching her up and over the handrail. Ingrid pivoted and would have plunged straight down to the concourse floor but for Nina's hand gripping her wrist.

Ingrid swung, wriggling. Nina pulled up hard against the barrier and huffed at the exertion. She tightened her grip on Ingrid's wrist but her hand wasn't all that strong and, it turned out, Venislarn geeks were heavier than they looked.

The shouts and screams, and the sight of a woman being thrown off the upper floor, lent credibility to the station-wide alarm and finally got people running properly for the exits.

Nina reached down with her other hand. Ingrid, still squirming, looked up with both panic and contempt. "So, you're the good guy, now?"

"Me? God, no," said Nina. "I'm a stone cold bitch." She wrested Ingrid's phone from her clenched hand. "And a sex kitten."

Nina let go of the wrist. Dr Ingrid Spence dropped and managed a half second of scream before slamming noisily and violently through the plastic and steel roof of a falafel stand.

"Mostly a sex kitten," said Nina and massaged her aching shoulder.

Morag pushed the man ahead of her as they climbed the stairs from the platform to the road bridge. She turned back to look at the wreckage. Wagons were mashed up against each other in a tangled heap. Red and blue and green cargo containers lay scattered across the area like God's Legos. There was no sign of life or movement from the locomotive engine.

Down on the platform a low shape lifted itself up.

Morag had seen pictures of *Zildrohar-Cqulu*, but pictures rarely did monsters any justice. They could never convey the movement of muscle, the oily flow of the alien body or the malevolent intent that lay behind its movements, its very being. *Zildrohar-Cqulu* — as long as a shipping container — moved on four angular legs with joints in all the wrong places, switching between standing upright and squatting on all fours from second to second. His wings, folded along his back, twitched, *yearning...* His head, vaguely simian in shape, was covered in scales of glistening chitin. Spear-like barbs, longer than a man, jutted forward from his cheeks and chin. The god growled and worked his four-piece jaw.

Zildrohar-Cqulu stood and put his forelegs-arms on the station building roof. He swung his bristled head towards the road bridge and produced a roar so multi-layered that it could have won an Oscar for best sound design. It was the roar of a blast furnace, of primeval monsters, of an unholy choir, of a petulant toddler. Morag felt it tug at her consciousness and, responding quickly, she dropped to her knees.

"*Yo-Zildrohar, meh skirr'ish. Perisa ghorsri Yo-Zildrohar.*"

The prayer of submission given, Morag felt the god's presence brush over her mind and move away.

"Lord! My Lord!" shouted a man on the bridge who then, without hesitation, flung himself over the edge and to his death.

"*Bhul*," whispered Morag and ran to the other two bystanders. She whipped the feet out from under the woman and then slammed the man against a lamppost before he, too, could throw himself off the bridge as a sacrifice to the Venislarn.

"Stay down," she hissed.

Zildrohar-Cqulu clambered over the station building, pulverising tiles under his huge claws and up onto the street that ran alongside the railway. Lights were on in houses nearby and Morag saw more than one door open.

"Don't," she said uselessly.

The Venislarn hoisted himself over the first row of houses with ease. Morag could not be sure in the streetlights' weak illumination but the god-creature appeared to be growing. He was waking but he had not fully risen. *Zildrohar-Cqulu* slipped over the roofs into the next street.

Morag ran after him.

Rod had been in some tight spaces before, both metaphorically and literally. The ancient tunnels beneath the Syrian desert sprang immediately to mind. But, right now, the dented and overturned cab of the Class 66 locomotive held a special place in his top ten list. It was one of those situations in which being a big man really wasn't an advantage.

He groaned and gasped as he tried to turn himself around and face the door. He couldn't find room to bend his elbows so he could bring his hands around, and his left foot appeared to be wedged in something. And, not terrible in itself but adding a sprinkling of irritation to the situation, his phone was ringing and he couldn't reach it.

He grunted, twisted and suddenly was able to push himself upward into a larger space. He yanked his foot free and booted violently at the upside down cab door. It gave on the fifth kick and he pulled himself forward and out onto the rubble-strewn remains of the platform.

Vivian was hurrying along the platform. He waved wearily at her.

"Where is it?" he said.

"*Zildrohar-Cqulu* was heading north. I think I saw Morag chasing after it."

"Okay," he said and then held up a finger. "Excuse me." He answered his phone.

"It was Ingrid," said Nina.

"What?"

"Dr Ingrid. She did it. Where are you?"

Rod wiped a line of blood from his forehead. "Bournville. Near the chocolate factory. Zelda-Val Doonican is out. He broke free of the train as I tried to drive it out of town."

"I've stolen a bus," said Nina.

"It's not a competition," he said.

"I'm coming to you."

"Why have you stolen a bus?"

"You know, YOLO. Um, question. How tall is a double-decker?"

"Twenty feet. I don't know."

"And the tunnels on the A38. How tall?"

"I don't know. Why?"

"Never mind. I'm about to find out." She ended the call.

"What's the plan, Mrs Grey?" Rod knew how to await orders.

Vivian looked at him and then at the general direction *Zildrohar-Cqulu* had left in.

"We declare an emergency. A chemical leak. We need these homes evacuated."

Rod nodded and discovered that nodding hurt.

"And we follow its trail," she said.

Morag dashed across a road, through the gap in an iron railing fence made by the passage of a god and into a well-lit car park at the rear of a huge square building that might have been a factory or might have been a college of the sort built in the decades that architecture forgot. Across the way, the elephantine Venislarn stood with its front claws on a white transit van, chewing on the unfortunate men who had been in it. A security guard whose commitment to his job was woefully misplaced ran towards the Venislarn, waving his torch about as though that would somehow make a difference.

Zildrohar-Cqulu issued a mighty chordal roar and the guard immediately fell to his knees and began to bash at his own skull with the torch. On the third strike, the torch went out and she did not see what became of him.

Beyond *Zildrohar-Cqulu* and the end of the car park stood a church and an apartment block. The noise the creature made was going to draw attention and the sanity-robbing power of his cry would soon have people killing themselves or others. Getting the god-monster away from the general populace and out of sight seemed the best plan.

"Hey!" she yelled. "Hey, *Yo-Zildrohar!*"

The Venislarn swung its spiked head about and regarded her with opalescent eyes. Morag instantly saw – instantly felt – that she was utterly beneath him. She was not merely insignificant; on a molecular level, an atomic level, she belonged to the order of things that were not worth paying attention to. Its head swung away and it began to head out of the car park.

"Hey!" she screamed. "Hey, *per muda khi umlaq!* Don't you turn your back on me!"

It was enough. *Zildrohar-Cqulu* turned, swatted the savaged transit van aside and roared. Morag felt his hatred, his real and physical hatred, stab into her. She summoned what Venislarn prayers she could bring to mind and recited them until the psychic assault lessened.

Zildrohar-Cqulu was stalking rapidly towards her.

Morag ran off to the side, aiming for an open freight service door in the square building. The Venislarn god followed, which was simultaneously what Morag wanted and a very bad thing indeed. Fear gave her speed but she was no match for the enormous alien. If she got to the service bay ahead of *Zildrohar-Cqulu* it would be only just, and then he would have her.

Nina ploughed a path through suburban Selly Oak, along a high street crowded with cars and the local student pub-goers. She kept one foot on the accelerator, one hand on the wheel, one eye on the road and, at the same time, flicked through the phone she had taken from Dr Ingrid Spence.

The woman had appalling musical taste.

266

Celine Dion, Luther Vandross, something called Enya and the Bee Gees filled her phone's music library.

"What the hell's a Bee Gee?" she said and then suddenly had to swerve to avoid a young woman in the road.

The bus bounced off a parked car, cut down a Belisha beacon at a zebra crossing and wobbled back into the centre of the road. Blue emergency lights reflected inside the bus from somewhere behind. Nina would have looked in her wing mirrors but she had lost both of them some miles back.

She continued to flick through Ingrid's phone until she found the music track she was looking for.

The freight loading bay in the rear of the factory was three feet off the ground to make it level with a parked trailer. Morag leapt up and dived through the door with a rare show of athleticism. *Zildrohar-Cqulu* bellowed behind her. A man in a purple boiler suit inside the entrance was trying to kill himself for his new god. However, he was attempting to do this by bashing himself over the head with a large box of chocolates and she imagined it would take him a long time to do any significant damage. Morag, selfishly if pragmatically focussed on her own safety for now, ran on.

There were stacked pallets loaded with cling film-wrapped boxes of chocolate throughout the warehouse space and, ahead, crisp strip lighting indicated the direction of the factory proper.

Zildrohar-Cqulu barrelled through the doorway, scooped up the chocolate-box-basher in his jaws and, claws grasping for purchase on the smooth concrete floor, galloped on in pursuit of Morag.

Morag had read once that the best way to escape from a charging crocodile (a creature which, despite appearances, could run faster than a human being) was to run in zig-zags and thus force the pursuer to make awkward turns for which it was simply not built. Though the horror on her tail was no crocodile – it was five times the length of any crocodile she had seen (and growing!) – Morag put her hope in dodging and weaving to keep *Zildrohar-Cqulu* always off balance and slightly out of reach.

Morag ran onto the factory floor – it was night and the machines were silent and the place deserted – and ducked down a left turn between stacks of empty packing cases and rows of machines that wrapped and boxed chocolate eggs. *Zildrohar-Cqulu* skidded round to follow her, sending egg boxes flying.

Morag cut right, under rollers of printed tin foil and alongside a series of box-building robots. *Zildrohar-Cqulu* thrashed through the sheets of tin foil and barged aside machines that had been bolted to the floor.

Morag lunged left between conveyor belts that were empty and still. She risked a glance back and saw that she had actually put some distance between her and the Venislarn. And that was the hell of her situation: she had to stay ahead of him but keep him focussed solely on her until whatever help was coming came.

"*Yo-Zildrohar! Pasp phe! Pasp phe!*"

She powered through a set of double doors and up a flight of stairs.

The loading bay door was part demolished. There were ruined shelves, scattered chocolates and blood smears around.

"I'm guessing he's here," said Rod.

Vivian would normally have chided a colleague for such a redundant and obvious statement, but with ripped and dirtied clothes and a cut drying on his forehead, Rod was possibly mildly concussed and Vivian did not believe in mocking the afflicted.

She crouched to examine the claw marks in the floor.

"He is getting bigger," she said. "As he grows, he will reach out mentally and draw in servants."

"Servants," said Rod.

"Locals. He is the tyrant of dreams and the speaker of men's souls," said Vivian. "He will draw people like flies to a bug-zapper."

"And do what with them?" he asked, pointing to the eyeless and legless man.

Vivian nodded. "His mind is unknowable."

"I don't like him," said Rod simply.

"We have no means to contain him," said Vivian. "We must simply do our best to find and... distract him and hope the powers that be can throw a cordon around this."

"Right, I'll get after him. There must be CCTV in this place."

"I will find the security office," she said.

Rod nodded tersely and headed off.

Vivian walked over to a fire alarm box on the wall and smashed the glass. With luck, that would drive any night staff from the building. She then took a minute to consider where the administrative and security offices would be if the factory had been laid out by a sensible person such as herself. She set off purposefully and, two minutes later, opened the door to a room of surveillance screens, public address systems and electronic door controls. Vivian sat down and calmly surveyed the closed circuit television footage.

She saw Morag. She saw Rod. She saw *Zildrohar-Cqulu*. She flicked an intercom switch.

"Rod. Miss Murray is in the development kitchens on the first floor." Vivian saw both Rod and Morag look up at her voice. "It is part of the chocolate experience, Rod," she said and then added, "Miss Murray, you might want to find somewhere to hide. I believe your only exit is blocked."

Morag could have kicked herself. Vivian was right.

A good portion of the Cadbury chocolate factory was given over to an interactive chocolate experience for the public. She had run through a Mayan village, a Victorian high street, an unlit cinema, and had now come to a large room that was some PR person's dream of what a chocolate factory should look like. Kitchen stations were set around for the rolling, moulding and sculpting of milk chocolate. Open vats of thick, liquid chocolate sat beside tasting stations and product demonstrations. And it was indeed a dead end.

Morag slipped between a vat and a set of storage cupboards a fraction of a second before the doors exploded open and *Zildrohar-Cqulu* burst in. Yes, he had definitely grown. He could barely fit through the double doors now and pulverised plaster rained off his back as he forced his way in.

With nowhere to go, Morag hunkered down, put her hands uselessly over her head, closed her eyes and tried to psychically project the idea that she wasn't there at all.

The risen Venislarn howled. The sound rattled the hanging kitchen equipment and set the windows humming in sympathy. Morag pictured the people outside, the crowds of curious drawn by the chaos, and what that sound would do to their minds if they got close enough.

Zildrohar-Cqulu padded across the room. It took Morag a second or two to work out what the strange and new rattling noise was. It was the Venislarn's breath. It was trying to sniff her out. The god edged closer.

"Let me try something," said Vivian over the PA.

A moment later there was light and sound. TV screens around the room came on, showing television adverts and images of chocolatiers at work — providing a narration to the tasks that ought to be going on at the various stations. Around Morag, machines came to life. Vats hummed, paddles stirred and conveyor belts rolled.

Zildrohar-Cqulu reared back and lashed out, smashing a workstation against a wall, sending wrapped chocolate bars flying. He stood upright, taller than a house, and ripped clusters of TV screens from the walls. The diversion had worked. It had him angry but it had distracted him and, if Morag was to escape, now was the moment.

She bolted and ran past the giant creature towards the door. She was not fast enough. *Zildrohar-Cqulu* turned, claws outstretched. Bowls of liquid chocolate, machinery and belts were swept up and round in a great tide that caught up with Morag and sent her tumbling. Something heavy rolled painfully over her leg and then a hot mass of sticky melted chocolate crashed over her. Panting, she skidded, crawled and threw herself into a corner. Wide-eyed and injured, she pressed herself up against the wall, grabbed a pipe for support and waited for *Zildrohar-Cqulu* to finish her off.

Chocolate dribbled down her face. The liquid, hot but not scalding, coated her entirely. Where her legs lay in the lake of chocolate that now covered the floor, she could feel the gloopy substance pulling on her skin, almost attempting to draw her down into the brown goo.

Zildrohar-Cqulu stood less than ten feet from her, chocolate spattered across his claws and torso, like a toddler let loose with cake decorating. He swung his head back and forth, sniffing noisily. His face barbs quivered. Morag looked directly into those irisless eyes and that restless inhuman mouth. He could simply angle his head forward and snatch her up.

And yet he didn't. Morag wondered insanely if he was averse to chocolate-coated food.

Zildrohar-Cqulu roared. Unholy phlegm spattered Morag.

"Heat vision perhaps," said Vivian from the PA. "*Zildrohar-Cqulu*, he of the flame-vision. You currently look and smell like chocolate."

Morag stayed perfectly still, happy to be one with the chocolate for the time being.

"We will work out what to do with you before you set completely. Rod should be with you at any moment."

And he was. Rod appeared in the doorway, gun in one hand, phone in the other. *Zildrohar-Cqulu's* head whipped round. Rod's face ran through a whole gamut of emotions — surprise, fear, resolve – in a split second.

"This way, lad!" he called and, with a wave of his arm, ran off again. *Zildrohar-Cqulu* obliged, sending a spray of chocolate in his wake. The monster wriggled through the doorway and was gone.

Morag sat there for a moment and then attempted to get up. "Oh, God. I'm setting." With a grunt, she pulled an arm free. Several pounds of molten chocolate came with it, leaving a fat hollow in the chocolate swamp.

Rod was a fit man but definitely built for strength not speed. He had to put in considerable effort to stay ahead of the pursuing monster. It was near impossible to maintain a phone conversation with Nina as he ran.

"What file?" he yelled.

"The Invertible Hymn of *Sanq'hu*," she repeated.

"And what am I meant to do with it?"

"Oh, Jesus *bhul!*" swore Nina.

There was a sound of grinding metal that sent ear-splitting feedback down the phone.

271

Rod leapt over a bannister in the stairwell, then another, taking two flights in two bounds. Above, it sounded like *Zildrohar-Cqulu* was simply destroying the stairs as he came.

"There's a police and fire brigade cordon around the factory. I just burst through it. Where are you?"

Rod bounced violently off a wall and dived headlong through a set of doors. "Warehouse F."

"Right. Coming to you."

"To me?"

Within the chocolate-encrusted folds of her clothing, Morag felt a buzz.

She peeled an inch-thick plaque of chocolate off her hands, levered open her nearly solid jacket and rescued her phone from the chocolatey reservoir of her pocket. She had received a direct message from Nina. There was a file attached. It read, INVERTIBLE HYMN (EDITED) – PLAY NOW.

Morag opened the file. There were perhaps droplets of drying chocolate in the phone's speaker but the music file played. It was vaguely musical. It didn't sound awful. It didn't sound particularly tuneful either. It sounded like a series of chords played rapidly on an organ or a synthesiser, a sound pattern that didn't follow any conventional melody or serve any purpose apart from checking every key on the keyboard worked. It was a non-tune, a backwards tune.

"Nina, you're a bloody genius." Morag hurried from the room.

The warehouse Rod had run into contained aisle after aisle of industrial shelving, laden with pallets of chocolate bars of all varieties, ready for shipping. Rod picked an aisle and ran. Behind him, he could hear masonry snap and crumble as the Venislarn titan blasted through the doorway and into the warehouse.

"Take a left," said Vivian's voice from a speaker, loud and echoing like the voice of a peevish God.

Rod took the left as instructed. He had twisted his ankle in escaping from the locomotive cab and now it screamed at him, threatening to betray him at any moment.

"Right," said the voice of God. He ran right.

272

Zildrohar-Cqulu thrashed through the shelves behind him, sending a clattering cascade of chocolate bars, selection boxes and snacks down from above. Directly ahead, a floor-to-ceiling roller door was slowly grinding open.

"It's not for you," said Vivian. "It's for Nina."

"Nina?" said Rod and then yelled in pain as his left foot truly gave out on him.

He turned. The ugly Venislarn god, with an accompanying shower of sweeties spraying before him, charged at Rod.

"Get out of the way," said Vivian.

Rod momentarily heard the growl of an engine, saw the flash of headlights and stumbled out of the way as a double decker bus sped into the warehouse.

Vivian could see on the internal and external monitors that the roller door had not risen high enough. The door buckled loudly and the top deck of the bus smashed apart, the roof peeling back like a banana skin. The battered lower half of the National Express double decker rammed into a set of industrial shelves and sent them toppling.

Zildrohar-Cqulu whirled in the carnage, ripping shelves apart, batting pallets away and generally adding to the chaos rather than escaping it.

On another monitor, a chocolate-coated figure shuffled rapidly but clumsily along the corridor.

"Where are you going, Miss Murray?" said Vivian.

Morag stopped, turned to the CCTV camera, waved her phone about and then pointed repeatedly at the camera. Vivian had no idea what that particular pantomime meant.

"I'm in the security office on the ground floor, along the corridor from the factory reception," she said.

The chocolate figure shuffled on.

Shelves fell. Chocolate rained from the heights. Rod knew that chocolate was bad for the health but, for once, he admitted there was a very real danger of it being the death of him. While *Zildrohar-Cqulu* battled falling shelving and a constantly shifting floor of discarded chocolate, Rod ran to the bus. The front end was buried deep in a compact pile of steel struts and plywood shelving so he hoisted himself up and through one of the broken windows further back. He dashed to the front of the bus. "Nina!"

A groan from the driver's cab told him that she was at least still alive.

"I hurt."

Glass crunched under his boots. A miasma of smoke, faint but thickening, filled the air. He shoved a metal stanchion aside.

"You drove a bus into a chocolate factory," he replied.

"And how many people can say that?" grunted Nina.

He levered a shelving board away and there she was. There was glass and chocolate everywhere and the cab was severely buckled around her but there was no blood.

"Want," he said, putting a hand to her cheek and checking her pupils. "How many people would *want* to say that?"

She held her right arm in her left. There was an ugly looking bend in her right forearm where there really shouldn't have been one. "Can you move your head?"

"Uh-huh."

"Do you feel any nausea? No? Can you feel your legs? Yes?"

She nodded. "I'd like to get off the bus now, please," she said.

"Okay," said Rod. "I'm going to hook my arms under yours and pull you out."

"Hang on," she quickly stuffed a handful of chocolate bars down her blouse.

"Really?"

"YOLO."

Rod leaned in and took hold of her – she really was a tiny itty bit of a woman – and gently hauled her out. She winced and gasped each time her broken arm was jolted.

"You know," he said. "YOLO is just carpe diem for people who can't spell."

"I thought carpe diem was just foreign for 'fish of the day'."

He slipped her legs over the lip of the cab and assisted her to the back of the bus and the emergency exit.

"Why would I have a tattoo on my arm that says fish of the day?"

"I dunno," she shrugged. "Thought it was an army thing."

He looked at her.

"You're definitely not concussed?" He pulled the emergency door lever and half-led half-carried her out.

"Shit, my phone," said Nina. "I need my phone."

"Priorities." Rod pulled her away from the diesel fuel that was pooling around the bus. "I'll get you a new one."

"But it's got the file on it."

There was an abrupt moment of silence. Rod looked up. Up in the rafters, *Zildrohar-Cqulu*'s head, itself as big as an elephant – how did he get so big? – was looking directly at them.

"Bugger," said Rod.

The Venislarn horror screamed, a noise that went beyond the merely animalistic into intelligent and purposeful hatred. Like a hooked barb, it penetrated his mind, his psyche, and pierced deep into his need to conform, to obey and to seek forgiveness.

Beside him, Nina was fervently muttering prayers.

With *Zildrohar-Cqulu's* scream-command inside him, Rod couldn't comprehend why there would be any need for prayer; the will of his god was clear and evident to him. *Zildrohar-Cqulu* demanded an act of atonement. He had wronged his god and he would have to pay. A sacrifice would have to be made. *Zildrohar-Cqulu's* biting truth had carved all doubt from his mind, excised it like a tumour. All was bright and clear now.

A sacrifice would have to be made...

He put a hand on Nina's shoulder. "*Per Yo-Zildrohar, me-asqh pas pherri khor llang'xi.*"

She paused in her prayers and looked at him with suddenly narrowed eyes. "Since when did you speak – Oh, *muda!*" She tried to pull away but Rod held her with gentle and implacable hands.

"Don't be scared," he said.

"This girl ain't scared of nothing," she spat back.

Easily ignoring her struggles, he placed a hand on her neck and pressed his thumb into her windpipe. She kicked against him. He twisted her broken arm. Her scream was a squealing gargle that vibrated against his tightening fingertips. It felt good to experience her so closely. Rod felt a sudden desire to open her up and know her insides.

"You will be assured a place in his kingdom," he told her.

275

Nina thrashed and clawed at his jacket. Rod paid it no mind. Her pain was temporary and could not be compared to the eternal glory in which she would soon reside.

Purple-faced, she held up his pistol and put it to the bridge of his nose. She had snatched it from his holster. Sneaky. The natural instinct to survive made him hesitate. He released his grip for a moment.

"Don't make me," Nina croaked.

Zildrohar-Cqulu padded towards them and snarled his encouragement. Of course, she must die, Rod realised. There was no point in getting squeamish when the rewards of service were so close at hand.

As he closed his grip about her again, music started to play from the PA speakers. It sounded like organ music although there was no melody, merely a succession of arpeggios and chords. It was an immediate distraction, its meaningless progressions cutting between the clarity in his mind and the reality of his actions. The gun was still pointed straight at his face.

He struggled to regain his focus. Why didn't she shoot him? Didn't he need to kill her? Where was his lord, *Zildrohar-Cqulu*?

He turned to look for his master. *Zildrohar-Cqulu* stood still and – Rod had to take a second look – he was shrinking.

"*Yo-Zildrohar?*"

The butt of the pistol slammed against his temple and, in a fleeting instant of unconsciousness, he lost his grip on the sacrifice. She stamped against his knee as she fell back and he fell too.

Rod gave no attention to the physical pain. His connection with the god was receding. He tried to reach for it and draw it back to him but it was like grasping at fog. The music was sending his god from him. Rod shook his head at himself in disgust. His god?

The foul Venislarn was drawing in on itself, returning to the size it had been in the cargo container. It was almost lost to sight now, no higher than the piles of strewn confectionery that it had brought down around it.

Vivian watched *Zildrohar-Cqulu* shrink and become still on the screen. Morag's phone next to the PA microphone continued to play the file Nina had sent her.

"It worked," she said.

"The Invertible Hymn of *Sanq'hu,* inverted," said Morag. "Or played backwards."

"A lucky guess."

"A lucky guess saves the day."

Vivian looked warily at her colleague and at the patchy layers of chocolate that still clung to her. "You may be tempted to hug me now or offer me a high five," said Vivian. "Don't."

"We won," grinned Morag. "This is our moment of victory."

"And this is Marks and Spencer," said Vivian, touching her suit jacket. "Don't."

Smiling had cracked the chocolate on Morag's face. She peeled off a strip and popped it in her mouth.

The police and fire crews all looked a little lost and unsure what to do. They had attended what was obviously a serious incident. There had been thunderous crashes, smashed windows and hints of fire but they had been given firm instructions to hold back and not intervene. Eventually, bored, they fell back on old favourites. The police bossed passing traffic around and told onlookers to keep back. The firefighters chatted up the prettiest of the onlookers and made unnecessary references to hoses and helmets.

The ambulance crews looked almost smug when four survivors made their slow way down the driveway and gave them something to do. Two of them needed no treatment. The older woman seemed perfectly untouched and there wasn't really any treatment the NHS could offer the redheaded woman for a chocolate gunking. The paramedics all but leapt upon the giant man with a bloodied forehead and obviously twisted ankle, and the petite woman with a broken arm.

From beyond the police cordon, Vaughn Sitterson approached Morag and Vivian, which was a peculiar thing to watch because, as a rule, he was clearly opposed to approaching or looking at anything directly. He approached them as though he was simply walking in their general direction and their presence was merely coincidental. He looked past them to the Cadbury's chocolate factory.

"This was a planned event?" he asked.

"Luring a wakened god into a chocolate factory, ramming it with a bus and sending it to sleep with a backwards lullaby?" said Morag. "No."

"I like to be aware of incidents before they happen," he said, apparently addressing the sky.

"Including unforeseeable incidents?"

"Especially those," he said.

"I would be the same," said Vivian.

"I think you should write the report on this one, Mrs Grey," said Vaughn.

Vivian nodded as though she had been given a singular honour. "We will need a clean-up crew to contain *Zildrohar-Cqulu*. I will ask *Yo-Morgantus* what he would have us do with him," she said.

"I gather *Yo-Morgantus* is incensed that another god of power came into his city without notification and would rather we sent *Zildrohar-Cqulu* to the furthest and coldest ends of the earth."

"Hull, then," said Vivian. "There is also the matter of the *Nadirian*. We found it."

"I know," said Vaughn, trying to sound superior and knowledgeable but unable to hide a certain sheepishness.

"If I wasn't so tired and covered in chocolate, I would slap you sideways," said Morag. "You put me in there as a canary."

"And you survived," he pointed out.

"Well," she said, "then I guess that deserves a pay rise."

"In these times of austerity and budget cuts?" he said. "At best, we can offer you alternative accommodation. Nothing as pleasant, I should imagine, but guaranteed to be devoid of Venislarn."

"Another time," she said. "I've got a daft neighbour to check on and I'm definitely going home to get out of these clothes."

"We could offer you a ride," said Vaughn, gesturing to the unmarked car he had come in.

"It's okay," said Morag, waddling uncomfortably toward the uCab that had just pulled up. "Got my own ride."

Nina and Rod sat side by side in the rear of the ambulance while the paramedics assessed their injuries.

"Ingrid was right," said Nina.

"Was she?" said Rod.

"You. You went all Sean Bean back there. Like in *Lord of the Rings* when he went all mad and tried to kill Frodo."

"And you would be – what? – the tiny little hobbit person with hairy feet I tried to kill?"

"I have beautiful feet," she said.

"Thank you though," he said. "For not shooting me."

She shrugged and winced as she jolted her arm.

"Couldn't kill you. You promised to buy me a new phone."

He thought on this.

"Aye. Sounds fair," he said eventually.

When the taxi stopped outside 27 Franklin Road, Morag had to peel herself away from the seat, leaving behind a whole-body chocolate imprint.

"You might need to get your god to clean that up for you," she told the taxi driver and got out. She looked up at the sub-divided house. There were lights on in Richard's ground floor flat. Her own flat was in darkness, as she had left it. There was a faint light from the second floor, a low glow through the mouldy curtains.

She made her plans as she walked in chocolate trousers up to the front door: strip, put the clothes in the washing machine (along with the two other soiled outfits she had put in there earlier in the week), actually put the washing machine on, get a shower, check that Richard hadn't done something as stupid as awaken or feed himself to the *Nadirian*, sleep or not sleep, then get the hell out of Dodge...

She barely had the key in the lock when the door was pulled open.

"You took your time," said Ingrid.

Morag looked at the wand in Ingrid's hand.

"I thought Nina threw you off a balcony," said Morag.

"Yes, that hurt," said Ingrid. "It really did hurt."

Morag noticed that Ingrid was slightly bent, hunched, as though she really wanted to curl up.

"Got some broken ribs and that's not put me in a good mood," said Ingrid. "What's that stuff on you?"

"Chocolate," said Morag.

"I won't ask. Which one's your apartment?"

"Upstairs."

Ingrid waggled the wand for Morag to lead. Morag sidled past her and up the stairs.

"Slower," grunted Ingrid behind her, taking the steps with difficulty.

Morag considered lashing out backwards with her foot but she had seen what a wand of *guirz'ir* binding could do when fully employed and did not want to contemplate what would happen if her kick missed.

Morag opened the door to flat two. Ingrid prodded her inside. Morag turned on the lights.

There was an August Handmaiden of *Prein* in her front room. More specifically, it was *Shardak'aan Syu*, the mistress and lover of Drew.

Morag must have been tired, because her first emotional response was to be impressed rather than terrified. The handmaiden had to squat a little to not scrape the eight-foot ceiling. Her armoured body and arched legs stretched from the front window to the beginning of the dining area. If the Venislarn were forced to obey the laws of space and time, they would have had to remove the front wall of the house to get her in.

"*Kos-kho bhul!*" swore Ingrid in surprise. "Who's that?"

Jagged armour plates shifted and rode across the handmaiden's body. A screaming baby face of porcelain came round to face them.

"Who is this little thing?" said the handmaiden in beautiful and precise tones.

Morag marshalled her thoughts rapidly. She felt a little giddy to be caught entirely between a rock and a hard place. A very, very hard place.

"*Shardak'aan Syu* of the August Handmaidens of *Prein*," she said, "may I present Dr Ingrid Spence, a colleague of mine from

Birmingham consular mission to the Venislarn. Ingrid, her ladyship *Shardak'aan Syu*, who I guess is here to exact revenge for me killing her sister on Sunday in Edinburgh."

The handmaiden's plates rotated angrily. "Murderer. You tricked me into offering a poisoned tribute to *Yo-Morgantus*."

"No one to blame but yourself for that," said Morag.

"You will pay, small human."

Ingrid held forth her wand. "I warn you, I'm armed," she told the Venislarn.

The handmaiden shifted and twitched, positioning her body to perceive the wand better. "This one is mine," said the handmaiden.

"Not today, she isn't," said Ingrid. "You need to leave, *sa vei-Prein*."

The handmaiden ground its plates together and brought its claws forward.

"You should not defy me."

"And on any other day..." said Ingrid.

Both the handmaiden and the doctor held their positions. Morag, although directly between them, was almost completely ignored.

"I was this close to her," Morag said to the handmaiden. "I had startled her. I wasn't even looking for her. I just happened to have the gun in my hands."

"Shut up, Morag," said Ingrid.

"I turned. She reared. I put both barrels in her mouth. I didn't even know her name."

The handmaiden growled and rose up as much as the ceiling would allow.

Ingrid twisted the wand. An invisible wrecking ball smacked into the handmaiden and pushed her back against the wall, smashing plaster and IKEA art prints. It wasn't enough. The August Handmaiden of *Prein* propelled herself at the two women, the circular and pink-toothed mouth in her belly wide open to consume them. Ingrid twisted the wand again. This time, the wrecking ball not only picked the creature up but powered straight through her, nearly destroying the wall with shards of exploded alien royalty. The largest fragment of shell bounced off the wall and rocked around on the floor. One of her amputated legs twitched and was still.

"Boom," said Morag softly. "Just like that."

"You got any more mortal enemies hiding in here?" said Ingrid. She sounded tired, so very close to collapse.

"No," said Morag. "Do you mind telling me what you want with me?"

"The *Nadirian*," said Ingrid. "I know it's here."

"What do you want with the *Nadirian*?"

Ingrid gave her a sour look. "You have deprived me of one incursion."

"Did you not see what that god did to the chocolate factory? We had a serious incursion, no mistake."

Ingrid shook her head. "I'm considering this Plan B. Where is it?"

"Top floor," said Morag.

"Good, then you're going to wake it and –"

"What's going on here?" said Richard from the doorway. "It sounded like an explosion."

Ingrid turned, wand in hand.

"Don't hurt him!" said Morag.

Richard looked at the pair of them and the bent stick in Ingrid's hand and the enormous splatter of gore and crustacean armour that coated half the room.

"Was there some sort of accident?"

"We're going upstairs," said Ingrid.

"Your aunt just cleaned this place," said Richard.

"Not important right now," said Morag. "This woman is dangerous, Richard."

"Why is she holding a stick?"

"It's a wand."

"Okay," said Richard.

"Upstairs," instructed Ingrid, "or the lumberjack gets it."

"Lumberjack?" said Richard.

Morag took him by the arm and led him to the stairs.

"You do know you're covered in chocolate," he said.

"It's been one of those days," she told him. "Just keep your head down, do what she says and, if you hear screams, start running."

Ingrid grunted with effort and she hauled her injured frame up the stairs. The door to flat three was ever so slightly ajar. Lamplight shone through the gap.

"You go in," Ingrid told Morag. "Junior stays out here with me."

"Go in and what?" said Morag.

"Wake it," said Ingrid. "The *Nadirian* can be contained, commanded even, once it has eaten."

"I see," said Morag. "It's like that." Richard looked at her blankly. "Run if you can," she said.

"No one's running," said Ingrid.

"Hide," said Morag.

Richard nodded.

Morag opened the flat door, stepped inside and then closed it behind her. A cat meowed in a dark corner. The thing in the armchair in front of her shifted and snorted.

"I must have dozed off," it said to itself.

"*Yo-Nadirian yos'kherrign bis-ghu!*" shouted Ingrid from behind the door, urging the *Nadirian* to consume what was before it.

Morag looked at the outline of the old woman in the chair and tried to force her mind to only think of it as an old woman. It was an old woman, not a creature from another space and time, not a thing of claws and tentacles, of wound-like orifices and misshapen limbs...

"No," she said and screwed her eyes shut.

"*Yo-Nadirian, treghhu shan-shan prui!*" Ingrid shouted. It was the linguistic equivalent of prodding a wasps' nest, needling a response from the Venislarn.

Morag felt a subtle but definite change in the atmosphere, a prickling of her skin, an electric tang in the air.

"What is that noise?" said the old woman-shaped thing.

"Got an image in your mind, Morag?" called Ingrid. "What's the most horrific thing you've seen? What monsters can you dredge up from your subconscious?"

283

"Shut up, Ingrid," said Morag.

The figure in the chair pushed itself forward, leaning heavily on the wooden walking stick. "Who are you?" she said. "Who let you in?"

Her accent was heavy or maybe her speech had become lazy with age. She wobbled forward in clumping orthopaedic shoes.

"*Yo-Nadirian, yos'kherrign zhul prui!*"

The static charge in the air rose exponentially. The air fairly buzzed with Venislarn magic.

The woman cocked her round head. Her unrealistic mound of grey hair quivered.

"Who is that?" she said.

"Mrs Atraxas, there's no call to be alarmed..." said Morag and then stopped herself.

There could be no reasoning with the *Nadirian*. This old woman wasn't the *Nadirian*. It was the shell it wore, its projected form into this world. If she pictured it with a handmaiden's claws or *samakha* gills, *Croyi-Takk* wings or a *presz'ling* anus-mouth then that would be the form of the *Nadirian* projection. But it would still just be the cloak the *Nadirian* wore.

An ornithologist using a bird-shaped glove as a parent proxy to rear orphan chicks had no idea what it was like to *be* that bird they imitated. The glove might emulate genuine animal communication but there was no actual communication. There was no comprehension, no more than an owl butterfly, mimicking an owl, knew what it was like to be an owl...

"Oh, hell," she said in sudden understanding. She tried to open the flat door but something held it firmly shut on the other side. Morag hammered.

"Open the door!"

"It'll be over soon," said Ingrid.

Morag slammed her fists on the door.

"Yes, but you're on *the wrong side of the door!*"

"What?"

Morag laid her head against the door. She wasn't sure how she could feel sorry for the woman who had wanted to kill her, but she did.

"You must be strong," Morag had told Richard on Tuesday morning.

"I must be," he had replied.

"I need to make it up to you," she had said.

"You must," he had replied.

"You've been very calm and understanding," she had said.

"That's the kind of guy I am," he had replied.

She had told Richard to 'bust some moves' on anyone who broke into his flat and he did just that, even though that person was her.

"You're like some kind of ninja," she had told him on Thursday.

"Yes, I am," he had agreed.

"You play an instrument?" she'd said.

"Absolutely," he'd replied.

"Bagpipes?"

He clicked his fingers.

"Got it in one."

And Morag had hit onto the bigger truth without realising it when she had said to him, "You're going to think it's bizarre but, this morning when you said you played the bagpipes, for a moment I just thought you said it because I suggested it, that you've got some kind of uncontrollable need to agree with people."

"Richard is the *Nadirian*," Morag said softly but, by that point, Ingrid had already started screaming.

Morag felt the energy build up in the room – and it wasn't electricity and it wasn't magic because they were simple words for human concepts and neither applied here – she felt it flow out through the door, through her, drawn in by the shape-shifting *Nadirian*. She found herself wondering how powerful an imagination Ingrid had. How many nightmares had that woman seen close up and stored in her memory? Morag concluded that the answer was probably 'lots' before she clamped down on that line of thought.

The screaming transformed into a pained and terrified cry for help and then the word 'no' repeated over and over and over again with increasing pitch and intensity. And then it became a wet bubbling sound that faded to silence but not quickly enough, not quickly enough at all.

"I have no mouth," Morag whispered to the door.

"What is that?" said Mrs Atraxas.

Morag turned to the little old lady, who really was just a little old lady. "It's nothing."

"Is it on the television or something?"

"Yes," said Morag. "Let's say that it was." She smiled. "I'm Morag. I'm your new neighbour."

Mrs Atraxas regarded her sceptically.

"I do coffee," she said eventually. "I do not do tea. I do not understand it."

"Life is full of mysteries, isn't it?"

When Morag had finished her coffee – 'finished' meaning that she had sat down and stared at the tar in her cup (and let a tortoiseshell cat wearing a knitted waistcoat savage her ankle) for as long as seemed polite before putting it down – she said her goodbyes and ventured out the flat door.

There was no Richard. There was no amorphous Venislarn horror. There was no Ingrid. There wasn't even any blood.

She padded downstairs, past her own flat where the exploded carcass of an August Handmaiden of *Prein* remained, and to the front door of flat one on the ground floor. She knocked nervously. Richard opened the door instantly as though he had been standing there, waiting. It was just Richard, the same bushy beard, the same body, stocky but veering dangerously close to fat.

"So, what happens now?" he said.

Morag didn't have a box woven from ivy in which to bind him.

"It's the weekend tomorrow," she said. "You get weekends off?"

"I do," he said.

"And what do you like to do at weekends?"

He mulled it over, shaking his head.

"Maybe," she suggested, "you like to take your neighbour out for breakfast and then help her clean up the mess in her flat."

"I do like to do that," he agreed earnestly.

"Then it's a date," she said.

"It's not a date," he said.

"No, it's not a date," she agreed.

Saturday

"The train derailment, believed to be caused by an improperly loaded container, led to structural damage in surrounding buildings. Several homes and businesses were evacuated while investigations and repairs take place. West Midlands Police say the matter is unrelated to a terror alert at Birmingham New Street station earlier that evening."

Maurice closed the news app and put the tablet down.

"And Miss Murray?" asked Sheikh Omar.

"Alive and well. You still think she is essential to our future plans?"

"I don't travel to the wild untamed lands to the north on a whim. She has, as our forebears might have said, spunk. She will fight the good fight when the time comes."

Maurice made a non-committal noise.

Omar finished buttering his toast. "It seems that our precautionary and personal evacuation to Barry Island this weekend was not entirely necessary," he said. "Still, better safe than sorry."

Maurice looked out of the guesthouse window. Rain drummed ceaselessly on the seafront promenade. "I don't like Barry," he said. "I never have."

"You can be deliberately cruel sometimes," said Omar blithely. "Now, be a dear and pass the jam."

Authors' Notes

YES, the Library of Birmingham is the largest public lending library in Europe. This is a good thing. It was indeed opened with great fanfare and then, less than two years later, had its opening hours decimated in a cost-cutting exercise. This is a bad thing.

NO, the Library of Birmingham is not home to a shadowy organisation that monitors alien-god behaviour in the city.

YES, the lower ground floor of the Library of Birmingham does run underneath the width of Centenary Square.

NO, the Library of Birmingham does not contain a secret vault full of forbidden treasures.

YES, Birmingham surrealist, Conroy Maddox, had several of his paintings confiscated by Scotland Yard during World War Two, because they suspected he was a fifth columnist and was sending coded messages to the Nazis through his paintings.

YES, the *National* Sea Life Centre is in Birmingham, over 100 miles from the sea.

YES, The Queen Elizabeth Hospital contains the Royal Centre for Defence Medicine for the treatment of people injured in military conflicts.

YES, there is an overlapping series of canal, road and rail tunnels beneath Snow Hill station.

YES, there is a rooftop garden café in Birmingham Children's Hospital.

YES, the Birmingham Jewellery Quarter has the highest concentration of jewellery-related businesses in Europe and, in that 1 km², produces over a third of all UK jewellery.

NO, none of the sex shops in Digbeth are fronts for dodgy fish-porn film studios. We checked.

YES, Bournville is a dry village. When the Quaker Cadbury family built their factory and village in the late nineteenth century, they decreed that no alcohol could be sold within its boundaries. That decree is still in effect today.

YES, there was a tornado in Birmingham on 28th July 2005 with wind speeds up to 130 mph. It uprooted 1,000 trees, removed house roofs, threw cars around and effectively destroyed Christ Church in Sparkbrook.

YES, the Cube's shaped cladding is meant to represent the city's industrial heritage and the glass interior the city's jewellery-making past.

NO, the Cube does not have any horrors from beyond living in the top two floors.

YES, the 'Birmingham Qur'an' was discovered in 2015 in Birmingham University's Mingana Collection (having been previously misidentified and catalogued with newer manuscripts). It is around 1400 years old and therefore is a contender for the world's oldest Qur'an.

NO, there is no department of Practical Theology at Birmingham University or Department of Intertextual Exegesis and they don't employ a Professor Sheikh Omar.

NO, the freight handling terminal in Nechells is not a secret operation for the transportation and handling of occult materials.

YES, the Balti triangle is a real thing.

YES, the Balti was invented in Birmingham and first served at Adil's restaurant on Stoney Lane in 1977.

NO, there is no Karakoram restaurant in the Balti triangle and certainly no restaurants in the area would treat their food or their customers in that way.

NO, Birmingham taxi drivers are not in the thrall of an imprisoned god. Birmingham taxi drivers are lovely people.

YES, Birmingham's St Philip's cathedral is the third smallest cathedral in the country but it does have some lovely Burne-Jones stained glass windows.

YES, Mike Edwards, cellist with Birmingham band ELO, was killed when a 1,300 lb hay bale rolled down a hillside and hit his van.

YES, Brummies do not say 'mum', 'bald' or 'tooth' but 'mom', 'bold' and 'tuth' instead.

NO, Nina is incorrect in thinking the original New Street building was built in the Dark Ages and modelled on a Nazi bunker. It was completed in 1967 and was instantly despised as ugly, brutal and not fit for purpose. The station was completely renovated and reopened in 2015.

YES, railsimulator.com does have documents to teach you how to drive a Class 66 diesel-electric freight locomotive. We do not recommend you try it.

About the authors

Heide and Iain are married, but not to each other.
Heide lives in North Warwickshire with her husband and children.
Iain lives in south Birmingham with his wife and two daughters.

Together, they are the authors of the surprisingly successful
Clovenhoof comedy novels.

Made in the USA
Middletown, DE
04 December 2019